TRASH

John David Hall

"This book is hilarious AND filthy. I blew a load while reading Trash at my desk at work." *NY Times Book Review*

"This is the best fucking novel I've ever read. I hope Wal-Mart has more copies." Anna Wintour *Vogue Magazine*

"I wish I'd gone to a sex club instead of marrying Sean Penn." *Madonna*

"My book club will not be the same." *Oprah Magazine*

"After reading Trash, I went back to my day job. Uncle!" *David Sedaris and Augusten Burroughs*

"I am going to teach John David about straight sex." *Britney Spears*

"I'd sooner stand in front of Brad and Angelina at another awards show than read another one of John David's stupid filthy books." *Jennifer Anniston*

"I'll be trying out for the part of 'Greg' in the movie version. I've already started practicing!" *Matthew McConnaughey*

"I hope I can achieve a 'non-pinpointable' accent. What a challenge." *Meryl Streep*

"I still have some of those flags at home if you want one." *Former Atlanta Mayor Shirley Franklin*

"I didn't even know what a booty bump was." *Michael Stipe R.E.M.*

Library of Congress Control Number: 2014908745
ISBN: 0615691930 John David Hall Photography
ISBN: 0615691935

To Kathy

Acknowledgments

Thank you Albie - you listened patiently, edited meticulously, and encouraged with love.

Thank you Rebecca Kilby for editing with care and discussing with your dry, deadpan humor.

Thank you to everyone who listened, encouraged, and took time to read my manuscript and make it better with your insightful feedback:

Jay Bernson, Erica Briscoe, Heather Dray, Tori Hall, Richard Hume, Rebecca Hooper King, Michael Martin and Dan Cameron, Leo Nieter, Janet Simpson-Templin, Amy Watson, and Brent Walker.

Chapter One

During the first spring Will lived in Atlanta, when week night drinks called his name, he and Kaleb sometimes went to Burkhart's. At Burkhart's, there is a pool room upstairs where, most times, a person could put their quarters down and get into a game. An elk's head attached to a dark paneled pool room wall might make a person feel like they were at someone's dad's house - someone's straight, deer-hunting, beer-drinking dad. That feeling quickly disappears when the lip-synched lyrics of drag performers float up the stairs and mingle with the cologne of gay men.

The drag shows were later in the week, and early in the week Dolly hosted a karaoke show while sauntering around in an evening gown with two balloons stuffed in her dress. Dolly capped off her ensemble with seventies heels and a Dolly Parton wig. While the karaoke singers performed, Dolly could be found next to the downstairs bar with an upturned shot glass in hand.

The bar was mostly empty, but Will and Kaleb could always find a way to keep themselves entertained. They were standing by the ATM downstairs, telling anyone who used it how much they loved guys with cash, when someone they knew came over to them. Will had taken him back to his apartment over the Thanksgiving holiday weekend. Will and the guy had never called each other, but they were friendly when they saw each other out. Will had no recollection of his name.

The guy asked Kaleb and Will if they wanted to go over to the Manhole.

Will said, "What's the Manhole?"

Kaleb and the guy gave each other a look.
Kaleb said, "It'll be fun, Will. I'll protect you."

"Protect me?"

Kaleb called shotgun, and Will sat in the backseat.

The guy zipped out of the parking lot in his little Civic, masterfully maneuvering the steering wheel while shifting gears and smoking a cigarette. He sped down Cheshire Bridge Road, past the adult entertainment venues with half-naked models gracing lit signs in parking lots as if to signal you're getting closer to the back pages of a magazine where for ninety nine cents a minute you can hear anything you want to.

Before *the Manhole* was *the Manhole*, the building was occupied by a restaurant. Before it was a restaurant, it was a train station. A deck in back overlooks a gravel parking lot and on the other side of the parking lot, train tracks cut through a wooded area. On this quiet Tuesday night, the loneliness was palpable.

There were few people hanging around *the Manhole's* dark corners. They weren't chatting or singing or playing pool like the guys at Burkhart's. They looked somber. And lonely.

Red lights cast a glow on thick hardwood floors. A bored-looking, shirtless bartender served their beers. Will couldn't stop looking at the strategically placed holes in the bartender's jeans. The bartender smiled at Will.

Will turned to Kaleb and pointed at two wooden boxes, painted black and worn with scuff marks, next to a doorway.

"What are those big black boxes for?" Will asked.

The guy looked at Kaleb and said, "he's really never been here?"

Grinning, Kaleb said, "go-go boys dance up there on Thursday nights, Will".

Kaleb's animated gestures and vies for attention seemed cartoon-like in a place like *the Manhole*. He popped against the sad surroundings like orange against blue.

The guy suggested they go have a walk around and watched for Will's reaction. Giggling and twirling around, Kaleb said "It'll be okay, just stay with me."

Kaleb held black, rubber, curtains back for Will as he stepped through a doorway that separated the front bar from the rest of the club. Disco music bounced off the walls of the empty dance floor, as if it would always be there.

To the right and up was an empty DJ booth. Will saw more boxes, presumably for go-go dancers, and a smaller bar in the back corner of the dance floor. To the left, beside the smaller bar that wasn't in use, were more rubber curtains and a doorway that was sealed off. The three of them walked across the dance floor to where two men were sitting on a bench that was attached to a wall. Will wanted to know their stories. Why they were there on a Tuesday night drinking and staring at an almost empty dance floor.

They walked past the guys on the bench and around to the other side of the wall. It was darker back there. The guy suddenly stopped in his tracks, causing Kaleb to bump backwards into Will. The guy and Kaleb both darted and left Will standing near someone who was backed against the wall with his pants down. In front of him was another guy, on his knees, giving him head. The guy standing up and receiving the blow job looked at Will for a moment, and then closed his eyes again.

Averting his eyes, Will turned and walked away quickly. The guy and Kaleb were both laughing when he found them in a hallway.

On one side of the hallway were two steps that led up to a poolroom that was lit only by one light over each of it's two pool tables. A row of windows along the outer wall reflected those two lights in the otherwise darkened windows. On the other side of the hallway was another bench, occupied by someone who was drinking a beer, smoking a cigarette, and studying the three of them.

Kaleb joked that the hallway was also known as the carwash.

Will laughed and said, "why is that?"

The guy and Kaleb looked at each other again. Kaleb did a twirl and gave a come-hither look to the guy sitting on the bench.

Will said, "I have to pee."

"He always does this" Kaleb said to the guy and then pointed to the end of the hallway, next to the door with the black rubber curtains they'd come through earlier.

The urinals were out in the open with no partitions. A single red light bulb drenched the white tiles in blood red.

Will found his two hosts and they crammed themselves back into the little Civic. The guy, smoking a cigarette and shifting gears with authority, sped down Cheshire Bridge Road back toward Burkhart's.

8

Chapter Two

The office Will worked in was on the eleventh floor of one of five non-descript downtown skyscrapers that were identical on the exterior. Will worked in Marquis One and the other buildings were named accordingly.

In the summer of 1997, during the dot com boom, Will began enjoying his eleventh floor window seat view from one of Inform's four floors in Marquis One.

Part of Will's job was helping clients with database searches, and his phone rarely rang more than ten times in one day. When he wasn't helping someone, it was his job to run searches and know the company's databases, which comprised a large variety of records.

"Will, Frank walked by your desk at one o'clock and looked at his watch," Craig said. "You better start leaving your apartment five minutes earlier."

Craig said "No one notices if someone doesn't make it here by eight or nine because of traffic, but your hours are one to ten thirty. Everyone knows when you try to slip in late."

"Yeah, I know" Will said. "Have you been to lunch yet?"

Craig quietly said "Noooooo – but a good looking man cruised me downstairs this morning. I'm going to go back down there and see if I can get him to follow me into the men's bathroom at the Marriot."

"Again?" Will said.

Craig was four years older than Will, conservative and clean cut, about five foot ten with brown hair and wire framed glasses. He sat down in the taupe colored, butterfly shaped guest chair at the edge of Will's cube.

Craig whispered, "There were at least six guys getting it on in that corner bathroom this morning."

"Craig, I haven't even had my Pepsi yet."

"Are you still drinking Pepsi just to annoy Frank?"

"While that is an added bonus, I really do like Pepsi better than Coke," Will said.

"Well, you better hide them when Frank's around" he said. "you know how he feels about being loyal to Atlanta companies."

"Well, you're doing your part" Will said "by servicing so many employees of those companies."

Craig grinned widely, put his hands in front of his face, and pretended like he was giving head to someone.

"Oh God, stop it!" Will said. "Go downstairs and give somebody head. I'll cover for you if Frank comes around."

"Thanks Will."

"Craig—"
Craig stopped and turned around. He looked like expected a smutty remark.

"Bring me a Pepsi when you come back up."

***

Later that evening, Will sat on the concrete steps that led up to the Buckhead apartment he shared with his straight, soccer playing roommate, David. Will lit his first cigarette of the evening. He saw Laura, his co-worker, whiz down the sloped parking lot with her roommate. They both jumped out of Laura's car, both looking like they'd just came from the gym, and each with a bag of groceries from Harry and Son's in their arms. Laura yelled from across the parking lot as they bounced up the stairs to their apartment in the B building. It was perpendicular to Will's, in the A building.
"Will! You better quit smoking!"
Smiling back at them, Will took a drag from his cigarette.

Habersham Court was in the heart of Buckhead, but it wasn't a posh Buckhead property. Instead, they were older buildings that looked like a two story cheap hotel. Remodeled on the inside, but the outside was still orange with a green roof. It was on the corner of Piedmont Road and Roswell Road, two of the busiest streets in Buckhead. If a person tried to come or go at the wrong time of day, it could take them an hour to move a mile in any direction.

Will grabbed his cordless phone and called Kim.

"I'm on the phone with Zach, we'll call you right back".

Within a minute the cordless phone rang.

Zach said "Will, we were just talking about you."

Will heard Kim light a cigarette.

Will, Kim and Zach were why three way calling was invented and all three felt they couldn't live without it.

"Will, is that a car horn I hear?" Kim asked.

"Yeah, you wouldn't believe the traffic around here" Will said.

Kim said "I'm so glad I didn't move into that apartment with you. No offense".

Will said "None taken. The street noise reminds me I'm in the city. It doesn't bother me."

Zac said "speaking of, I'm off Monday. Can we come see your office?"

"Yes! Come see it! I can tell you about it all day but you have to see it to believe it" Will said.

"Didn't you say there's a full size pool table with purple felt instead of green" Kim said.

"Yes, and pinball machines, foosball and table top shuffleboard" Will said. "There's even an exercise area and the bathrooms have showers in them."

"You landed in the lap of luxury when you got that job" Zach said.

Kim was the opposite. She was a gregarious and open book for all to read while at the same time wanting to know everyone's story including the very core of what made them tick.

"I'm happy for you" Kim said "you were diligent about sending resumes and interviewing over the summer.

I'm happy for you too, Will" Zach said. "I have something for you. I'll bring it to you on Monday."

Chapter Three

Will wanted to see why Kaleb had referred to the hallway at the Manhole as "the carwash." The black rubber curtains really did look like the ones at a carwash. That Friday night, after work, Will went back to the Manhole. This time he went by himself.

The hallway was so packed that once someone entered it and got swept into the crowd with no room to turn around, they had to keep moving forward. Hands came out of nowhere, grabbing crotches and asses. It was difficult for Will to discern who was groping who – pretty shirtless boys, well built, middle aged men, or trolls in desperation.

On Will's second walk through, he waited and made sure he was behind a hot guy with a hot ass before he got swept into the moving crowd and groping hands. The tightly packed crowd of hungry men slowly pushed it's way forward, forcing Will's erection into the guy's jeans for the duration of his second trip through the carwash. A periodic smile over the shoulder and a hand reaching around to grab his crotch, told Will it was okay.

It was late, close to three, when the hallway finally began to clear out. A pretty, shirtless boy remained in the middle of the hallway among the thinning crowd. Three men, on their knees, surrounded the pretty boy and each took turns sucking his dick. The pretty boy smiled at Will, who sat down on the bench to watch the show. Someone unzipped Will's jeans, pulled his dick out, and began stroking it. The pretty boy walked over and sat down next to him. Will was so turned on when the pretty boy started stroking his dick, he came in a couple of minutes.

The pretty boy whispered "nice" in Will's ear before Will, embarrassed, jumped up and zipped his jeans. He hadn't intended for it to go that far, and especially not in public.

By two o'clock that Monday afternoon, Craig was already telling Will about his downstairs bathroom excursions earlier in the morning. Craig was in the guest seat at the edge of Will's cube, mimicking giving someone head, when Zach and Kim walked up.
"Will, this place is insane" Zach said.
Kim said "Look at this view."
Will said "Kim, Zach - this is my co-worker Craig."

As they all exchanged handshakes, Laura walked over from her cube which was in direct sight of Will's, past two rows of cubes that were indented and walled. Will and Laura often made faces and laughed silently unbeknownst to the people on the other side of the partitioned wall.

"You're Kim" Laura said. "Are you the one that almost moved in with Will?"

Laura's light blue eyes and shiny black curls shined in the afternoon sunlight.

"Yes, that's me." Kim said. Kim's Little Five Points alterno exterior (nose ring, burgundy hair, bag slung over her chest) didn't hide the dignified social graces she naturally exuded.

Laura said "I live in the same building. We love it over there."

"Now where are these apartments again?" Craig asked.

When he wasn't telling Will about sexual encounters in hotel bathrooms, Craig's demeanor could be that of a lady from the old south.

"I can't place them" Craig said.

Laura said "On the corner of Roswell and Piedmont – in the middle of everything."

"That's why I didn't want to live there." Kim said.

Laura said "It's not for everybody, but we love it."

Craig said "Those little orange apartments?" He made a face.

"They're not bad" Laura said in her mellifluous, upbeat voice. "They're really cute inside."

Craig said "Will, you should take Zach and Kim up to twelve and fourteen".

"That's exactly where we were going" Will said. "Do you mind covering for me while we're at lunch?"

Craig grinned widely. "Just don't do anything I wouldn't do."

"What was that all about" Kim asked as they waited for an elevator next to the wall to wall glass that was the fishbowl looking into the rows and rows of blinking lights on servers lined throughout the data center.

"That all looks so high tech" Zach said, staring through the glass.

"Craig cruises the downstairs bathrooms during his lunch breaks" Will said "I'll tell you about it at lunch."

On twelve, Will introduced Kim and Zach to his boss Frank, who stopped playing pinball just long enough to shake their hands.

Kim said "This pool table is bigger than my dad's" as she lightly touched the purple felt. And look at that wood".

"And the claw feet" Zach said. "Oh. My. God. Look at his place!"

Kim said "You weren't kidding about this place were you Will?! Foosball and table top shuffleboard?!"

"Zach, come look at this gym" Kim said, looking at Will with her serious, piercing brown-green eyes. "Will, do you realize how lucky you are?"

Will said "Go look in the bathroom".

Kim's expression told him she was impressed with the sleek tiled floors, club track lighting, changing area with lockers and showers. Will led them around a large aquarium, enclosed by a wall that separated a quieter TV Lounge. Three Jetson's cartoon butterfly lounge chairs in primary colors, red, yellow, and blue, lined the wall of windows that looked eleven stories down to Peachtree Center Avenue.

Will said "Let me show you the receptionist area and then we'll go".

On the fourteenth floor, the receptionist's desk was in the middle of a circle of shimmering, aqua fiberglass walls. The reflection of the track lighting bouncing off the shiny, black tiled floors and hitting the fiberglass walls was almost dizzying.

Zach and Kim wanted to go to a quiet restaurant on Peachtree. Two in the afternoon, after the lunch rush, made for relaxed conversation in the mostly empty restaurant. A person could almost hear the relief from the staff that another lunch rush was over as the sound of dishes being separated and loaded made it's way to the dining room. To Will, who was forever jarred by close contact and noisy crowds, it was a luxury rather than an inconvenience to have lunchtime after lunchtime.

No sooner had the waiter given them their menus and stepped away did Kim pull out a pack of cigarettes from her shoulder bag and ask about Craig and his comment.

"What was he talking about?" Kim asked, repeating Craig "Don't do anything I wouldn't do? We're just going to lunch." She gave Will an I don't get it look.

"Wait Kim" Zach said "I want to give Will his gift".

Zach pulled out a small box and handed it to Will. Inside was a shiny, silver business card holder with Will's initials engraved on top.

Will said "I'm really just Customer Service you know."

"You'll go higher" Zach said "I know how you are Will".

Will gave them the full scoop on the licentious goings on in the hotel bathrooms. All the cruising and dick sucking. He told them about one bathroom just inside the Marriot where sometimes there were four or five guys going at it even before lunchtime. Someone would stand guard at the entry, alerting everyone else when a cleaning person or someone else was about to walk in. Everyone quickly pulled their pants up and resumed normal positions – pretending to be urinating in front of a stall or closed in a different stall. A look and a lingering hand on someone's own crotch from someone standing at a urinal reciprocated by a newcomer would set the mid-morning orgy in motion all over again.

Kim, insatiably inquisitive and a psychology major at Georgia State University, was fascinated with the sociology of it. Zach may have been fascinated with other aspects, but he was a master at not letting it show.

"Just be careful, Will" he said "that's all I have to say about it."

Chapter Four

On Thursday nights at the Manhole, there were two well muscled go-go boys who danced on boxes on either side of the door that led to the dance floor from the main bar. Will found that Thursday nights were laid back enough without the crowds of weekend nights, but there were still plenty of people around and fun to be had. Every time he walked through the door toward the dance floor, one of the dancers mussed his carefully attached golden hair (not just the president but also a member) and smiled at him.

At the far back corner of the dance floor, Will put his jacket down on another box that wasn't occupied by the shuffling tennis shoes of a cute young dancer. From that corner, he could see who was coming to the dance floor from the front of the bar, as well as who was going behind the wall where he'd seen naughtiness going on before.

Will noticed a collegiate, rosy cheeked, brown haired boy came through the door from the front and walk toward the hallway. The boy wore a navy pea coat and he had the easy stride of suburban money. A minute later, Will saw the cute boy go behind the wall. Will followed, and found the kid surrounded by three other guys, all grabbing him. The brown haired boy grabbed Will's crotch and the two of them pulled their dicks out. While the three other guys looked on, the cute boy and Will stood and faced each other. They shot at about the same time. The boy pulled Will close and whispered "thank You" in his ear before briskly walking back to the front and out the door. When Will got home, he noticed a circular stain on the tip of his shoe. He tried to wash it off but it left a faded circle in the black leather. He stopped trying to wash it off and decided he liked seeing it there.

"Will, I meant to tell you, your friend with the tattoos is cute".

Craig, in the guest chair at the edge of Will's cube, legs crossed, sipped coffee and periodically gazed down at the street below.

Will said "Zach is cute. I agree."

"Well you tell Zach I want to –". He licked an imaginary dick in the air.

"Quit it. There comes Laura." Will said. "And besides, Zach can be an island. It takes time for him to open up. So to speak."

Craig did it again. Will gave him a look just as Laura got to his cube.

"Hey Will. You're right" Laura said "Kim doesn't look like I'd imagined."

"Is Zach the one you were telling me about?" Laura said "you shared an apartment with him in college?"

"Yep, that's him. I'm surprised we didn't ever run into you at U.G.A."

Laura said "and now we not only work together but we live at the same apartments! It's a small world!"

"Well aren't you two just the cat's meow" Craig said, moving across to his own cube. "I need to get this research finished for Frank by the end of the day." The way Craig said it, Will could imagine a lady walking back into her kitchen, wiping the sweat from her brow with the back of her hand before wiping both hands on her apron. Put upon and overworked by the men folk and not appreciated for it.

When Craig was seated with his back facing them, Laura and Will, smiling, rolled their eyes at each other.

"Your friends are cute Will. They look artsy like you" Laura said over her shoulder, her black ringlets bouncing as she walked over to her own cube, documents in hand.

Back at his cheap hotel apartment building, with evening traffic winding down on Piedmont and Roswell Roads, Will sat on the front stoop and lit a cigarette. He could see the Tower Place building with its hard, mirrored angles lit vertically by neon green lights. Some of the lights didn't go all the way to the top or the bottom, making the mirrored building look like it dripped green against the blue dusk sky. The blond in Building C, on the other side of the parking lot, wore only tight jogging shorts. He was busy making dinner, bending over occasionally. Will dialed Kim, but wondered if it might have been better to wait until the blond finished cooking his dinner. Will was halfway hard by the time Kim answered.

"We were just talking about Craig. We'll call you right back."

"He is a good guy" Will said, hard on gone but still watching.

"So does he really cruise the downstairs bathrooms all the time?" Zach asked.

"He's down there a lot." Will said.

"Do you still go down there?" Kim asked.

"Not necessarily for sex. There are real reasons to go there – like lunch. If I happen to get cruised by somebody who works close by that knows about the bathrooms, I'll go in for some fun" Will said. "But it doesn't happen that often anymore."

"How do you know they work close by and know about the bathrooms?" Kim asked.

Zach interjected "You just know."

Kim said "How?"

Zach said "Will –"

"Well. Hm. I don't know" Will said. "It's a look they give you."

"Anybody could walk by and look at your crotch" Kim said. Will could hear her light a cigarette.

"Yeah, but – " Zach started.

"It's just a look" Will said. "It's hard to explain but you know it when you see it."

Chapter Five

Thursday nights proved to be Will's favorite at the Manhole. Now, both go-go boys mussed his blond hair as he passed through. Like his black Halloween cat, Frieda, he enjoyed the attention for a moment before darting away. What if one of the go-go boys pulled his hair off? How would he explain it at the Hair Club?

"Yes, the hair was attachéd securely, but this particular go-go boy was very strong. He wouldn't give it back."

As Will walked toward a glass sliding door that leads to a back porch, a man sitting in the corner caught his eye. He smiled at Will like he knew him, and Will walked over to him.   Handsome, mid forties Will guessed, the man had thick dark hair with some salt and pepper coming in. His skin was somewhat weathered but it didn't detract from how handsome he was. It may have added to it. He had a cute puppy dog expression and Will surmised that in his younger years the man probably looked like one of those cute and fresh faced English school boys that he admired so much. The man drew Will into his arms and said "Hi". The man's smile was warm and inviting.
Will said "do I know you?"
"You look like a lot of the boys I've seen in California, but we're not in California are we?" the man said.
Will said "judging from the swampy humidity, I'd say no".
"I'm sorry" the man said. "Where are my manners? "My name is Daniel".
When he smiled at Will, his head was held high and tilted backward, his expression gently probing. Expectant.
"I'm Will".
Daniel repeated it back in a non-pinpointable non-accent.
"Will. Is that your first name?"
"Yes."
"I like the way you said "yes" Daniel said. "I've missed that about the south."
"Thanks."
Not sure what to do with the attention, Will pulled out his cigarettes. Daniel lit one for him.
"I like your name" Daniel said
Daniel lit his own cigarette before drawing Will into his arms.
Will said "Thank you. Is Daniel your first name?"

Daniel said "I love hearing you talk". "Thaaaank Yooouuuuu". It was gentle mocking. "And yes, Daniel is my first name."

"I hope you don't mind." Daniel's voice was deep, intelligent, like his brown Labrador retriever eyes, and a little commanding. Not commanding in a bossy way, but commanding in a mesmerizing way. Memorable.

Will said "I don't mind".

"So Will" Daniel said "What do you do here in Atlanta?"

Will said "I work for an information brokerage."

'I'm sorry, I don't know –"

"It's a huge database of public records used mostly by attorneys and government agencies" Will said.

He'd grown used to confused expressions when telling someone where he worked. The idea of an information brokerage wasn't something most people knew about.

"It's my job to know how to navigate the database and help users find their information."

"I know nothing about computers" Daniel said "But it sounds very interesting. Did you go to school for this type of job?"

"No" Will said "I graduated from U.G.A with a degree in Art and Photography."

"Photography?" Daniel said, perking up. "What kind of pictures do you take?"

"Took." Will said "Nudes and half nudes – mostly in black and white."

"You're not taking pictures now?" Daniel asked, his tone fatherly and his head lowered.

"Who's got time with a full time job and those go-go boys calling my name after work?" Will said.

Daniel said "I like the image of you taking pictures of naked boys" and moved Will's hand on top of his own crotch. Will felt a hard on in Daniel's jeans.   Daniel kissed Will and said "I guess the cigarettes don't bother you?"

Will said "Nope".

"Let's go outside" Daniel said, taking Will's hand and opening the sliding glass door.

It was a warm, May night and Daniel and Will made themselves at home on the empty deck looking over the gravel parking lot. Will liked Daniel, so he asked him the Stephanie (one of his best sidekicks in college) question guaranteed to get the personality revealing started.

"What's your favorite book?" Will said.

Daniel looked surprised. "I don't think I've ever been asked a question like that in a place like this" he said. "Let me think about that."

"While you're thinking I'm going to go inside and get another beer" Will said "Want anything?"

"Whatever you're drinking" Daniel said.

Inside, Thursday night was at its peak. The dance floor wasn't full, but it was thick with guys dancing their troubles away. Will was happy to be going back outside to talk to a nice man. He was different than most everyone he'd met at the places he'd been hanging out. Will sensed he was making and becoming a new friend. It felt seamless.

Daniel said "It would be hard for me to pinpoint one favorite book" as Will handed him his beer.

"Thank you" he said and reflected a little longer. The lull, like all lulls, left Will not knowing what to do. He began shifting, nervously.

"I like to read historical books" Daniel said. "And autobiographies." His answer satisfied Will- Daniel wasn't a schmuck.

"What is your favorite book, Will?"

"Catcher in the Rye" Will answered without hesitation, still enjoying the sound of his own name ringing in his ear.

"Is that what you read? Fiction?" Daniel asked.

"Mostly" Will said.

"So tell me, have you lived in Atlanta your whole life?" Daniel reached in his pocket for his box of cigarettes.

Will pulled a pack from his jeans pocket. Daniel lit Will's first, and then his own.

Will said "I grew up in Rome, I went to school in Athens, and then moved here to Atlanta last summer."

"Rome, Athens - it sounds so glamorous". Daniel said.

"Doesn't it though" Will said. "It couldn't be more opposite. Rome was like living in a very narrow tunnel. Athens was liberating. I'm hoping Atlanta is even more liberating."

"I know what you mean" Daniel said. "I'm from Macon. I just moved back to Georgia a few months ago after spending most of my adult life in California.

"I've always loved the idea of living in California" Will said.

"You look like a California boy" Daniel said. "Before you noticed me I watched you. I thought you might be from California – the blond surfer haircut and the way your faded jeans hang low on your waist. You have that look."

Will wondered if he was being played, but took the compliment at face value. If he was being played, it was enjoyable.

"Thanks" Will said, proud of himself for standing out.
Daniel mussed Will's hair and he jerked back.

"Ah – so you like it to stay perfectly unkempt I see" Daniel said "So you are like those California boys."

He smiled at Will warmly and kissed him.

Will turned around to put his cigarette out and looked out over the parking lot. Daniel turned and stood beside him.

Will pointed to his car, parked on the end of the left side of the gravel parking lot.

He said "that one's mine."

Daniel said "The shiny white one? You're proud of it aren't you."

Will said "Yes. I just got it a few months ago from a girl who had recently joined the Peace Corps. She wanted out of corporate life and sold her car at a bargain. She'd taken pristine care of it but I still cleaned and waxed it as soon as I bought it. There was one flaw which was a worn hole in the center arm rest. My mom took the arm rest to an upholstery shop - that was the final touch that made the car perfect."

Daniel smiled at Will affectionately.

"That was very sweet of your mom." he said.

Will said "She raised me to love cars. I can usually tell you, even at night from the headlights alone, the make and model of a car in the distance on the highway. Except SUVs have really thrown me off." Daniel continued smiling at Will.

'Which one's yours?"

Daniel pointed to a black Mitsubishi Eclipse at the far right of the gravel parking lot.

"That's my car over there" he said. "I bought it just before I moved back to Georgia. There's a story behind it, but that's a story for another time."

"It's pretty" Will said. Daniel's low, quiet voice made him feel safe.

Daniel moved behind Will and put his arms around his waist.

He said in Will's ear, deeply "my last name is Payne, and some people say I'm a pain in the ass".

He pulled Will's ass close to his crotch. Over his shoulder Will said "Ha. Ha. You're amused with yourself, aren't you?"

Daniel replied with an overly exaggerated "Ha. Ha. Ha."

"Would you like to go to my house for a while?" Daniel asked.

Will turned around and said "Okay".

"My friend Rudy is here visiting from Los Angeles" Daniel said. "He's staying with my roommate, Rob, and I this week". "Rudy is staying in the guest bedroom, and since it looks like he met someone here earlier, I don't think we'll be seeing much of them tonight."

Daniel and Will kissed again and went inside to look for Rudy. After all the introductions were made and it was decided who was riding with who, the four of them were all off to Smyrna where Daniel lived in a house with his roommate Rob.

Daniel and Rob's house in the burbs was lovely. Daniel explained that he and Rob dated briefly in college and had become friends. They'd been friends ever since and bought this house together a few months prior when Daniel moved back from Los Angeles.

Daniel and Rob's house was just different enough from the typical Atlanta suburban home, and not in a subdivision named "Eagle's Trace" or "Hunter's Landing". The suburbs were full of houses that all looked alike with beige carpet and beige walls inside. It irritated Will how little thought must have gone into those cookie cutter worlds that looked prefabricated and cheaply done.

Once inside, the first thing Will noticed was a shiny, black, baby grand piano in the living room.
"Do you play" Daniel asked.
"Not since high school --" Will stopped himself. "I was eighteen when I stopped taking lessons."
Upstairs, there was a small den attached to Daniel's bedroom. Will pointed toward a big, gold "D" on the wall and said "What is this?" Charmed by Will's interest, Daniel said "Do you remember the Mary Tyler Moore show?"
"Yes."
Daniel said "When I was young and first moved to L.A., I asked a friend of mine to find me a "D" just like the "M" in Mary Tyler Moore's apartment. It was on my wall the whole time I was lived in Los Angeles, reminding me that 'I would make it after all' as the theme song goes."
Will couldn't help but smile.
In Daniel's dimly lit bedroom Will saw a sculpture of a male torso made dramatic by backlighting. There were two well executed charcoals of male nudes on one of his walls. Will got a kick out of seeing this kind of thing in a suburban home that one would expect to be occupied by a family.
Daniel and Will sat on the bed and kissed again. Will wondered how he would get his tee shirt up and over his head without the hair going with it. Daniel started to unbutton Will's shirt and Will said "I'll be right back".

Standing in Daniel's bathroom, looking in his mirror, it wasn't only his hair (or whoever's it had been) that worried Will. He had no muscle tone. None. Daniel hadn't seemed to notice.

In Rome, days had been structured around eating without regard to nutrition. In Athens, days had been structured around assignments and cigarettes. In Atlanta, Will had a growing sense that he was about to be tossed on a treadmill if he wanted to stay. Many of the gay men he'd encountered - and he'd encountered more in the past few months than his entire life - made a V-shaped torso their top priority. Will slid his tee shirt over his head, careful not to disturb the hair.

They spent some time in Daniel's bedroom before strolling through the backyard where Daniel pointed to plants in Japanese inspired landscaping and named them for Will who heard nothing as he watched Daniel's black cocker spaniel chase a carelessly tossed tennis ball.

Neither showed signs that they wanted to end the night and on his way home, in the wee hours of the morning, Will went the wrong way on I-285, the perimeter that circles the urban sprawl that is Atlanta. Will didn't care. He lit a cigarette and rolled his window down. He turned up the radio and drove all the way around I-285 in the middle of the night.

It'd been almost a year since he and his friend Stephanie had indulged one of their infamous all nighters in Athens. Though Will loved the structure and routine of office life after class schedules that changed quarterly and frenzied scrambling before exams, he welcomed this reminder of his days in Athens when throwing a wrench in a routine by staying up all night and excitedly anticipating what the future might hold while most were in bed asleep became the routine.

The next day on the elevator, Sarah immediately noticed Will's red eyes. Sarah worked with Will until she got promoted to marketing and moved to fourteen. A cute, thin, mid-twenties northerner, Sarah had moved to Atlanta for two purposes – to build a career and find a husband. Sarah was a pleasant and constant reminder that Atlanta would be nothing like Rome. In Rome, at the office, a female co-worker might call her husband (probably Lloyd or Billy) to check on the kiyuds.

"Lloyd, if ya'all go to Wal-Mart, be sure to get --"

In stark and welcomed contrast, during Will's first week in Atlanta, as he trained from Sarah's cube, she took a break and checked one of her mutual funds online. Will found it refreshing to be sitting at a desk on the eleventh floor of an office tower with a woman who thought about her own money instead of unplanned offspring and Wal-Mart.

On Mondays, Sarah usually found Will to tell him about who she'd been out with that weekend. On Fridays, she usually found him to tell him who she was going out with the upcoming weekend. That afternoon Sarah showed up at his cube. She wanted to know why Will was so tired looking and he didn't hold out on her.

"So what does Daniel do?" Sarah asked, sitting in Will's guest chair, eyes wide and expectant, right leg crossed and swaying, and an always present coke can in her right hand.

"Well - he doesn't do anything."

"He doesn't do anything? So he's independently wealthy?" Sarah grinned widely.

"Not exactly. He gets money from disability." Will said, feeling like he might be exiled back to Rome.

"Why is that?" Sarah's smile faded.

"An illness" Will said. "He had surgery years ago and the illness altered his life."

Sarah said "Do you really want to date someone in that situation?"

"Why not?"

"He has no income except for disability and no potential for future income" she said.

Will's phone rang and immediately he knew from the seven seven zero area code that it was Daniel.

Will said "I bet that's him".

Sarah got up to leave and said "talk to you later" over her shoulder as she walked away.

"You know we're breaking the three day rule" Will said, barely giving Daniel time to say Hello.

He said "I know. But it doesn't matter".

Will was glad they were on the same page. If two people like each other, and they know that, then does it matter how many days go by before one calls the other? A friend asked Will that once and it stuck.

Will and Daniel made dinner plans for Saturday night.

"Will has a boyfriend" Zach said as soon as Kim picked up.

Still tired from the night before, Will was on the front stoop, smoking a cigarette and admiring how Tower Place dripped green in the night sky. The blond wasn't at home and his blinds were turned.

Kim said "Are you serious or are you getting ready to tell me about some guy that blew him at the Manhole?"

"He has a date."

"Thank God" Kim said "You little shits have five minutes and then we're (Kim and her roommate, Diana) going to go pick up dinner."

"Who is he, how old is he, where'd you meet him, what's he like?" Kim's first round of questions.

"His name is Daniel, he's forty eight, he just moved back to Georgia from L.A." Will said "Let's see. He's very handsome and we really hit it off."

"Where'd you meet him?" Kim said.

"The Manhole".

"Will –"

"I know, I know" Will said "But he's different. I really think so."

"How is he different?"

"I don't know" Will said. "He's smart. He reads books. He has a big "D" on his den wall just like Mary Tyler Moore had an "M" on hers."

Kim laughed as she exhaled. "I like that" she said.

Zach laughed too.

"Is he really forty-eight?" Kim asked.

"Yes" Will said "And I think you'd really like him."

Sing-songey, Zach said "Will - has - a – boy - friend".

"I want to hear more about this person" Kim said "I'm calling you both back in an hour and you better answer your phones."

Chapter Six

For their first date, Will and Daniel went to Après Diem in the Virginia Highlands neighborhood. Après Diem was a restaurant and bar that sometimes felt like a European coffee house. Lone hipsters reading books at smaller tables alongside parties of ten who were eating, drinking, and laughing merrily. Kim and several of Will's other friends often met up at Après Diem. Daniel loved it there, and Will loved hearing his tales from his former life in L.A. He'd seen someone who played the dad on a popular TV show at the local bathhouse. He'd been arrested with several others at a cruisy beach for public indecency.

Daniel said, laughing "We all fooled around in the back of the police van on the way to the police station."
Daniel's lover of fourteen years eventually cheated on him, and things turned ugly.

"That's why I bought the car I did" he said. "Because my ex wanted one like it. I thought it would be the perfect thing to do – buy that car and then move to Georgia with it."
He told Will about his illness and the surgery that followed. He'd woke up from surgery with a colostomy bag attached which he had to keep for months.

"You have no idea how debilitating it is to your self image to have a bag while most of your gay male friends are still maintaining their Adonis physiques" he said. "It feels like non-existence".

Daniel looked so vibrant and the sparkle in his dark brown eyes was so bright, it was hard for Will to understand he'd been through so much. But sometimes when he looked at Daniel he could see it.

The Manhole began having wrestling matches on Thursday nights and Daniel and Will liked to go. Manhole employees would put mats on the dance floor, cover them with oil, and have two hot men in wrestling gear go at it. Daniel sat on the wooden bench attached to the wall at the end of the dance floor. Will sat in front of him, between his legs, while they enjoyed the match. Daniel liked it when Will wore jeans with holes so he could maneuver. The matches were a tease.

Over the next couple of months Daniel and Will saw each other regularly. All seemed well until one Friday night in July when Will's cousin Paul visited from Rome. Paul was straight, recently divorced and still depressed. He'd been hanging out with guys in Rome who were closeted, but still followed him around like desperate and lovelorn puppies. Paul had dark good looks and an athletic body which attracted both men and women. Paul and his friend met Daniel and Will at the Manhole.

While the four of them stood at the front part of the bar having drinks, it was obvious to Will that Daniel wanted in Paul's pants. The more Daniel salivated over Paul, the more jealous Will became. And the more jealous Will became, the more he realized how much he liked Daniel. He was attached and it seemed he realized it all at once while Daniel made advances on someone else. Will felt like a fool.

Will excused himself to go the restroom and took his time, taking a stroll through the mostly empty hallway, or carwash, or hall of shame as he'd most recently heard it called. It was too early for the jam packed crowd and the lasciviousness that went with it, but there were some guys around. Will didn't resist when two cute ones stopped him and began kissing him. He made out with one while the other got down on his knees. When he'd had enough oral attention from both guys, Will walked away.

Accidentally on purpose, Will didn't zip his jeans back up all the way. He waited to finish buttoning his shirt as he easily strolled back up to his group at the front bar. Daniel noticed Will's jeans and when he looked up to meet Will's eyes, Will was ready with a satisfied gaze and the beginnings of a smile. Daniel flinched so slightly, only Will would have noticed – and that's hat he'd wanted. The exchange was that much more satisfying because Paul and his friend never even knew it. Five uncomfortable minutes later, Daniel said it was time to call it a night.

Paul and his friend asked Will if he wanted to go with them to a bar called Stormy's. Stormy's was a bar that sat on top of a small hill at a busy intersection in a turn of the century craftsman house. Paul's friend drove and Will sat in the back seat.

Paul carried a book by Oscar Wilde with him and he read quotes from it on the way to Stormy's. He stopped reading often so that he could put his head out the window, closing his eyes as the wind whipped across his face and through his hair. Will didn't understand why Paul acted the way he now did. Paul had graduated from college around the same time Will had, found a job in Atlanta around the same time Will found one, but somehow ended up back in Rome hanging out with gay men that were afraid to be gay men. Will suspected that Paul's divorce broke him, and that his ex-wife had introduced him to drugs. Will wondered if Paul would ever revert back to the way he'd been when they were younger – athletic and assured with the world ready to step aside for his entrance.
Will, in the backseat, silently wished Paul would just roll his damn window back up.

Stormy's, the bar in a house, was crowded and Will wanted to leave. Paul and his friend suggested Backstreet, a twenty four hour, seven day a week, multi-level dance club in Midtown Atlanta which was known for debauchery and drugs. Will had no interest and declined. He hoped Daniel was fuming and he was more interested in going home and checking his answering machine.

Betty, Will's tuxedo cat, who Will thought possessed a stronger intelligence and personality than many humans, hurried to the door to greet him. Betty stretched and made a meow purr that sounded like a little kid trying to immolate the purr of an engine. She raised her right paw up as she stretched, as if to say "hello, I want to reach out and touch you".

Will picked Betty up and carried her with him to the answering machine. Betty purred while Will grew disappointed by no calls from Daniel. Still carrying Betty, he went to his bedroom and closed the door. Frieda, Will's tense and nervous black cat, stayed perched on his bed. With her round, gold, saucer eyes, Frieda watched him as he detached the hair, washed his face, and got ready for bed. Once he was in bed, Betty and Frieda snuggled up on either side of him and purred. That's how he fell asleep most nights.

***

Wednesday night, Daniel called Will at work. He made a polite amount of small talk before getting to what Will had anticipated.

"Will, I think our relationship is becoming more friend-like than boyfriend-like" He said, the quick wit in his voice replaced with a flat finality.

Will said "this is because of Friday night?" He felt his voice tighten.

"I had already been thinking that" Daniel said. "Friday night just confirmed it."

"You were drooling over Paul" Will said. "It made me mad."

"I know" Daniel said. "I was attracted to Paul and I'm not ashamed of it. What you did reminded me so much of my ex. We were together fourteen years and he did those kinds of things all the time. I can't go through that again."

"I'm sorry" Will said. "I won't---"

"Will, I feel like I've known you far longer than I have" Daniel said. "I love you as a friend and I adore Kim and your other friends. I don't want to lose your friendship or theirs, so if you need time--"
Choking back tears, Will said "Of course. Let's stay friends."

"I'm going to Macon to visit Will's mom and dad tomorrow" Daniel said. "I'll be there through Monday and I'll call you when I get back."

By the time Will left work for the night, he'd already decided that while Daniel was away visiting his parents, he'd think of some way to win him back over.

Will didn't want to go straight home after getting dumped by Daniel. He thought about calling his friend Kevin, who'd grown up not far from him in Rome.

Kevin was five years younger than Will and he'd moved to Atlanta before Will. In that couple of years, Kevin had ferreted out several underground clubs where one could enjoy the seedier goings on in Atlanta's gay nightlife. Will always had a fascination with what he imagined must be going on in these types of places and Kevin enjoyed the role of guide. He introduced Will to the parts of Atlanta's gay nightlife that were just under the radar.

Kevin identified with a subculture within the gay subculture that called themselves bears. He had a youthful face and exuberance that made it hard to believe he was part of a subculture that exalted hairy, smelly, trucker armpits. Kevin ended enough sentences in a high, questioning note rather than a low, statement note that he often got called a valley bear. Will and Kevin not only shared a love of Atlanta's grittier side, they also shared a fear of the consequences for exploring it's grittier side - H.I.V. and other STDs. Often times, at the end of a night, one or the other of them would say "you're right, I'm never doing that again and I'm getting tested soon."

Will called Kevin and they agreed to meet at The Eagle. The Atlanta Eagle was another bar inside a former house, but not obviously so like Stormy's. At the front of The Eagle, which faced Ponce De Leon Avenue, was an addition of space that was so industrial and store front in its appearance that it obscured the early 1900's Victorian house that comprised most of the club. That addition of space occurred before The Eagle was The Eagle, and a heterosexual strip club resided in the space. The area that was thoughtlessly added on (like most of Atlanta) was where the stripper poles had been located. There is a concrete step that leads up to the rest of the club, which is drastically different in its architecture and style. While the added-on space, which is now a dance floor and bar area, feels like a warehouse industrial space, the back of the bar is comprised of thick wooden paneling, thick wooden door frames, and an ornate staircase leading up to a roped off second floor apartment. The rooms on the lower level were the living and dining areas of a once elegant home. The fireplace in what was once the Parlor or Dining Room is now painted black and there is a motorcycle parked on the hearth. The thick paneling on the walls is painted black and there is a pool table in the middle of the room with a single light hanging on top of it.

Will and Kevin liked to sit on the staircase and watch the pool games while drinking their beers and talking about the guys who were cruising around the pool room. The pool room had doorways, but no doors, on three of its walls. From where they sat on the staircase, they could see through a doorway to the poolroom and across to another doorway on the other side of the poolroom. This one was next to the front entrance, giving them a peek at who was just coming into the club. A third doorway on the opposite side of the fireplace led to rooms in the very back of the bar. Those were dark rooms where the smell of poppers permeated the air. Someone could also get to those rooms by the hallway that was just in front of the staircase.

Will and Kevin noticed it when someone walked past them and into the dark rooms, and then instantly turned up in the pool room. It signaled the guy hadn't gotten the action he may have hoped for when he entered the dark room.

Will laid out the whole spiel for Kevin – Paul, Daniel's drooling over him, Will's hallway excursion. Kevin laughed at the hallway excursion and said "I know everybody likes Daniel—"

"But you don't" Will said.

"It's not that. I don't dislike him" Kevin said "It's just that - well, he's kind of old."

Kevin made that face. That scrunched up face people make when they don't want to say it, but somebody's got to say it.

"The age difference didn't ever bother me" Will said.

"I know" Kevin said "I'm sorry to say this, but I just don't see it. Wouldn't you rather have some tattooed, pierced alterno-boy?"

"Like that one over there" Will said, nodding at a lean machine in combat boots, propped against the motorcycle watching the pool game.

"VaVaVoom" Kevin said. "Even though he is kinda skinny."

"I wish I could be that lean" Will said. "How do people have bodies like that?"

Kevin said "He's too thin. He needs to put on some weight."

"You and your bears"

"Don't worry about Daniel" Kevin said. "You can do better and he was taking up our Raging Burrito time anyway."

"Mmmmm, let's go to Raging Burrito tomorrow" Will said.

"Mmhm, now that you don't have to give all your time to that old man" Kevin said.

"He's not an old man!"

After Will and Kevin finished their drinks, they walked down dark, moonlit sidewalks, under canopies of huge tree limbs, back to their cars parked on side streets behind the Eagle. Lights from nearby skyscrapers shone through the branches of the old trees. Kevin said "Walking through here at night reminds me of New Orleans".

"I've never been there" Will said.

"What! You've never been!"

"Nope".

"We should go to Southern Decadence" Kevin said. "If not Southern Decadence, you should go to New Orleans sometime anyway. It's a lot of fun."

Will had heard of Southern Decadence, New Orlean's end-of-summer party where anything goes. It sounded like the back room at The Eagle, or the hallway at the Manhole – only out in the open and unashamed. Will knew he wasn't ready for it but he was too embarrassed to say so to Kevin.

"So dinner tomorrow at Raging Burrito?" Kevin said before getting into his white SUV.

"Yep" Will said.

Kevin said "I'll pick you up at the kitty around six".

The kitty was a heavy, bronze statue that was perched comfortably, one front paw draped over the other, outside the Marquis Tower that Will worked in. It faced the street corner at Peachtree Center Avenue and Harris Street. Whenever Will and Kevin went to lunch (lunch to Will– the six o'clock hour meant dinner to most) Kevin drove down Peachtree Center Avenue and turned right onto Harris Street, parking in the furthermost left lane. Will slid off the kitty's back, where he'd been sitting, relaxed in the early evening and people watching – business men and women leaving work, walking briskly among tourists strolling from their hotel to a restaurant.

Raging Burrito, a restaurant that Will and Kevin frequented, was in a little strip mall called Midtown Promenade on the corner of Monroe Drive and Piedmont Avenue in Midtown. Or, the epicenter of Atlanta's gay universe.

Across Piedmont Avenue is Ansley Square, home to Burkhart's, the gay Laundromat, the naughty gay store where lube and DVDs, among other things, were sold. Various other gay bars and businesses have come and gone over the years, including a gym called Bootcamp.

Midtown Promenade, where Raging Burrito is located, isn't as blatantly gay as all things with "Ansley" in their names are, but because of its location alone, it's pretty damn gay.

Kim was always on the lookout for cheap, tasty, and trendy places to eat in Atlanta. She took Will to Raging Burrito during his first week living in Atlanta and he loved it. Huge, delicious burritos served by alterno, college age servers and cashiers. Atlanta's more liberal, intown families ate elbow to elbow next to tanned, muscled, gay men with their perfect 50's flip haircuts and biceps.

That weekend, it was time to visit Rome again. If Will didn't visit regularly, he began getting the phone calls:

"Well, I wondered if you were still alive."
"Well, I guess you forgot us."
"I don't even know what you look like, it's been so long."

At his mom's house, like someone going home for Christmas break, it was all too easy for Will to revert to a sullen teenager. He slouched in a chair in the den, worrying over Daniel and telling his mom his troubles.

Will hoped Daniel would have a change of heart while he was at his parents. He and his mother watched a Hollywood movie Daniel had been in.

Will's mother, in her cool Bea Arthur demeanor, told him he'd have a stroke if he didn't stay still and stop worrying so much. It wasn't the first time she'd told him that.

On the drive back to Atlanta that Sunday, Will went over the things he'd say to Daniel when he called.

Daniel called Will Monday night after work

'What did your mom think of the movie?"

One could always tell more by what Will's mother didn't say. Daniel could have acted his ass off in the movie, but he'd jilted her son. And no matter what her son may have done wrong, she wouldn't be impressed with the movie.

"She liked it."

Daniel said "Will, I hesitated to tell you this because I didn't know how you'd feel about it, but it sounds like you've accepted the idea of us as friends."

Daniel told Will he'd gone out to the only gay bar in Macon on Saturday night and met someone.

"His name is Trey" Daniel said "And he's so cute and sweet. We ended up spending the rest of the weekend together."

After work, Will's cordless phone was busy like a switchboard. His best friend Rebecca, Kim and Zach, Kevin, back to Rebecca. Everyone agreed that Daniel was an ass. Cigarette after cigarette on the front stoop long after the blond across the way had turned off his lights and gone to bed. Telling Rebecca you'd been rejected was like telling your own mother. Her vitriol was cool and even.

"What is this *Trey* person like?" Rebecca said.

"I don't know anything about him yet" Will said "and I'm sure Daniel will tell me all about him. If Daniel has a clue that I'm still hurt or upset, he's not showing it."

"Wait until he sees you in person" Rebecca said flatly. "The tension in the air is thick enough to cut with a knife when you're upset about something. You won't be able to hide it."

Will could hear Rebecca exhale (and he could practically see her roll her eyes) as she said "God what a pretentious name – Trey."

Chapter Seven

Will and Daniel continued to talk on the phone daily and because it was over the phone, Will, who flushed and blushed and gave himself away with his facial expressions, was able to keep his hurt ego from Daniel.

Kim, a psychology major at Georgia State, loved to analyze. Over the phone. With a cigarette. She and Will often did just that and Kim wondered if Daniel really knew Will was still hurt. Perhaps Daniel enjoyed having his ego stroked. Kim also wondered if Daniel didn't use his past in Los Angeles attract younger men.

"To some young guy from South Georgia like Trey" Kim said "Daniel must seem like hitting the jackpot."
Will hated admitting he'd felt the same way.

In late July, Daniel asked Trey to move in with him.

"I hope he decides to" Daniel said. "We love each other body, mind, and soul". Will felt like throwing up on his cordless phone.

"Any plans for your birthday next week?" Daniel asked after finally being met with silence after his last comment.

"The usual crew" Will said "Kim, Zach, Kevin - plus a couple of people from out of town are meeting at Après Diem for dinner and drinks."

"Who's coming from out of town?"

"Rebecca and her boyfriend Joey" Will said.

"I'd love to meet them" Daniel said "You've talked about Rebecca several times."

"And Stephanie" Will said. "Stephanie coerced me into skipping Art History with her one fall day during his first quarter at U.G.A. From that day on, they were inseparable."

Daniel said "When you said a couple of people from out of town, I thought you might have meant Paul."
For a moment, Will felt for Trey and what his future must hold.

"Well please tell everyone hello for me" Daniel said. "I didn't realize this was a milestone birthday coming up when I made plans with Trey. Boy I'd love to be turning thirty again."

At Après Diem, no one asked about Daniel and Will didn't mention him. A party of ten, all seated around one of the big, round tables. Will didn't even feel close to thirty and he enjoyed as much, if not more, youthful energy and hope for the future than many twenty year olds.

Will was surrounded by friends, gifts, and laughter in his new city, and he still ached for that special person to share it all with.

By the time everyone was splitting up to leave, Will was on his third beer and ready to talk about Daniel. Stephanie, as nocturnal as she was in college, was ready to go somewhere, have drinks, and talk about him too. Stephanie was a sensitive, headstrong, brilliant minded, OCD battling, devourer of quality books and art. She was a genius of a painter and debater. She was also a child of money and could be a pain in the ass when she didn't get her way. The OCD battling and love of getting their way was their big, true connection. That and their equally matched moxie. Stephanie was tall with a fair complexion, dark hair, brightly lit brown eyes, and a determined gait. Stephanie's dad was also from Rome, and he knew Kim's dad.

It seemed like Stephanie had passed on to Kim the role of watching out for Will when he'd moved from Athens to Atlanta. The role wasn't a full time job in Atlanta as it had been in Athens. In Athens, in college, Will rarely had any money. Stephanie's dad paid for their lunches and dinners for three years. In Atlanta, Will had an income, but he wasn't any better at keeping up with finances. Kim, like Stephanie, came to the rescue at various times.

One night Will couldn't get money at an ATM because, as usual, he hadn't written down transactions in his checkbook. He had no idea how much money he had or how much money he'd spent. Kim, sensing he was embarrassed, pulled out a one hundred dollar bill and handed it to him.

"Go flash that at the bartender" she said.

Will and Stephanie went to Burkhart's, but the poolroom was too busy for them to get into a game right away. They wouldn't be able to exercise the skill they'd learned in college that they would "take with them for the rest of their lives" as Stephanie justified it one night when they'd shunned homework to drink beer and play pool.

Stephanie was expected at her aunt's house in Decatur, a ten minute drive from Midtown, where she was to spend the night. Stephanie suggested they go to Will's apartment, a ten minute drive to Buckhead, so she could use the phone to check in with her aunt. At Will's apartment, they could think of a game plan.

"Sorry, I don't have a cell phone yet" Will said. "You're doing fine" Stephanie said "You're just getting started. I don't have one either and I don't really like them – but in a situation like this it sure would be handy." There was a message from Zach on the answering machine. He wanted to be in Atlanta celebrating with Will and Stephanie, but Athens was over an hour away and his car had died. The beer buzz that Stephanie and Will had going was just the thing to jumpstart an impromptu drive to Athens.

Stephanie drove Will's car to Athens and straight to Zach's apartment, where he was ready to go.

With Zach in tow, Will still sat in front, lighting cigarettes for Stephanie and himself periodically. When Will's bladder called, as it often did, Zach and Stephanie waited in the car and giggled as Will made his way through the crowded Waffle House.

On the drive back to Atlanta, Stephanie half sang along with the radio, and half talked to Will and Zach. She was the only girl Will knew that could drive a stick shift. She had an air of confidence that made driving back to Atlanta at two AM with their Athens friend in tow, just for the purpose of drinking, seem like any other Saturday night.

"Will, where are we going when we get back to Atlanta?" Zach asked.

"Backstreet" Will said and quoted their sign "Always Open and Pouring."

"I don't know if I've ever been to Backstreet" Zach said.

"I went a couple of Times in the 80's" Will said. "And didn't go again until just last year. It seemed like a different world than what I remembered."

Will said "Now, if you watch from the balcony that overlooks the dance floor, it's a sea of chiseled, masculine chests. I couldn't figure out how they had the energy to stay up dancing all night."

"Drugs Honey." Zach said without hesitation.

"But how did they get those bodies?" Will asked.

Zach said "I don't know what those guys do during the week. It sounds like they're probably working out every day. But I can tell you what they're doing on the weekends."

Will felt naive. Zach's ecstasy fueled raves when he and Will had been roommates were long behind him, but it had left him more experienced. Will had never done anything more than smoke pot, and he hadn't even done that in years.

Backstreet was comprised of three floors. The bottom floor was the dance floor which was practically impossible to move through on a weekend night. Just a couple of steps up from the dance floor was a bar, and up an entire flight of stairs and perpendicular was another bar and a balcony that overlooked the dance floor. On that second, middle level, and through a doorway, was the main bar that ran almost the entire length of the main room. Just beyond the main bar were two pool tables which were the first things someone saw after gaining entrance and stepping around a dividing wall.

Everyone came and went through the parking lot entrance and above that entrance was a deck so that people could see the line which most weekends extended around the parking lot and to Juniper Street.

Atlanta police guarded the door as someone in drag, but dressed down for work, checked IDs, made change, and stamped hands. Between the main bar and the bar overlooking the dance floor was another flight of stairs that led up to the third and top level. There was yet another bar and a small stage for Atlanta's infamous drag performers. Seating and tables in front of the stage allowed drag queens easy access to patrons. They delivered heavy handed and snarky quips to audience members who'd driven an hour or more for the abuse.

Will shivered at the idea of having the spotlight turned toward him while Charlie Brown or Lilly White wrapped her curly, painted nails around a plastic drink cup and spat obscenities at him. He watched fearfully from behind the bar as insult after insult was hurled by a drunk, aging, drag queen who ended many sentences with "Up in this trailer, bitch".

One of Will's worst waking nightmares was the idea that one night, one of those drag queens would dig one of those long, curly red finger nails into his hair system (Rebecca never failed to squeal and say "I love how they call it a system!), take it off and then wave it around in the air before tossing it to another drag queen.

"I'd be the Frasier Crane of Backstreet" he thought.

"Let's just hang out here and play pool for a while" Will said to Zach and Stephanie before they got too far into the club.

Zach started toward the bar for drinks and Stephanie said "I can't believe little Zach! He's buff!"

"I told you".

"Yeah, but damn!" She said. "I had no idea. That six pack! Those arms!"

"He's been working hard" Will said. "Did you see his tattoos?"

"How could I not!"

Will and Stephanie watched a pool game and adjusted to the sudden cacophony after the comparable quietness of almost four hours in a car. She was still going on about Zach's transformation when he approached, drinks in hand and smiling. Stephanie was caught off guard.

"I was just telling Will how great you look". She flushed a little, and stared at the floor like Princess Di.

"Thanks Stephanie" Zach was all smiles.

"How long did that take?" She asked.

While Zach told Stephanie how he formed guns and six packs at the local, frat boy heavy, Gold's Gym in Athens, Will couldn't keep his eyes off of a shirtless, lean torso with dress pants hanging just so, and a fedora casting just enough shadow to compliment a strong jaw. Stephanie waved her hand in front of his face and yelled "Are you in there!" like she had so many times in college.

"Put some quarters down" she said "And maybe we'll end up playing him." Will began digging in his jeans pocket.

Stephanie said "He is hot Will. I like those vintage dress pants he's wearing."

Will couldn't get over the bodies running around the smoke and tan filled zoo of debauchery at three AM. He was mesmerized. He'd tried in the past to make one of those bodies for himself by attempting to survive on rice cakes and exercising. But it hadn't worked.

Twenty minutes later, Stephanie said "We lost the game Mister", bringing Will momentarily back to earth.

Stephanie turned to Zach - "Do you two want to go see who's dancing since Will would rather look at half naked men anyway?"

The three of them made their way through the thick crowd of shirtless, ripped chests and bug eyes to get to the landing that that overlooks the dance floor. There was so much energy, smoke, and music in such sharp contrast to the three a.m. sound of crickets where Will had grown up. Had he known this world was here waiting for him the whole time, he may have just skipped college and moved straight to Atlanta.

Will wondered when gay night life transitioned to this from the 80's, shoulder pad wearing queens he'd been met with during his first introductions to Atlanta. He was overwhelmed by what he saw now and wanted badly to be a part of it. Will was happy for Zach that he'd been able to achieve one of those bodies, and at the same time, he felt left behind.

Gay guys were now light years ahead of straight men in terms of musculature and physique. Maybe gay men, because they are outsiders from the beginning, naturally have more of the grit and determination needed for a meticulously maintained physique. Were gay men, fueled by vanity and a need for acceptance, working hard on themselves while their straight counterparts were sitting on the sofa, watching the game, drinking beers and ignoring their wives? Leaving them sex starved?

Surveying the sea of muscled tan chests dancing and rubbing against each other, Will wondered how a straight man could ever feel justified in looking down at one of these people. In fact, shouldn't straight men be looking up to gay men? Look what gay man had managed to do, in spite of.

Will's obsessing was halted by Stephanie's hand in his face again.

"Jesus Will, ARE YOU HERE OR NOT?!" she said. "Come on, we want to go upstairs".

They left the thumpa thumpa of the beat, the glowsticks and the light show below them for the quieter but still packed cabaret upstairs.

Those curly fingernails of Charlie Brown's were wrapped around a plastic cup, just like Will remembered. She spewed insults at a spotlighted straight couple who were at one of the round tables in front of her stage.

Charlie Brown was also Backstreet's Cabaret's namesake, and she didn't disappoint when delivering her trademark quips.

Charlie Brown asked the guy to stand up and unzip, standing back from him while the spotlight moved to his crotch. Egged on by the audience, the guy, shaking his head and looking to his girlfriend or wife for approval, reluctantly unzipped his jeans. As soon as he was unzipped, Charlie Brown abruptly and without warning jerked the guy's jeans down to the floor, bringing cheers from the audience as well as people standing beside the bar and beyond.

The straight guy was a good sport while Charlie Brown's curly nails pulled at the back of his briefs, drawing more applause from the audience.

Those same curly nails waved around the front of the guy's briefs, showcasing his package a la Vanna White. Charlie Brown turned up her plastic cup and excused the guy back to his table and girlfriend.

Stephanie, a seasoned painter and painting major, giggled at the mural on the wall beside the stage. Cartoon color replications of photos of stars all sat on top of one another. Cher turning back time. Madonna in a leather biker's hat, arms crossed and folded, a cigarette dangling from her freshly pumped lips a la Tom of Finland. Elvis and Marilyn. Elton John and Peg Bundy. Peg Bundy? Charlie Brown's photo was, of course, stenciled in among the other stars. Peg Bundy?

Zach went for more drinks while Stephanie and Will stayed close to the double glass door that led outside. Through the double doors, the deck was visible on top of the entrance, where cops and cashiers were still busy checking IDs and taking money.

Still a thick line to get through at the bar, Will and Stephanie reasoned that Zach, understandably, enjoyed the attention his new guns and tight stomach got him.

Stephanie said "I hope you're having a good birthday despite what happened with Daniel."

Will said "You know, I am enjoying myself. Who would have thought that I'd be ringing in my thirties with the unlikely combination of you and Zach and Backstreet – and at almost five AM."

"I know" Stephanie said. "Who would have seen that one coming. Just a couple of years ago, we'd be at The Grill in Athens at this time of day, eating French fries and feta, trying to figure Zach out.

"He is a closed book" Will said.

"But this isn't the same" Stephanie said in an upbeat tone. "I have a feeling you'll have this Daniel out of your system pretty quick. Look around you – this isn't Athens or Rome. There are lots of boys around for you to choose from."

"You can subtract the ones that would surely run when the hair comes off" Will said, the alcohol raising the maudlin.

"I'm kind of getting used to your new blond hair even though it bothered me at first" she said.

"Thankfully everyone doesn't have the artist's eye for detail that you do" Will said. "I hope not."

Zach, grinning widely, approached with their drinks. Ordinarily, Zach wasn't one to seek out attention, but he soaked it up.

They walked to the crowded outdoor patio and managed to find a spot. Through the waves of drunken chatter they looked up at the tips of skyscrapers lighting up the Atlanta sky.

"Zach, we were talking about Daniel while you were gone" Stephanie said "Have you met him?"

"No, but I want to meet him and his idiot boyfriend."

"Zach!"

Stephanie hadn't seen this side of Zach. Kim and Will experienced it nightly on the phone. He had to be comfortable with someone before he used that acidic tongue around them.

"Well. I do want to meet him. Who would act like this? Like anybody can go from dating to friends to someone moving in this quick." Zach said.

"Plus, I want to see what Daniel looks like" Zach said.

Stephanie lit a cigarette for herself and one for Will.

"I want to see what he looks like too" Stephanie said "Will, didn't you say he looks like an older Brian Hayes?"

"He does look like Brian Hayes" Will said. "His faced is shaped very similar – same puppy dog, questioning brown eyes."

Zach said "Who's Brian Hayes?"

"Will photographed him a lot for his senior exit show and I helped" Stephanie said. "We both had little crushes on him. Sometimes we wrote lyrics from Morrissey songs on fruit or canned food and left it on his doorstep in the middle of the night."

Will said "God, we're such stalkers."

"He liked it" Stephanie said.

"I know. He used to call me the next morning and ask me all kinds of questions about you" Will said. "He ended up with a crush on Stephanie."

"Yeah" she said. "I'd decided he was a goof by then though."

Stephanie smushed her cigarette butt with one of her trademark big, clunky white shoes she wore with jeans.

"We should take Daniel Payne some fruit" Stephanie said. Will was looking up at the lights of the skyscrapers against the sky when her words hit him. Will looked at Stephanie and she looked at him with a little "I dare you".

Stephanie looked at Zach with a little "Why not?"

Zach looked at Stephanie in disbelief.

They both looked at Will.

"Let's do it" Will said instigating an immediate and joyful clapping of hands and squeal from Stephanie.

"Well it's not really the middle of the night anymore, Will" Zach said. "It's after six."

Stephanie said "You're right Zach! I hadn't even noticed it's getting lighter out here!"

"We won't be able to sneak up his driveway and leave any fruit on his doorstep if it's daylight" Will said. "We've only done this type of fruit delivery in the middle of the night, stealing away like thieves."

"Well we'll just have to ring his doorbell and hand-deliver it to him" Stephanie said. "Then I can meet this Daniel."

Zach said "Yeah!"

"I can't believe we're doing this" Will said. "But since we are - I hope Daniel and Trey are planning to sleep in and have a relaxing Sunday morning."

"Where does Daniel live?" Stephanie asked.

"In Smyrna" Zach said.

"How far is that?"

"Probably twenty minutes on the interstate." Will said.

"Then we better get going" Stephanie said.

Will said "Are we really going to show up at Daniel's house on a Sunday morning, drunk, carrying a piece of fruit with Morrissey lyrics written on it?"

"Daniel doesn't get Morrissey lyrics" Stephanie said without hesitation. "Not since he dumped you and hooked up with someone else so quickly."

The sun was up as the three of us walked down Juniper toward the side street that Will's car was parked on.

"I want to drive again" Stephanie said. "And whoever sits up front has to light my cigarettes".

They tried to think of just the right fruit to take to Daniel on the way up to Smyrna. Stephanie finally suggested they take him a watermelon.

"Because Will said Daniel likes to lie by the pool a lot" she said.

"And that way, I can point out in front of everyone that it's the neighborhood pool and not his own pool."

Will and Zach couldn't help but laugh.

After exiting the interstate, they stopped at the first Kroger grocery store they saw in Smyrna. The hot, July, morning sun beat down on the itchy hair system on top of Will's head, which had already undoubtedly soaked up every bit of cigarette smoke in Backstreet that could be soaked up by someone's hair system.

The cashiers in the mostly empty store gave them a look as they passed. All three were drunk and giggling as if they were children in church and given strict instructions to be quiet. Will, Zach, and Stephanie that is, not the cashiers.

The three of them had tears in their eyes from laughing when they finally took their places in line with a carefully chosen watermelon in tow. Shaking with laughter, Zach missed the conveyer belt when he attempted to put the watermelon on top of it, sending the watermelon straight to the tile floor where it shattered into pink and green pieces. Zach, not moving a muscle, his arms still open as if he were still holding the melon, said "Will, did that really just happen?" The three of them, still wearing their sunglasses, couldn't control themselves and started laughing even harder. The justifiably surly, but not as surly as she could have been, cashier suggested they go pick out another watermelon. Stepping over the sticky mess, Will and Stephanie tugged at Zach, urging him back toward the coolers.

When the shiny white Celica finally pulled into Daniel and Rob's uphill driveway, the sun was shining, the sprinklers were watering the well manicured lawn, and a Sunday edition of the Atlanta Journal-Constitution Newspaper was neatly wrapped in plastic, lying beside the concrete driveway.

Stephanie said "Okay, Zach I want you to carry the watermelon. We'll stand on either side of you and I'll ring the doorbell."

Zach said "Oh Lord. Are we really doing this Will?"

"Will" Stephanie said "don't start acting all bitchy."

The three of them, Zach in the middle holding the watermelon, stood in front of Daniel and Rob's handsome, two story brick house. Stephanie rang the doorbell. Nothing. She rang it again. Nothing.

"Will" Stephanie said "Which room is Daniel's?"

Will walked around to the side of the house with her and pointed out Daniel's room while Zach stayed stationed with the watermelon "In case he comes to the door" Stephanie said.

'It's getting heavy" Zach said.

"Okay you can put it down" Stephanie said.

Stephanie yelled up to Daniel's window "Daniel, Oh Daniel. It's Will and Stephanie. Please come down we have something for you." Nothing.

They walked back around, both of them hoisting the melon back into Zach's outstretched arms, and took their positions on either side of Zach.

Stephanie rang the doorbell a third time. They heard footsteps before the door finally opened. A shirtless Daniel stuck his sleepy, confused head outside and said "Yes?"

After scanning the three of them, Daniel looked at Will and said "Will? I thought I heard your voice out here."

Smiling, Stephanie took the lead. "Hi Daniel, I'm Will's friend Stephanie and this is Zach." Daniel looked at Zach, still wearing sunglasses and holding the watermelon. Stephanie, still smiling and in her sweetest voice said "We brought you a watermelon."

Daniel said "Zach is it?" Zach nodded. Daniel said "That looks heavy, would you like to bring it inside?"

As always, Will silently admired the black baby grand in the living room as they passed on their way to the den and kitchen. The den and kitchen were open and to the right were stairs that led up to the bedrooms.

"Zach, you can just put that on the counter" Daniel said.

"So you're Stephanie?"

"I'm sorry, where are my manners?" Will said. "Daniel, this is Zach and Stephanie. They are friends of mine from Athens."

Stephanie gave Will a look.

"I see" Daniel said "And you're in town for the weekend?"

"Yes" Stephanie said. "We're here celebrating Will's birthday."

"Will, I have something for you" Daniel said and started upstairs. "Do you mind waiting while I go and get it?"

He didn't invite anyone to sit down. When Daniel was up the stairs and out of sight, Stephanie whispered to Will. "Don't be so bitchy."

While Daniel was upstairs Stephanie surveyed his house with her astute artist's eyes. Zach looked like he'd slipped into catatonia.

Daniel returned with an envelope with Will's name on it.

He said "I had to get you this card. I thought of you immediately."

Will tried a genuine laugh, but it came out sounding resentful.

Stephanie said "I hope we didn't wake you."

"As a matter of fact you did" Daniel said "and Trey is still asleep."

"Who is Trey?" Stephanie asked. She didn't sound convincing that she didn't know.

"He's Will's boyfriend" Daniel said. "Will knew he was here for the weekend."

They all seemed to notice at once that Zach had turned catatonic. Stephanie sensed it and began working toward an exit.

"Well, we are very sorry for disturbing you and Tripp" She said.

"Trey" Daniel corrected her.

"Will he be coming downstairs? I'd love to meet him" Stephanie said.

"No" Daniel replied flatly.

Will said "Oh, but you should bring him down to meet everyone."'

Daniel kept his gaze on Stephanie.

"I'm afraid not."

Stephanie said "Daniel, Will told me how much you enjoy lying by the pool every day, so we thought it might be nice if we brought you some watermelon to enjoy while you're out there."

"I don't eat watermelon" Daniel said, derailing Stephanie's plan for a snobbish community pool comment. "But my parents love watermelon. Would you mind if I gave it to them?"

"Of course not" Stephanie said.

"Well Daniel, we better leave you to your Sunday morning" Stephanie said. "It was very nice to meet you."

Chapter Eight

Daniel called Will the next week after driving Trey back to South Georgia and giving his parents the watermelon.

"Are you sure you shouldn't be afraid of this person" Daniel's parents asked him.

The more Daniel and Will talked about the Sunday morning visit, the more they laughed about it. Daniel, always curious, wanted to know all about Stephanie and Zach. Somehow, after the watermelon visit and Stephanie's heartfelt advice, Will's romantic feelings for Daniel dissipated. Their friendship instantly became the light and easy friendship that Daniel had hoped for. Daniel became a regular fixture among Will's group of friends. Outside of that group of friends, when talking to strangers as both Will and Daniel often did, if someone asked them if they were dating or how they became friends, Daniel began with "The Watermelon Story" as it came to be known. Daniel beamed whenever he replayed it.

Will and Daniel talked on the phone daily, sometimes several times. Daniel worried about his roommate Rob's growing penchant for rough trade and his frequent visits from The Smith brothers.

The Smith brothers were two rural, roughneck, straight brothers. One late teens and one early twenties. Rob paid one or both of them to spend the night some Saturdays. The Smith brothers, for Rob's payment, would allow him to suck them off unreciprocated. Sometimes the Smith Brothers would spend an entire weekend at Daniel and Rob's house. Daniel worried about the potential of robbery, or worse, by these two guys.

The four of them - Stephanie, Zach, Daniel and Will - met up again in late August. They all met Kim and her roommate Diana at Après Diem for a late dinner one Sunday night. After dinner, everyone went their separate ways except for Zach and Will.

"Where should we go" Zach asked.

"I'm not sure" Will said. "Bars are open until four so we've got options."

"I want to see The Manhole" Zach said, surprising Will.

"It's Dress Code Night" Will said. "You have to take your shirt off to go to the dance floor or anywhere in the back."

"Like the hallway" Zach said, laughing.

"Definitely the hallway" Will said. "But hey, I think they start letting everyone back, shirtless or not, after two. What time is it?"

"One."

"Let's go over there" Will said "We can have a drink at the front bar until two when they stop making people take their shirts off."

"Do they do that to women too?" Zach asked.

"I don't think I've ever seen a woman at the Manhole on take your shirt off night."

Zach laughed again. "Is that what the Manhole calls it Will, or is that what you call it? Take your shirt off night."

"That's what I call it" Will said. "That's what it is. But I don't ever go on those nights. Those guys are so cut."

"The are?"

"They're like the guys at Backstreet when we were there with Stephanie" Will said.

"Then we're going" Zach said.

The floors of The Manhole were littered with empty water bottles, neon colored plastic wrist bracelets, and dimming glow sticks. Most everyone had dilated pupils. Though Zach was sporting big guns and a six pack himself, he didn't take his shirt off to gain entrance to the back of the club. They both ordered beers and sat down at the front bar. It was only half an hour until two o'clock.

There was a guy sitting beside the entrance to the dance floor. Based on how someone was dressed, or not dressed, he either allowed entrance or not. At two AM, he picked up his stool and went away, allowing the men with shirts but and apparently no gym membership access. They'd been waiting to get to the back with the Adonis's and who knows what else might be going on. It was tantalizing, knowing the kind of things that went on in the dark corners of the Manhole, knowing that only men who were confident with their shirtless torsos were allowed back, and knowing you couldn't go in. One could only imagine that those bodies might be entangled in.

Will and Zach let them all pass before they went back. No sooner were they at the dance floor than a muscled, dark haired, shirtless man walked over to Zach. Will gave Zach a smile and walked back toward the hallway.

The hallway wasn't the traffic jam orgy that it could be on Friday or Saturday nights, but there was plenty of naughtiness going on amidst the bug eyed party boys. Will sat on the long bench where Kaleb and he sometimes stationed themselves to have beers and entertain themselves on slow weeknights.

There was a guy leaning against the outside wall of the pool room, making out with someone. His make out partner had his back to Will, and the guy leaning against the wall eyed Will over his shoulder as they kissed. Will laughed and jumped up, starting toward the bathrooms. The guy who'd been eyeing him pushed the other guy out of the way and walked toward Will. Smiling, he grabbed Will's crotch. He had piercing, light blue eyes, and a shirtless, lean, muscular frame. Will noticed a wild look in the guy's eyes as he, still holding onto Will's crotch, shoved Will against the wall and kissed him. He pulled at Will's belt and kissed him again. When a hand went up Will's neck and into his hair, he suddenly pushed the guy away. Will looked back as he walked off, to see what he could have had if he weren't so afraid. The guy stood in the middle of the hallway, arms outstretched, with a "What did I do?" look on his face. His light brown hair was mussed just so. Will thought he was sexy.

Will got himself another beer and went back out to the dance floor. He'd never been to Mardi Gras or Southern Decadence, but he imagined this is what it must look like during both – a party gaining it's second wind before ever really losing it's first. Zach was dancing with the same guy. He was handsome, Will thought. He liked the sight of Zach with someone older and sure of himself.

Will wandered back around to the hallway, where he saw the blue-eyed guy had resumed making out with his friend. When the blue-eyed guy saw Will, he pushed the guy off of him again and went back over to Will. The blue-eyed guy grabbed Will's crotch again, resumed kissing him, and put his hand in Will's hair again. But this time when Will jerked backward, the guy pulled a hair out. The blue-eyed guy stood, in the middle of the hallway, holding a strand of blond hair between his fingers. He smiled at Will as he dangled the expensive follicle in front of his face.

"What's this?" he asked, smiling broadly. Will felt himself turn red.

Attempting to deflect, Will said "What's your name?"

"Greg". His voice struck a chord in Will. "What's yours?" the guy asked, still smiling and holding the strand of hair up in the air like a trophy.

"Will."

"Will" He repeated it back, still smiling like a Cheshire cat.

Finally, Greg dropped the yanked hair and pulled Will in for another kiss. He grabbed Will's crotch and said "I know you have it, but do you know what to do with it?"

"Yeah" Will shot back. He had no idea what to do with it.

Greg said, "I'm not so sure about that" as he backed away from Will, putting on a show of staring at Will's crotch.

Will said "Leave with me."

Greg backed up against the wall, where he'd been making out with someone when Will first saw him.

"You're just going to tell me to leave with you?"

"Will you leave with me?" Will said.

Greg studied Will's face for a moment. He pushed himself off the wall and swaggered past him. He stopped halfway down the hallway and turned halfway around, looking back at Will over his shoulder.

"Well?" Greg said.

Will shrugged his shoulders. He didn't know what Greg was doing. "Are you coming?"

"I'm here with my friend" Will said, not yet believing his luck. "I should tell him I'm leaving."

Still standing in the same place, Greg sighed and made a large, come along gesture.

Will thought Zach must still be around because he'd walked by once when he and Greg were making out. Will found Zach on the dance floor and told him he was leaving.

Greg, relaxed, arms folded, leaning against a wall, said "Is it okay for you to leave now?" as Will approached.

Greg lived in non-descript, flat-roofed, brick apartment complex just a few blocks away. Will could make out the shiny black lacquer of the dining room furniture on the way to Greg's bedroom. It seemed so glamorous to Will. A hot, muscled man living just down the street from the Manhole with his other gay roommates. They could do what they wanted, bring men home any time, and even use cheap, tacky furniture. No one could tell them what to do or even impose good taste on them. If Stephanie had thought Daniel's world was fool's gold, she would have, without hesitation, deemed this a gutter. Will wondered if Greg and his roommates even fooled around together.

Greg's bedroom was neat but cramped. Not intended for his metal canopy bed, flush in a window corner. Greg turned the lights down low and excused himself to go to the bathroom.

"Pick something out" he said, opening his five disk changer and gesturing toward his CD collection. Indecisive and nervous, five CDs seemed like a task to Will. Greg's collection contained plenty of pop from the era - Sugar Ray. Semisonic. Matchbox 20. Mixed in with those was an R.E.M. CD. Will was pleasantly surprised to see it, and put it in.
From the hallway, Greg said "Just pick something."

Will grabbed four other CDs with no thought to the names. Naked, Greg positioned himself on his bed and waited for Will. Will undressed. He'd worn a shirt that buttoned up the front. Otherwise, he'd have left Greg like that while he went in his bathroom and carefully pulled his tee-shirt up over the hair. It would have ruined the moment.

Will fucked him like that and came within a couple of minutes.

Greg went to the bathroom again and returned with a warm, wet hand towel. He turned the music down and the light low.

"That's my side of the bed" he said, pointing to the outer side of the metal canopy.

When Will returned from the bathroom where he'd washed his face, used Greg's mouthwash, and ate his toothpaste, he crawled across the foot of the bed to the passenger's side. Greg drifted off to sleep while Will lay next to him, hair itching, surveying his room.

On the wall opposite Greg's bed was a black and white poster. A lean, cut, mid-twenties model, jeans riding low on his hips exposing a washboard stomach. He was pulling his tank top over his head. "Not All Men Are Created Equal" the caption read. Welcome to Atlanta, Will thought.

Marky Mark smiled down at Will from the wall on his side of the bed. It was the Marky Mark poster from the nineties. Him scrunching his Calvin Klein briefs in his hands, revealing the most muscular legs of his life. Huge arms and washboard abs. Kim had said she would pay one thousand dollars for that particular poster if she could find it. And she would have. Will couldn't wait to tell Kim he'd not only seen the poster, but fucked in front of it.

Will focused again on the "Not All Men Are Created Equal" poster. Such a long, lean torso. It commanded attention. Will guessed that everyone, whether they cared to admit it or not, had either wanted to touch a body like that or have a body like that of their own. He wanted both. It was hard for Will to fall asleep with another person in bed. He worried about every movement and every little noise, concerned that he might wake the other person, at the cost of his own sleep. The hair itched.

The R.E.M. CD finished and another CD started. It was louder and it woke Greg up. Will told him that he was leaving, so Greg got up and put on a robe and a pair of glasses that were lying on his nightstand. At The Manhole, he'd looked so youthful and wild eyed. Now, he looked like someone's groggy father who'd been woken up in the middle of the night. Surely he'd stolen those glasses from the set of The Rockford Files. Greg gave Will a hug and a goodbye kiss at the door. Will was taken by Greg's impeccable manners combined with his animalistic behavior in bed.

When Will got home, Zach wasn't there. But the next morning, he was asleep on David's brown, plaid sofa. Zach wouldn't give up any details about his night, except that he had walked all the way up Lenox Road to Will's apartment. As disconcerting as it sounded, Will knew that getting information out of Zach that he did not want to give up was impossible. Something had happened with the person Zach went home with, but Will and Kim may never know what prompted Zach to walk home.

Over the next couple of weeks, Will thought about Greg and one weeknight, after having drinks with Kaleb at Burkhart's, Will drove past the Manhole and toward Lenox Road to see if he could remember which apartment building Greg lived in. When he was sure he was at the right non-descript, brick complex, he left his phone number in Greg's door. The next Monday night, David and Chloe stepped beside Will on their way down the front steps. Will smoked an evening cigarette as they walked past. Chloe said "Oh, Will – someone named Greg left you a voicemail. I saved it."

She turned and gave Will a knowing smile as they jogged away with their lean, runner's bodies.

Greg's voice wasn't what Will remembered. It was a little higher. A little thinner. And it resonated through him. He could swear he'd heard it a million times before. He liked hearing Greg say his name. He listened to the message again. "Will."

"That voice" Will whispered to himself "that voice." He loved hearing it.

It was the next evening before Will felt brave enough to call back. He dialed Greg's number from work, and got his voicemail. Will was sure he wouldn't hear from Greg again because of how awkward and nervous he must have sounded while leaving the message. Greg called back later the same night, after Will was home and laughing on the phone with Zach and Kim. He was outside smoking and watching the blond across the way's nightly show - making and having dinner in only his jogging shorts.

"I'm sorry I didn't call you back sooner" Greg said. "I was out of town". He sounded cool and composed.

Nervously, Will said "Work or pleasure?"

Greg said "I went with some friends to Southern Decadence in New Orleans".

It shot through Will, and he didn't know why. The wildness of Southern Decadence and the wildness of Greg. All at once.

"Oh" Will said "My friend told me about Southern Decadence not long ago. He said it's a lot of fun."

Greg said "It--" his voice drifted. "It is a lot of fun." He said "I don't think I could do that again for another year though. I'm pretty worn out."

"What is Southern Decadence?" Will said.

"It's—" Greg, though he remained cool, couldn't find words.

"Maybe your friend should tell you about it" he said.

Will and Greg made a date for that Friday night. Greg said he worked until eleven PM at The Hilton. Since they worked similar hours, they made it a late date. Greg suggested they meet at Blake's, the stand and model bar on Tenth Street across from Piedmont Park.

At work the next day, Sarah easily picked up on the extra spring in Will's step. She was in the guest chair of Will's cube before lunch.

"You have a date" she said, sipping her can of Coke. Will never knew how she constantly drank Coke yet still had a lean body like David's and Chloe's. He was afraid to tell her that though this one wasn't disabled, he carried people's bags to their rooms at The Hilton. Will thought it was hot, being a bellhop in a big hotel. He'd already imagined the ways Greg's lasciviousness might emerge while showing strangers from out of town to their rooms.

"You wont' like this one any better than Daniel" Will said sheepishly. "He's a bellhop at The Hilton."

Sarah's crossed leg was really going now. "Really" she cooed, smiling. "He must look like a model then."

"He is gorgeous" Will said.

"What's his name?"

"Greg."

"Where'd you meet him?"

"You don't want to know."

"You met him at the Manhole didn't you." Sarah laughed. "When's your date?"

"This Friday" Will said. "And I've got nothing to wear and I really want to buy that Acqua Di Gio I've been smelling whenever I go into Lenox Mall."

"I'm always in favor of buying new cologne" Sarah said.

"Mr. Turner". Neither one of them had noticed Frank walking toward Will's cube. Sarah tensed up likeBettyand Frieda when they see a cat outside the living room window. Frank dropped a stack of papers and envelopes on Will's desk. They made a thump. Frank looked at Sarah and Will.

"Would you print labels for these envelopes, put invoices in them, and have them all in the outgoing mail by the time you leave on Friday. There were at least seventy-five. Maybe one hundred.

"I'll do it" Will said.

Frank looked at Sarah, then back over at Will. "U. G.A. huh?" he said. "My daughter's going to Tech."

Frank tilted his head and stared at Will's hair for a few moments before giving Sarah a look and then finally skulking away.

"His daughter is eight" Sarah whispered.

"I know" Will whispered back.

Sarah whispered again "I hope she ends up dropping out of high school."

"Because she gets pregnant" Will whispered back.

Sarah almost spit out her sip of coke as they chuckled.

"I'm going back upstairs but I still want to hear more about this hot man later."

An hour later Sarah's name appeared on Will's phone display.

"I walked over to the Hilton during my lunch break" she said. "I didn't see any name tags that said 'Greg'".

"I can't believe you did that" Will said "And he doesn't work until three".

By Friday evening at six, most everyone had gone home and Will had completed most of the busy work that Frank had given him. He didn't mind it. Will had a lot of nervous energy and at times, he welcomed the chance to keep his hands busy in an effort to keep his mind from obsessing. It rarely worked for very long.

Ginger, Will's co-worker who spent many work hours on the New York Times Book Review's website chatting with other book snobs, brought her legs down from the top of her desk and walked back to his cube.

"Will, are you at all bothered that Frank gave you all this work to do instead of Craig?"

"Not really" Will said. "This doesn't bother me. I think I've even read somewhere that monotonous work can be good for the soul."

"You're kidding me".

"No I'm not" Will said. "I'd rather do this than run around kissing Frank's ass all day like Craig".

Ginger let out a hearty laugh.

"Well I'm going home, Will. If I were you I wouldn't take this kind of shit off of Frank".

"It's okay" Will said. "Have a good weekend."

This was the first time Frank had assigned a task like this to Will. Without this busy work, he'd be pacing and going downstairs for a cigarette every five minutes in nervous anticipation of his date with Greg.

After Ginger left, someone at the The Hyatt Hotel's rooftop pool caught Will's eye. The pool area was empty except for one lean, muscled man who swam in Speedos. Back and forth he went, deliberate and graceful. His muscles worked in concert with every movement.

Mesmerized, Will sat in his cube, facing the window, and watched him swim back and forth until he finished, dried off, and pulled his cargo shorts up over his Speedos. The peaceful spell was broken with Craig's exuberant return.

"I've been on the thirty seventh floor of the Westin with a hot married man from Virginia!"

"Where'd ya pick him up?"

"The bathroom at the Marriott across from the Sports Bar" he said.

"The one you and that guy you told me about go to."

"We don't go to that one anymore" Will said. "He showed me another one at SunTrust Plaza with a door that locks."

"Oooooh. You better show me where that one is."

"I will. And my friend told me that sometimes they have about six or seven guys in there.

"A lunchtime orgy!"

"Tell me about the guy at the Westin" Will said.

"Well" Craig started "We were in the bathroom across from the Sports Bar but someone came in. We stayed really still and quiet in the stall until they left. I think it was a cleaning person. Anyway, John asked me to come back up to his room at The Westin."

"John?"

Craig did that positively evil laugh he does. "Uh huh" he said.

"That was a close call" Will said. "I'm glad you didn't get caught."

"Will - could you imagine if security came up here and told Frank that I was being held for public sex!"

The very idea of it made Will laugh out loud.

"Well – his dick was about that long."

Craig demonstrated with his hands in the air.

"What'd you do with him?"

Craig said. "We sucked each other's dicks for a long, long time and then we jacked each other off.

"I wish you could have seen him – tall, dark, and married."

"Mmmmmm" Will said. "Married is so hot."

Craig laughed again and said "uhh huuuhhh."

Will looked twice to make sure it wasn't Blanch Devereaux sitting in front of him.

Craig grabbed a CD out of his desk drawer and proudly showed it to Will.

"Have you heard this yet?"

Will looked at it and let out a little laugh.

"That's Cher, Craig."

"I know. Barry says this is going to be huge."

Barry worked on fourteen in Marketing with Sarah. He and Craig had been friends since college.

"Speak of the Devil" Craig said as Barry approached down the row of empty cubicles.

"Hi Will."

Will could swear he saw those little diamonds, like in advertisements from the 1950's, coming off of Barry's Hollywood white teeth and heavy starched shirt. Will smiled and said hello, but didn't break from his envelope stuffing.

When Barry and Craig began talking in Craig's cube, Will went back to obsessing about his date with Greg. Once in a while he tuned in to their conversation. It was a routine for those two on Fridays - Barry relentlessly trying to cajole Craig into going out after work.

"But I'm really tired Barry" Craig said. Barry's back was to Will, who winked at Craig. He would never tell Barry the reason he was tired was because he got picked up in a hotel bathroom downstairs and then went back to a married man's room for the better part of the evening.

Barry didn't let up on him. "But after Taqueria Del Sol, we're going to The Man-hooole". He practically sang it.

"Oooooh", Craig cooed. The carwash."

Craig looked at Will and said "Will, you know what the carwash is don't you?"

Barry turned to face Will. Will shrugged his shoulders.

"Oh Will!" Craig said. "You go to the Manhole don't you?"

"Yes".

"And you don't know about the hall of shame?"

"What's that?" Will said, barely able to keep a straight face.

"Well, let's just say it lives up to its name."

Barry finally conceded and offered to walk Craig downstairs. The two of them said goodbye and for the next hour and a half, Will's hands worked while his mind wandered. What would he say to Greg. How to disrobe and get into bed without pulling the hair off. How hot Greg's ass was.

Windows down and music up, there was a hint of autumn in the early September air as it swirled around on Will's drive up to Buckhead. The daily gridlock had been over for a couple of hours and presumably most of the commuters were in bed for the night. At ten PM, people like Will were getting themselves ready to go out and experience Atlanta's other side.

When he got home, Betty greeted him at the door with her outstretched arm and meowpurr. Frieda walked over from the window sill she'd been perched on, watching for him to get home. David and Chloe were in their respective zones – him working on an apple computer and she avidly reading a science book. Will took comfort in their daily dedication to running, studying, and each other. They could be doing anything they wanted on a Friday night but they chose to stay in and work.

Chloe looked up from her book and smiled at Will. "Greg called" she said.

Chloe, rolling her pencil under her chin, watched Will as he walked over to the machine. She was all ears.

"Will, this is Greg. I just wanted to make sure we're still on for Blake's at eleven."

Will looked at Chloe and said "Thanks".

He attempted to act like it wasn't a big deal, but it was a feeble, transparent attempt. That voice.

Once inside his room with the door closed, Will switched to high gear. Frieda managed to slip in before he closed the door and now she was perched atop his bed, watching him.

Off with the hair, then the clothes. Quick shower, then dressed again - faded jeans with a slight hole and a new V-neck Banana Republic sweater to counter the old jeans. Brown double-holed leather belt that his mom had worn in the 70's (it was a men's belt) and his favorite ankle length cordovan boots (Stephanie had told him they were cordovan. He didn't know.) A squirt of Acqua Di Gio - into the air, followed by a quick walk through and turn around in the air. Never sprayed directly on, as he'd learned behind the cologne counter at Rich's as a teen. Finally, back on with the hair.

Frieda's round, gold saucer eyes followed Will back and forth like a tennis match. He gave her a pat on the head and took off. Chloe looked him over, tilted her head while rolling the pen under her chin, and smiled a smile that said "Interesting. I'll let you slide – this time."

She told him to have a good time. David, half noticing he was leaving, said goodbye too. Will didn't ever take it personally that David was either engrossed with an apple computer or laughing hysterically at an episode of Southpark.

There was a gravel parking lot across Tenth Street from Blake's and it was already full, so Will parallel parked on Myrtle Street, just off of Tenth. Will got his first ever cat call walking down Myrtle Street toward Tenth Street and wondered if the hole in his jeans was too slutty. He reasoned that since Greg had put his naked ass in the air for him within ten minutes of bringing him home, that the hole (in the jeans) was not too slutty.

Will didn't see Greg among the sea of gorgeous men downstairs at Blakes, so he made his way to the back of the bar and the stairs that led to the second level. The staircase was packed and there were two drunk drag queens trying to push their sequins and feathers past the tans and pecs that crowded the small passage.

"Girl, she ain't right!" Will heard one of them exclaim as he braced the side rail in anticipation of one of them slipping on their heels and tumbling downward. Those types of queens made him nervous. So rowdy and shameless. He feared that one of them, eyes trained to detect plastic surgery and fake hairlines, would figure out his hair and snatch it off. He could see bright red fingernails waving his one thousand dollar hair around while someone screamed "Girl, look at her weave!"

Will held the side rail tightly as he made his way past the drunken ladies as quickly as possible, the whole time the macabre image of one of them grabbing his hair replaying itself in his head.

Finally upstairs, Will shot over to the bar. Beer in hand, he remained stationary in a corner and watched for Greg to walk by. He didn't see Greg, but he felt like he had to have the time in the corner with the beer before he could venture any further. When he did venture further, and all the way around the downstairs and upstairs of the bar, he still didn't see Greg.

Will's apartment was dark and the TV was off, but Chloe came out of David's room in her PJs and whispered that Greg had called.

"He said he couldn't find you at Blake's and asked you to call him" she said. Chloe stood in the living room and listened to Greg's message with him before going back to bed.

"Will, I'm so sorry about Blake's. I should have known it would be too crowded."

Chloe smiled and said "Good night Will."

Once Chloe was back in David's room and Will was in his own, he called Greg. He would have been embarrassed for Chloe to hear how nervous he sounded when he talked to him.

"Will" Greg said "I'm sorry for the foo pas".

Will tried. He bit his tongue. But it came out.

"Faux pas?" Will said.

"Whatever" Greg said "If you don't mind getting out again, I could meet you at Burkhart's in twenty minutes."

Will stood in the middle of the two downstairs bars at Burkhart's looking for Greg. He looked all around, but didn't seem him anywhere.

"I watched you walk in" Greg said, giving Will a good scare as he walked over to him.

The sheer, cable sweater Greg wore showed off his muscular and pale torso. Will had never seen anyone wear such an overtly sexual piece of clothing – in real life. In public. And look so hot in it. He was practically hard and stumbling for words when Greg said "Let's go back here. It's quieter."

Greg led Will to a little afterthought of a back bar that had apparently been added on. The ceiling was lower and a TV played above the bar. The bartender was laid back and there were only a few people around.

Greg was right. It was quiet and cozy. Will could barely keep his eyes off of Greg's nipples showing through the sheer sweater.

Greg said "Let me buy you a drink since I messed up with Blake's. What would you like?"

When Will asked for a beer, Greg said "just a beer?"

"Why, what are you drinking?"

Greg looked at the bartender and said "May I have a Golden Texas Margarita?"

Greg nodded to Will and said "And a beer for him".

Will felt like he had when his brother, six years his senior, got his first car and Will was still riding a bicycle.

Greg pulled Will in close and said "Finally, I'm glad you made it." Will was hard before the bartender had the margarita ready. Greg looked at him, amused, and smiled. Greg kept his leg against Will. Full hard on. Greg offered Will a sip of his drink, and Will made a face before giving it back to him. He directed Will's attention to a movie that played on the large TV screen above the bar.

"Recognize that?" Greg said.

Will said "That's the Suntrust Building! I can see that from work!"

"This movie was filmed in Atlanta" Greg said. "I forget which Baldwin brother that is."

Greg said "Tell me again what you do at work."

Greg appeared disinterested as Will told him about his job. He asked who Will's friends were and where he hung out.

Greg said "I wondered because I don't see you at The Manhole every weekend."

Will thought the every weekend part of that statement was odd, but kept his mouth shut. Did Greg go to the Manhole every weekend? Did people go to the Manhole every weekend?

Will told Greg about Kim and Zach, Rebecca and Stephanie. Greg said "Don't you have any gay male friends around here?"

"Oh yes" Will said. "Kevin, Kaleb, Daniel". He gave him a brief description of each and told Greg how they'd met.

"Is that all?"

"Yeah?" Will said. "Why?"

"Two of those you already knew before you moved to Atlanta."

He said. "You've been here a year and you've only made one new gay male friend?"

Will was glad so many of his friends from home lived in Atlanta too. It made it less daunting.

Will said "I hadn't thought of it that way" and continued looking for buildings in the movie that he recognized. He felt Greg's eyes on him.

Greg said "You really are beautiful" and kissed him. He saw that Will was instantly hard again and grinned, canoodling Will's legs with his own under the bar.

"How old are you Will?"

"I just turned thirty" Will said without mention of the Watermelon Story. "And you?"

"Thirty-five, thirty six" Greg waved his hand dismissively. "I don't know."

Greg turned his attention back to the big screen TV.

"What!" Will said. "You don't' know!"

Greg stroked him through his jeans, smiling.

"What do you want to do when we leave here?" Greg asked.

Too shy to say what he really wanted, Will said "I don't know". The indecision irritated Greg.

"Okay" he said. "Let's go to the Manhole when we finish their drinks." Greg continued stroking Will while they finished their drinks.

There was a tent in Will's jeans when Greg stood up and said "Ready?"

Will said "Couldn't we wait just a second?" and looked down at himself.

Smiling broadly, daring him, Greg said "No."

He pulled Will up from his barstool and drew him in for another kiss.

"You can walk right behind me" he said softly and powerfully enough to leave Will helpless while leading him toward the front.

Midway through the front of the bar, which was also visible from the second level, Greg stepped away from Will, leaving him standing center court, tent fully visible. Greg turned back to smile. Will was panic stricken like a deer in the headlights. Greg laughed and pulled him back in.

The Manhole, like most weekends, was full of chiseled men showing off their bare chests. And even with all those men around, Greg only paid attention to Will. Hand in hand they walked down the unusually sparse Hall of Shame to the poolroom. Will hadn't noticed before, but there was a small, cut out window in one of the walls of the poolroom. The window was the kind one might see in the cafeteria of an elementary school, sometimes forgetting someone was on the other side of it. Someone was behind this window as well, preparing bar food for Heretic patrons. Greg walked up to the window and ordered chicken fingers.

"Want anything?" he asked over his shoulder.

"Uh – uhm, no" Will said, almost having an Alice in Wonderland moment. He kind of wondered if the window, and the person behind it serving food, would be there next time he was at the Manhole.

"I never got a chance to eat after work" Greg said through a cheek stuffed with chicken.

Ordinarily, Will would have flinched and tried to hide it. But on Greg, talking with a cheek full of food was emasculating. Will made a mental note to ask Kevin if this was what rough trade meant. Will wished he could be that type of person. The kind who can talk with their mouth half full of food and not care. Will used several napkins during a meal, each bite filled with anxiety that something may run out the side of his mouth and land on his shirt. It was oddly out of character, how Greg talked with his mouth full. The rest of his manners were impeccable.

Greg finished his dinner and walked over to one of the two pool tables where a game was already in progress. He put quarters down and said to one of the players "Can he play the winner?" while nodding at Will. The guy looked like he would have agreed to most anything Greg asked for.

Greg cheered Will on and though Will was a confident pool player, he missed shots he ordinarily wouldn't have. He loved being around Greg and at the same time, he was nervous and self conscious around him.

Someone Greg knew came into the pool room and sat next to him. With Greg's attention momentarily diverted, Will made a couple of shots before his opponent won the game. Greg stopped talking and cheered him on more. Embarrassed, Will excused himself to go the bathroom.

When Will returned, he felt like he was walking up on the end of a private conversation. Greg's friend continued talking, apparently about someone he'd been dating.

"He's already ready to get married" the guy said.

Greg said "Oh, I know how that is."

Will felt ridiculous.

After the guy left, Greg let Will coerce him into one more drink.

"I have one roommate moving out tomorrow and another one moving in" Greg said "I've got to be in bed at a decent hour."

Greg, like a kid with a new toy, kissed Will again and then watched his erection grow.

Greg said "You're not coming home with me tonight."

"I want your ass again" Will said.

"Wooooo!" Greg said. "Look at you!" He stepped back and leaned carelessly on the pool table.

"Well" Will felt himself turning red. "I do".

"When did you have it before?" Greg asked. Will knew his face was flushing red.

"What?" Will said.

"Just kidding" Greg said "So we met here. Is that right?"

Will began to stomp off toward the bar, Greg grabbed him on cue, and pulled him back in.

Laughing, Greg said "You're cute Will, you really are."

He said "You could walk through here with some attitude if you wanted to."

Greg said "How old are you again?"

"Thirty".

"You're a young thirty" he said. "Didn't you get any experience in college?"

Will said "How old are you again?"

Greg pushed him off and sighed. "Go get our drinks."

"I'll be right back."

Will didn't attempt any attitude in his walk. They had their last drink of the night and Greg messed with Will's head some more before he said he was ready to call it a night.

"You be careful going home" Greg said.

"But I want to go to your house." Will said.

"No" Greg said. "I told you I have to get up early tomorrow. Or today," He looked at his watch.

"I'll walk out with you." Will said.

In the parking lot, Greg kissed Will again and when the tent grew in Will's jeans, he grabbed it. Smiling, Greg pulled away from him. Will stood still, looking after Greg. Greg, shaking his head, walked back over to him. He kissed Will again and said "You won – this time."

Will loved being in Greg's apartment again. When they passed the darkened dining room with the shiny, black lacquer dining room set, Will could almost hear the infamous, local Atlanta TV ad - 'tell 'em the Wolfman sent ya'.

Greg's bedroom was mildly messy in a busy person kind of way. It probably wouldn't have taken ten minutes to straighten it up. Will felt, in that regard, they were on an even par.

Greg asked Will to pick out some music and excused himself. Instead of looking through his CDs, Will wanted to take in more details about his room. A pair of jeans was carelessly tossed across his bed. Thirty one inch waist. He was six years older than Will and three waist sizes smaller. Will looked at himself in Greg's dresser mirror.

"All those yummy breakfasts Grams made me – bacon, eggs, buttered toast and jelly. It's all right here."

Interrupting the conversation in Will's head was a naked Greg standing in front of him. "Are you just going to stand there looking at yourself all night or are you going to pick out a CD?"

Ray of Light was already in Greg's CD player and Will went with it.

Will excused himself as well, undressing and crawling into Greg's bed when he returned. Greg was asleep.

Will lied in Greg's bed as still as he could, trying not to disturb Greg. He couldn't sleep. The damn hair itched. He lied still, taking in Greg's room. An out of date computer with party beads draped on the side of the monitor. The monitor was that beige-gray color. They were everywhere. Dresser drawers open with clothes overflowing. The Marky Mark poster beside him. He'd forgotten to tell Kim about it. The poster on the opposite wall. Not All Men Are Created Equal. The long torso and the tight abs. Ray of Light was the soundtrack for Will's late night musings, earning Madonna a Grammy in the background.

> Travellin' down my own road
> Watchin' the signs as I go – oh –oh

Will thought about the weekend before, when he and Kim had gone to Athens to hang out at the one gay bar with Zach. Boneshaker's. It was late and the crowd was thinning out and Will sat himself down next to Michael Stipe. He tried pretending he didn't know who Michael Stipe was, saying things like "Oh, you're a musician? You should keep that up – you might be able to do something with that one day." And "I would have guessed you were an accountant."

Michael Stipe was a good sport.

When Will asked Michael Stipe how he felt about Ray of Light, he said "She's very nice. She likes to talk about herself."

Michael Stipe watched Will's reaction, and Will knew the game was over. It was game over for this night as well. When the CD finished and another one came on, it was much louder. As it was happening, Will remembered the time before, but it was too late to do anything about it.

Greg rolled over and said in a surly tone "turn that down, it's too loud".

Will used it as an opportunity to excuse himself. He dressed quickly. Greg, groggy and wearing his white terry cloth robe and James Rockford seventies bifocals, began walking Will through his apartment and to the door. They ran into what must have been one of Greg's roommates on his way to the bathroom across from Greg's room. Greg gave him the same kind of look he'd given his friend in the poolroom at The Manhole. The look said "have you ever had one of these?"

In the kitchen, Greg unlocked the back door that opened to the parking lot, hugged Will, and gave him a kiss.

"I'm sorry" Greg said. "I'll call you."

Will sat on the front stoop smoking, looking at the drippy green lights on the Tower Place office tower, wishing the blond across the way hadn't gone to bed so early, when Zach and Kim called. They were having so much fun laughing at Will's attempt to pick up Michael Stipe (he eventually asked Michael Stipe for a date. He was politely turned down.) and Kim's impromptu three AM rendition of I Touch Myself at the Athens Krystal Drive Thru, Will thought he would get by without hearing them sing "Greeeeggggg".

"Will's in love" Zach started.

Kim said "I think he may have a boyfriend."

"You two--" Will lit another cigarette.

"Tell us about your date the other night." Kim said.

"Yeah, did you get a piece of his ass?" Zach said, laughing.

"Zach, Will's ruined you!" Kim said.

Will said "No, I didn't get to fuck him."

"That has happened on dates before, Will" Kim said.

Zach laughed. "You haven't seen the guys at the Manhole".

Will said "Even if he brushes up against me I get hard. It's terrible."

"Were you in public Will?"

"Yes." The two of them started cackling like hens.

"Oh My God, Will, did you walk around with a hard on all night?" Zach asked.

"That's what I was going to say!" Kim chimed in.

"Not all night. But several times, yes. And Greg milked it. Well he didn't milk it, but I wish he had."

"Will."

"Sorry Kim".

"Why didn't you get two get it on?"

"He fell asleep" Will said "He said his roommate was moving the next morning and he had to get up."

"Don't worry about it" Kim said. "He brought you home didn't he?"

"Yeah".

"You're fine."

"Will has a boyfriend – Will has a boyfriend." In unison.

"Cut it out." Will said.

Before he could tell them the other details of their date, Stephanie called on the other line.

"You've got five minutes" Kim said.

Greg called that weekend and he and Will made plans for a weeknight date. It was a Thursday night and they met at the Armory, which was a bar next to Backstreet. Both Backstreet and the Armory had been around for years and because of their close proximity, their names were synonymous.

Greg's friend Lou met them at The Armory. Will wondered if Lou was there to help Greg assess him. Will was so irritated that Greg had brought a buffer, he watched one of the TV Screens more than he participated in their conversation.

Footage from the previous years' Atlanta Pride Festival played on the TV screens. Greg watched the footage with a faraway look in his eyes.

"I remember that" he said as the camera panned around a group of guys. Watching the video, remembering the weekend, Greg was a million miles away. His sadness grabbed Will.

In the Armory parking lot, as Adair drove off, Greg pulled Will tight and gave him a Hollywood kiss. Will had never starred in someone's rearview mirror before. Greg held Will close and said "You better stay away from me - before you get yourself in trouble."

Will's next date with Greg was at Backstreet on a Tuesday night after work. Greg wanted to visit a Tarot reader. Again, Greg was with a friend when Will arrived.

Backstreet was quiet and empty. Hearing a clank or an echo in a place where one typically only hears thunderous beats under layers and layers of voices and laughter – it felt haunted simply because of the void of energy that had been there only days before. It was difficult to imagine the sea of souls that would be swimming around these walls so aimlessly in just a few days.

"This is Will" Greg said. "He works at Inform. The way Greg said Inform, with an exaggerated tone - Will guessed they'd been talking about him and where he worked.

Greg said "The person who reads cards didn't show up tonight. I'm sorry, I should have checked."

Greg's friend didn't stay long and Greg asked Will if he wanted to have a drink at Burkhart's. Will followed him over there and they sat on the brick patio that Daniel always admired.

"It's nicer than many in L.A." he'd said.

A hint of autumn was in the air. When some cute boys walked by, whispering and giggling, Greg quietly referred to them as sissies. Will enjoyed Greg's bored dismissal of the fresh faced, tan boys.

"Is your friend familiar with Inform?" Will asked.

"Because of me" Greg said. "I interviewed there last year."

"For what type of job?"

"Working in their data center" He said. "I didn't ever got a call back."

"I didn't realize you did that type of work" Will said. "I'll watch the job board at work if you want."

Greg remained unaffected. Will almost thought he had over-affected, unaffected.

Greg told Will that he'd been a contract IT person who went around to businesses and maintained their computers. As Greg recounted his experience with computers, he sat up straight and spoke to Will as if he were in an interview. He wasn't flirting or being cute. This was serious. Will wasn't sure Greg even knew his demeanor had changed. He appeared almost nervous for the first time since they'd met.

Will and Greg kissed on the dimly lit patio, with backlit gargoyles and gnomes tucked in nooks and crannies watching them. The promise of fall in the air not only soothed the recent heat, but it, as always, tinged the air with electricity.

Greg said "How do you feel about three ways?"

Will replied with a question mark expression.

Greg laughed and said "I don't mean tonight. But in general?"

Will said "They sound like fun."

"You've never had one?"

"Well – no. Not exactly."

Greg took a step backward and sighed. "You've really never been in a three way?"

Will said "no", concerned he'd done something wrong by not having ever had one.

"I don't like jealousy" Greg said. "You'll have to be able to deal with three ways."

"I won't get jealous. It sounds fun."

Greg said "And one more thing." He hesitated.

"You know how they always put those disclaimers on products? It might be dangerous because of -- ?"

"Yes" Will said, oblivious to what was coming.

"I have one of those disclaimers" Greg said "I'm H.I.V. positive."

Chapter Nine

Later, in October, the sun sprinkling light through ready to fall leaves, Greg called Will on a Thursday. He wanted to know if it would be alright to move their Friday night date to Saturday.

Will arrived at Greg's apartment at seven as planned. Greg dressed casually, like he had on their previous two dates – jeans and a long sleeve button down shirt. Greg suggested they rent a movie and stay in. Will loved the idea of no buffers and time alone. Perhaps it was the night to make his own disclaimer and show Greg his bald head.

Will drove to Ansley Mall where they looked around for a movie to rent. Will noticed Greg's breathing was heavy - labored like that of an overweight person. Greg quickly grew irritated with Will's indecisiveness and it was real irritation, not flirting. Greg grabbed a chick flick and turned the cover over for Will to read. Rather than read about the movie, Will thought more about the semen on the inside of Greg's arm. It was in *that spot* on his arm – that spot that most every man didn't realize they didn't clean while showering at least once. Will guessed it was why Greg moved their date from Friday to Saturday with such short notice. Will wondered if the reason Greg breathed like a three hundred pound man scarfing down a Big Mac was because he'd been up all night.

Will said "Sure. That one looks good."

It was the first time Will had seen Greg's apartment at a normal hour and with the lights on. There was a large - huge, replica of a Nigel painting on the living room wall. It was the first time Will had been in Greg's living room.

The more things his friends, and normally himself, would have found unacceptable about Greg, the more these things charmed Will.

Will didn't come from a family with money, he came from a family that struggled. But he'd spent so much time around families that did have money, some of their ideas were ingrained in him.

For example - it's better to go for substance over flash. Always choose a slightly worn Brook's Brother's shirt over a new trendy shirt. The Brook's Brother's shirt will last, and not ever go out of fashion. Things like that. The same applied to books, music, art, cars – everything. Everything about Greg's apartment was the opposite of what Will had learned, and Will wanted to soak it all up. Every shiny, black lacquer bit of it.

Will mentioned that he'd never seen the apartment except in the dark, in the early morning hours. Greg offered a tour and when they got to his room, he turned the light off and closed the door.

"We're not going in there tonight" he said.

Ordinarily, Will thought that meant "try me and maybe we will." But Greg's tone was serious. He sounded tired.

The movie was barely a distraction and Will laughed at all the wrong places. After their pizza and Will's beer (Greg wasn't drinking) Will attempted small talk. He was too nervous, confused, and sober to make any disclaimers of his own. The only thing Will was sure of was that Greg appeared exhausted.

Deflated, Will went into the end of another date more confused than when it began.

"This was nice" Greg said "We should do it again". He gave Will a quick kiss at the kitchen door before saying goodnight.

Though he was impatient, Will stayed curious about knowing what would happen if he didn't call Greg. Would Greg call him? If Greg didn't call for a week, and they talked, Will would wait a week before calling Greg. He tried to let Greg set a tone and go with it. Will found that Greg didn't go more than two weeks without calling, and Will liked that. He felt a connection. To him, it meant Greg wasn't so into him, but wasn't ready to let him go either.

Kim and Rebecca questioned why Will hung on, and he didn't have a good answer for them. Kim was especially vocal about her concerns over Greg's H.I.V. status, and she told him this often when she wasn't hounding him about her upcoming Halloween party.

The Saturday night of Kim's Halloween party, David and Chloe were out of town. A rare opportunity to have the apartment all to himself, he played quiet music (not the usual for him) and walked around naked (not the usual for him). He took liberties getting ready.

Will had invited more friends to spend the night after the party than he had room to accommodate. On their way to Atlanta to spend the night were his best friend Rebecca, her boyfriend Joey, Patricia, her current boyfriend, and finally Zach. Will hadn't planned, and he did not know where they all might sleep.

When Will's phone rang, he thought it might be one of his friends, lost in Buckhead, asking for directions. Instead, it was Greg. Will's "hello" was followed by a nervous, choked "Oh, hey Greg."

Greg apologized for the late notice and asked Will if I'd like to go to a Halloween party with him. Silently, Will stomped and kicked the wall as he told Greg that he already had plans.

When Greg told Will about his costume – a Roman gladiator with a skirt, a tent grew immediately in his vintage pants. Will could clearly imagine clutching Greg's well muscled legs and ass in his gladiator skirt.

No sooner had Will hung up the phone than the doorbell rang. Still fully erect, Will grabbed a towel to hold in front of him and opened the door. It was Patricia and her boyfriend.

Will, towel in front, opened the door and quickly turned around. Over his shoulder Will said "You two make yourselves at home. I'll be right out." He walked quickly back to his room and closed the door behind him. Within seconds, Patricia was knocking on his bedroom door.

"What are you doing in there?"

Will sat down on his bed next to Frieda. She looked up at him with her big, gold, saucer eyes. Frieda, a presumed victim of rough handling as a kitten, stared up at the only person she trusted and purred. Frieda sat still and watched.

"I could have fucked Greg. In a gladiator's outfit. " he whispered to her. "But instead I'm locked in my bedroom while my pants deflate. What is wrong with this picture?"

Will thought of what Greg had said at Burkhart's –

"you need to break out of your bubble. The friends you grew up with - and moved down here with" Greg had said.

Will finally emerged from his room, tent free, and sat down with his first two guests. They had driven four hours.

Next to arrive at Will's apartment were Rebecca and her boyfriend Joey. Rebecca dressed as a Superstar and Joey, sporting fake blood, was a victim.

Rebecca used glitter and glue to spell Superstar on the back of her denim jacket. Rebecca, a red head, wore a long, platinum blonde wig. The five inch heels she wore made her eye level with Will for the first time ever. It was a jolt of WTF every time he looked at her - her dark brown eyes peering out from a glowing pallor of skin and hair.

"Rebecca said "Where's Zach?"

"He called to say he'd meet us at Kim's" Will said.

The five of them squeezed into Will's two door Celica and drove to Decatur where Kim and her roommate Diana, also in college, lived in a brick ranch house.

Alone in Kim's backyard, Will told Kim about Greg's call. And his frustrations.

Laughing, Zach said "I heard Greg and ass, so I knew you two were back here."

Zach, a talented hairstylist, had managed an authentic Shaggy (from the Scooby Doo cartoon) hairstyle. His green t-shirt and brown pants were unmistakable Shaggy.

Kim, smushing her cigarette butt with her shoe on the cement parking pad, said "Greeggggg called Will and asked him to go to a party with him."

Kim said "Tell Zach what Greg's wearing. I have to go check on everyone."

"Will, I know that has to be driving you crazy" Zach said.

"Yes, and as soon as we're done here and everyone is back at my apartment, I want to go to The Manhole so I can try to find him."

"Ok" Zach laughed "I'm game."

Will grabbed Zach's arm and said "He's wearing a gladiator's outfit. I *will* fuck him in it."

Back on Kim's front porch, which was popular for smoking, Zach spotted Rebecca. The two of them giggled, bringing back memories of Athens. Rebecca twirled around in her Superstar outfit, dark eyes peering from behind the whiteness. Gays and Rebecca were like moths to a flame.

Rebecca said "Let's go see what everyone is wearing!" and the two of them went inside. It didn't take them long to find a winner – Kim's roommate Diana.

"How perfect is that?" Rebecca said. "The pillbox hat and everything".

Zach said "My favorite part is the blood on her jacket. Hers is definitely the best costume here".

"I have to hand it to her" Rebecca said "not many people could pull off a Jackie-O costume, but she did."

Kim's friend Gina arrived wearing simply black with a large mirror hanging on her front and back side. She was accompanied by a boy in his early 20's with pale skin and strawberry blond hair who no one at the party had met before.

Zach said "There's Gina".

"Oh yeah" Will said "I didn't recognize her at first. Who's that boy she's with?"

"I don't know" Zach said. "But I want to find out."

Will said "He is cute."

"He's mine, Will, you're fucking Greg later. Remember."

"What!" Patricia said in a high pitched squeal. "Who's Greg?"

"I've told you about him" Will said. "We've gone out a couple of times."

"What! I didn't know about this! Who is he!"

As if a day hadn't passed since they were in college, Rebecca, Will's discomfort, blew a smokescreen by doing another twirl in her Superstar outfit, igniting more giggling from Zach.

"Let's go get a beer" Rebecca said, looking Will directly in the eyes with an impish smile that said "you're rescued, let's go."

Crowded into Kim's kitchen was an entire grouping of people who must have been associations Kim had made since she'd moved to Atlanta two years ago. There was a clear shift between her older friends from Rome, and her newer (literally) younger, skater friends and their girlfriends. Kim's roommate Diana, remaining with the new set of friends and bridging the gap, perhaps channeled Jackie O more than she realized.

Rebecca said "I have to know, how did you get the bloodstain on the jacket to look so perfect."

Quiet, as if she were culpable of something terrible, Diana whispered "ketchup."

Rebecca's smokescreen was successful, and conversations had all taken a different turn when she and Will returned to Kim's front porch. Patricia had *that look* on her face, creamy complexion and perfectly made up, she looked like an angry doll. When she clutched her beer close to her chest, as she was then, something was up. Someone had said something to her, and she'd taken it as an insult.

Rebecca broke the ice.

"What happened?"

Patricia looked like she might cry. Her chin quivered.

Zach said "Gina asked her if she was dressed as Barbie."

Rebecca and Will gave each other a look, drew in deep breaths, and sighed. Patricia put her beer bottle down and went inside to the bathroom. Zach, Will, Joey, Rebecca, and Patricia's boyfriend all looked at each other, confused.

Will said "even if it was intended as an insult, is it really such an insult?"

"That's what I thought!" Rebecca said. "Who wouldn't want to look like Barbie!"

For the rest of the evening, whenever Mirror Gina and her boyfriend came near, Patricia, clutching her beer against her chest, glared at her intensely. If Gina noticed, she wasn't bothered.

As one o'clock drew near, Will suggested his group call it a night and go back to his apartment. Zach took Patricia and her boyfriend in his car, so Will could tell Rebecca and Joey what their plans were. Rebecca agreed to cover while Will and Zach went to The Manhole.

"Is there more beer at your apartment?" Rebecca asked.

"Yes".

"I'm good then. Let me tear Joey away from 'the man' over there. Joey's bent his ear about his military days for over an hour now."

The man, as he called himself, was one of Kim's original crew from Rome – dressed suavely, in a suit, with a cane and a fedora. He was – the man.

Back at Will's apartment, Zach, Patricia, and Patricia's boyfriend were already having another round of beers. Because the apartment was small, it was impossible for Zach and Will to slip out unnoticed. They could hear Patricia say "where are they going!" as they walked quickly down the front steps towards Will's car.

The gravel parking lot behind the Manhole was full and Will spotted Greg's car immediately. They parked at Sundown Café on Cheshire Bridge, where several Heretic patrons parked when the Manhole's lot was full. Sundown Café, like most businesses, had long been closed. Will and Zach walked a short distance across Peachtree Creek and to the Manhole. They waited in line for almost ten minutes when finally the doorman told everyone in line that the club was at capacity.

Zach patiently listened to Will rant as they drove back to his apartment.

"I've spent too much time pulling plans together for everyone else" Will said. "Patricia especially has never minded ditching me to go satisfy her own – her own - instant gratification!"

"That's a nice way of putting it Will" Zach said with a laugh. "Speaking of instant gratification, can we stop at that Krystal?"

With the smell of fast food permeating the car, Will and Zach drove up Piedmont toward Roswell Road, still busy with lights and cars and twenty-somethings driving from one party to another.

"I guess I really am a terrible host" Will said. "ditching my guests when there's nothing much to eat there."

"But there's plenty of beer" Zach reminded him. Underneath, Zach was, most times, sensible. Sensible wasn't Will's strong suit – often times his head was in the clouds instead of doing things like planning where everyone would sleep.

Rebecca and Joey, Patricia and her boyfriend – they all brought sleeping bags and pillows. All friends since their teens, this wasn't new territory for anyone. That left Zach without a place to sleep and Will suggested he sleep in David's empty bed since he was out of town.

Alone in his room, in his boxers, t-shirt, and de-haired, Will got in bed and curled up with Frieda. Betty had been Rebecca's cat in Athens, and she was in the living room, nestled among Rebecca's things – suitcase, soaps, perfumes. When Rebecca visited it was like a perfume counter exploded in the apartment and the delightful smells remained for days after the visit ended.

The street lights on Roswell Road shone through the closed blinds, making Will's room appear as if it were subtly lit with narrow lines of light. He fell asleep with Frieda by his side, purring, and Betty in the living room, basking in Rebecca's presence.

Greg called that Tuesday night and asked Will if he'd like to have dinner that weekend. Will guessed by Greg's tone what was coming. Still, he hoped that if he wore just the right sweater and just the right cologne – Greg might change his mind.

That Saturday evening when Will arrived, Greg met him at the door with a kiss and hug. He seemed in a hurry, already grabbing his keys and telling Will he wanted to leave right then because the restaurant he wanted to go to got crowded early on Saturday nights.

Greg drove to Cowtippers, a steakhouse in a barnlike building in Ansley, the gay epicenter. Greg made a stop on the way to the restaurant – he got cash out of his bank's ATM.

As Will sat in Greg's car, still running, he noticed two things - Greg's car was idled too high. Will knew that because of his own rural upbringing. He also noticed an excitement, bordering urgency, with which Greg withdrew his money.

"He's getting cash for later you dumbass" Will whispered to himself. "He's going out after he dumps you."

Cowtipper's was as rustic as one might expect, with Mountain logs lining the walls and wagon wheel chandeliers. The place was bustling as Greg had predicted. Greg made polite small talk throughout the western themed appetizer.

Greg took a deep breath, put his elbows on the table, and said "Will, I'm going to do for you what I wish someone had done for me a long time ago. I want to offer you my friendship."

"Okay" Will said "Is it –" Greg cut him off.

"Will, there's nothing going on here. It's one sided."

Will knew it was coming, but hearing the words cut right into him. The sea of voices and clanking dishes all around slowed down so that it sounded like he was under water.

Greg said "I know you like being around your friends from Rome who live here, but you need to break out of that bubble. I will bring you into my group of friends."

Will didn't realize how cold Atlanta could be. A lot of other guys would have dropped him without making an offer like this. He didn't know yet how hard it was to break into Atlanta and he had no idea what Greg's offer meant. He raised a half hearted smile, unable to think of anything except that he didn't get what he wanted. Greg offered to be his ally. His mentor. A hot, popular mentor. Will didn't see any of that.

A middle aged man bumped into Greg's back as he walked passed on his way back to his own table. Will saw a flash of recognition come over Greg's face as he looked after him. Will also thought he saw Greg's appetite being whetted. It was the first time Will felt like Greg was looking at someone else, in that way, while they were out. Greg may be a whore of the most venereal kind, but at the same time, he made an art out of being a gentleman. Will was instantly incensed at the downgrade to friendship status, and the immediate division of attention that went with it.

Will said "I still want to fuck you."

Greg put his fork down. He was silent for a few moments.

"No" he said.

"I can handle it."

"No."

"I want to fuck you like an animal." Will didn't see that one coming any more than Greg did. Greg was silent for a moment, and then took a deep breath.

"No Will. No sex."

"Will" Greg said "about once a month, me and about ten of my friends – we all come here to Cowtipper's and we have a great time. I meant what I told you on the phone before – I haven't known you long but I do already love you, as a friend."

"Thank you for your offer" Will said. "I do want us to be friends. But tonight I'll be out licking my wounds, so to speak. Don't be surprised if you see me at the Manhole."

Greg nodded in a sincere way Will recognized – he'd seen it done by older people in Rome when he was a kid. He knew it was real. The nod said "of course, do what you need to".

Greg said "I won't be at The Manhole tonight. It's all yours."

That Monday at work, as if to punctuate being dumped over the weekend, Frank dropped a stack of invoices and envelopes on Will's desk. They made a thump as Frank stood, smiling at Will.

"Mr. Turner, you exceeded my expectations the last time you handled these. So here are some more."

Frank made his usual comment about U.G.A. as he turned to skulk away. Ginger overheard and brought her legs down from her desktop and tore herself away from the NY Times Reader's Forum so she could walk over to Will's cube.

"So Will, I see Frank's given you another important assignment." She followed that with a hearty laugh.

"Isn't your ottoman getting cold over there?" The person in the cubicle between Will and Ginger let out a chuckle.

"Gosh Will, aren't you the bitchy one today." Ginger sat down in his guest chair.

"Sorry" Will said. "It was a crappy weekend."

Ginger said "Where's Craig?"

Will made the universal sign for cock sucking, making a fist next to his air filled cheek. Ginger threw her head back and let out another hearty laugh as she walked back over to her cube.

Will's phone rang and it was Kevin's number on the display.

"Raging Burrrrritttooooooo".

"Okay, I wish I could go now. I don't want to be here today" Will said.

"You'll feel better when I tell you about the new place I found."

"Tell me now."

"It's a sex club."

"Ooooooh. Pick me up at the kitty at six."

That evening, Will sat on top of the heavy, modern, bronze sculpture. One sat on either side of the entrance to the office tower he worked in, and the four other towers that were identical to it. The kitty relaxed on it's stomach, head up, one front paw lazily resting on top of the other. The kitties sat perched atop the concrete stairs leading up to Marquis One's circular drive with a lit fountain in the center. The sculpture Will sat on top of was at the corner of Peachtree Center Avenue and Harris Street. He watched for Kevin's white Jeep Cherokee to round the corner. Will loved being perched, like the cat he sat on, watching the people down below. When he saw Kevin turn the corner and turn his hazards on, he slid down the big kitty's side and hurried down the stairs so Kevin wouldn't hold up traffic.

As Kevin drove down Piedmont, and downtown became midtown, he told Will about his recent trip to San Francisco.

Raging Burrito was full of midtown muscle boys and Kevin had a challenge keeping Will focused on their conversation

"Hey!" Kevin said "Pay attention!"

"Anyway", Kevin said as a college age alterno-kid served their burritos, "I was in a sex club in San Francisco and I was messing around with a guy."
Now he had Will's undivided attention.

"And when things started really heating up, he stopped and said "Wait, I better suit up.""

"What does suit up mean?" Will asked.

"It took me a second too" Kevin said. "He meant he was going to put a condom on. I thought it was so hot."

"You did?"

"Yeah. It was so much better than in L.A. around all those guys who are so ready to bareback."

Will thought about what Kevin said as he studied horseshoe shaped triceps on a perfectly smooth, tan guy who stood in line. He wanted a body like that.

Kevin said "Oh hey, I went to the Eagle last weekend to hang out with my friend Tom and tell him all about my trip. He goes to San Francisco a lot. While Tom and I were at The Eagle, we ran into someone we both know named Stephen. Stephen gave me a pass for a sex club that he and his partner have opened up."

Kevin, relaxed in his chair with one elbow resting on the table, casually ate his burrito while talking to Will, as if they were discussing their friends or their jobs. Kevin and Raging Burrito with a backdrop of well muscled gay men was something Will looked forward to. He worried over his burrito, as if the entire restaurant would go silent and fingers would point at him if he dropped a piece of food on his shirt.

"I hope this place is better than I.T." Will said.

"You went there on a Tuesday, right?"

"It was practically empty" Will said.

"Well duh." Kevin said.

"Valley Bear."

"Yeah, I know" he said "But Imagine all those mazes and dark corners filled with horny men. If you'd gone on a weekend that's what you'd have seen."

"It was a random, spur of the moment decision to go on a Tuesday."

"Well you should go with me to the Looming and check it out. If for no other reason, Stephen is doing the music and he has great taste. Like me."

Smiling, he chomped a nacho to punctuate.

"The Looming?"

"That's what Tom said!"

"Yeah, The Looming. The name sounded kind of weird at first but it's growing on me" Kevin said. "so why were you having such a bad day at work earlier?"

"Oh, Greg dumped me."

"You kinda saw it coming though didn't you?"

"I did, but I kept hoping he'd change his mind."

"Ah, I'm sorry. I know how it is" Kevin said. "I was in love with this guy named Phil who lived in Australia forever it seemed like. He was H.I.V. positive too, and there's just something about those guys. Phil would always go swim in the ocean every morning – it's like they know they have to rise above a lot of things and make every minute count."

It was the first time anyone had truly encapsulated what Will was feeling. Kevin was right. Greg had crossed a line that Will hoped never to cross, yet he was still fascinated with the other side of it. At the same time, he was magnetized to the health and vitality permeating from the men all around him - with their muscles and their glows.

"So you'll go to The Looming with me Friday night and check it out?" Kevin said.

"Yeah, I guess so. But what if one of us walks up on the other getting a blowjob or something? That'd be weird." Will said.

Kevin laughed again and said "This club is for *men* only. You'll have to get over it."

That Friday night Will drove to Kevin's apartment off Ponce and rode to The Looming with him.

"By the way, did I mention we have to go to a kiiiinda bad part of town?" Kevin scrunched up his face on kinda. He had a way of scrunch face apologizing during the word that started the pill portion of the sentence.

"Uhm, no."

"Stephen told me if you go down Courtland you'll get stuck in Esso traffic."

"What's Esso?"

"A hip hop club on Courtland. If you *happen* to decide to go back to The Looming *on your own*, remember this route so you can avoid that traffic."

"Are you still in a bad mood?" Kevin asked.

"It's been a crap week. Not only did Greg dump me, but someone sideswiped me on Piedmont last night."

"Did the police come?"

"They did, but he didn't fill out a report. I didn't get it."

"Just relax and enjoy The Looming. There's nothing you can do about it tonight anyway. I wouldn't let it ruin a good visit to a sex club."

"You don't know how anal I am about my car" Will said.

"It'll look as good as new" Kevin said. "Remember to go down Argonne and turn right on Pine Street. This gravel parking lot is where we're gonna park."

"It looks like a warehouse" Will said. "Or wait, did this used to be an auto repair shop?"

"Something like that" Kevin said. "Let's go see what's inside. When we get out, hurry to the door. There are a lot of homeless people and shootings around here."

At the front of the building with faded white paint was a tinted glass door with that grooved, silver metal handle like you'd seen on any one story Acme Inc office building. In small, stick on, gold letters leaning toward the right, was THE LOOMING. Plain Arial font, or something like it. Kevin tapped on the glass door lightly. A moment later, a shaved haired guy in a white tee shirt and jeans opened the dark tinted door just far enough for Kevin and Will to come inside.

Kevin said "I only have one invitation. Is it okay if he comes in too?" and gestured toward Will.

"Sure" Stephen said. "If I can just get both of you to fill this out."

He handed them each a Xeroxed sheet which asked only the basics – Name, Age, Address, Phone number, E-Mail address and who referred you.

"That'll be ten each" Stephen said when they finished filling out their sheets.

"After tonight, if you want to come back to see us, just fill in your name and e-mail address on the clipboard here at the desk whenever you come in. We're not open during the week and it's always ten dollars on Friday and Saturdays."

Stephen sat down on a barstool in front of a painted black podium with a small adding machine on top. He used a pen light to count singles from a zipper bank bag he kept in the back of the podium. Will didn't register any of Stephen and Kevin's quick chat about music as he took in the dark surroundings in this front area that was only lit by a dark light. Green aliens and stars glowed on the walls, the thick, padded, shag carpet felt squishy after having just walked across a gravel parking lot and then onto a concrete sidewalk. There was a lava lamp on the podium. It was as if they'd stepped out of concrete Downtown Atlanta and into a teenager's basement love den. Kevin held back floor length hanging beads from a doorway so Will could walk through.

"Have fun guys" Stephen said, behind them.

"What is that smell" Will whispered to Kevin after they walked through the beads.

"You mean the Nag Champa?"

"What's that?"

"It's just incense. I have a ton of it at home. You can have some if you want it."

"Do you like it?" Kevin said.

"I don't know." Will's voice trailed off as his eyes adjusted to the dark room they were now in. He heard hushed voices but couldn't tell where they came from. It sounded like they'd stepped into a rainforest. Croaks and chirps all around. Was that a monkey?

Kevin said "This must be some kind of jungle area. Look, there's a fountain over here."

Will thought he'd heard running water.

"Those chirping and monkey noises are probably coming from a speaker hidden somewhere. Stephen and his lover really went all out on this place." Kevin said.

Will felt like Betty and Frieda creeping down low like when they saw a cat outside the living room window. As his eyes adjusted, he could a gargoyle and tropical plants were lit by a small light underneath water in a fountain. He could see men coming and going, and standing in line for a restroom in a far, dark corner.

On the other side of the jungle themed area were more beads and a doorway that led to an area that was lit more, mostly by the flicker of a big screen TV.

In an area to the left were three different thrift store (Will assumed) sofas arranged in a U shape. Two of the sofas lined walls made of concrete blocks that had been painted white. The white paint was fading. The back of another sofa acted as a room divider between this TV area and a walk through. A big screen TV sat high atop a tall TV stand at the open end of the U. The porn on the big screen TV wasn't like any Will had seen. There was something about the porn – it wasn't more hardcore in it's content, but something about it's realism gave it that you're not supposed to be doing this excitement that someone gets when watching their first porn – an excitement that doesn't seem to ever happen again. Perhaps it was also that instead of being at home, in private, with the blinds turned, this porn was on a big screen, in a warehouse building where strangers walked around eyeing each other with hungry looks. It was as if, when a person walked into the Looming, there was an understood rule that conversations should be kept to a low whisper. Will thought he smelled a joint, and he thought he heard the sound of someone moaning.

Kevin said "I'm going to go see what's back there" and gestured toward a row of black, rubber curtains like the ones at the Manhole. Will walked the opposite direction, past the area with the big screen TV and back in the direction from which they came. Will noticed two doorways. The one on the left was the one he and Kevin had just come through and it went into the jungle themed area. Will walked through the doorway to the right. It led into a tight, mazelike hallway that was also only lit by black lights. Plastic, blow up doll aliens were fucking in a corner. The maze led to a small area with refreshments. Canned cokes, sprites, and a water cooler. No alcohol. There were two guys, shirtless and sweaty, standing by the cooler with their drinks. The two guys spoke in hushed whispers. It sounded like the two guys were talking about someone they'd just had sex with. Unlike bars, like Burkhart's or even The Eagle, no one laughed or talked loudly at the Looming. All the conversations Will encountered were hushed and whispered.

Will saw the flicker of a TV screen on the doorway to an adjoining room. He heard the sounds of porn coming from the TV. He stepped into the room and the first thing he saw, to his left, looked like an art installation - multiple television sets placed haphazardly with metal tubing, netting, and even brush winding throughout and all around them and enclosed with chain link fencing. Across from him he saw a mirrored wall, and to his right three guys seated on a black, leather sofa. The three guys were all feeling each other up while watching a variety of porn on multiple screens on the opposite wall. Will began to feel like the entire place was an art installation, and he was a part of it. So far, the Looming had assaulted Will's senses and he loved it.

Will left the room with the TVs and went through a doorway to his left with more beads. He was back where he and Kevin had started in the jungle area. He'd circled the place completely except for the area that Kevin was now in. Will walked through the sounds of chirps and jungle life again, this time noticing again the gargoyles lit from underneath, the water ponds and someone getting fucked on a bench that was hidden behind two large plants.

Will emerged on the other side, in the open area beside the larger TV area. To his right he'd seen several guys coming and going to the area Kevin was in.

On the other side of the curtains, Will saw an orange and white construction horse with a blinking light on top. Through some more rubber curtains was an area with only a motorcycle in the corner. It was a chopper and a guy sat on it while another kneeled on the worn concrete floor in front of him, giving him head.

There was a draft that came through the Looming that was a reminder that it was a building made from concrete blocks with concrete floors and probably no insulation from the cold outside. The sex all around chased the reality of the cold away.

Music played on unseen speakers, periodically interrupted by the sound of a prison alarm.

Next to the room with the motorcycle was another room where Will heard chains rattling and moans. Timidly, he moved over to the doorway so he could see past the backs of the men who were blocking it. In the middle of the dark room was a sling, hanging from a ceiling. Seven or eight guys stood around the sling, watching someone who was only wearing a jockstrap and combat boots get fucked, each movement making the chains attached to the sling rattle. Will stepped backward and bumped into someone.

Kevin said "Oh, sorry. I didn't know that was you. It's so dark in here."

Will and Kevin went to the cooler and had some water, where they both agreed that they would be visiting The Looming again.

Kevin said "I can only imagine what this place is like around two or three in the morning."

They didn't go anywhere after The Looming. On the way home, Will thought about what he'd seen there. He was surprised to see David still up and working. Chloe had gone to bed.

 David, for the first time since Will had known him (they'd shared an apartment for just over a year) was pensive and somber.

"Will, did you let someone sleep in my bed on Halloween weekend?"

"Well—" When Will said it, it wasn't cute like Samantha when she got in trouble on *Bewitched.*

 "I meant it when I told you that you've been the best roommate I've ever had" David said. And he had said that, on the way to Will's office on a Friday night. Will had just bought his car and David drove him downtown to drive his old one home.

"I just can't believe you'd do that" David said.

Will's throat tightened. He began to see how upset David was.

Because David and Chloe were always in a hurry and his bedroom and bathroom reflected that - it didn't occur to Will that they would even know someone had slept in his bed. It had rarely been made.

Now, looking at David, Will began to see the lack of respect in letting someone sleep in his bed, and not telling him.

"I'm moving out at the end of the month" David said.

Will didn't attempt an argument and said only "I'm sorry. I'm so sorry" before retreating to his bedroom.

The next day Will met Kevin at Raging Burrito. He somehow always had a way of making Will forget about it, whatever *it* was, and just have a good time looking at the midtown muscle boys.

"You know" Will said. "one night, David and Chloe went through the Tom Bianchi coffee table book that Kim gave me. They kept telling me that I could make my body like any body in that book. That it was within my reach. They'd look at a photo and say "oh, he probably just does this exercise" or "oh, he probably just really works out that part of his body".

When I think of something like that especially, I hate the feeling that I screwed them over.

Crunching his ice, Kevin said "eh, he'll get over it. Don't worry about it. He probably just wanted an excuse to move out anyway."

"What!"

Kevin laughed and held out his cup. "Go get me some more Dr. Pepper."

David's Dad came down to Atlanta from Rome and helped him move out the Saturday after Thanksgiving. David's dad gave Will a look, so he cleared out, not knowing where to go.

Kevin was out of town. Kim had a house full of skater friends and no roommate ideas.

Stephanie had once told Will 'Don't ever be afraid to go eat by yourself. Just take book with you if you couldn't find anyone to go with you."

Will picked up a Southern Voice, the local Atlanta gay newspaper, and took his time eating, reading the articles, and looking out of the window.

Reading, and the cloudy, gray day, calmed Will. The want ads were, as usual, the most entertaining. He decided his would say "Gay male and two cats seek roommate for 2BR/2BA in Buckhead." He'd leave out the part about the building being old and orange, located at a busy intersection.

By early evening, when Will got back, David and his dad were gone. Will stood in the empty apartment, his bedroom the only furnished room, and wondered if he was really such an asshole that someone would just up and move out. He thought he knew the answer, and it was depressing.

Will's phone rang and it was Greg's name on the display. Greg could hear in Will's voice that he didn't know what he was going to do about a roommate. He told Will about a friend of his, an ex-marine, who he thought he remembered saying would be looking for an apartment. He said he wasn't sure and not to get his hopes up, but he would give the guy a call. Will liked the feeling of Greg looking after him, and still somehow, it added to the melancholy of the empty apartment.

"It hasn't been the best week for me either" Greg said.

"What happened?"

"I don't work at the Hilton anymore."

Greg hesitated before saying "No call, no show."

"That doesn't sound like you" Will said.

"It's not" Greg said. Greg hesitated again and for the first time, Will heard what sounded like fear in his voice.

"I blacked out" he said. "I was at a party----with some guys"

Greg sighed "they thought they were going to get me to—"

After a few moments, Will said "you blacked out—"

"I blacked out. We'd all been up all night partying and I have no idea what happened after I blacked out."

It was the first time Greg had said it – that he stayed up partying all night. At once, Will felt concerned for him and turned on.

Will said "could you maybe talk to someone and get your job back?"

"I tried that already" Greg said. "Even though this was the first time, they can't hire you back after a no call, no show."

Greg said "That's okay though. I was planning on working retail over the holidays anyway. I've got that covered. It's the blacking out ---"

"Sounds like it's time to reel it in a little" Will said, as if he knew what he was talking about. He only knew the phrase because he'd heard his mom say it when she'd felt like her drinking was getting out of control.

"A friend of mine referred me to a therapist" Greg said. "I'm going to start AA".

"That really is reeling it in" Will said.

"But I won't give up X".

"What?"

"I won't give up X" Greg said. "I'll give up alcohol, coke, anything – but not X."

"I've never done coke or X" Will said, feeling suddenly ashamed for having not done any hard drugs.

"Coke's okay" Greg said, non-chalantly. "But X - X is my lover. It – never does me wrong."

"So, it –"

Greg cut him off.

"But—"

"I don't want to talk about it anymore Will." He said. "I want to hear more about what you've been doing and then I have to go to bed. I have to be at the mall early tomorrow."

"Kevin took me to the most insane place" Will said "I loved it."

"Oh yeah. What place is that?"

"The Looming" Will said.

Greg was silent for a moment.

"Did you say The Looming?"

"Yes, I don't even know how to describe it" Will said.

"I didn't know that place was still around" Greg said, stealing Will's thunder and sounding far away.

"You've been there?!"

"It's been a while" Greg said.

"Will, do you like that kind of thing?"

"It was my first time there" Will said. "But I *loved* it!"

Greg chuckled quietly.

"Why is that Will?"

"There's a motorcycle area with those orange and white construction zone horses. There were even orange blinking lights on top of one. And that lounge area with all the TVs playing porn. You can get lost in there and it's sex all around."

"Yeah" Greg said. "the different themed areas - it adds to the fantasy, huh."

"Well dear, let me let you go" Greg said. "I have to get some rest for work tomorrow."

"You'll be okay" Will said, knowing he sounded as protective as a doe on the woods.

Will sat outside and had one more cigarette before bed. He couldn't believe the things Greg had told him. He wanted to know what exactly it was those guys had thought they were going to do with him. And what they did to him after he passed out. As sad as he was for Greg, he still got hard at the thought of him partying all night with a bunch of guys. Did that mean he was even wilder than he had been with alcohol alone? Will tried to imagine what Greg must be like on something besides alcohol. And, in trying to imagine Greg getting passed around by a bunch of horny men – Will was hard.

His phone lit up with Zach's number. If it were Zach or Kim's number, the other one was probably on the line as well. He turned the ringer volume down and stared at the green, drippy building in the not so far distance. The sound of Greg's voice danced around in his head.

The next Saturday, Will drove to Rome and gathered furniture he'd stored at his mom's house. From things he'd grown tired of before, he put together enough items to make the living room at his apartment a somewhat aesthetically pleasing space. Most noticeable – A vintage, black, fur-covered S shaped chair from the nineteen sixties. A friend of Will's mom's had given it to her when he was young and he'd claimed it as his own. It looked like furniture he'd seen in magazines he'd seen in his teen years.

Will bought a sofa from a friend, Rebecca. Also from Rome and also friends with Kim, Diana, Kevin and Zach, Rebecca was someone Will spoke to regularly. The sofa had been in Rebecca's family home. It was simple and pretty, and it had some shine and some color. David's sofa had been brown and dulled, calling up images of third or fourth generation hand me downs that had been slept on in a frat house for years. Will had hated to see David and his brown, plaid sofa go. He hated to see Chloe go. But he moved forward by cleaning, making order, and gaying up the place.

For Christmas, Kim bought Will a terra cotta Corinthian column from a store on Amsterdam Avenue in Midtown that was going out of business. Will went back to the same store and bought a round piece of glass and that completed the gayest coffee table ever. It all came together nicely and now David's abrupt move and the drama that went with it had been transformed into a fabulous gay living room. Lemons to lemonade.

Earlier, when Kevin helped Will unload his furniture, the one-liner jokes flew about the sexual possibilities of living with an ex-marine.

Before Kevin left, he said "you better call me as soon as he leaves and tell me if he was any good."

"Really, you think?"

"Where have you been?!" Kevin said. "placing a roommate ad means you want to get laid."

Greg's friend, Alex, showed up promptly at eight. Alex reeked of the Eagle, no-nonsense, sometimes believable machismo. He wore old jeans that were tight, but not obscene, with a white t-shirt, camouflage jacket, and lace up work boots. Kevin would have loved him. Will thought he was okay and didn't get the impression he wanted sex. Nor did he get the impression he would be moving in.

Alex told Will about a time when he'd lived in midtown and been held up at gunpoint.

"I'm leery of moving back into town" he said "I'm happy at my place in the mountains, but I've been thinking of renting a place in town as well. I wanted to see your apartment and the location."

Alex said "Greg's a good guy. He's a good person to have as a friend."

"Where did you meet Greg?" Alex asked.

"The Manhole."

"So you went home with him?"

"Yes."

"That's how Greg and I first met too" Alex said.

There was silence as they looked into each other's eyes. Both of them knew they'd wanted something else with Greg.

Alex spoke first, his tone taking a somber note.

"Once or twice a year, I can get Greg to come up for a weekend at my house in the mountains. He's never made it through a whole weekend."

Alex sighed.

"Around ten on Saturday night he'll say he better get back to Atlanta. That's how it always goes."

A look of sadness washed over Alex's face and stayed there throughout their visit and even as they said goodbye.

As soon as Alex left, Will grabbed a jacket and cigarettes. He sat on the front stoop and called Kevin.

"Did he bust into your apartment and yell "get down on your knees boy!'"

Will told him about the visit.

"You should probably listen to him."

Later that night, feeling lost and not quite sure what to do with himself, Will decided to give The Looming another try. Will forgot how it was that Kevin had weaved and dog-legged, as Kevin called it, his way through the one way downtown streets to get to The Looming. He'd been preoccupied over his newly wrecked and still unrepaired car.

For his second foray into the underground world of free sex in a men's only club, Will followed the directions on the flyer that Stephen had given him. The directions were straightforward and simple with the only catch being Esso traffic, as Kevin had warned and as the flyer also warned.

When Juniper Street turned into Courtland Street at North Avenue, Will was met with slow, thick traffic. There were shiny wheel spinners all around, purple lights beneath luxury SUVs and a cacophony of driving bass from different songs coming from different vehicles. If he were a person who was afraid of black people (and they do still exist) he might have been alarmed by men and women, dressed in club clothes, walking all around, directed by a bouncer's glow sticks. The traffic was slow but it moved.

Finally, will turned left onto Pine Street and a long haired guy in jeans and army jacket waved him into the gravel parking lot of the Looming with his flashlight. Will ran through the cold, December air to the front door. Seconds after knocking, he heard the latch. Stephen smiled and welcomed Will inside. Stephen glanced around outside as he closed and then locked the blacked out glass door.

Alone at The Looming, Will stayed later this time. He picked up more of the unspoken language – long looks by those who liked being watched, sometimes followed by an arm of someone drawing him into a group. He noticed what happened if someone tried to join a group who wasn't welcomed – their hand was simply removed but no big deal was made. Will walked around and watched but he didn't instigate. He either waited to be invited if he liked the show, or, he moved on if no interest was returned. Will liked it when a hand reached out and drew him in. He liked the eye contact. He liked the unspoken. To him, it said "this is our place. It's just for us."

That next Saturday, Will met with someone who'd responded to his online ad. His name was Brandon and he had just been hired as a Customer Service Rep at a company near the perimeter. Brandon and his friend Joseph drove over from Birmingham to meet Will and check out the apartment.

Laura came over to help Will break the ice. She not only gave Brandon and Joseph a thumbs-up, but also assured them that Will was a good person. Will got a call from the leasing agent that Monday after Brandon sent her his information.

"I really think he'll be an asset to you" she said.

Will believed her and asked Brandon to move in whenever he wanted to. The day after Christmas, Will got back from Rome late at night to find the apartment dotted with Brandon's furniture. Will's own aesthetic blurred the line between minimal and vacant, and he had an immediate and negative reaction to Brandon's additions. Will adapted and later admitted he liked it that the apartment now looked like someone lived there.

That Monday, as Will sat on the floor leaning against the sofa that had been Rebecca's parents, Brandon walked in and sat down on the sofa behind him. Although Brandon's effort to get to know Will was kind, there was something in it's self awareness that made Will so uncomfortable he had to leave the room.

Safe inside the bathroom in his bedroom, Will turned on the overhead fan and called his mother in Rome.

"What's he doing that's so terrible?" she asked him.

He whispered into the phone, speaking as if Brandon had committed a terrible crime.

"He's sitting on the sofa. Trying to get to know me."

Will's abrupt exit rolled off Brandon, who didn't take it personally. Despite Will's initial rudeness, the two of them settled into a routine of casual friendliness and mutual respect for one another's space. With David, Will had been the neat one. With Brandon around, Will felt like a slob.

Whenever Brandon left the apartment and passed Will, sitting on the painted concrete steps that led up to their front porch, he commented on how many cigarette butts were in the ash tray. Around Brandon, Will felt like one of those people who seems to always be smoking out in the back of a vocational school. Or a health care worker on break, smoking a cigarette next to a patient in a wheelchair attached to an I.V. Brandon was the Felix, Will was the Oscar. Soon, Brandon's ponytail and oversized sweaters were gone and in their place was a low calorie diet, stylish, fitted clothes, and a sexy haircut. Atlanta got him.

Will and Greg continued to talk regularly, and Kim and Zach continued to dramatically feign utter abandonment when they couldn't get Will to answer when he was on the phone with Greg. Since he didn't mind clicking between calls with most people, they knew when the machine didn't' pick up and there was no answer, he was on the phone with Greg. When they did leave messages......

"Oh my God Kim" Zach said "We're not Greg. Will won't ever call us back."

"You better call us back you little shit" Kim said.

Zach and Kim both sang in unison "Greeeegggggg" before bursting into laughter. Kim would soften it with a "seriously, call us back" before the click of the sound of them hanging up.

The heaviness in Greg's voice when he'd told Will about losing his job at the Hilton was gone. He sounded better. Like himself. Will asked how his therapy was going.

Greg hesitated, almost as if he'd forgotten he'd told Will about it.

Greg said "I quit going."

"What happened?"

"I couldn't sit and listen to all that psychobabble" he said.

Will didn't know what to say.

"Don't worry about me" Greg said "I just had to get a handle on my partying."

Greg wanted to know if Will had been back to the Looming, and he had – a couple of times. He told Greg about a guy there who he'd bottomed for in one of the stand up, plywood booths with moons and stars cut out. Will liked how it looked when he walked near one of those booths, and from the way a hand was wrapped around the edges of the moon and star cut outs, he could just about tell what was going on inside. He'd found out for himself that those cut outs were a good place to hold onto when inside one of those booth's getting fucked.

"We even drew a little crowd" Will said, proud of his newfound worldliness.

"What did he look like?" Greg asked.

"Well built. Suburban. Probably lives OTP with a girlfriend somewhere."

Greg chuckled. "You know what Will – you're probably right."

Will blurted out "the thing I really can't get over about the Looming is all the hot guys. All those hot muscle guys that I never thought I could get close to are a dime a dozen there."

"Really" Greg said, his low, as if he dared Will to prove it.

"I haven't been in there in a while. Maybe I should go back in and check it out."

"I keep thinking about what you said about X" Will said. "I've heard before that it makes sex feel better than it already does. Is that true?"

Greg said "Yes. It's not even in the same ballpark."

"So that's why you said 'X is like your lover. It never does your wrong'?"

"Did I say that?"

"Yes."

Greg chuckled again.

"It's true. Sex on X is out of this world. You should try it sometime."

"My only experience with drugs was smoking pot in my early twenties" Will said. "I did it a lot back then, but then it started making me paranoid. I'm afraid if I tried X I'd get in some bad state of mind and not be able to get out of it."

"That's why you should try it with someone you trust the first time" Greg said. "then if you do start feeling paranoid or whatever, they can talk you out of it."

"I want to try it" Will said. "Will you do it with me?"

Greg hesitated. "I'm not sure about that" he said.

Greg said "Let me think about it."

Later that week, will asked Kevin about X. He agreed with Greg that ecstasy was a lot of fun, but he'd never had sex on it.

Will asked Daniel, who told him that while he'd never done it himself, he'd heard, while living in L.A., that sex on ecstasy was mind blowing.

Will, knowing how much Daniel had loved the sex clubs in L.A., said "the Looming is mind blowing."

"Hmmmmmm" Daniel said.

"Since you're curious about The Looming" Will said "And I'm curious about X - - "

"Yes?" Daniel said, sounding like a father again.

"Well, maybe you could stick around and make sure I don't go crazy on it".

"So you've decided for sure you're going to try it?" Daniel said "I don't know if that's such a good idea."

"Pot" Will said.

"I hear you" he said. "When were you thinking?"

"Soon."

"Well, I'll babysit you and we'll see how it goes" Daniel said with a sigh. "But promise me you won't make this a habit".

"I won't."

The next evening at work, Kevin picked Will up at the kitty and they went to Raging Burrito.

Through the chomping of chips and salsa, Kevin said "yeah, Daniel's right ya know."

Will didn't want him raining on his parade, and his pout showed it. Kevin laughed.

"No, no. I don't mean never do X. It's fun. Just don't turn into one of those skinny bug eyed boys who are out doing it every weekend. And whatever you do, don't ever let anyone talk you into doing meth. People go crazy on that."

"They do?"

"Oh My God!" Kevin said.

"How old are you again?"

He said "I knew a guy once who was completely normal until he got on meth. He started acting really, really crazy after that and then we hardly ever saw him anymore. When we did see him out, he just looked really sad."

"Okay" Will said "We'll make a pact. No crystal meth – ever."

"I wasn't going to do it anyway, but if it makes you feel better, I'll make a pact with you. You wanna pinky swear?"

"Shut up" Will said "Hey, I bet it'd be fun to take X at the Looming."

"I was thinking the same thing!" Kevin said "But you said you were gonna do it with that old man."

"He's not old."

A cute alterno boy brought their burritos and Kevin sent Will to refill his drink.

"Half coke and half Dr Pepper" he said as Will almost tripped over himself walking through the beautiful, fresh from the gym muscle boys.

"I have to start working out" Will said as he handed Kevin his drink.

"Hey, now I do need someone to help me do that" Kevin said. "Let's get buff, pinky swear!"

"You were going to tell me about some guy that fucked you at the Looming". As soon as it came out of Kevin's mouth, they both realized there was a family next to them.

"Well" Will started, in a lower tone. "He was hot."

"And—"

"And, he used a condom."

"Good" Kevin said "Now get to the good stuff."

"He was pretty built but not thoroughly like these guys."

Kevin made a face.

"What?" Will asked.

"They're *too* perfect" he said.

"No they're not." Will said.

"Anyway" Will lowered his voice again. "He looked straight. Like he probably lived up in Cobb County or somewhere with a girlfriend."

"Oooooh. I like those types".

"Yeah, me too" Will said.

"Keep going."

"The first time I met him, I was sitting on the leather couch in that room with all the TVs behind the chain link fence.

"Don't you love that room" Kevin said.

"Yes!" Will said "I was sitting next to two guys and we were all—"

Will stopped to check on the family next to them. He lowered his voice more. "The three of us were – pleasuring ourselves and watching the movies."

"Built suburbanite came in and he kept watching me instead of the movie" Will said "He nodded toward the TVs and said 'Looks like fun, huh?'"

"Oh my God that's so hot" Kevin said through his ice.

"The guy said 'want to go out there?' and I said 'sure'".

"The guy took me by the hand and led me to the back".

Will said "You know those things – they're made out of plywood and painted black and have the moons and stars cut out of them?"

"Yeeeeaaaaah" Kevin said, wincing. "I wish those were a little more private."

"He took me in one of those and told me to pull my jeans down. By the time he had the condom unwrapped, we had an audience."

"You got fucked at the Looming while a crowd watched?!"

The mom at the next table gave them a look.

Will said "yeah."

"What have I done!" Kevin whispered. "You'd never even been in one of those places a few weeks ago and now you're getting fucked in front of strangers."

"I like it there." Will said, still talking low. "I notice some weird, different thing every time I go in there."

"Just how much have you been going in there?" Kevin asked, now leaning back in his chair with one arm around the back of it, chomping his ice.

"I don't know. A couple of times."

"Uh huh" Kevin said. "Go get me some more Coke."

"And don't forget to mix it with Dr. Pepper."

Two muscle bears, as Kevin called them, sat down at the table next to theirs. From the drink machine, Will turned to look back and Kevin raised his eyebrows.

"There's just so many odd things in there" Will said "like that mannequin with the long black wig holding out a serving tray with little packs of lube on it."

"Next to the big screen TV?" Kevin said "they never put condoms on that tray".

One of the muscle bears looked over.

"I think about that damn Cher song every time I see that mannequin" Kevin said "Strrrrrooongg Enuff-uhhh!"

Kevin loved making fun of that CD. He didn't own it, but who needed to. Most every gay establishment they went to had it on heavy rotation as if no other CDs existed.

"And what about those glow in the dark aliens painted on the walls?" Will said.

Kevin said "What about those alien blow up dolls they've set up to look like they're fucking!"

"Oh, I know!" Will said "And that bathroom that's sort of in the middle of everything—"

Kevin said "The one with 'feelin' free' written in that glow in the dark paint? Yeah, that's a song."

"What is the name of that incense again?"

Kevin said "Oh, the nag champa?"

"Yeah".

"I'll give you some of mine. I burn it all the time."

"I love that stuff."

"You know" Will said. "Nine out of ten men there are hot. They just want sex. No 'can I buy you a drink?' or 'what do you do?'"

Will said "They just want sex. I'm terrible and nervous about making conversation anyway, but I love sex! You walk around and it's nothing to see someone bent over a motorcycle getting fucked, or a group getting it on near the big screen TV, or—"

"Or you getting fucked in a box!" Kevin said.

The muscle bears were unmistakably tuned into Will and Kevin's conversation. They hadn't spoken to each other in the past few minutes.

Kevin said "I can make you a CD with a lot of the music they play too. Stephen does have great taste in music. That's how I know him really. He DJs around town."

"Don't get too caught up though" Kevin said. "Remember it's just a scene."

Back in Will's office it was quiet. The phone didn't ring that much normally, and even less so over the holidays. The only call he got was from someone who noticed a discrepancy in their data. She was known in Will's group for finding discrepancies in the data and calling immediately to report it. He assured her he'd get the record corrected and she went on to tell him about another error she'd found.

Claudia, a manager in Will's department who was also exacting, described this caller as an asset.

"She finds the errors before anyone else does" Claudia had said once.

To Will, the lady's calls were not a nuisance. He treated her, and anyone else who called, well. He was glad to take her calls and get paid for it. And getting paid for it, he could stay in the city. And in the city, he could go have sex after work.

After the call with the lady ended, Will picked up the phone again and called his friend Jill, a pretty and hilariously irreverent girl he'd worked with briefly after college.

Will remembered that Jill mentioned recently that she's tried X - and loved it. Jill said she'd call him back in five minutes. In two minutes, Jill called back and asked Will when he wanted to pick up the X.

They agreed to meet at Steak and Shake at the West Paces Ferry Road exit on I-75 at four o'clock in the afternoon on New Year's Eve.

Will hung up the phone, excited, and whispered to himself "my first drug deal!"

He wanted to call someone and tell them. Someone who wouldn't freak out. He dialed Zach's number and told him what he'd done. Or was going to do.

"Will" He said "I never thought I'd see the day."

"I know, I know" Will said. "I just want to see what it's like".

"You know" Zach said "I never took it for the sex even though I always heard sex on X was some kind of crazy, good sex."

"I remember" Will said. "You took it for the all night raves".

"Yeah" Zach said "And everyone who did used to get all huggy feely toward the end of them."

"Did it ever make you paranoid?"

"No" Zach said "It's not like pot. You'll be fine".

After Will hung up with Zach, he called Kevin.

"My friend is getting me X!"

"I want some!" Kevin said. "When?"

"New Year's Eve."

"Hey, I forgot to tell you" Kevin said. "the Looming's going to be open tonight. They don't usually open on weeknights so I guess this is just because it's the holidays."

"Hm, on a Wednesday night" Will said. "Are you going?"

"No, I can't" he said. "I have to work early tomorrow. I just thought you might want to drop in."

"I wish you hadn't told me" Will said. "I should really stay home."

"So you're going?" Kevin asked.

"Yeah, I want to see what it's like there on a weeknight."

"I bet it'll be fun" Kevin said. "There probably won't be a big crowd there though. But the ones who are will be ready for a good time I bet. Let me know how it is. I may want to go in there next time they're open during the week."

"So you told me so I can go scope it out for you?" Will said, pretending to be offended.

"Yeah, pretty much."

Will said "I must help you out then."

On the phone, at the office at night, Will laughed out loud without worrying that someone might be bothered. The floor was empty. It didn't dawn on him that Frank, who went home around six most days, might walk up. He did, for the first and only time, with someone Will had never seen. Will was sitting in Craig's seat with his feet propped up on his desk, talking (and laughing loudly) on Craig's phone with Kevin. Frank smiled an I caught you smile and introduced Will to his friend. Will was as stunned as someone who'd been caught singing into their hairdryer.
Within a minute they were gone.

Kevin still laughing, said "where'd you go?"

"Uhm, my boss just walked up."

"Oh My God!" Kevin said. "I thought he went home around five or six every day. Wait, I know he does because you always want to wait until he's gone before I come pick you up for lunch. Why is that anyway?"

"Because I'm only supposed to take thirty minutes" Will said. "He must have been giving a friend a tour of the office space. Sometimes you see someone after hours, giving a tour."

"Waaahh" Kevin said. "I want an office like that. I love that purple pool table."

"You work in a sexy downtown office already."

"I know, but I still want a purple pool table."

Will said "Hey, it's ten. I'm getting out of here."

Kevin said "Let me know how the Looming is".

Will gave Kaleb a quick call before he left and, as always, Kaleb was up for meeting at Burkhart's. All through Will's U.G.A. years, Kaleb was always around although he was never enrolled in school or working anywhere. Somehow, he'd managed to carry this feat into Will's current Atlanta working years. Kaleb felt that he deserved attention just for showing up, and in most cases he got it. He had a natural and lean musculature that had been accentuated by minimal exercise when not smoking cigarettes and eating fast food. His face was pretty, his cheekbones defined, and his eyes deep set. He had the kind of plentiful but fine, dark but not too dark hair that could be cut, colored, and styled any way one could imagine.

Kaleb showed up at Burkhart's wearing jeans and a cable knit sweater. His hair was its natural color and cut into messy, college boy bangs. It was a refreshingly casual look on Kaleb.

After two drinks, Will was ready to go.

"Thanks for meeting me out" he said. "It's been a long day. I better call it a night."

It was almost one o'clock when Will pulled into the Looming's gravel parking lot. There were plenty of cars in the parking lot, but Will easily found a spot. He ran through the cold air, feeling warm from the vodka, and knocked on the blacked out front door. Stephen quickly let him in, and began rubbing his hands together.

Will had gone around once when, in the area with the motorcycle, a group of shirtless guys pulled him into their group. They immediately began working on his zipper and shirt buttons. Will let them unzip his jeans and go down on him, but he was more shy about his shirt buttons. He would not be shirtless next to those worked out bodies.

Later, as Will passed by the area with the big screen TV on his way to the bathroom (Rebecca had heard on a sex talk radio show that peeing immediately after sex reduced risk for transmission of STDs) Will ran into Greg. Greg wore a fitted but not tight red sweater and khaki pants. Greg looked almost preppy but the cut of his clothes made him sexy.

Seeing Greg in what Will sometimes felt was *his* place took him by surprise. Seeing Greg in clothes that were more conservative than revealing, in a place where anything goes, almost gave Will an instant hard on. Greg sauntered up to Will and rubbed his hand up Will's chest where his shirt was still unbuttoned.

Greg said "having a good time?" and smiled at Will wryly.

Quietly, Will said "yeah."

Greg smiled broadly and said "what have you been doing?"

Still tongue tied, and now hard, Will said "I don't know. You?"

Greg said "I went to three different holiday parties tonight. I decided at the last minute to stop in here."

"Holiday parties?" Will said "the week between Christmas and New Years?"

Greg smiled devilishly. "Yes, Will."

A muscle guy in leather chaps (no jeans) walked past, staring hard at Greg as he did.

Greg, still looking back at the guy, said "excuse me".

Seconds later, the leather guy had Greg pinned against a wall, grinding him through his khakis.

Will went into the bathroom, attempting to regain some composure while there. When he came back out into the main area – the walk through between the big screen TV and the curtains that led to the back, Greg and the leather guy were still going at it. Will backed up, hoping Greg hadn't seen him, and went through the doorway that led to the jungle themed area. Will walked through the sounds of birds, water, and men fucking, and through the beaded curtains to the front.

"Leaving so soon?" Stephen said.

"It's kinda late" Will said.

Stephen stepped around the podium to the area where he put people's coats. He stood behind Will and helped him put his jacket on.

In his car, still cold until the heater warmed up, Will cursed himself for being too nervous around Greg to pounce on what he thought may have been an opportunity to have sex with him. He hit the steering wheel, yelling at himself.

"Why are you such a dumbass?"

The next night, Thursday, was New Year's Eve. At work, Will's phone had been silent all day except for calls from his friends. In the early afternoon, while Craig and Ginger were still around to cover, Will slipped away for an early lunch break. Instead of going to the food court downstairs or meeting Kevin outside, he walked to the parking deck, got in his car, and drove up I-75 to meet Jill.

Jill, slender and tall, looked gorgeous in a pair of faded jeans and plain white tee shirt. Her dark straight, wispy hair whipped across her face in the wind as she got out of her boyfriend's truck and ran up to Will's car. Dawn was one of those girls that could sparkle and look fully made up with a few swipes of mascara – and she did sparkle against the gray winter sky. The sounds of cars rushing in the sparse traffic on the interstate was soothing.

"These are Mercedes, and they'll rock your world" she said.

Jill's lack of fear about the pills made Will less afraid himself.

Will said "thanks for getting these for me."

"Just call me lord" Jill said, laughing and turning her head so the wind blew her hair out of her face rather than into it.

"It's cold out here and he's waiting for me. Have fun!" She said before running back to the truck.

Not long after Will was back at work, Frank called him into his office.

"You can take off at eight tonight." he said.

Everyone had been leaving early, and Will has happy to be given the go ahead as well.

"Thanks" Will said "And sorry about he loud laughing and everything when you came in last night."

"That wasn't laughing, Will" Frank said, leaning back in his chair with his feet propped on his desk, flipping a pin top on his desk through a makeshift goal.

He stopped and looked at Will.

"That was something that could shatter glass."

"But that's not the point." Frank went back to his desktop football goals. Will tensed, ready for a reproach.

"The point is you were sitting in Craig's cube talking on his phone."

Will braced himself for the rest of what Frank had to say. He stopped again and looked up at Will, amused. Half smiling. It was Frank's favorite part – those seconds just before delivering the punch line while the person still thinks their in trouble.

"And that's a good thing. You were logged into your phone which you could hear if it rang and see if it lit up."

Frank spun the pin top around. He stopped the pintop sharply and said "I don't care what you do as long as you're logged in to the phone and available to our customers – and you were."

Will sighed, relieved.

Smiling, Frank said "have a good New Year's Eve" and before Will walked out of Frank's office, he gave Will a look that said "but not too good."

By four o'clock most everyone was gone and the floor was quiet. Still overcast and cloudy, Will spent a lot of the afternoon staring out of the eleventh floor window at the people below, hustling and bustling around downtown, anxious to get to their New Year's Eve destinations. He could feel the energy in the cold air below.

At six o'clock, Will felt secure enough that the still silent phone would remain that way while he went downstairs for a cigarette. He doubted that anyone on the west coast would call and if by chance they did, he'd see a voicemail when he returned and call back promptly.

The patio downstairs was between his building, Marquis One and the Marriot Marquis Hotel. The Marriot Marquis Hotel's belly jutted out in the sky along with the lights of the Hilton across the street.

An Asian woman, probably late twenties, who cut hair at the salon on the ground level, was also outside smoking. She was a couple of tables over, and she was polite, but she didn't make an effort to talk. Will liked her. It was as if they had a mutual understanding that they were out there to smoke, relax, and not intrude on each other's thoughts or waste words with gratuitous small talk. Rarely finishing a cigarette, the Asian woman left the patio and walked back inside toward the salon. She would probably be at the podium in front, reading her magazine, the next time someone walked by.

Alone now, smoking a cigarette and staring up at the stars past the Marriott Marquis' lit rooms, Will looked over at the lit rooms in the Hilton. Will stared up at the Hilton, imagining Greg working there, wearing his uniform and rolling luggage to guest's rooms. Will thought of Greg's impeccable manners and handsome, boyish face, smiling as he received a tip from an out of town businessman. The out of town businessman, now married in Will's imagination, closed the door behind Greg, pulled down Greg's uniform pants, and pounded his ass.

Back upstairs in the office, Will stared out of the window at the glowing blue dome atop The Hyatt. It soothed him, along with the smoky air coming from the exhausts of cars passing down below on the street. He thought about going out later with the pills he'd bought from Jill and looking for Greg. Greg would probably be at the Manhole, Will guessed, looking for someone to ring in the New Year with. Will walked over to Craig's desk, sat down, and called Kim.

"I wouldn't" she said. "After the conversation you two just had this week, it might seem obvious that you were out looking for him."

"I knew you would say that" Will said.

"Didn't' you say you're going to hang out with Kaleb and some of his friends?"

"Uh huh".

"Don't sound so excited!" She said.

"I appreciate that they invited me, but I'd rather be somewhere else."

"It's better that way" Kim said. "There will be plenty of time over the three day weekend for you to run into Greg somewhere without it looking like you intended to."

He knew Kim was right. He left work at eight, drove home, showered, and met Kaleb and his friends. One of them drove a four door sedan, speeding up the interstate, too close behind other cars. Will was sweating, nervous, and irritated when they finally got to Chattanooga.

At Allan Gold's, Will rang in the new year with Kaleb and his friends. They didn't know that in his head, Will had been somewhere else most of the night.

It was almost five am when Kaleb and company dropped Will back off at his car. Once inside, and after the ice covered windshield was clear enough to see out of, Will drove over to the Looming. Thought it was well after five am, the parking lot at the Looming was still full of cars. Inside, there were plastic cups scattered about the floor, shirtless men walking around with satisfied afterglows, and other shirtless and naked men still going at it. It looked like a good time had been had by all and if it still looked like this, Will grimaced at what he must have missed. He went straight to the back and was drawn into a group of guys who were in the furthermost, darkest part of the club. Within a minute Will's jeans were down and two guys were taking turns giving him head. He reached down and felt their shoulders, muscular and smooth. Someone from behind pulled him onto his lap and started on his ass. Will allowed a lubed finger and that was all. A minute later Will shot down someone's mouth, pulled his pants up, and started toward the bathroom. Ten minutes after he'd entered the club, he was back at the front asking Stephen for his jacket.

Grinning, Stephen said "leaving so soon?"

"I'm beat" Will said. "Thanks".

"Glad you had a good time."

It was two o'clock pm on New Year's Day when Will finally getting out of bed and checked his messages.

Kim and Zach: "Hey Will. Call us back. We want to hear what you did last night."

Kim: "He's probably still got somebody there."

Zach: "Will! Throw your trick out and call us back!"

Laughter, then a dial tone.

Daniel: "Well, well. It looks like someone stayed out late last night. Call me back sleepyhead."

Rebecca: dial tone. She hates leaving messages.

Kevin: "Let's go get something to eat and talk about last night. You won't believe the hot man I picked up." Afterglow in his voice.

Will called Kevin back and they agreed to meet at Fellini's on Ponce in half an hour. Realistically, He knew it would take forty-five minutes to shower and drive to midtown.

"Don't dally" Kevin said. He knew Will would be late. Will laughed.

"Dally?"

"Yeah" Kevin said "You've never heard dally?"

"No!"

"Ah! It means don't do whatever it is you do when you say you're gonna be somewhere and then I'm sitting there waiting for you by myself."

"You knew I was a lit major didn't you?" Kevin said.

"Little details like that somehow get pushed aside in our conversations. Sorry, I forgot."

"I'm sure that'll be the case at Fellini's. Hurry up – I'm getting hungry."

Fellini's was full of people. The usual Ponce De Leon oddities mixed in with fresh faced Emory college students. Like Raging Burrito, their food was served by college attending hipsters.

Kevin did indeed have himself a good time the night before with someone he'd seen around the Eagle but hadn't had the nerve to go up to.

"So, did you take the pills?"

"Not yet" Will said. "I decided to go with Kaleb, Wayne and Harry to Allen Gold's in Chattanooga."

Kevin said "Why'd didn't you just stay in town?"

"I thought it'd be better to go out of town with them. I don't know – to stay out of trouble maybe. I haven't been able to stop thinking about Greg since I saw him at the Looming last week."

"Yeah, I kind of figured" he said "did you have a good time?"

"Eh, I hope no one noticed that I kept checking out. I kept wondering what was going on here" Will said "and as soon as they dropped me at my car, at five am, I drove over to the Looming."

"You did?! That late?!"

"Yep" Will said. "It looked like things had been crazy earlier in the night."

"I bet" Kevin said. "Did you have fun?"

"Some guys blew me while some other guy fingered me" Will said. "I shot down somebody's throat and then I was out of there in ten minutes."

Kevin looked around at the tables next to them. No one was paying attention.

"You know it occurred to me, after that last time at Raging Burrito - we might want to tone it down if we're going to talk about that place when we go out to eat" he said.

"Why?"

"Because!" he said.

"I was kidding" Will said. "I thought the same thing."

"Well" Kevin said "I was going to say that I like I.T. better for that reason. You can at least go in a little booth and have some privacy there. It can be too much of a free for all at the Looming and sometimes it's hard to tell whose hands are on you."

Back at his apartment, Will sat outside with his cordless phone and cigarettes and returned phone calls. Daniel told him he'd spent New Year's Eve at home with his roommate Rob.

"That's what old men do" he said. "You'll find out one day. The lines and the crowds just aren't worth it."

"I feel a little like I robbed myself of a New Year's Eve" Will said.

"I'm feeling a little antsy myself" Daniel said. "Are you planning to go out tonight?"

"Well, it is still only Friday" Will said.

"It might be a good time for you to meet me somewhere and I'll stick around if you want to take that pill."

"You'd really babysit me?"

"Yes, I said I would" he said "Just make sure you take it early enough so that it's a couple of hours later when I leave you. By then we should be able to tell how you're going to react to it."

"Then let's meet at the Eagle tonight" Will said.

"Hmmmmmm" Daniel said. "the Eagle. I haven't been there in a while. Will it be difficult to find parking?"

"I don't know" Will said "there's usually plenty of parking around there."

"What time would you like to begin this foray into drugs?

"Nine o'clock" Will said.

Parking spaces were much scarce than Will predicted.

"I almost gave up and went over to I.T." Daniel said while they waited to have their coats checked by the burly muscle bear at the coat check just inside the side entrance.

"Thank you for doing this. Now that I've decided to bite the bullet, I'm ready."

They both seemed to notice, at the same time, an odd kind of party energy in the rapidly thickening crowd.

"It looks like the party carried over from last night and never really stopped" Daniel said as they got their tickets for their coats and started toward the front bar. Will bought Daniel a beer.

"Thank you" he said.

"It's the least I can do for my babysitter" Will said. "I want to hang around in front of the staircase and watch people play pool."

"You mean under the sign that says 'No Parking' Daniel said.

"Yes".

By the end of their first beer, Daniel was already chatting with a cute guy. Will gave them a chance to be alone, and went to buy more beers. He stopped to look at the dance floor on the way to the bar.

"He's right" Daniel said to himself. Relaxation somehow intermingled with excitement swirling about. Round two was in the air.

A few minutes later, Will interrupted just long enough to hand Daniel a beer and then excused himself to the bathroom.

Daniel stopped him and whispered "are you?"

Will nodded yes and said "I'll be back in a minute."

Will went into the one bathroom with a door. It was underneath the staircase that went upstairs to a roped off section of rooms. Will locked the door and dug around in the small hip pocket of his jeans. He held the little bag up to the light and looked at the Mercedes symbol on the pill. He bit the pill in half and carefully put the other half back in the baggie and put the baggie back in the hip pocket.

Back outside, Daniel's friend excused himself to go the bathroom.

Daniel said "did you do it?"

"Yes."

"Do you feel anything?"

"Not yet" Will said "it's supposed to take about half an hour."

"What do you think of him?" Daniel asked.

"He's cute."

"He wants me to go home with him" Daniel said "but I told him I'm taking care of you tonight."

"Thanks Daniel" Will said "And look. See that guy over there?"

"Uhm hm" Daniel said, salivating at his naked chest.

"Those guys are a dime a dozen at The Looming" Will said. "And all horny. You'll be glad you went there with me instead of home with that guy."

"I feel kind of fuzzy" Will said.

"Fuzzy?"

"Warm? Fuzzy? I'm not sure. It's not bad though. Definitely a good feeling." Will made a goofy smile.

Daniel said "Mmmhmm."

Daniel's friend rejoined them and Will was unable carry on a conversation with either of them. Everything looked pretty. The low light hanging over the pool table was now glowing and warm. Every glisten of sweat on the shirtless chests that passed by sparkled.

"Daniel, let's leave" Will said abruptly, interrupting his friend mid-sentence.

"Are you okay?" Daniel said.

Will whispered back "more than okay."

Daniel quietly and politely untangled himself from his new friend, who understandably looked confused.

They started toward the coat check.

Daniel said "can I follow you over to The Looming?"

"Yes" Will said, his voice void of animation. "I parked my car on the side of the street by the parking lot. I'll stay there until I see you pull up."

When Will got in his car and cranked it, he was taken at how neat it looked when the headlights popped up.

"Wowwww" he said to himself.

The cool, blue and green interior lights looked brighter than ever. It felt like he was sitting in a warm, shiny, white oasis that he'd never seen before. He clutched the wheel and said "I love this car!"

He noticed someone behind him waiting for a parking space but it wasn't someone waiting for a parking space it was Daniel waiting for him to pull out.

"Oh, oops" he said as he slowly backed up, careful not to hit either car that had sandwiched him in.   After a couple of back and forths, he drove slowly up Argonne and stopped at the red light.

"That's so fucking gorgeous" He said. "that is the most beautiful fucking place on earth."

He gazed at the Krispy Kreme donuts store across the street. Green, white, red against the night sky – it was electric. He felt tingly and euphoric. A peace and calm he'd never known came over him. A sense that everything was okay. More than okay.

Will stayed still and watched a moving silhouette of hairy men in black leather against the bright lights of Krispy Kreme as they quickly crossed in front of him on their way to The Eagle.

"It's all so fucking gorgeous" Will said to himself as the light turned green and he crossed Ponce. Will turned right on North Avenue and then left onto Courtland Street where he quickly hit traffic backed up from Esso. He looked up and saw his office tower, Marquis One, next to the Marriot Marquis.

"That's where you go to work everyday" he said to himself. "I love it."

Will thought of where he was going, and what would be going on inside when he got there.

The ubiquitous bass from the SUVs with their black lights underneath - all around him, people making their way into the club. They were slowing him down from getting where he wanted to be, and at the same time, he loved it all – the sparkle and the jewelry and the music and the excitement. Those horrible hummers he complained about.

Soon Will was being waved into the gravel parking lot of the converted old building that was now home to the Looming by the long haired guy in the army jacket. He guided Will in to an open parking space. Just after ten, and the lot was already filling up.

Daniel sauntered over to Will from where he had been waiting in his car and said "I remembered what you said about the Esso traffic so I came the back way.

"Wow" Will said. "I thought you were behind me. I forgot the back way."

Will made a weird, nervous little laugh that he hadn't heard come out of himself before.

"Let's get you inside" Daniel said.

Stephen let them in before they had a chance to knock.

While Daniel filled out his paperwork, Will savored the smell of the Nag Champa.

Will and Daniel walked through the beads and through the doorway that leads to the jungle area. From there, a left would take them toward the room with multiple TVs, and a right would go through the jungle area and then through a doorway that opens to a walk through next to the area with the big screen TV.

"How are you feeling?" Daniel asked.

"Good. I think. Uhm, yeah. Good." Will said.

"This sort of reminds me of a place in L.A." Daniel said.

Will nodded.

"I think you probably know your way around here pretty well" Daniel said. "I'm going to explore but I'll check on you in a little while."

Normally, the Looming didn't open until twelve. But Stephen had given out flyers with holiday times. Even at twelve, it normally wasn't this full. The feeling in the air was much like the one at the Eagle. Like it was time for round two and no one had even thought of stopping after just one night. Will hadn't seen the Looming so full, and, Will hadn't seen the Looming so fully. Will noticed lights and sounds and plants that he'd not noticed before in the jungle area. His senses were bombarded.

Will walked to the left, through a doorway, and through another. He sat down on the leather couch in the video room next to the refreshment area and watched the multiple TVs behind the chain link fencing. The porn seemed hardcore for this early hour. He was ravenous for sex - like he could do everyone in the club and still not get enough. The guys around him stroking got him hard.

Not worried that a hard on would show, not here, Will stood up and walked back to the middle TV area where hardcore porn was playing on the big screen. He walked through the black, rubber curtains that separated the main area from the back of the club where the motorcycle, orange construction horses, stand alone boxes, slings, and that darkest area he'd been the night before were.

Someone from a group of guys around the motorcycle pulled Will in. Within seconds his jeans were unzipped and someone went to work on his dick. The warmth of the guys mouth colliding with the tingling sensation of the pill was - "I could stay here forever" he thought.

Behind Will, someone lightly caressed his back, moving his hand across his ass and up and down his leg. Will liked it, and then it stopped. When he turned to see who it was, Daniel winked, over his shoulder, as he walked away.

Will zipped up and walked back out into the middle area, or, the walk through, and then back through the little maze to the other TV room. He loved that room with its many TVs all tangled in wire playing porn.

As Will walked in, four other guys were walking out – two in jeans, one in leather chaps, and one in only a jockstrap and boots, who was being led by the others.

Will sat back down on the leather sofa and the guy next to him said "they're taking him out to a sling. Want to go watch?"

"I'm fine right now" Will said.

a pale, rosy cheeked kid who looked about twenty sat down next to Will. He had dark hair, an athletic, lean body, and cute collegiate looks. He was about five foot eight. Michael introduced himself to Will. Michael's thick southern accent was the loudest thing in the Looming. A tall, cute, black guy named Nicholas walked in and sat down on the other side of Michael. The three of them chatted so much the room cleared out.

Michael suggested the three of them go to the back. They walked through the now thick crowd of men and back to the motorcycle area where Michael blew Nicholas and Will, and the other guys who began watching. The sight of Michael, fresh faced and collegiate in appearance, on his knees giving head to shirtless, hungry men – Will almost came.

Will heard a whisper in his ear and it was Daniel.

"It looks like you're doing okay. It's getting late so I'm going to go now."

Will turned and smiled at Daniel before Michael stood up, pulling both Nicholas and Will back toward him.

"Interested in getting out of here for a while?" Michael asked.

Nicholas looked at them both and said "I live close by."

Michael grabbed Will and said "come on".

The three of them stepped past the rubber curtains and into the walk through, which was full of people, some having sex. Someone stopped them and asked to speak with Michael. When he was finished, the guy looked at both Nicholas and Will. He said "Don't let anything happen to him."

Stephen, busy checking people in, quickly stepped around and got their jackets.

"Coming back guys?" he asked.

Nicholas said "Yep, we'll be back."

Will noticed that Michael could barely stay still.

Nicholas wielded his new civic much like that 80's guy that Kaleb had taken Will to the Manhole with that first time. Will wondered if it was some kind of gay protocol to be able to whiz around Atlanta's many nonsensical streets while shifting the gears of a manual transmission.

Nicholas noticed Michael shivering and said "the heater heats up pretty fast and we'll be at my apartment in just a second."

On the short drive over to the highrise Nicholas lived in on Peachtree (George and Weezy's building on The Jeffersons) Will learned that Nicholas was an architect and Michael was a student but he'd dropped all his classes.

Inside Nicholas's tenth floor apartment, the living room window showcased Downtown Atlanta's late night lights. Nicholas led them to his bedroom where he and Michael undressed their lean, athletic bodies. Will held back.

Nicholas threw Michael on his bed. No one mentioned a condom as Michael's pale, muscular legs went over Nicholas's muscled brown shoulders. It was the first time Will had seen such an aggressive bottom – not even Greg. Michael slapped Nicholas's chest while he fucked him. Will thought Michael might be too wild and untamable to fuck, until Nicholas pinned him down and fucked him.

Neither heard Will clumsily excuse himself before going into the bathroom.

With the door closed behind him, Will examined himself in the mirror. He didn't half mind what he saw, but "what the hell is on my head?" And that fat has to go. Nicholas and Michael had lean, hairless physiques. He felt ashamed for being squishy and practically non-human for having pubic hair. How was it that two people in the next room who were fucking like animals, undeterred by the risk of H.I.V., made Will feel so – so much like an animal? The question was still in his head as he noticed again how strange the blond hair looked sitting on top of his head. Will heard his name.

"I'll be right out" Will said, flushing for effect.

Will opened the bathroom door and Michael grabbed Will's crotch as he stepped into the shower and turned the water on.

"Everything alright?" Nicholas asked from his connecting bedroom, pulling up his jeans.

"Yes" Will said "I guess I'm shy about getting naked in front of people, even considering where we all just met."

Nicholas, pulling a handsomely tailored sweater over his head, said "I understand." He smiled at Will and said "How long have you lived in Atlanta?"

"Almost two years" Will said.

"You'll be fine" Nicholas said. "It just takes some time to get used to it."

The three of them exchanged e-mail addresses and phone numbers on their way back to The Looming. Inside, the party was at its peak. Everywhere Will turned was an orgy and he'd barely got the second half of his pill down when someone pulled him in. The guy was tall, blond, and lean with clear definition, but not muscular and pumped like a lot of the other guys. The blond had been getting fucked by two other guys and now he unzipped Will's jeans. The blond drew Will in closer and when Will asked him if he had a condom, someone put lube on Will's dick. Someone behind Will pulled his jeans down to his ankles and started rubbing his ass while the blond put Will's dick inside of him. Will fucked the blond while the blond sucked the guys in front of him. After the blond came and Will pulled out, he turned around and kissed Will's cheek.

"I have to go get cleaned up. Thanks" He said.

Will watched his lean, long body gracefully glide through the sea of muscles and machismo, moving more like royalty than someone who'd just bent over for strangers in a sex club. Will recognized the blond's frame, and it was his own.

It was five o'clock before Will was home and in bed. His dreams were vivid and surreal. That afternoon, though Greg had warned him he'd feel wiped out and devoid of energy, he woke up feeling strangely alright. He called Greg, but he wasn't home.

After a couple of hours of lying around and listening to music but unable to stay on task long enough to get anything done, Will saw what Greg had meant. His energy was low. Greg called back around dinner time and Will went out to the stoop to have a cigarette and talk to him. It was that time of day in the winter when darkness sneaks up without warning and people still have their blinds open and their lights on, unaware they are on display.

Will felt strangely relaxed while they chatted. As he recounted the previous night to Greg, he felt he might have been acting a little like Betty and Frieda after they've been to the vet – prancing around like they're number one because they've been out of the house and had a latex finger up their ass. He caught himself and tried to hold back, but he'd fucked without a condom and felt like a member of the club even though he'd had a nagging worry about it in the back of his mind all afternoon.

"You know I really wouldn't mind going back tonight" Will said "and I still have another pill."

"You mean you're ready to do it again tonight?"

"I had so much fun last night" Will said "and besides it's only Saturday. I don't have to be at work tomorrow."

"Neither do I" Greg said "do you think your friend could get you any more pills?"

"I'll find out."

Jill laughed and said "yep, call me Lord. Sorry but we the rest last night. Try to give me a couple of days notice like you did last time."

Will called Greg back.

Greg said "I'll try and shake some trees."

Will hung up with Greg and lit another cigarette, releasing every draw with a new feeling of worldliness, knowing that his hot friend was shaking some trees, and they'd probably rolling and fucking later.

Greg called back as Will finished his cigarette. He couldn't find any either. Will offered to split the one pill with Greg.

"That wouldn't do either of us any good" Greg said.

"But just half of one of these last night—" Will started

"Will, it was your first time. And believe me, I won't feel anything from half of one."

"Maybe we can find something at the Manhole" Greg said. "Don't worry, I'll find some way to get stupid tonight. Meet me at the back bar at ten thirty."

As Will looked around the back bar of the Manhole for Greg, the light hit a small, shiny earring that sparkled and caught his attention. Will instantly recognized Greg's strong jaw from the rear, three quarter view. As Greg turned around and smiled at Will, blue eyes piercing through him and earring sparkling along with his mischievous smile, Will was taken aback. Greg wore a sleeveless, black mesh shirt. Will couldn't move for a moment. Would someone really wear something like that? And how could he possibly be so hot that he could pull it off? But Greg was that hot, and he was pulling it off.

Instantly, in Will's mind, Greg had catapulted to rock star status. After the previous night at the Looming and during his phone conversation with Greg earlier, Will had felt like the big man on campus. Now, Will descended at a record pace. He felt like a wallflower. A wallflower who was attempting to run with someone way out of his league. The that Will saw in Greg's eyes as he drew him in for a hug told Will that Greg had easily read everything written across his face.

"Would you like a drink?" Greg asked, grinning and self assured. Will couldn't take his eyes off Greg's pale defined pecs through the black mesh.

"Will?"

"Uhm. Uh – yes"

"What are you drinking tonight?" Greg asked.

"Beer" Will said weakly, still feeling like someone had knocked the breath out of him.

"You're already dropping down to beer?" Greg asked.

"Well – I –"

Greg turned to order their drinks.

By the time they'd finished their drinks and Will had clumsily attempted, unsuccessfully, buying pills from a stranger, Greg suggested they go over to Fusion. Fusion was a club for circuit boys, or the chiseled chest smooth beauties who could be seen squeezed onto the dance floor at Backstreet in the wee hours of a weekend morning, eyes bugging and jaws busy chewing gum.

"Let's take our own cars" Greg suggested "In case we want to leave separately."

The suggestion sent waves of disappointment through Will.

Fusion was like someone had carved out only the dance floor full of ripped male torsos, bug-eyes and water bottles from Backstreet and stuffed it into one small location. Greg could see that Will was too inhibited to go on to the dance floor and suggested they get drinks.

"I'll go check things out first" Greg said before confidently striding through the sea of bobbing muscles and Hollywood smiles. When he returned, they sat on one of those round, velvet covered seats like the ones in hotel lobbies and watched the party around them. Greg caught Will eyeing a muscle guy's ass as he shook it in time with the music and gave Will a grin.

"Let's finish up our drinks and go on over to The Looming" Greg said "I don't think we're going to find any pills here anyway. It looks like everyone's already got their party going".

Again, Greg suggested they drive separately. Again, Will sank inside.

The previous night, the Looming had been festive and celebratory – wild. Tonight the mood was dark. It was as if the energy turned hardcore along with the videos.

Greg and Will sat on one of the three sofas near the big screen TV. Two men were standing and passing a bottom back and forth on the screen.

Greg said he could smell marijuana and asked Will if he could tell where it was coming from. Will smelled it too, but he kept watching the guys pass the bottom around on the screen. Greg grinned at him.

Greg said "Did you take your pill?"

"I took it all at once this time" Will said.

"Is that why you're getting quiet?" Greg asked.

"I think so" Will said.

He wasn't sure what was happening. The night before when he'd taken half a pill he'd felt euphoria like never before, but tonight was like someone holding a mirror up to him. All his insecurities about Greg and his own body were amplified. He felt ashamed to be sitting next to Greg, his pale musculature peaking through the black mesh. Will felt like he was all love handles and insecurities, unsuccessfully camouflaged with faux blond hair sitting on top of his head like processed sugar on top of a birthday cake. He felt like a bowl of jell-o sitting next to a lean cut of meat.

In his younger years, Will had discovered the harsh self awareness that marijuana can bring and immediately stopped using it. Now, he felt that same self awareness but ten fold. He couldn't move. He couldn't speak. His mind raced into its darkest territories and as if on cue to match its frantic dash into darkness, the atmosphere at the Looming turned darker as well. The Looming felt eerie and the party atmosphere of the night before had been replaced by a palpable raw hunger. Greg studied Will in his frozen state.

He said "I'm going to go walk around. Will you be okay?"

Will looked at him and said in a voice more serious than he knew he owned, "Yes."

As Greg stood up to walk away, a man who may have been the only other man in the Looming hiding his chest behind a shirt, sat down next to Will. Greg nodded at the guy and then looked at Will as if to say "There you go." It infuriated Will.

Will felt like no one would believe, especially Greg, that he'd been invited to leave with Nicholas and Michael, then fucked a beautiful, shirtless blond when he'd returned. Now, as Greg oozed sex out of his black mesh tank top, Will felt foolish, flabby, and inexperienced.

Greg sauntered off toward the maze that led to the refreshment area and the room with multiple TVs, his walk incensing Will even more.

Will ignored the man sitting next to him as well as the others on the two other sofas that comprised the U shape around the big screen TV. He was sitting on the sofa against the drafty concrete wall with a good view of who was coming and going from the back area behind the black rubber curtains where the motorcycle, standing boxes, and construction horses were. Opposite from the night before, the porn on the big screen did nothing for him as the ecstasy pill hit him head on. He lit a cigarette and continued his downward spiral into his own psyche. He heard loud moans coming from behind the rubber curtains and the next time someone walked through them he made it a point to notice what was going on behind them. There was a table with lit candles around it and someone tied down on top of it. A cross hung on the wall beyond the table. The person lying on the table was getting spanked with a paddle and his moans were turning into yells. Will heard chains rattling in the sling area.

As the atmosphere at the Looming grew more brutal, so did his relentless self examination. He began thinking of his current state in every imaginable way and from every possible angle. He was sitting in a sex club surrounded by cut, hungry men, while he was carrying at least an extra thirty pounds of flab on his small frame. And wearing fake hair No, not fake hair. A piece. The euphemism that he normally used to give himself break in his world was now replaced with hard honesty.

"You've got a fucking wig on your head" Will thought to himself as he blew smoke. "You're a fucking loser. A loser driving a car with a big dent on the side because you've been going out and spending money on alcohol and covers instead of using the insurance check to get it fixed. White trash people do that – drive around in a wrecked car having spent the payment.

The Looming was getting busy and Will worried that someone might notice him - frozen and staring off into space. He tried to get into the porn on the big screen as people came and went around him but instead, he continued beating himself up.

"Did you see Greg's body tonight? Did you really expect someone like *him* to be interested in someone like *you*? You'll never be the type of person who is free enough to just waltz in here, get with three other guys and then lead a bottom off to a sling to fuck him the way those guys did last night. You'll never have a body like that and you'll never have enough balls to strut around here shirtless. You're in a place with *men* and you are not a *man.*"

His mind raced around like that for a while and he lit himself another cigarette. He didn't know how to make the torture stop but he did think he could get up and walk. He couldn't make himself move. He tried to get lost in the porn again, but it didn't work. He hoped Greg would come back soon and sit down and talk to him so he wouldn't feel like such a freak, but he didn't.

The night before, hours passed like minutes. Tonight, time stood still in an awful place. He could feel a cold chill coming from the concrete block wall behind him.

A guy carelessly flipped the black rubber curtains aside and easily strode through them to the main area. He sported a well defined V Shape, big arms and a tight stomach. As well as a satisfied smile and afterglow. Still walking, the guy turned up the plastic cup he was carrying and pat the last bit of ice out of the bottom of it and down his open mouth. He carelessly kicked a half exhausted balloon out of his way as he sauntered off toward the maze that Greg had gone off to. A moment in time that lasted a mere fifteen seconds that would be forgotten by the guy in a mere fifteen seconds had just etched itself into Will's memory like a blueprint.

Inaudibly, Will said to himself "You *will* turn yourself into that."

As he stubbed out his cigarette in the thrift store ashtray on the thrift store coffee table in front of him, he reminded himself that he'd never get that kind of body by smoking cigarettes, not exercising, and by eating fast food. He wanted that body. He wanted Greg to look at him like one of those guys. He resolved himself to quit smoking.

Will stared at the last bit of smoke coming up from the squished cigarette butt and thought "I'll give these things up. The cigarettes. The fast food. Even the meat – I'll become vegetarian. I'll do whatever I have to do but I want a body like that".

This will never happen to me again.

He repeated it to himself before finally standing up from the sofa where he'd been sitting, frozen, for how long he did not know. The man sitting next to him whom Greg had silently suggested he hook up with seemed unbothered or unaware by Will's lengthy and still silence.

Will slowly got his footing and walked back through the maze toward the refreshment area. Shyly, he started into the room where all the different size TVs were playing. There were two men sitting on the leather sofa, one of them smoking a cigarette. Greg was lying, comfortably draped across both guys, his mesh shirt wadded up in his hand. It was an obvious afterglow for all of them. Greg saw Will but didn't move.

He said "Will."

Will couldn't speak and he backed out of the room and into the refreshment area. He heard Greg say, sounding confused and irritated, "Will?"

Will stood still in the refreshment area, momentarily frozen again. He walked toward the front and through the beads to where Stephen sat at his podium.

Will barely heard what Stephen said to him as he handed him his jacket and unlocked the front door.

At his apartment, Will turned on a space heater that maintenance had left earlier in the day when the heat stopped working. He shivered under his comforter, grinding his teeth. Betty and Frieda curled up in a yin yang beside him.

The next afternoon, the Will who woke up wasn't the hopelessly optimistic Mary Tyler Moore throwing her hat in the air because as long as you try hard everything will be alright Will. It was the first time he'd felt such a feeling of doom. Truly hopeless. He called Stephanie, who'd warned him not to try X.

"You know what Will, we've all got problems" she said "is this what you want? Do you think it's glamorous? to go down?"

He didn't know what Stephanie meant. How could one weekend of trying X be considered "going down"? He still didn't get what she'd meant when Greg called later that night. Will cried on the phone with him, told him how hot he looked in his shirt, but couldn't hold a conversation.

"I knew it wouldn't be the same the second night" Greg said "But your mind was made up".

Chapter Ten

"Mr. Turner".

Will could hear Frank coming down the aisle. It was Tuesday after New Year's, and Will still didn't feel completely like himself.

"Did Craig tell you we're having a meeting at three this afternoon with Amanda?"

"We're having a meeting?" Will said.

Frank didn't say anything but instead looked over at Craig's cube. "Where is he at?"

"Getting a bagel. He'll be right back".

"Ah" Frank eyed Will for a moment before walking away.

Half an hour later when Craig sat down in Will's cube eager with anticipation to tell him about some bathroom orgy with five men in dress slacks who wore wedding rings, Will cut him off.

He whispered "You *really* have to start carrying a cell phone so I can let you know when Frank's looking for you."

Startled, Craig said "Why? Was he looking for me?"

"Yes. I told him you went to get a bagel so pretend like you enjoyed a nice, delicious—"

"Well, it was delicious but it wasn't a bagel" Craig said "When was he looking for me?"

"Half an hour ago."

"Did he seem mad?"

"He wasn't smiling" Will said

Craig said "You must be nursing a pretty serious hangover from the weekend."

Will threw Craig off by turning it back around to his bathroom excursion. Craig perked up.

Ginger, Craig, Johnny, and Justin, who was in their group but seldom heard from, all met in Frank's office at three o'clock with Amanda, the VP of Sales. Amanda, intelligent and sporting stylish suits with skirts, put everyone at ease with her salesperson's personality and relaxed manner. One got the impression she could intimidate, but chose not to.

The meeting was the usual rigamoroo – sales look like this. Goals look like this. What are your concerns? Is there anything I can help you with? After Ginger came back with a response followed by Craig kissing Amanda's ass for a few minutes, Frank took the lead for the rest of the meeting.

"You're all familiar with our division in California. I hope so." He said "Justin, you know who I'm talking about, right?"

"Okay" Frank said, pacing and talking "as you all know-"

"As you all know – that division is growing."

Your interaction with the reps there will increase."

It was difficult for Will to stay focused. It was a cold, crisp, sunny January day and the sunbeams were bouncing off the round, mirrored Hyatt Hotel. From the floor to ceiling windows in Frank's office the hotel looked close enough to reach out and touch against the clear blue sky. Ginger tapped Will's leg and whispered.

"What about that Will, we're going to L.A."

Will tuned back into Frank who said "with more interaction, it'd be helpful for you all to know what it is they do. That's why you'll be cross training with them.

Amanda watched Frank speak, nodding in approval.

Will and Craig smiled, excited. Both of their wheels already turning. What trouble could they get into in Los Angeles.

"Justin" Frank said loud enough to make him take notice. Frank paused again – something was coming.

"Justin, you can stay here and man the phones."

Frank quickly went into the proposed dates for travel while Justin looked confused without a chance to absorb or respond. Frank, Johnny, Craig, Ginger and Will would be flying to L.A. the last Wednesday in January.

By MLK day weekend, Will still hadn't smoked a cigarette since the night he went to the Looming with Greg and sat frozen on the sofa. He hadn't tried X again. When Will reflected back on New Year's weekend, he thought of euphoria and sex, followed the next night by brutal, unforgiving mirrors.

Will went to Burkhart's the Sunday evening before the MLK holiday. The crowd was low key and if there was a drag show he'd missed it. Shortly after buying a drink he was approached by someone who claimed he was a personal trainer. He was cute enough – blond, toned. He looked like he hadn't slept in a while and Will wondered why someone who made a living teaching others how to get fit would be at a bar with a sleep deficit. He thought he might know the answer and asked the guy what was going on at Backstreet. Five minutes later, they were in Will's car on their way to Backstreet. The guy said he could find X once they got there.

At Backstreet, the personal trainer did indeed know several people who just so happened to have drugs. While Will waited at the front bar, the guy went off to make a transaction. A girl sat down next to Will.

"Have you ever done coke?" she asked him.

"No" Will said.

"Me either" she said. "I've never done coke."

Will looked to his left and then his right, hoping the personal trainer was back around. Will considered if it might have been a bad idea sending a stranger off in a bar with cash. The girl made Will nervous. He wished she'd go away. The girl grabbed Will by the arm forcefully, drew him into her face, and with a look of intense determination said "Do you know where I can find any?"

"What?" Will said.

"Coke."

Will couldn't help laughing.

"I really haven't ever done coke so no, I'm sorry, I can't help you" He said.

After almost an hour, Will finally found the personal trainer with several people in a lounge area on the top floor. They all looked like they were rolling. He drew Will in and asked him to sit on his lap. Will asked him where the pills were. The trainer slipped two in Will's hand and Will stood up.   "Where are you going?" he asked.

"Don't you think I should go in a restroom to take this?" Will said.

"You're fine here" the guy said.

"I better go take this in private."

Instead of going into a restroom, Will walked outside and got in his car. Will took a pill and pulled out of the Backstreet parking lot. He' d forgotten the guy's jacket was still in his trunk.

Will turned right out of the parking lot onto Juniper Street, a one way street that would turn into Courtland Street. In a few minutes, Will was stuck in traffic, outside of Esso, staring up at the skyscraper where he worked. The pill hadn't hit Will yet as he said hello to Stephen and handed him his jacket.

Less than half an hour later, Will knew the pill was a strong one. There weren't even ten people coming in and out of the dark shadows of the Looming's themed areas. He felt himself sinking into that self aware and brutal state he'd been in the last time he was there. Before it could start he got up, went to the front, asked Stephen for his jacket and left.

Will couldn't shake the brutal self examination and it felt like all the demons in hell were out and in his car with him. It was one o'clock and though his brother normally woke up at five o'clock to go deliver mail, Will dialed his number from his new cell phone.

"Will, are you okay?" His brother, Jim, sounded groggy. Will could hear his wife in the background asking who it was.

"Yes" Will said, not recognizing the voice that came from his mouth.

Jim took a deep breath while he tried to wake enough to talk.

"So what is it?" Jim said, sounding more concerned than agitated. He had, after all, known Will his whole life and up until that point Will had never given him a meltdown phone call in the middle of the night.

"I—I—I don't know" Will stumbled. "I think that, well, I think that I'm horrible."

"Why do you think you're horrible?"

"Because I get to live in an apartment in Buckhead and even though it's a crappy old apartment it's still an apartment in Buckhead and you know in mom's house the kitchen counter is starting to look all warped down the middle like it's drooping so why should I, after she sent me so much money in college that she didn't have to give me, why should I get to live in a place without some crappy drooping kitchen counter and she still has to?"

Jim took another deep breath. Will heard him say something to his wife.

"No Trudy, it's Will. Now please be quiet so I can hear him."

"Jim, it's one o'clock in the morning."

"Is it now Trudy. Thanks for letting me know that." Will could hear him say.

"Will, I don't know. Why are you worried about this now?"

"I don't know" Will lied, hearing a voice he definitely recognized coming from his mouth. It was the tone he'd used since he'd been able to talk - not wanting to tell on himself. Hearing a familiar voice and his own familiar response, he immediately felt better.

"It's okay" Will said "Thanks for picking up your phone."

"Where are you at?" Jim asked.

"On my way back to my apartment" Will said.

"Where have you been?"

"Backstreet".

"I've heard about that place" Jim said "You better go on back home."

Late the next morning, Will lay in bed feeling, as Greg had said – wiped out. He remembered he'd volunteered to work MLK Day. When he got to he went downstairs to get a sandwich. Back at his desk on eleven, he couldn't stand the smell of the sandwich. He stared at the sandwich like it was alien and offensive. He slid the sandwich back into it's bag and folded it back up.

"Craig, do you want this?" he asked.

"You don't want it?"

"No" Will said. "I'm not as hungry as I thought." Will said.

Will heard a co-worker who sat on the opposite of the cube wall that Craig faced, chuckle. She was the one who always commented on Craig's khaki shorts and "schoolboy" backpack audibly enough for him and everyone else to hear. She said "coke" loudly before chuckling again.

"Not exactly" will thought to himself, but glad to see she still thinks she' s a know it all. Still, the comment made him paranoid. Frank came by Will's cube with a manager of another department. They chatted with Will for a minute, which was unusual, before eyeing him and going back to Frank's office. Though he sometimes dropped busywork on Will's desk, Frank's usual style was to leave Will alone. Will wished he hadn't volunteered to work, or at least had the good sense to not take ecstasy on a school night.

It was almost the end of the week before Will felt completely like himself again. Will and Daniel regularly chatted around nine or nine thirty, during the slowest part of the night. Daniel was excited about Will's upcoming trip to Los Angeles, often saying "be sure to go here" and "be sure to go to this place." What bars to stay away from, what sex clubs to visit.

"I wish I could go with you" Daniel said "and be your personal tour guide. I love Los Angeles. I have so many great, and not so great, memories there."

"I guess so" Will said "you lived there for how many years?"

"Twenty five" Daniel said.

"And you had a fourteen year relationship there. Made a movie there. Found out you had an illness there. You've spent your entire adult life there." Will said.

"You *have* been listening" Daniel said, his chipper tone tinged with maudlin.

"Of course I have!" Will said. "I love your stories about L.A. I love hearing how you worked for that company and instead of eating out during your lunch breaks you went to he bathhouse – and that's where you ran into the actor you told me about.

Daniel reminded Will who it was he'd seen.

"Seems like a lifetime ago" Daniel said, his voice sounding far away.

"I do wish I could go with you and see it all through your eyes for the first time.

The next evening when it was time for Will's lunch break, he dropped his car off at a body shop. Kevin picked him up from the body shop and drove to Raging Burrito where he reminded Will what the guy in San Francisco had said.

"Pack condoms" Kevin said.

The next week, on Wednesday, Kevin stood waiting on his front porch, suitcase beside him, for a cab to arrive. It was crisp, cold, and sunny. The sky was blue and the air was dry. Will breathed in the air and thought about how nice it would be to come home and drive his car once the ugly dents were fixed. Will hadn't forgot how he'd tortured himself about it on New Year's weekend, and, he hated driving it the way it was. He still had not smoked a cigarette since that night. A gust of wind came up and he turned his head down, so the hair wouldn't fly up.

"The damn hair" he thought "this is probably a preview of the next few days in California."

The cab ride was just over twenty dollars. Will felt guilty as he paid the driver, knowing if I'd gotten an earlier start he could have taken MARTA. The body shop would be expensive and he had little cash on hand for the trip.

As Greg settled in at work, reading e-mails and eating a sandwich, his phone display lit up with Greg's number. Mouth still full, Will picked up and said a garbled hello.

"Will, this is Greg."

He quickly got the rest of it down and said "hey Greg".

Greg didn't usually call in the mornings. And he didn't usually call Will at work.

"I think you said that today is the day you go Los Angeles" Greg said. "I hope you have a wonderful trip."

Will was caught off guard. Greg had remembered.

"Thanks" Will said "how have you been?"

"Not bad" Greg said. I don't to keep you, but I also wanted to ask you - would you bring back a *David* magazine if you happen to see one."

"I bet I'll see one" Will said.

"Bring any of the gay rags you run across if it's not too much trouble. I love reading the ones from other cities."

"It's no trouble" Will said. "They're flat. Easy to pack."

Greg's call caught Will off guard. In his excitement over the trip, Will's mind wasn't occupied with Greg's rejection. Will head was in the clouds at the idea that Greg thought of him, and remembered when he was going out of town.

"If you could be happy just being friends with him, you wouldn't have got so excited about that call" Will said to himself, unable to do a thing about it.

At four o'clock, suitcases in tow, Frank, Johnnie, Ginger, Craig and Will went downstairs, walked through Peachtree Center Mall to an escalator that took them to the Peachtree Center Avenue MARTA station. Less than an hour later, they were inside Hartsfield-Jackson Airport.

After they were all boarded on their plane, Ginger complained audibly that none of them were seated together. Will settled in with his magazines next to a pretty, blond, soft spoken lady. She had a window seat and Will sat next to the aisle. The outer rows were Will's favorite. Though the lady next to him was petite and soft spoken, he sensed a power underneath. Her hair was shoulder length and neat, but not severe. She was put together and dressed stylishly – crisp but not militant. On the four hour flight, it seemed like she took a genuine interest in Will. She asked what he did, what the purpose of his trip was, how long he was staying. Will liked this person. As they approached Los Angeles she insisted they switch seats.

"You have to see the lights at night as the plane gets closer" She said "they are beautiful."

"Thank you" Will said.

"You don't have to thank me", she smiled "I get to see it for the first time through your eyes."

As the plane approached LAX, the lights of Los Angeles were beautiful indeed, just as she said they would be. Will gasped.

The lady, right leg crossed and chin resting on her knuckle, still smiling, said "it still takes my breath away too. So flat and it looks like the lights stretch on forever."

At the carousel, while Will's group waited for their luggage, he saw the pretty blonde walk up to an equally handsome man who'd apparently been waiting for her. They hugged and kissed. He already had her bag. As they turned to walk away, she noticed Will and walked over to him. She gave him a warm hug and said "good luck to you."

Frank watched the exchange and watched Will, bemused. Will didn't care. He felt a little extra spring in his step as he walked through LAX for the first time. Remembering that Daniel had suggested being on the lookout for celebrities at the airport, Will stopped in his tracks and let out a loud gasp. The other four stopped and turned around. They looked at him with WTF expressions on their faces.

"I'm sorry" Will said, looking at Craig. "I thought I saw Cher."

Ginger laughed heartily while Frank and Johnnie gave each other a look and turned back around.

"Will" Craig said "what if we *really did* see Cher". Craig came up beside Will and whispered "wouldn't that be something!"

Frank turned around and gave Will another look, but this time he smiled.

At the car rental place, Frank asked for the biggest SUV they had.

Will whispered to Ginger "he got the most expensive one?"

"Don't worry about it" she said "geez Will, you need to get out more! You're not paying for it, are you?"

At eight o'clock, the traffic between the airport and Santa Monica was still thick. Ginger asked Frank for his cell phone so she could check in with her two teenage kids.

"Hopefully they haven't destroyed anything" she said as she dialed from the middle of the back seat between Craig and Will. Ginger rarely put on her inside voice while she was on the phone with her kids.

"Did you remember to take out the garbage? Is your sister at home? Are the doors locked?" She went down the list.

It took about half an hour to get to their hotel across the street from the Santa Monica pier.

"It's late guys so you're on your own for food" Frank said as they pulled into the parking lot.

Soon after checking into his room, Will walked across the street to McDonald's. Johnnie was already in line. It occurred to Will that in a chain restaurant that was exactly like thousands of others of its kind, everything around him – the air, the people, the murmur of the conversations – it was all worlds apart from what he was used to.

Back in his room Will called his mom in Rome.

"No matter how late it is" she'd said "I want to know you made it there."

He called Daniel, who was still up watching TV and smoking pot. He knew exactly the hotel they were in.

"I know that area like the back of my hand" Daniel said.

Will ironed his clothes for the next day, putzed with the hair, and went to bed where he fell into a deep, peaceful sleep.

The next morning he met the other four downstairs for breakfast. Will loved it that he didn't have to pay for breakfast, he could have as many eggs and as much orange juice as he wanted, and his room would be made up when he got back that evening.

On the ride to the office the next morning was Will saw California for the first time in day light. The sky was blue and the air was crisp. The houses all had such flat yards.

At the office, the next eight hours were dry, but Will did his best to pay attention during the training sessions – the reason he was there. But he couldn't wait to get out and see more of the surroundings. During a break he stepped outside with Ginger to a long patio that overlooked a valley. Will didn't think he'd ever seen such a clear blue sky. He often noted the crisp days at home because they were such a welcome relief from the humidity. He wondered how, with days like this being the norm, anyone in California could stand to spend them inside.

At lunch, Frank drove to a restaurant he knew and pointed out Nicole Brown Simpson's house on the way. They saw the front door and hedges that had been described in the news so many times. After lunch Frank drove through the Hollywood Hills and showed them Mulholland Drive.

The wind blew constantly and every walk from a car to a building and a building to a car was a threat to Will. What would he say at the Hair Club – in California?

"The winds are really strong out here. My hair is somewhere – maybe in the Hollywood Hills – turned reclusive and watching old films from it's glory days."

In the afternoon as they were shown more features of the software they were there to learn, Craig took every opportunity to kiss someone's ass. Ginger and Will rolled their eyes at each other and during their afternoon break, they joked that Craig had to have something to do since he couldn't spend the day crawling around on bathroom floors of hotels, giving blowjobs.

After work, the four of them met Amanda at a restaurant across the street from their hotel and down the Third Street promenade. Walking down the promenade at dusk, the sky glowed. It was just dark enough to make streetlights and the lights of buildings pop against the blue twilight. There was a casual attitude that put Will at ease.

After dinner everyone split up. Will, by himself, breathed in the night air and walked along the promenade.

Friday morning at breakfast, Ginger asked Frank if he would expense a tour of the stars homes and other landmarks.

"I don't want to go by myself though" she said. Neither Craig nor Johnnie volunteered. Frank and Ginger looked at Will.

"Oh, come on Will" Ginger said "I know it's cheesy and touristy but I think you'd enjoy it."

The rest of the training on Friday seemed to fizzle along with everyone's end of week attention spans and desire for a change of scenery. No one complained when Frank was ready to go by three o'clock.

"I want to beat the traffic back to Santa Monica" he said.

On the ride back to the hotel, Craig contemplated out loud the possibility of getting himself a job at the facility and moving to California, name dropping this or that person who he'd felt had shown interest in him.

Craig, Ginger, and Will lingered in the lobby to discuss the rest of the weekend. Ginger made sure Will knew what time to meet her in the lobby Saturday morning for the bus tour. Craig and Will arranged a time to meet with Daniel's friend Rudy that same night in West Hollywood.

Back in his room, and as on most Fridays, Will was happy to ditch the hair for the weekend. He threw on some jeans and a baseball cap, walked across the street for more fast food, and then headed toward the promenade. He wanted to feel that Friday afternoon turning into evening excitement he knew so well from their eleventh floor office back home – the hustle of people leaving the law offices and government offices in the office tower, rushing through and around groups of tourists milling about the Peachtree center mall on the ground level.

In Santa Monica, it was easier, more laid back – but the anticipated excitement that Friday night promised was the same in any city, Will guessed. It was so thick in the ocean air he thought he could taste it. Everyone seemed tuned in to tuning out their co-workers and ushering in whatever the weekend had to deliver.

At eight, Will met Craig in the lobby and they asked for a cab. It was dark and on the ride to WeHo Craig still chattered about the idea of moving to California.

"Well I know Frank would recommend me if I wanted a job, he said."

Will gazed out the window of the cab. He saw a famous street sign that said "Beverly Hills 90210."

Craig said "Well, don't tell anybody just yet. I haven't decided if this is something I want to do or not."

As they got into West Hollywood, Will noticed a two story, glass walled gym mixed in with the gay bars, all within walking distance. Lean, muscled men left the gym and walked up the street with their gym bags among the freshly perfumed boys in their club shirts.

"Pecs and biceps are the name of the game no matter what city you're in" Will thought to himself as he and Craig stepped out of the cab and onto Santa Monica Boulevard.

The first bar that Will and Craig ventured into was called The Revolver. If the revolving door in the front of the bar weren't kitsch enough, on several TVs scattered throughout were Alexis and Crystal Carrington bitch slapping each other in repeated loops. Julia Sugarbaker leaned over a pageant contestant, railing at her with Suzanne Sugarbaker's past accomplishments as Suzanne Sugarbaker looked on from behind. The giggles from the boys in the bar rolled in waves that seemed to grow in concert with Julia's crescendo.

Mickey's was a larger bar with tables along an open air side facing the sidewalk. Boxes were located throughout Mickey's with gyrating muscle boys in revealing shorts on top of them. Unlike Will, whose lack of manners often times got him in trouble, Craig had impeccable manners. He and Rudy got along well and made conversation. Craig took on the role of host, keeping the three of them engaged.

While Craig and Rudy talked, Will noticed some of the interactions going on around them. In Atlanta, if someone younger or more attractive wasn't interested in someone else, they made a show out of how much they were *not* going to talk to that person so there would be no doubt in anyone's mind – as if even the slightest interaction would mark them as spoiled meat. Here, in what was presumably a gathering of some the most shallow people in the world, it seemed like the point didn't have to be driven home so hard. It looked to Will like when the L.A. boys weren't interested in someone, they truly just didn't notice them as they kept on moving. It was as refreshing as the lack of humidity in the sparkling Friday night air.

When Craig was in the restroom, Rudy asked Will if he still wanted to go to the bars in Silver Lake. Will was hesitant about what Craig might think of him, and worried he'd tell people at work. He told Rudy.

Rudy said "isn't he the one that sits across from you at work?"

Will threw his head back and laughed.

"That's right" Will said "you and Daniel talk pretty often. He told me that."

When Craig sat down Will said "Rudy's offered to take us to Silver Lake."

Craig looked at Rudy with a question mark.

"What is Silver Lake?"

Rudy looked back at Will.

"Cheshire Bridge" Will said "like The Manhole?"

"Will, you naughty boy – ha, ha, haaaa. Whyyyyeeevvvaaaaah would you want to visit that part of town. Craig's sinister laugh was unmistakable.

Will shrugged and said "I don't know. To check it out."

"Uh huh Will" Craig went on "I know what you want to check out – ha, ha, haaaa."

"That's very gracious of you to offer, Rudy" Craig said "But I'm going to stick around here and see if a friend of a friend shows. You two go and have a good time."

A group of muscle boys passed on the sidewalk and Craig turned back to Rudy.

"I've seen a few of those muscle boys pass by since we've been here. Is there a club nearby they're all headed to?"

"Firehouse" Rudy sounded tired. Or bored. "It's a large dance club."

Craig looked at Will and said "Probably like Backstreet, huh Will."

"Nothing's like Backstreet" Will said.

"It doesn't get going until about midnight" Rudy added.

"Well, that part is like Atlanta" Will said. "What time do they close?"

"Two thirty."

Craig said "Will, why don't you meet me at Firehouse at midnight. That should give you plenty of time to *check out* Silver Lake and it will give me time to see if Barry's friend is going to show."

On the short ride over to Silver Lake, Rudy told Will about the area. About the earthquakes he'd experienced. Delivering mail in the hot sun. They passed a club with a long line outside.

"What's that?" Will asked.

"If you want to go in there I'll have to just drop you off. I don't feel like going in."

"I don't want to go in there" Will said. "Just curious."

There was hay on the floor, still photos of naked men on the TVs, and few patrons milling about The Faultline in Silver Lake. Rudy explained that the club didn't get going until midnight as well.

Will and Rudy had a beer and talked more about Daniel, until Will noticed a young, despondent looking boy.

Rudy observed from the bar as Will chatted aimlessly with the boy, unable to elicit even a giggle. Rudy allowed Will's self indulgence for the length of their beer and then suggested they leave.

"I've seen that kid before" Rudy said "I think he's a hustler."

Rudy looked at Will as if he had been born yesterday. "Are you sure you want me to drop you at that sex club?"

"Yes. Daniel told me it's one of his favorites."

The mostly empty sex club did have a nice outdoor patio that was lost on Will as he hadn't grown into an appreciation of horticulture as a thirty year old growing on twenty. He fucked a tan blond guy using the lube and condom provided by the attendant at the front entrance. Afterward, the same bored looking attendant called a cab for him.

Back in WeHo at the now crowded Mickey's it took Will a few minutes to find Craig. He was chatting someone up at the bar and Will guessed it was Barry's friend.

"No, he didn't show" Craig said quietly before turning around and introducing Will to his new friend.

The atmosphere had turned festive while Will was at Silver Lake. The crowd was thicker, louder, and Craig's beer was really working on him.

"Will, do you still want to go to Firehouse with me?"

Will nodded toward two muscle boys walking past in tank tops and said "Uhm. Yes."

Craig let his sinister southern laugh of his and told his new friend they were leaving.

Craig and Will, excited and chatting, walked the few short blocks and around to Firehouse. It seemed a luxury, being able to walk between such different worlds.

They paid a doorman a cover and entered Firehouse on the street level. There was a long bar to the left with several shirtless patrons coming and going. A model beautiful bartender in a tank top served cocktails and beers. Craig and Will ordered beers, both anxious to see what was behind a set of double doors past the end of the bar where cut, shirtless men came and went. Will recognized their restless behavior and bugged eyes glowing white through whatever means of a tan they'd acquired. The majority of the wired up beauties were carrying water bottles rather than cocktails. Greg came to mind and Will made a mental note to grab some of the gay rags by the front entrance on the way out.

Like the dance floor at Backstreet on a weekend night, on the other side of those double doors was a sea of chiseled chests and bright white smiles. The whites of eyes peeked out from tanned, handsome faces bouncing up and down in time with the heavy beats.

Craig said "Haaaa haaaaa haaaaaa Will, look at this."

Will said "Let me go to the bathroom really quick" though the hair wasn't attached to his head but still back in his hotel room – it was a habit. The habits going on in the restroom couldn't be ignored. In Atlanta, the bug eyed shirtless boys waited in line for a condo to do their bumps. In Los Angeles, groups of chiseled men and boys were gathered around the sinks doing their bumps and lines in full view of everyone.

Will remained at the corner of the dance floor and surveyed the crowd just like he did in Atlanta. He smiled when he noticed Craig in the middle of the dance floor dancing with a group of guys, and Will wasn't sure if the guys knew it or not. For a reason Will didn't know, the sight of Craig dancing with a group of guys who may or may not have known touched him.

A shirtless, pale, lean, and muscled guy wearing black pants and a black derby hat danced up to Will. If he hadn't smiled and looked into Will's eyes, Will would have assumed he was about to dance right past him on his way to someone else. He grabbed both of Will's hands and started moving backwards on to the dance floor. Will had just enough of a beer buzz to allow himself to be led to the middle of the dance floor.

"You're a good dancer" the guy said.

"Thanks" Will said as they guy pulled him in closer, grinding his hips against Will's. They danced like that for a while and Will observed they guy's long, lean torso. He had personality and his smile sparkled among the bobbing tan chests.

They guy pulled up Will's sweater slightly and put a finger in each of his sides.

"What are you—" Will started.

"Just checking" the guy said.

It was the first time Will had been physically checked for fat by someone at a club – or anywhere. Did the guy have calipers in his back pockets for verification – in case they decided to leave together? Before Will knew how he felt about it, the started pulling him toward the side of the dance floor where he'd been standing with his friends.

"I want you to meet my friends" the guy said.

Craig appeared and danced up behind the guy, wrapping himself around him, and grinding him as he danced.

"Willlll, he's cuuuuuuute" Craig said, unphased by the look of confusion and agitation on the guy's face. Craig continued wrapping himself around Will's shirtless dance partner and began feeling him up front and back. There was a look of defeat in the shirtless guy's eyes as he untangled himself from Craig and rejoined his friends on the other side of the dance floor.

Craig said "He was a hottie Will! Why'd you let him get away?!"

Will made his way across the dance floor and toward the guy who was now talking to his friends. He saw Will coming and stepped toward him.

"I like you" he said "but not him" and gestured toward where they'd been dancing.

"I'm not with him like that—"Will started, but one of the guy's friends pulled him away before Will could finish.

Ginger rang Will's phone bright and early the next morning. Rather than pick up the receiver, Will laid still and wondered if he really was back in his hotel room about to go on a tour of the stars homes that he wasn't interested in. Shouldn't he be at that hot, shirtless guy's apartment which Will was certain must be a duplicate of Michael Mancini's swank beachfront condo on *Melrose Place* and he was certain if it wasn't for Craig he'd be in the shirtless guy's bed watching the ocean waves break through floor to ceiling windows while the hot guy showered after their third round of sex.

"I'll go but I'm not wearing the fucking hair" Will said to himself as he reached for the phone when Ginger called back. He could hear the disappointment in Ginger's voice as if she knew already he was hung over and in no shape to go.

"No, I'm fine" Will said. "But I'm hungry. Do we have time for breakfast first?"

"You and that breakfast" Ginger said, laughing. "Go stuff yourself."

One of the first places the van stopped was Rodeo Drive. Ginger noticed Will shy away, and asked if he was intimidated. Rather than answer honestly, he answered vaguely.

"What's the point in going into a store when you can't afford one single thing in it?" he asked.

The first part of the tour included the homes of Sandra Bullock, Lucille Ball, and an aging film star who the tour guide told them complained about the tour bus driving by.

"But if you look up the driveway to the left, you can see him picking up his newspaper" she said "this is a rare occurrence.

Ginger whispered "yeah right".

The driver pointed to the balcony outside of the apartment building that was used in *Pretty Woman*. As they walked on the sidewalk outside of Mann's Chinese theater, Will and Ginger took each other's photographs kneeling over a star in the sidewalk. Will had to admit, he was kind of enjoying himself. And though Will was enjoying himself, he began to notice an itch. Not just any itch – a crazy bad itch.

By the time the sight seeing part of their tour was over and they were headed up to the Getty Museum, Will couldn't think of anything except that itch. In his rear. He'd past uncomfortable was well into misery before they even reached the Santa Monica hilltop where the Getty Museum sat. The view of the Pacific Ocean and San Gabriel mountains was breathtaking, and so was the white museum. Ginger tried to convince Will to stay and take in the museum when he told her he wasn't feeling well and wanted to catch the next ride back to the hotel.

"Will, you just want to grab a nap so you'll feel like going out again tonight" she said as he moved around uncomfortably, unable to scratch the offensive area in public.

"No, I really don't feel good" Will said

Ginger, disappointed for Will, said "I wish you'd stay here. You've never been to L.A. and who knows when you'll get to see it again."

"I'll call you later when I wake up" Will said, spinning around and grabbing the nearest docent who gave him directions out.

The ride back down the hilltop and to the hotel seemed to take hours. As the van neared the hotel, there was one more stop to make. Will felt like he could have kicked the those last passengers (a lovely senior citizen couple) out of the van, thrown the driver out of his seat and floored the gas himself. It. Was. That. Bad.

Once Will was finally inside his hotel room and inside the shower, he was finally free to inspect. He felt something though he didn't know what. Though he cleaned with a fury of Joan Crawford who he'd seen slapping Christina over and over the night before on the TVs at The Revolver, this new foreign thing would not be scrubbed away. Confounded, worried, and thousands of miles away from his doctor, Will collapsed on the crisply made hotel bed and fell asleep.

That Sunday, the flight home seemed to take longer than the flight going out. It was raining in Atlanta when the plane landed.

Chapter Eleven

"You're going to need a little surgery" Dr. Bernard said as he walked around his heavy, thick wooden desk where he had been talking into a recorder. He sat down in a guest chair beside Will.

"What kind of surgery?" Will's eyes moved between Dr. Bernard eyes and the top of his neat desk - a shiny clock and shiny pens which reflected from the surface of the wood.

"Condyloma" Dr. Bernard said as he handed Will several brochures. Will searched his eyes for answers but the technical explanations he gave me weren't the answers Will was looking for. Why was this happening? Will hadn't been unsafe, according to Daniel's four levels of what's safe and what's not safe. They went like this, with 1 being most unsafe and 4 being the least risk:

1 – anal bottom

2 - anal top

3 – oral giving

4 – oral getting

"This is transmitted by skin on skin contact" Dr. Bernard explained "and it's very contagious."

"Do you smoke?" he asked.

"I quit January 2nd."

"Good for you" he said "smokers are more susceptible".

"It's a rather large area and there will be some pain involved." Dr. Bernard sounded serious. "I'll give you some medication for that."

Will was still in a daze as Dr. Bernard walked him to the receptionist at the exit desk.

"She'll set up your surgery and I'll write you a note for work. You will need a few days."

At home, Will felt like calling someone. But who? With a problem like this?

Greg said "you need to pay attention to how this is transmitted. When is your surgery?"

"It hasn't been scheduled yet."

"Well let me know when it is" Greg said, sounding concerned, but not surprised. "You'll need someone to drive you and I can do that. How did you hear about Dr. Newman?"

"My regular doctor said I needed to go see a special butt doctor, so I looked some up. It was a random choice. He's hot."

Greg laughed. "I think he is too. I like his thick silver hair and blue eyes."

"How do you know him?"

"I had the same surgery about two years ago" he said "I ran into him recently when I was doing community service at the hospital."

"Wait, what?"

"I was out with a guy one night who got pulled over. He had some X on him so even though I wasn't driving I still had to do community service. It wasn't that big of a deal. That's when I saw Dr. Newman at the hospital."

On the day of Will's surgery it was Kim who drove him. Though he loved any excuse to be around Greg, Will chose the comfortable and familiar. And though Greg lived close to Will in Buckhead, Kim drove from Decatur to Will's apartment, from Will's apartment to the hospital, and then back to his apartment again.

In the post op area, someone kept saying "Mr. Turner" loudly in his ear, irritating him more each time she said it.

"Now the morphine will make you a irritable" she said.

"No fucking shit." Will said.

Kim said "that's one hundred percent Will" with a laugh. "He's awake. Don't worry."

"Where's my hat?" Will slurred his words. The nurse grabbed the plastic bag and handed it to Kim.

"It's right here." Kim was warm, smiling and laughing. "You look fine Will. You don't have to worry."

On the way back to Buckhead he asked Kim to stop at Smoothie King. Still groggy and beginning to feel like a Mac truck had ran through his ass, he took one of the pain pills Dr. Newman prescribed as soon as they walked in the door. Kim tucked him in, told him how clean his apartment was and thanked him for letting her do her laundry.

"Call me later when you wake up" was the last thing Will heard before falling into a deep sleep.

It was dark and Will didn't know what time it was when he heard his phone ring. It must have been before eight, he thought, because he still heard rush hour traffic outside his bedroom window on Roswell Road.

"How is the patient?" Daniel's voice sounded warm and familiar.

"I have to pee" Will said "I'll you right back"

Twenty minutes later he called Daniel back.

"I can't pee."

"That's normal" Daniel said "did you try running water?"

"Yes. And my ass hurts."

"Did your doctor give you anything for pain?"

"Yes" Will said. "I took one when Kim and I got here this afternoon."

"It's probably time for another one. Take one of those and take a warm bath. I'll be up for a while longer so call me back and let me know if that works."

Will loved warm baths anyway and while he lay in the bathtub trying to relax and the pill started working on him, he thought about Greg and how much he wanted him. When it finally flowed he didn't understand why a hard on came with it. He stood up, flicked the drain and ran the shower. Will cleaned himself well before slowly and carefully walking back to his bed.

"Your suggestion did the trick" he told Daniel. It was well after nine and getting close to Daniel's bedtime.

"I thought it would. Now, is there anything I can bring you in the morning?"

"I can't think of anything."

The next morning, Daniel waited until Will had plenty of time to sleep in before calling.

"I was afraid we might have to take you back to the hospital for a catheter" Daniel said "I'm glad the bath worked."

"What's a catheter?"

Daniel laughed. "You really don't know what one is?"

"No."

"Ahhhh. Be happy you were able to pee. How do you feel this morning?"

"Pregnant. Now I can't do number two."

"Well I have to tell you, I don't feel so old now." Daniel laughed again. "Should I get you a laxative old man? Maybe some Correctol?"

"I'll get up and unlock the door for you."

"Will Betty and Frieda try to get out?"

"No. They're afraid of it out there. I don't think I blame them."

Will dozed, on and off, and later heard Betty doing her meow-squeak at Daniel as he came through the front door with plastic bags rustling. He stopped to pet her and Will could hear him talking to her. Daniel rarely met a pet that he didn't bond with immediately. He loved it that Betty acted like a dog, greeting visitors at the door.

Daniel stood at the doorway of Will's room for a moment, smiling broadly.

"I think you almost look cuter without the hat or the hair" Daniel said.

That one comment soothed much of Will's pain. As Daniel pulled out the contents of the Kroger bag – laxatives, juice, ice cream – the doorbell rang.

"Are you expecting someone? That cute Zach maybe?"

"Do you mind answering it?"

Daniel grinned.

"Don't turn the front door into a glory hole" Will joked, weakly.

Daniel was back a minute later with a bouquet of cookies.

"From your friends at work" the card read.

Daniel sat on the side of Will's bed and rubbed his swollen stomach. He looked good. His always thick hair was cut shorter and gelled up. His tanned face, nor his smile lines, nor his wise brown eyes detracted from an eternal boyishness he possessed.

"If you aren't able to go to the bathroom today we still may have to take you back to the hospital."

"The nurse said the pain pills were a blessing and a curse. They take the pain away but they also cause constipation."

"I told Rob about this. I hope it's okay" Daniel said.

"I don't mind."

"Last night we remembered that a friend of ours had been through this. The first time you go – it will hurt."

"Greg said the same thing."

"Oh" Daniel raised an eyebrow. "You two are talking again?"

"Yeah." Daniel's look of concern changed to very concerned.

Daniel brought a pain pill into Will's room and sat on his bed talking for a while. He had been busy putting his list of Oscar picks together. He wanted Gwyneth Paltrow to win for *Shakespeare in Love*, which they'd gone to see with Rob over the holidays. Rob, Daniel's roommate and an English teacher, had laughed out loud throughout the movie while Daniel and Will gave each other "Was that really so funny?" looks. To Daniel, who still had his Screen Actor's Guild card, the Oscars was like the Superbowl for football fans. He beamed with excitement as he talked about his choices for winners. Will hadn't seen many of the movies Daniel talked about but the sound of his voice calmed him, as he explained who Andrea Bocelli was. Daniel kissed Will's forehead before he left and Will understood for the first time how a sexual first encounter and romance can turn into sweet friendship. He felt loved.

Will lay in his bed, Betty and Frieda on either side of him, and looked out of the window at the cold, gray, February sky and traffic coming and going on Roswell Road. He could feel the pain pill working its magic. He thought about what Stephanie said about Daniel on his birthday weekend. In Will's defense, she'd called Daniel fool's gold. Will knew now that Daniel wasn't fool's gold, but instead, he had a heart of gold. He hadn't talked to Stephanie since New Year's Day when he'd called her upset about Greg.

"You know what Will, we've all got problems" she'd said.

That was over six weeks ago and the longest they'd been without talking. He picked up the phone and dialed her number.

"I heard you went to Los Angeles" Stephanie said abruptly "How was it? Did you go to many museums?"

"My co-worker Ginger and I went to The Getty" Will said.

"Did you see any photography?"

"Well, I had to leave early"

"Is that the only museum you went to?"

"Well, yeah".

"Do anything else?"

"Another co-worker, Craig, and I went to West Hollywood. A really hot guy at a place called Firehouse danced up to –"

Stephanie cut him off.

"Will, I head about your surgery too. I hate that and I have to tell you – I just hate to see your light go out."

"I don't under –"

Stephanie cut him off again.

"I have to go. Bye Will."

"What a fucking bitch."

Will could hear Kim exhaling smoke over the phone. It was almost six o'clock PM and already dark outside. He could hear the bumper to bumper traffic outside on Roswell Road. The sounds of it gave him comfort – hearing the world going on outside around him even though he was down.

"What the hell does that mean?" Kim said "I just hate to see your light go out".

Though they were talking over the phone, Will could easily see Kim's face scrunched up as if to say "that's so stupid".

"Daniel thought I was cute without the hair" Will said.

"Awwwww – you are Will. I don't know what you're worried about". Kim was instantly lighter and laughed. "I want to hear about your visit with Daniel, and then talk about Stephanie some more, but first I want to know if you've been able to dook".

"No and my stomach is huge and every time I *try* to go it hurts so much I feel like I might pass out."

"What does Daniel say about that?"

"He wants me to go back to the hospital if it doesn't happen soon."

"I have to say I agree with him." Her tone was serous.

"I think I'm going to try another warm bath" Will said.

Moving like a pregnant woman in the final trimester, Will slowly got himself out of bed, walked to the bathroom, and started warm water in his bathtub. Once he was finally in his bath and beginning to relax, the phone rang. It was Patricia's name on the display. He pressed the 'talk' button.

"Hey Will, what are you doing?"

"Taking a bath" Will said "The surgery was rougher than I knew it would be and –"

Now Patricia cut him off.

"He wants to break up" she said.

"I'm sorry, I am. But right now I can't –"

"HE HATES ME AND I HAVEN'T EVEN DONE ANYTHING WRONG!" Her voice shrieked so loudly, Will took the receiver away from his ear. He lay in the warm bath, bubbles all around him, candlelight flickering on the Pepto Bismol colored tile walls and white porcelain. He held the cordless phone over the side of the bathtub – Patricia's pain still mega phoning through the receiver.

He pressed the 'talk' button again and the phone went silent.

Daniel called after nine when it was nearing his bedtime.

"Were you able to?"

"The only thing that went down the toilet today were two of my friendships – Stephanie and Patricia."

"What happened?"

"It looks like Stephanie's leaving me behind and I'm leaving Patricia behind. I'll tell you about it later. My stomach hurts and my ass is killing me just from trying to go."

"How long has it been now?"

"Since the night before my surgery. Almost three days."

"Will, we'll have to take you back to the hospital if you haven't gone by morning." Daniel wasn't coaxing him – he was telling him.

The next morning Will thought he felt as close as a man could feel to giving birth. Something was going to happen and every minute that passed the pain became worse. Daniel said he would be at his apartment in the afternoon if there was no change. Before that could happen, hunched over and moving like someone who'd suffered decades of back pain, Will slowly walked into his bathroom. He pushed for a resolution like he never had and when it finally came he stood up, dizzy with pain, and fell down across the threshold of the doorway and into his bedroom floor. He gasped for air and breathed heavily – the natural human instinct for repair. An hour later, his phone rang and he crawled over to it. It was his neighbor and co-worker, Laura.

"I have a little care package for you if you feel like company."

"My room is gross" Will said "but come on over. The door is unlocked."

Shaky, he pulled himself up by the doorframe, cleaned himself, and sat down on the side of his bed. He wished he could clean up before Laura came over. Moments later, he heard a knock at the door followed by Laura's cheery voice. She appeared in his room like a ray of sunshine, her good perfume blasting through the smell of sick stillness. When she saw him she threw the care package down and raced over to his bed. She put her arms around him and drew him in protectively. He sobbed uncontrollably.

Later in the week, healing but still raw, Will was able to sit in the living room and have company over. He needed the pain pills, but feared what they might do to his digestive system. He needed food, but feared what might happen if it got stuck. Liquid and fiber were the only things he considered safe enough to have. He stopped eating meat partly because he'd always wanted to and partly because he imagined that by its texture alone it was more likely to grab on to something inside and hang on.

Early the next week Greg came over with a frozen pizza. It was the first time he'd been to Will's apartment. Will's roommate was out and Greg sat on the edge of the S shaped chair and talked to Will, who sat on one end of the sofa with a blanket draped across his legs. Greg burned the frozen pizza he'd brought with him. Will had looked at the sheet of bread and cheese with terror, afraid of what it might do to him.

It seemed, for the first time, that Will was more relaxed than Greg. Under a blanket and relaxed by a pain pill, he chatted with Greg easily. It occurred to Will that now they had something in common – an STD.

Chapter Twelve

As Will healed over the next few weeks, he did not forget the worst pain he'd ever known. He swore off meat and anything else he felt might slow down his system or even grind it to a halt. He ate plums and salads, replaced Pepsi's with bottled water, and began walking at nearby Chastain Park, where Buckhead moms determinedly pushed their toddlers in expensive strollers down paths carved through the plush southern landscape of hundred year old trees and neatly manicured grass. By spring Will had lost twenty pounds, his skin glowed, and his eyes were brighter.

His friend Rebecca said "You've inspired me! If you and my brother are both starting new fitness routines at the same time, then I have to get on board too."

"What does he say about his routine?" Will asked.

"That he's uncovered muscles he never knew existed" Rebecca said.

"I've noticed around my waist" Will said "There's a negative space between my arms and my waist that I see now. I feel so much better than before."

"You know how to bounce back Will. I've always said you're resilient."

Rebecca put together a routine that very week and started on it.

Will made up goals for himself and didn't tell anyone. Kim would soon be going to Europe with Gina's boyfriend Devin and one of Devin's friends from school. Will's goal was that by the time they returned from Europe, Kim would notice a difference.

Will walked and jogged at Chastain Park in the mornings before work. He loved seeing the mommies jogging along pushing their strollers, the privileged kids in expensive summer clothes taking their tennis lessons from hot twenty something instructors, and the presumably old money in mall track suits power walking. It was a little slice of Atlanta heaven that he'd never taken advantage of and it provided calm for him like he'd not known before.

Since there was nary a soul around the office at ten at night when finished work, Will began using the exercise equipment on the twelfth floor. He would not have felt confident enough to use it in the daytime. Three nights a week, he changed clothes in the men's restroom room with its sleek black tiled floors, black tiled walls, and track lighting. Working at a job that many considered menial didn't matter to Will. What mattered was that during these workouts, as Will gazed out the vertical windows with darkness on the outside and reflections of the pool table, and exercise equipment on the inside, it all belonged to him. No one was around except the fish in the aquarium.

There was a framed poster on the wall and a toned, tan man in a muscle shirt and shorts was in row after row of photos. In each photo he illustrated the correct execution of an exercise and instructions were printed below each photo. Will checked the poster on the wall before each session and tried to mimic the man's movements. He often walked over to the poster between sets to make sure he was getting them right. There were two large TVs hanging from the ceiling. *Daria's* premature kept Will company while he exercised.

Daniel and Will talked almost every night during Will's last hour at work. Daniel had a goal of his own. There was a straight man that Daniel gardened with and Daniel wanted to suck his dick. Daniel reminded Will that it was a low risk on the "scale of four" in risk taking. Daniel kept Will up to date on the latest with his roommate Rob, and his increasing appetite for rented dick from the straight, rough trade, Smith brothers. Daniel grew more concerned.

Will talked to Greg less often – every couple of weeks. Will sometimes called him spontaneously and out of the blue like he would any of his friends, and other times, Will waited to see if Greg would call. Greg always called before two weeks went by. Will hoped to finally be satisfied with a friendship and nothing more, when Greg called him one night in April.

"Will, how are things going with you and your roommate?"

"I like Brandon" Will said "He's a good person and he has a hot boyfriend who's here a lot."

"The reason I asked" Greg said "Is that one of my roommates is moving out. I know you were struggling back in December and I just wondered."

Will felt like dropping the phone. Would that mean that he'd get to fuck Greg on random Tuesdays if he moved in?

"How much are you paying there?" Greg asked.

"Three eighty five" Will said "I pay more because I'm in the larger –"
Greg cut him off.

"It's two twenty five here for the master bedroom and bathroom. It only has a shower though."

"Are you kidding me?"

Greg laughed. "It's section eight. Do you know what that means?"

"No."

"It just means this apartment complex keeps the rent low and always will because of the little pocket that it's located in."

"Oh."

"What about my cats?"

"Oh yeah" Greg said. "There's more than one?"

"I have two."

"Ordinarily I try to keep it pet free and smoke free here" Greg said. "How are you doing with the smoking?"

"I haven't smoked since January 2nd" Will proudly proclaimed, forgetting that he might not want to bring that weekend up.

"Good, good for you." Greg sounded impressed. He let out a sigh.

"You can bring your cats if you decide this is something you want to do."

.

"I don't think it's a good idea." – Will's best friend Rebecca.

"I don't think it's a good idea." – Kim and Zach

"I don't think it's a good idea." – Daniel

"Woohoo! I won't have to drive all the way up to Roswell Road to pick you up anymore!" – Kevin

"You'll be at The Manhole every night" – All of the above.

No one said what Will wanted to hear. "Of course! Go live with Greg and follow him around like a sex starved seamen because you know you want to and hey, you might actually get to fuck him once in a while."

Kevin suggested they talk about it over a Raging Burrito the next night. The next night at six Will left Justin (warm body) in charge and went downstairs to sit on top of one of the big gold kitties in front of Marquis One. The evening sun shined down and spring air whisked around the hustle and bustle on the street below. In the sun, Will fell into a trance like he could only do when he was completely at ease with the sun shining on him. He let himself feel the city around him, reminding him that he was no longer in the narrow tunnel that was his hometown, like many must feel about their own hometowns.

In Kevin's white Jeep Cherokee (the Laredo – not the square kind), Kevin told Will about the shootings at Columbine. They didn't talk about it long in favor of their own chatter about sex clubs, music, and men.

At Raging Burrito, Will could barely keep his eyes off the biceps and V-Shapes all around. He looked at them more, studied, and made a mental note to check each part against the exercise poster at work.

"Are you going to talk to me?" Kevin asked more amused than frustrated.

"Sorry."

"He *is* hot." Kevin conceded "What are you going to do about Greg?"

"I went over to his apartment to have a look."

"Wait, I thought you'd been over there a few times."

"I have but I hadn't seen the bedroom that will be opening up. So to speak."

"Oh, I thought maybe it was a free for all over there!"

"Watch it!" Will said "We'll scare off another family. But yes, if it's a free for all, then that would be my first reason to move in."

"I met the roommate who is moving out" Will said "He was nice enough. Greg chided him for moving in with his boyfriend with the idea that it would be all roses and white picket fences forever after."

"Yeah, I have to agree with him there. That never happens" Kevin said.

"The bedroom was okay. And mildly depressing."

"Why?"

"It just has a stand up shower and no bathtub."

"I'm pretty sure I've been in those apartments" Kevin said.

"I'm sure you have" Will smirked as a college aged girl with piercings and tattoos put their burritos on the table.

"Hey, can we get some more chips?" Kevin grabbed the last handful and handed the kid the empty container.

"Why don't you go get me a Coke and then you can see that guy's arms again."

Will looked the guy's arms over really good again before he sat down with both their drinks. He remembered someone telling him that two thirds of building big arms was building triceps.

"Yeah" Kevin said "I don't like the beige carpet, beige walls, cookie cutter apartments either. And a stand up shower." He made a face.

"They're not my favorite either" Will said. "But these are close to highways and the rent's a lot cheaper than what I'm paying."

"What's Section 8?" Will asked.

"Those are Section 8?" Kevin asked.

"Yeah. What is it?"?

"I don't know. I think that means government funded or something."

"It doesn't matter. I already called and left him a voicemail before you picked me up. I told him I wasn't moving in."

"You did?! Why did we just talk about it then?"

"I don't know" Will shrugged "It might have been a disaster. I'm too into him."

"Eh – you're probably right" Kevin scrunched his face up. "I was hoping I wouldn't have to drive up to Roswell Road anymore though. Waaaah."

"There's one other thing" Will said.

"Oh God" Kevin said "There's more?"

"Not related. An e-mail came out at work. Inform is for sale."

"What does that mean?"

"I have no idea. But everyone says they're updating their resumes."

"It could be nothing" Kevin said "Sometimes companies get sold and nothing changes."

Over three weeks later, when Kim and Devin returned from Europe, Will was noticeably leaner. Rebecca's brother had been right – muscles were being uncovered that Will never knew existed. He was getting attention from men *and* women like he never had before. He knew he'd reached his goal but I still wanted Kim to notice. He wanted her approval.

The Friday after she returned, she met Will and Kevin at the Tara theatre on Cheshire Bridge. *The Blair Witch Project* was playing and all three loved getting spooked. According to the hype, they'd get spooked. Will wore a smaller tee shirt than usual. Kim didn't say anything and Will had to ask.

"Can you tell I've lost weight?"

"I was going to say something but wasn't sure if you wanted me to" she said.

The next week when Zach and Kim called for one of their regular weeknight trash talk filled phone fests, Will told them he'd call back later after exercising.

"Will, you're being so good." Zach said.

"You are doing really well" Kim conceded "But does that mean you're not going to talk to us on the phone at night anymore?"

"No!" Will said "I only stay after work to exercise three nights a week."

For Will, to even tell them he was exercising was a big deal. He liked to stay secretive about things until there were results.

The next week on one of those nights when Will didn't exercise, he met Kim at Après Diem after work. Après Diem was the closest thing to Athens Will had seen in Atlanta. It was a place a person could go have a cup of coffee or a glass of wine alone with their book, and no one noticed or cared they were alone. Music floated through carefree conversations, rosy, candlelit faces, the sound of old wood floors and old jazz music.

Will and Kim talked about Daniel, Rob and the Smith brothers (Kim loved hearing about the Smith brothers), Kim's roommate Diana and their friend Rebecca, who'd moved away to Birmingham. There's never a quiet moment between Kim and Will – she loves to know what's going on and he loves to talk about himself. Kim's tone was serious when she asked about Greg, who Will hadn't seen since he'd visited his apartment, still undecided if he would move in.

"You still talk on the phone don't you?"

"Yeah."

"You're not over him are you?"

"No."

Kim's piercing brown green eyes were full of concern.

"I just hope you're not doing all of this – the exercising, quitting smoking, and (she looked at Will's plate) now it looks like quitting meat – so that you can get his attention."

"It's for me. I like the attention I've been getting. I feel good. But yes, when I'm walking around Chastain Park I'm hoping Greg will notice a difference and maybe rethink things."

"I'm so glad you didn't move in with him Will" she said "I know you don't want to hear that."

Kim's cigarette was firmly in her hand. She clutched it tighter whenever she made a serious point, eyes staring straight into you.

Will wasn't ready to go straight home from Après Diem so he stopped in The Manhole. The Thursday night go-go boys were no more but there was still the Thursday night sizeable, but not too crowded, crowd. Still feeling the effects of the beers he had with Kim, Will bought another and casually strolled back toward the dance floor, his shrinking waistline increasing his confidence. He watched from the side for a couple of minutes before starting toward the back, where naughtiness goes on behind the wall. He stopped in front of the bench and turned around to watch the crowd dancing again. A set of hands reached around from behind him and covered his eyes.

An exaggerated, deep voice in his ear said "Hey Boy, want to get that ass fucked tonight?"

"Sure Kaleb. Who are you going to find to do it?" Will said without moving. The hands were still covering his eyes.

The voice, less mocking and with less fake machismo, said "this isn't Kaleb."

The hands slid down to the tops of Will's shoulders and turned him around. Greg smiled a devilish smile at him. Will's saucy coolness was instantly replaced with tongue tied nervousness.

"Oh! Hey!" He let out a big sigh.

"Will, I didn't scare you did I?" Will could only think how much he loved hearing Greg say his name.

"I was sure it was Kaleb dicking around."

"I got ya."

An awkward silence followed as Will tried to regain himself.

"You look good, Will."

Will quietly got out a "thanks".

"I saw how guys were looking at you when you walked in. I watched you for a minute before I walked up" Greg said.

Greg wore khakis and sweater. It always made Will laugh inside when he saw Greg dressed so conservatively. He looked like one of those handsome faces smiling at you from a Sunday Rich's or Macy's circular in the AJC. Will knew what a wild animal lay beneath.

146

"Where have you been tonight?" Greg asked.

"Après Diem with Kim".

"Is she the one I met at Burkhart's that time?"

"Yes" Will said, remembering Greg had said that he needed to break away from that comfortable set of friends.

"What about you?" Will asked.

"I just stopped in on my way home. I went to see Avery, my dealer."

Will didn't know what to say.

"He got us ecstasy for the Cher show next week" Greg said proudly.

"You're going to see Cher with your dealer?"

"He has a crush on me" Greg said, smiling coquettishly.

Will sensed the opposite was true. He reached for daggers.

"Cher?"

"What, you don't like Cher?"

Will smiled weakly.

Greg stepped back in mock surprise.

"They're good seats" he said. "I thought we might be sitting in the grass since it's at Lakewood."

Greg sighed and shrugged.

"No, no" Will said. "Lakewood just reminds me of going to shows when I was younger and it was always so hot and muggy."

Greg gave him a look like he didn't buy it.

"And whose shows would those have been?"

"The Cure. Siouxsie. You know."

Greg looked bored. Will had attempted to act somehow superior to him in that tired, outdated way that kids do when they're sure no one's heard of the group they're listening to yet. If Will had realized he was doing it, he would have looked bored too.

"I like Cher" Greg said proudly. Something about the way Greg took ownership of it – Will liked it.

"Hey, see that guy over there?" Greg gestured toward a skinny, pale, greasy and rank looking guy who looked like his big jeans hadn't been washed in weeks.

"What about him?" Will asked, shrugging.

"He's friends with a friend of mine. He's into that same kind of music you were talking about I think. Want me to introduce you two?"

New Year's Weekend at The Looming flashed through Will's mind along with the so-so guy who'd sat down next to him that Greg had gestured toward. A blind fury washed over Will and he shot Greg a look. Greg reached over and barely touched his hand. When Will started to get hard, Greg gave him a wicked smile.

"I'm going to the back" Greg said. "Nice seeing you. Don't have too much fun tonight. It *is* a school night."

Still smiling wickedly, Greg subtly nodded toward the greasy skater guy before turning to walk away. Will got himself another beer and resumed his position on the side of the dance floor, growing irritated that Greg had suggested, again, that he go hook up with someone who was, in Will's mind, a crappy Ford when he knew he was, or could be, a tightly made Japanese import. Following that up with the unarguable display of how easy it was for Greg to get Will hard just made him that much more angry. And horny. Will started to walk back to the end of the dance floor but Greg popped back up.

"Let's go hang out" Will blurted out.

"No." Greg looked at Will in momentary disbelief at his audacity. "No."

"Why not?"

"Will" He looked down and shook his head. He looked back up and said "Will, I was just thinking the other day how glad I am that we've almost made it to a year. We'll have been friends for a year."

"Greg, it's just sex and I still want it. It doesn't mean we can't be friends."

"You know that's not true."

"Yes it is."

"Will. You can't *just* have sex with me and you know it."

Will shook his head.

"But I can. I can."

Greg said "I just came in here to check things out on my way home. I'm going to go get off and then I'm leaving. I'll talk to you soon."

Before Will could say anything, Greg turned and walked off.

Will quickly drank his beer and went back up front to order another. He did walked around but didn't see Greg. Will walked past the pool room, but Greg wasn't there either. If Greg could suck some random stranger off in the pool room then what the hell is wrong with leaving with me, Will thought.

Will gave up and left the back area for the front bar where he wanted to finish off his beer and leave. Greg was at the front bar and when he turned around and saw Will he slumped his shoulders and started shaking his head.

"Will" he started. The bartender looked at Will and then Greg with a question mark.

"Sure, I'll have another beer" Will said. Greg gave the bartender a look. The bartender didn't seem to notice and smiled at Will. Begrudgingly, Greg said "yeah, give me one too."

Never one to count his money or pay attention to how much he had, Will pulled some wadded up bills of his pocket. A couple fell to the floor and Greg picked them up and handed them to him.

He said, or slurred, "that's my boy" as Will paid the bartender.

"I'm sorry Greg" Will said, embarrassed.

"Enjoy the rest of your night" Greg said, tapping his bottle against Will's as he turned to walk back to the back. Deflated, Will sat at the bar table in the corner beside the sliding door that goes to the patio where he'd first met Daniel. He drank his beer and pelted himself mentally for being so stupid. As he was finishing his beer, he saw Greg, keys in hand and hair mussed, briskly walk toward and then out the front door.

Chapter Thirteen

Two weeks passed and Greg didn't call. Will didn't call him either. Ashamed of the way he'd acted at The Manhole, Will wrote him a letter of apology full of excuses and explanations. Will met Kim for lunch on a Saturday when they were both in Rome visiting their families. They went to Schroeder's, Rome's liberal minded restaurant – quilts and artwork draped the walls of the high ceilinged space on Broad Street where college age alterno kids like the ones at Raging Burrito (these kids had nowhere to go after their shifts except the cluster of apartments in downtown Rome where several of them lived and hung out) served sandwiches with melted cheese in plastic trays. Classic Rock is on the juke box and *Louis Louis* is played often. I imagine Steve Jobs would have liked to get stoned and be at Schroeder's for a while.

"You need to get over him" Kim said, lighting a cigarette.

"I know. But I still want to fuck him."

"Why? What good will it do?"

"Maybe if I fuck him enough it will be out of my system."

Kim leaned over, laughing. "Will, we're not in Atlanta. Try not to scare anyone too bad."

"I just don't see it" Kim said, looking out the window at Broad Street and taking a draw from her cigarette. She shook her head as she exhaled.

"He's okay cute but nothing beyond that. And he wore those tacky red jeans that night we all met him at Burkhart's." She made a face and they laughed.

"I know. And I'm hooked" Will said.

"I know you are" Kim said "And the problem with you and me is that we usually don't stop until we get what we want."

"It has been said, hasn't it?" Will said, partly ashamed.

"That's not necessarily a bad thing" Kim said "but I'm not sure we should do that with people."

"I'm sure, and we absolutely should not" Will said.

"Aren't you at all worried about H.I.V.?" Kim asked.

"I want him that much. And according to Daniel's four levels of risk—"

"Oh, mmhm" she said, drawing her cigarette. "Tell me those again."

"The least risky is receiving head, the third is giving head, the second is being on top, and the first, most riskiest, is being on bottom and taking loads."

"There's still risk involved, Will." Kim locked eyes with Will. It felt like Kim was looking right through him.

"Yes there is. And I will gladly take it if given the chance."

Kim looked out at Broad Street and back to Will.

"How are you going to go about this?"

Will pulled out the letter.

"Have you mailed this?"

"No."

"Good." Kim looked worried but still laughed as she began reading.

"Wait, first - why a letter? Why can't you just say these things to him?"

"I get tongue-tied when we are in person. I can write how I feel much better."

She began reading. Then nodding and reading.

"I'm glad you apologized for that night at The Manhole you told me about." Kim laughed and shook her head.
"Will that was obnoxious."

Kim stopped reading and looked at Will.

"It's pretty brave to put this in a letter. It leaves you awfully vulnerable."

"I don't mind".

Kim suggested Will take out a couple of things but left the overall message intact.

"It's not like I could stop you from sending this. I have to admit I'm curious to see how he responds."

The rest of their lunch was spent with Kim asking Will if he thought she was terrible for spending so much time with Devin while Devin's girlfriend, who also Kim's best childhood friend, was away at school. Will didn't see how he could say "yes" when Kim afforded him so much carte blanche for terrible behavior of his own.

Early in May, Greg called Will. His tone sounded opposite from the last time they'd spoke, in person, at The Manhole. It was much softer.

"I have an interview for a Computer Operator job downtown" Greg said, his voice full of boyish pride.

"Congratulations!" Will said "Sorry I was no help in getting you one of those jobs where I work. It's not from lack of trying though. I told a guy who works in the Data Center about you and he still tells me he's watching for an opening whenever I see him."

"Is that the one you used to talk to outside when you still smoked?"

"Yes. His name is Herb. He's gay too but you'd never know it. He wears mostly denim and he's very soft spoken. He spends a lot of time at Home Depot and working on his house."

"Will. About that letter—"

Will hesitated. "Yeah-"

"I haven't ever had any friends that I had sex with. I've never mixed the two."

Will hesitated. "Yeah-"

"Do you really think you can handle it?"

No hesitation. "Fuck Yes."

"No jealousy?"

No hesitation. "No."

"Would you like it if I showed up at your apartment in nothing but a trench coat?"

No hesitation. "Uhm, Yeah."

"So do you think I can call you or you can call me and just ask for sex?"

Will was hard.

No hesitation. "Yes."

"I think I might like this idea" Greg said, a smile in his voice.

Will stepped back against the living room wall and sighed.

"You just sound so determined" Greg said "Like you really are sure of yourself—" His voice trailed off.

"I can handle it" Will said.

"No. Jealousy." Greg reminded Will.

"No jealousy." Will repeated.

Kim was the first person Will told. She didn't try to discourage him. Instead, she instantly and firmly reminded him how to get what he wanted.

"Will - Make. Him. Call. You."

Will could see the cigarette, firmly between Kim's fingers, punctuating each word.

After two weeks, Greg hadn't called Will. Kim, however, did call Will at work one Friday afternoon in late May.

"You better not tell me you're working out tonight after work."

"I'm not. I'm finished for the week."

"Good. You can meet us for dinner. Zach Will be down here."

"Where are we going?"

"It's called Harmony. It's a vegan restaurant way the fuck out on Buford Highway." Kim laughed. "You know how Zach's gotten. He won't even chew gum if he thinks it has some random part of a cow in it."

"Okay. I'll look the place up but it will be ten thirty before I'll be there."

"I've already checked" Kim said "they'll still be open. And don't be late! I know how you can be."

At ten thirty Will met Kim and Zach in a little hole in the wall hidden in a run down strip mall on Buford Highway. Everything was in a little hole in the wall in a run down strip mall if it was on Buford Highway. Many times, those places turned out to be treasures – inexpensive, delicious food and a quiet place to talk.

He was curious to try this all meat free Chinese food where the chicken, steak, and fish were all made to taste like chicken, steak, and fish although they were really tofu.

Kim and Zach were plenty impressed at how Will's little body was coming along. Just like Kim had sweetly demanded that Will meet them there for dinner, she sweetly demanded that Zach and Will go with her and Devin to Panama City Beach in June and stay with her at her grandmother's beachfront penthouse condo. Will and Zach both looked like they were afraid they might get beat up.

"God" Kim said "you're both such little shits. It's PCB, not Alcatraz." Kim reached for her phone.

"I'll just call Kiki (Kim called her grandmother by her first name) and say 'hey, Will and Zach want you to buy an apartment at a beach they like better. Maybe Key West or something. This one's not gay enough."

"Have you and Greg got it on yet?" Zach asked.

"No" Will said, his frustration apparent but not so much so that he wasn't still beaming from the praise they gave him over his newly lean physique.

"You haven't called him have you?" Kim's eyes were piercing into Will. Though he hadn't called Greg, he flushed with guilt because someone was looking at him (with a look that said you better not have) expecting him to say he had.

"No."

"Will." She was stern.

"No!"

"He hasn't Kim - I can tell" Zach chimed in, laughing. Zach's arms were completely covered with tattoos now and Will even saw some coming up out of his T-Shirt onto his neck.

"How can you tell?" Kim asked.

"I just can" Zach said "you can always tell when Will's guilty. It's written all over his face."

"Will smiled and said 'what *is* written across my face? That I have the guilt of a Catholic, the shame of a Jew, and the scruples of a whore?'"

"You better not call him" Kim said again, shaking her head as she pulled her ever present notebook out of her bag. "I'm gonna write that one down."

The three of them caught up, laughed at the aluminum foiled take outs that were folded into shapes of chickens, and as they often did, Kim and Will tried to convince Zach to move to Atlanta. A good sport, Zach played along until finally asking how he was supposed to pick up his growing clientele and move them to Atlanta. Finally, Zach yawned which meant "shut up about it."

After Will said goodbye to Kim and Zach, and as he drove down Buford Highway toward Buckhead, he dialed Greg's number. He didn't know why he was doing it, especially after promising not to.

Greg sounded buzzed. And not unhappy to hear from Will.

"Since we've only done this at my apartment I'm going to come over to your place." Greg said.

Greg heard a car horn followed by what could only be the giggling of Kim and Zach. He looked to his left to see Kim and Zach in Kim's SUV, which she wielded with authority as she drove around using hand sanitizer constantly and playing music loudly. They were stopped beside Will at a red light.

"Who were you talking to on your cell phone Will?!"

He couldn't even get a word out before Zach said "Oh My God Kim he *was* on the phone with Greg!"

"How do you know that Zach?"

"Look at his face."

"Will?"

"Well—" (never as cute as when Samantha did it on *Bewitched*).

"I knew it!" Zach shrieked.

"Who called who?" Kim's tone was as serious as an interrogation agent's. Will hesitated and Zach broke in "he called Greg."

"Will Turner!"

The light changed, Will shrugged his shoulders, smiled and drove away quickly. Laughing, he took a deep breath and hoped they'd turned to go toward Decatur before they could get stuck at any more traffic lights together.

At the apartment, Brandon and his hot retail boyfriend were gone. Check. Greg showed up looking like a hot mess. Check. Will led Greg back to his bedroom where the lights were low and Sade sang softly.

They undressed quickly and Will handled Greg's ass in a way that must have said he knew a little bit more of what to do with it. Before they'd barely got going, Greg pushed Will off and told him to stop. Greg put his hand to Will's forehead looked around the room almost like he didn't know where he was. Greg shook his head and stood up in Will's room, only lit by the street light outside and the light from the stereo. Greg pulled his jeans back on and walked over to the light switch.

In Will's bathroom, Greg turned on the light. He mussed with his hair and adjusted his V-neck sweater with no tee shirt underneath. Will sat on the side of his bed, turned on the lamp beside it, and watched Greg in his bathroom, wondering if he'd seen too many boy band videos. Why else would he be wearing a V-neck sweater and no tee shirt at his age. Greg's eyes looked wild and a lighter blue than usual in the bathroom mirror. Will watched Greg as he fussed with his hair and admired himself.

Greg came back out and sat down beside Will on the bed. Will opened his bedroom door so Betty and Frieda could come and go. Betty jumped on the bed between Greg and Will. Frieda hid underneath. Greg pet Betty with more affection than Will guessed he possessed for an animal.

"Will, what are you on?"

"What!?"

"What are you on?"

"Oh my God!" Will said. "Nothing!"

"You're on something." Will knew why Greg thought he was on something but he didn't know if he should tell him that he was really just that ravenous for him. Greg continued petting Betty. She did her little purr squeal that sounds like a toddler trying to immolate a race car. Greg petted her tuxedo coat and said "I like this cat."

So he was human. Had he not been subject to Betty's infinite charms, Will might have suspected otherwise.

"You're on something" Greg said again. "You're not usually like that."

"Like what?"

"Like you were just then. You're on something."

The phone rang and Greg jumped up to grab it.

"Hello" he said, playfully, and grinning at Will like I've got your phone and what are you gonna do about it.

"This is Greg. Who is this?" Greg said coquettishly. Will knew Kim and Zach were on the other end. Greg handed the phone to Will. When he heard Zach and Kim on the other side with music that could have only been from Backstreet in the background, he felt like someone must be pulling the strings of his life. If he didn't believe in coincidence he would have sunk into schizophrenia.

"Will, we're at Backstreet looking for X. We haven't found any but some guy said he would sell us meth."

"What?! No! Don't do that!" Will heard the phone being shuffled around.

"Get your ass over here" Kim said. Will heard Zach in the background. "He's got com-pa-neeeee."

"Will is Greg at your apartment?"

"Yes." Greg was back in Will's bathroom admiring his wired reflection.

Kim said flatly "Fine. Call us later".

Greg sat back down on Will's bed. Will sat down beside him.

"I was at The Manhole earlier" Greg said. "I was introduced to someone who thought I was a model."

Will tried to sound impressed and wondered how it was he could feel sad for someone whose company he spent most of every day feeling hungry for.

The phone rang again and Greg grabbed it. Will could hear Kim on the other end.

"Will, get your ass to Backstreet now. Zach and I are buying meth."

Smiling smugly, Greg handed the phone to Will. Will didn't know why those two had decided to go ape shit on him tonight of all nights.

"I'm not coming out and don't do that. Kevin said never do it. It makes people crazy."

Will sat back on his bed beside Greg.

"How dare you presume to ask me to come over here and not have drugs for me?" Greg asked, a wicked, mocking tone in his voice.

Will was stunned. That was the last thing he expected Greg to say.

"I'll call them back and get—"

"No, no" Greg said "It's too late. You could have fucked me all night and into tomorrow. This was nice but it's not what I'm looking for tonight."

They sat silent while Greg pet Betty. Will loved just being with him.

"Will. I'll never be in love with you."

"I know that" Will said weakly.

"Do you? I'm not so sure about that." He gently grabbed Will's chin and pulled his face around so that he was looking in Will's eyes. "Do you know that?"

Greg stood up and started toward the living room. Will followed him.

"Let me call them back and –"

Greg turned around and held his hand up.

"Not tonight Will".

Will stood on the front porch and watched Greg get into his car.

"You need to move closer into town" Greg said as he got in.

Will, exhausted and deflated, went back inside and stood in the middle of his room. His bed was messed up but nothing had happened. The lamp light was romantic but nothing was going on. He was tired and confused. The phone rang again.

"Will Turner." It was Zach.

"Are you two still at Backstreet?"

"No. We wanted ecstasy but all we could find was meth."

"Is Greg still there?"

"No. I guess you're happy now."

"Will." Zach sounded drunk.

"What?"

"You know."

"What?"

"Zach?"

"Kim doesn't think you should have sex with him because he has H.I.V."

"I'm going to bed."

"Are you mad at us for real?"

"I'm tired. Good night."

The next weekend, Kim wanted Will to go with her to a consignment shop on Moreland Avenue. Groovy Girl was in a stand alone building on a part of Moreland past Little Five Points.   The two of them had lunch at Flying Biscuit in Candler Park after. Kim was in high spirits. Instead of her usual old jeans, tee shirt and bag slung across her chest, she wore a yellow, feminine baby doll dress and black Mary Jane's with little white socks. Her hair was neat and when her hair was neat, her bangs were precision. She was glowing and her brown green eyes were shining.

"Will, are you going out tonight?"

"You know I probably will. Why?"

"Devin and I were talking about going to Backstreet and rolling."

"God" Will said "Ever since I rolled in January you've all been talking about doing it. I'm a terrible influence."

Kim laughed.

"Hardly Will. Zach and I had our own experiences with drugs when we were still in our teens."

"But that was years ago and it didn't last" Will said. "I feel bad for getting this all going again."

"I don't think rolling at Backstreet is going to turn us all into hardcore drug users" Kim said.

"Don't go to the Manhole. You'll just run into Greg."

"And you know I have an uncanny ability to find X."

Kim laughed.

"True, but Devin loves hanging out with you and so do I.

Kim could be infectious when she wanted something, making those around her want it for her (whatever the "it" was at the time) as much as she did.

Will napped in the afternoon and that was one of his favorite things in life – waking in the evening from a deep sleep in the afternoon, not knowing what the night might hold, but certainly knowing he felt recharged enough to go find out.   He took his time showering and dressing in one of his now standard tight shirts. He met Kim and Devin at Backstreet at eleven o'clock.

Kim bought drinks for the three of them and they stood on the second floor landing watching the dance floor. There was already a thick crowd but it wasn't impossibly push and shove. They decided to go dance on the opposite side of the dance floor so that they could see the big jeaned party kids under the DJ booth.

"Zach says that's where to find drugs" Will said as they walked down the stairs.

"How come Zach lives in Athens but knows where to find drugs in Atlanta?" Devin asked, laughing.

"That's Zach!" Kim and Will said, unintentionally in unison.

It was rare, being on the dance floor in the thick of it and still able to move freely. Kim smiled goofily at Devin as they danced and Will could have sworn Devin smiled goofily at him as they danced. Will kept his eyes on the kids under the DJ booth, noticing the ones with water bottles that couldn't stay still. When he saw what he knew was a transaction happen, he pounced on the big jeaned kid who'd supplied. Will asked the kid if he knew where he could find any ecstasy. The kid said he could get two pills and asked Will to go back to his friends for a second while he got them.

"Got fifty dollars?" Will said to Kim as he walked back up, Cheshire cat smile across his face.

"Will you're kidding me. Already?!"

"Sweet" Devin said, smiling at Will.

"How many, two?" Kim asked.

"That's all he had" Will said.

"Will, stay and roll with us. We'll keep you straight if you start thinking too much."

"I don't know" Will said. "Let me know how these go and maybe."

Kim stuffed cash into Will's jeans pocket and he pretended not to notice. Someone from the DJ booth walked halfway down the stairs and tossed glow sticks into the crowd. It sent a ripple of frenzy through the crowd as people scrambled for glowsticks. A video screen was slowly lowered from the ceiling. It was just over the area where Kim, Devin, and Will danced. People whistled and yelled, seemingly louder and in time with each bit of the image on the screen that became visible as it was lowered.

In army green Capri pants, simple black heels and a simple black tank top, a lean forty one year old Madonna flirted and teased the camera with the same self assuredness she'd exuded in the early eighties wearing other simple black tank tops. While glow sticks swirled with the beat of *Beautiful Stranger* and the crowd yelled and whistled more, Will walked through the new electricity and back over to the big jeans wearing kid. Without missing a beat as he bounced up and down, the kid had Kim's cash in his own pocket and two pills in Will's hand in a flash. Will slipped the pills to Kim before the first chorus began.

> If I'm smart then I'll run away.....
> But I'm not so I guess I'll stay....

"Will, go back and see if he can find you one".

Kim looked at Will and put more money in his pocket. As Will walked back over to the kid, someone grabbed him. He turned around and the sight of Greg in the black mesh shirt he'd worn on New Year's Eve threw him. Greg grabbed Will's shoulder, instantly making Will halfway hard.

"Will, do you know where I can find some really good ecstasy?"

"Well—I, I just got some but it was for my friends over there."

"You didn't get anymore?"

"No, Will said. But I—"

"That's too bad. I really wanted to do ecstasy tonight".

Greg shrugged and smiled at Will as if to say "your loss" before disappearing into the crowd. Will looked around for the kid but didn't see him. He went back over to Kim and Devin.

"Will, who was that guy you were talking to? That wasn't Greg was it?" Kim asked.

"Yes" Will said.

"Oh God that shirt Will".

Will loved Greg's trashy clothes.

"Have you taken your pills?" Will asked.

Kim handed him a water bottle and they both smiled.

"Did you find another one?"

"No" Will said. "Hey, don't be mad but I'm going to leave. I need to get out of here."

"Will, don't worry about him. Stay and hang out with us."

"I may be back" Will said "But I gotta get out of here right now."

Will cursed himself all the way back to his car and all the way back to Buckhead for being too stupid to see an opportunity right in front of his face and not pouncing on it. Will had never known such a level of frustration at having something he'd never wanted more slip through his fingers twice in the span of a few weeks.

"Greg's as slippery as you are naïve" Will said to himself in his car, pounding the steering wheel.

It didn't feel like Sunday evening, and the end of the weekend, when Kim called Will.

"Devin played video games all day" Kim said "and I watched T.V. It really does wipe you out."

Kim said "this morning when the sun was coming up and we were leaving, Devin and I sat in my car for a little while before we left. He said something that I haven't been able to get out of my head."

"What was that?"

"There must be serious consequences for feeling this good."

"About the X?"

"Yeah. What else?"

"I hadn't thought of it that way" Will said. "Maybe he's right.

I forgot to tell you this yesterday" Will said "Probably because we were having fun and I just haven't wanted to think about it – will you help me out with a favor similar to the one in January?"

"You mean take you to the hospital?"

"Yeah. I guess I should say exactly like the one you did in January."

"Oh Will. I'm so sorry."

"Dr. Bernard said I just happened to have a really aggressive case. But he said this time wouldn't be anything like the first time. Not nearly as painful."

"When are you going to do it?"

"He wants me to do it soon."

"Will you still be able to go to the beach with us?"

Will said "What if, since it won't be nearly as bad, I schedule it for a few days before the beach. He'll write me off work anyway."

Kim laughed.

"Will, what are you telling your boss and co-workers?"

"Well, Daniel and I have discussed this at length—" Kim laughed and cut Will off.

"I love Daniel" she said.

"Me too" Will said "I'm glad we're friends."

"So Daniel told me that hemorrhoid surgery is practically the same thing."

Kim laughed out loud.

"Oh God! Will, that's hilarious!"

Kim laughed.

"I'd rather them think I'm an old man with hemorrhoids than a dirty whore with an STD. Lesser of two evils."

"That really is funny Will. I wish I could tell Devin about this."

"NO!"

"I won't, I won't. Don't worry."

Kim was still laughing.

"Of course I'll take you" she said. "Can I do my laundry again?"

Chapter Fourteen

By June, Will's vegetarian diet and regular workout routine were solid new habits that replaced his hold habits of smoking cigarettes and eating fast food. Will moved with more confidence as he got used to the daily looks he received. His post adolescent appearing nipples barely poked through his tee shrits like a boy on the verge of manhood.

Will completed his pre-admittance at the hospital on a Friday afternoon and went straight to work still wearing his jeans, tee shirt and baseball cap. Since no one blinked an eye, he decided then and there to quit torturing himself with the itchy hair and leave it behind. His second butt surgery, as he, Kim, and Shane had began referring to them, was scheduled for the following Wednesday.

Though Dr. Bernard and his light blue eyes assured Will this surgery would not be nearly as painful as the first, Will prepared for the worst. The apartment was immaculate in case he didn't feel like cleaning for a while. He was well stocked with laxatives and prune juice, and on his last visit to Rome, his mom gave him a little T.V. for his bedroom in case he were to lie in bed for days.

None of that was necessary because Dr. Bernard was right - it was nothing like the first time. Dr. Bernard still order no strenuous activity and suggested Will take it easy the first few days. Will lay in bed watching movies that Zach and Kim, avid movie watchers, suggested. He took the pain pills that Dr. Newman prescribed and enjoyed his immaculate room as the summer sun broke through the blinds. He braced himself for the inevitable and when the inevitable came, it wasn't pleasant but it didn't knock him down. It stung.

Since Will was handling the second surgery so much better, he was able to help Daniel out. Daniel's connection for marijuana had disappeared and he was looking for a hook up. Though he was indifferent about pot, Will always knew where to find it. On Saturday, Daniel convinced Will that his butt was in fine enough shape to ride to Athens with him and visit his old college class mate Lisa and her girlfriend Jo who always looked like she'd just rolled out from underneath a car.

The Will had known at U.G.A was as disciplined and clean as a marine. A straight "A" student and respected photographer. The Lisa that now lived with Jo in their duplex didn't seem to care so much. Will tried to get used to this new incarnation as Daniel and Lisa passed a joint back and forth. Jo came out of the bathroom gruffly complaining that *someone* left the seat up while looking straight at Will.

"I thought you probably pee'd standing up" Will shot back without flinching or raising his voice. Daniel and Lisa laughed so hard that Jo turned red. Though she tried to spar with Will, the only time she offended him was when she unwittingly used the "N" word in reference to something else.

"I could see the vein on your forehead pop out" Daniel said on the drive back to Atlanta with his Joni Mitchell CD playing.

"I know you hate that word and that's why I used your butt as an excuse to leave. I know your butt it is fine."

"You just wanted to use my butt".

"You are doing much better this time around" Daniel laughed. "I'm glad to see it."

Daniel told Will that he used to listen to the Joni Mitchell CD, *Court and Spark*, when he lived in Los Angeles. He said that he would listen at night for his lover's car to "come up that hill", just like the lover in Joni's song.

Will loved hearing Daniel talk about his past life in Los Angeles as much as Daniel loved reliving parts of it as they rode back to Atlanta in the dusk golden hour.

Kim and Zach called Will throughout the afternoon and evening on Sunday and reminded him to pack. The plan was to drive overnight and get to Panama City Beach early the next morning. At ten that night, in the dark in driveway of Kim's brick ranch house, the four of them - Kim, Zach, Will and Devin – put their bags in the back of Kim's SUV. Kim showed everyone a generic notebook she'd labeled with a Sharpie.

"I want to write down all the funny things everyone says while we're there" she said.

Kim loves to document *everything* with writing, recording, and making videos.

Though he was most likely out of the woods, Will still cringed at the idea of a trip to the bathroom.

"This trip is going to be all about Will's butt" Kim said after their first pit stop.

When they got to Panama City Beach, bright and early Monday morning, the four of them, tired and sluggish from their drive, collapsed into the overstuffed furniture in Kim's grandmother's penthouse condo. Devin, Zach, and Will oooh'd and ahhh'd at the accommodations while Kim plopped on a piece of furniture like she owned the place, which she kind of did, and used one of the white remote controls to flip channels on one of the white televisions hanging form the ceilings.

"I hope no one minds" she said "but I watch court TV constantly whenever I'm at the beach."

A deck that ran the length of the fourteenth floor condo overlooked the ocean and the three bedrooms and two bathrooms were separated by a large living room and dining room. Light from the large windows reflected off shiny, white marble flooring and white furniture so that even though you were inside, you always knew you were at the beach. Kim faithfully registered the one-liners that flew between the four of them like ricochets. The brightness all around and the sense of non-reality that the beach can bring cut through the ill feeling a person might have after a sleepless night in a car. The coffee tables had several magazines lying about, all with photos, old and new, of Dana Plato along with stories of her cruel descent into drugs and then death. The magazines were the only spot of darkness in an otherwise light bright world.

Driving to the beach in the middle of the night reminded Will of impromptu trips to the beach on Sunday nights in his childhood. Also like his childhood, he spent a lot of time going back and forth to the condo and making drinks for everyone.

On the beach, Kim channeled a 1940's sunbather in her vintage one piece and sunhat, comfortably perched in a chair with *Vogue* magazines spilling out of her straw bag. It was rare that she ever looked like the money she came from. Devin, pale and tattooed, lay on one side of Kim, face down on his towel, raising his head up at times to laugh out loud at the crass jokes Kim and Zach made about people around. Devin was cute but not toned like a gay. He wasn't into it and didn't care. His strawberry blond hair and innocent blue eyes made him seem as submissive as Zach and Will.

In the late afternoon Kim went up to change and the three boys looked up at the penthouse, guessing its value. What they all agreed on was that it seemed permanently out of their reach. Kim came back down with sheets of acid. Fearing a lifetime in an asylum, Will remained the designated drink mixer while the other three took acid. From the descriptions of their hallucinations, Will had made the right choice in keeping his troubled mind away.

It was Will's first time at a beach when he wasn't ashamed of his shirtless body. Instead, he was proud of it. The water and the air and the exhilaration that came with his newfound health were in sharp contrast to the surgery in January. Will didn't care if he could never afford a condo like Kim's grandmother's because the body he now had made him feel like the world belonged to him anyway.

The occupants of the thirteenth floor apartment probably didn't think it was so funny when Kim, Zach, and Will periodically and loudly asked where security was.

"I need a drink!" followed by quiet giggles from Devin's direction – not loud enough to be heard by the other tenants, and just loud enough to egg the other three on.

On their last afternoon Zach finally relented to Kim's demands for a haircut. Zach was the only one who Kim, among others, trusted to cut her hair. On the drive back from Athens, Kim would often say to Will "do you mind driving my car?" She knew he loved it though he crouched over the wheel and reminded her repeatedly that "these things flip over" when they got to the interstate.

Kim sat on a dining room chair moved to the middle of the marble floor, towel draped around her with thick dark locks falling on top of it, while Devin lay shirtless and smoking on the balcony. Will sensed that Devin wished he was somewhere else, perhaps with his girlfriend Gina, as much as Will longed to be somewhere winning Greg over.

That Thursday, Kim and Devin sat in front, smoking cigarettes and playing music, while Zach and Will sat in back, silently gazing at the north Florida and South Georgia scenery as palm trees were replaced with pine trees.

Back at his apartment, in a genuine moment of "I feel so good I don't care if he says no", Will called Greg and playfully demanded as if Greg were Kim or Kevin.

"Let's go to lunch."

"Your surgery must have gone well."

"I'd say it did. I just got back from the beach."

"Didn't I tell you it'd be a lot better this time?"

"Yes you did" Greg immediately picked up on the chipper tone and absence of worry in Will's voice.

"What time do you want to have lunch?"

"It doesn't matter. I'm off til Monday" Will said.

"Do you know where Roaster's on Lenox Road is?" Greg asked.

"Nope."

"It's very gay" Greg said.

Will complained about the country cooking (add bacon, butter, hogjaw, fatback) while he enjoyed the flavors and Greg told him about his new job.

"Congratulations - in case I forgot to tell you" Will said.

"Thanks" Greg said "it's just what I wanted.

"After a week of training during first shift hours, I will work Monday through Friday, three PM to eleven PM. Those are *my* hours."

Will saw Greg beaming for the first time since they'd met. Will sensed that Greg wasn't bragging, but felt accomplished instead. Will surmised that Greg perhaps wasn't sure he'd feel accomplished again.

"And" Greg said "it's a no-brainer. The job should be easy and it's a slow shift. They told me to bring a book during downtime if I wanted to."

Will was envious of what sounded like a stress free job and mornings free.

"What's going on over at Inform? Have you heard anything?"

"Nothing official yet" Will said "but the rumor mill is going strong. From what I hear the people in my group will get their notices toward the end of the year."

"Do you know what you're going to do after that?"

"I've been thinking of applying for an online customer service job at Inform's spinoff company on the tenth floor. It sounds like they are doing well and it will keep going."

"Is that something you'd like doing?"

"I think it would be a nice job for anyone and I think it's true that you can learn about a company no matter what position you are in there – whether you're in the file room or all the way up to CEO. But I do enjoy what I do now helping clientele of long standing accounts."

Greg nodded.

There was a pause. Will looked down at his plate, busying himself meticulously moving meat away from vegetables just like Zach.

"How was the Cher show?" Will asked.

Greg didn't' stop chewing when he answered. Will, always afraid of food running out of his mouth or a piece of spinach stuck in his teeth, kept an arsenal of napkins at close range at every meal. He admired what he considered Greg's fearless nonchalance by chewing with a cheek full of food. Will thought it was masculine. He was reminded of 1970's detective shows where a cop is in a 70's car, parked, eating fast food. Wearing sunglasses. He thought of the glasses Greg kept by his bed and *The Rockford Files*.

"You went to see Cher with Avery didn't you?" Will asked innocently, finally managing to pull off some nonchalance of his own.

Greg stopped chewing. Will pretended not to notice the intense look coming from Greg's eyes now.

"Do you still have a crush on him?" Will asked.

Greg stopped again put his fork down. He shot Will a long look.

"No" Greg said "he's just my dealer."

Back at work the next week, Will immediately began an effort to get himself hired at the spinoff start up company on the tenth floor.

Will saw new person in the data center on eleven where he worked. He paid attention to the patio outside and caught Herb, the denim clad straight acting operator who he'd hoped might be helpful getting Greg hired. Herb was as surprised by the new addition to the data center as Will was since a hiring freeze had been in effect for weeks.

"He's not picking it up" Herb said about the new guy. "He's not learning the job."

"What exactly does one have to know in order to be a Computer Operator in there?" Will asked.

"If you can follow directions you can do the job" Herb said "you'd have no problem with it."

Will thought about what Greg had said at lunch - "It's a no brainer and second shift is slow. They let me bring a book if I want". Since it was not Will's ambition to rise in the corporate world but rather just be in it far enough to be covered by it, this second shift computer operator job sounded like heaven to him. He imagined that much of the pettiness and politics that were sometimes difficult to ignore didn't exist on a shift where two or three people monitored systems after hours. He began watching the data center and chatting with Herb regularly about the new guy. He did this in addition to his efforts to get hired at the start up company.

Will told Greg over the phone that he'd shown interest in both jobs that Sunday afternoon as he drove back to Atlanta from a visit in Rome. He'd called to wish Greg good luck on his first day of training the next day. In another moment of spontaneity, Will asked if Greg wanted to get together later in the evening. Greg asked what time and when Will told him after drinks with Kim, Devin, and Zach, Greg asked if he could join them. Pleasantly surprised, Will said of course.

At Buddies, a bar on Ponce De Leon Avenue where people played pool and TVs above the bar played porn, Will told Kim, Devin, and Zach that someone was on the way over and it was a surprise who.

"Daniel!" Kim said.

"Greg!"

Kim's smile faded. Devin and Zach stopped the clowning they'd been doing since Will got there.

"I kind of want to see what he looks like" Zach said quietly.

Devin chimed in. "Me too. I want to see this Greg."

Kim nervously looked through her purse for money and asked Devin what kind of drink he wanted. Devin, Zach, and Will looked at each other like they were in the doghouse before cutting up again.

"I don't know about this Greg" Devin said "let's just tell him I'm your boyfriend."

"Is he going to be wearing those red jeans?" Kim asked with a little too much vitriol spilling through to be playfully mocking. She handed Devin his drink.

Greg walked in a moment later wearing blue jeans and a button down shirt. After introductions were made, Zach got quiet and Devin didn't giggle as much. Kim was ice cold.

Greg politely asked if anyone wanted anything before going to the bar himself. Kim shot daggers at Will as he racked pool balls like a pro, like Lisa had taught him in college.

Greg encouraged Will during the first game and Will was relieved that he'd finally grown comfortable enough around Greg to play an acceptable game of pool in front of him. Greg asked Will what he was drinking before walking over to the bar. Will, no longer willing to rack up the calories that went with beer, asked for a vodka cranberry.

"This will insure your win on the next game" Greg joked to Kim, Zach and Devin as he started toward the bar.

While Kim, Devin, and Zach stayed at a bar table, Greg and Will stood on the other side of the pool table next a wall painted with murals of sports stars. As the second game was wrapping up and Will and Greg had remained distant from the others, Greg lightly laid his hand on top of Will's. Will was instantly hard and Greg, smiling, looked down at his crotch.

"I better be going" Greg said "I have an early day tomorrow."

"Can I come over?"

Greg continued smiling wryly at Will.

"Hadn't you better check with her?" He nodded toward Kim.

Will let out a sigh, point taken, and said "I do have to tell them goodbye".

Will walked over to the others and told them that they were leaving. Devin and Zach nodded but Kim barely looked him in eye.

Quietly, she said "have fun."

Greg walked over and everyone said a polite goodbye.

Will followed Greg from one distinctively trashy street, Ponce De Leon, over to another trashy street with it's own separate and distinct identiy - Cheshire Bridge Road. Greg lived in the thick of it. It was still early, before nine, and Greg's roommates weren't in. He told Will to pick out a CD while he went into the bathroom. Will grabbed the first thing he saw without looking.

Will sat on Greg's bed and took in the surroundings. The posters no longer intimidated Will. He felt he was well on his way to one of those bodies. Greg's room seemed smaller than Will remembered and there were stacks of clothes around.

"I've been cleaning out my closet this weekend" Greg said as he walked back in. Adjusting the volume on his stereo, Greg said "I'm surprised you chose this."

To Will, it sounded like everything else he'd ever heard at Backstreet.

Will let Greg pull off his baseball cap and then his tee shirt. Greg paused in front of Will, lightly touching his long, lean torso. Greg sucked air between his teeth and shook his head in approval. Greg undid Will's belt and dropped to his knees in front of him.

Unzipping Will's jeans, Greg looked up and said "still in boxers?"

Greg pulled Will's dick out and for once, took his time sucking it. When Greg got back up he took his own shirt off and stood in front of Will.

"How do you want it?"

Without hesitation, Will said "on your stomach."

Greg undressed while still looking over Will's body with approval. The sight alone of Greg naked and face down on his bed could have almost made Will come. Will carefully got on top of Greg, and took a bottle of lube from its apparent home on the window sill at the head of Greg's bed. He worked some lube into Greg's ass, making him groan and arch upward. Greg's muscular arms were folded under his chin and Will outlined them with his own as he sank into him. The sight of Greg's muscled arms with his own growing biceps on top of them was the most aroused Will had ever been. He finally felt a part of what he was doing – like he could *be* as well as *have* what he was drawn to. He never liked the idea of enjoying a body like Greg's without first having one of his own to bring to the plate.

Greg shot first.

Lying on their backs, side by side, staring up at the ceiling, Greg spoke first.

"I'm sorry".

"I'm not worried about it" Will said. "I should get out of here. You have an early day tomorrow."

"I can sleep this off" Greg said.

Will hoped he was only talking about the drinks from earlier.

"I hope training goes well this week" Will said.

"It should be a breeze. Seven to three and then my regular shift begins next week."

They lay like that for a couple of minutes and Greg said "Will—".

Will turned to look at him.

"I'm chasing things that don't exist. It's just a fantasy—".

His voice trailed off. It was almost inaudible.

"I don't get it" Will said, turning back to face the ceiling.

Greg looked over at him and smiled.

"I hate to kick you out but I better go to bed."

Will stood and began pulling his boxers and then jeans up, this time uninhibited by being naked in front of Greg. Will sat down next to Greg and pulled his tee shirt over his head. Greg slid Will's baseball cap over his head, backwards. Will made a face and turned it around.

"I knew you'd hate that" Greg said, smiling "I know how you like it."

After a quick kiss at the door, Will was back in his car and his cell phone, which showed several voicemails, was already ringing.

"Get your ass back over to Buddy's!" It was Devin on Kim's phone. Will could hear Zach in the background, which meant Zach had had a few.

Chapter Fifteen

Since they'd got back from their trip to Panama City Beach, Will noticed rainbow colored banners hanging on the sides of main streets like Piedmont Avenue and Peachtree Street. CELEBRATE was written across the banners in white capital letters. It took Will's breath away the first time he saw them and he felt an excitement welling up inside every time after. Though he'd never been to a Pride celebration and had no plans to attend this one, he knew he could not live in a place like Rome again by the idea alone that it was possible to see those banners alongside the city streets.

One evening at work, Lisa called Will at work to see what he was doing on Pride weekend. When he told her nothing she said "Oh no no no, we're going to have to change that."

Will's apartment was a home base for Lisa, Jo, and their sleeping bags. Daniel was the next to call and tell Will that not going to any Pride festivities was not acceptable. He convinced Will to take Friday evening off so that he and Will could go to the park and admire all the beautiful men.

"But there's always beautiful men around?" Will said.

"My dear, you really have never been to Pride have you?"

That Friday evening, Will and Daniel met Trey and one of his friends at a little Italian restaurant in Midtown on Peachtree Street. Trey, whom Will had referred to a job at the start up company on the tenth floor, told Will there was about to be an opening in his group. Daniel was visibly delighted at how well Will and Trey now got along – and he wasn't dating either of them.

Will, Daniel, Trey, and Trey's friend all covered their ears at the abrupt and loud approach of motorcycles. The sounds of backfires and worn mufflers rudely echoed off the open patio of the restaurant, making it feel less like a quaint Italian restaurant and more like a tailgate party. When the motorbikes finally came into view, the unexpected and aggressive assault on the ears wreaked havoc on the eyes as well - choppers, leather and proudly exposed women's breasts all came together in an I dream of Jeannie boing moment leaving you feeling like "did I really just see that?" Trey and his friend wore flabbergasted expressions of their own.

Daniel smiled easily and said "dykes on bikes – thank you for allowing me to see it through your eyes for the first time." He was speaking to all of us.

After dinner they all walked the short distance to Piedmont Park. They met up with Lisa and Jo who immediatley shared a joint with Daniel. They all strolled around and just like at Raging Burrito with Kevin, Will was barely able to hold a conversation because his attention was constantly diverted to beautiful triceps, beautiful biceps, and beautiful abs. He was so taken with all the Adonis physiques and the sheer volume of gay men and women all gathered in one place. Couples walked, hand in hand, holding each other. He hadn't realized that it took on a different meaning, to be seeing this kind of thing out in broad daylight, and in a park setting. In dark bars, there's a feeling that something is there for a reason. Outside – it felt different. Almost like running around naked. Every moment that passed felt like you were getting away with something. You kind of expected someone would step in and say "you can't be doing this." But that didn't happen and it was the most liberated Will had ever felt, stepping from one moment to the next, arrest avoided – and not necessary.

At once, Will felt like he belonged and at the same time, he felt a deep sense that something was missing. He wanted badly to be one of those exercising their right to hold hands with and kiss their special person in public. He was overwhelmed by feelings of newfound liberation mixed with intense sadness

Daniel told Will he'd enjoyed every aspect of a Pride celebration that could be enjoyed during his time in Los Angeles. He suggested Will go out over the course of the weekend and experience the crowds.

Saturday night, Will and Kevin went to Burkhart's for "one drink" as they often said. They had their next one at the Eagle. Will felt an energy in the air unlike any he'd known before. He wondered if it was what Daniel meant when he talked about the specialness of Pride weekend. You could just feel it.

Kevin didn't feel it. He grew tired of the crowds and reminded Will that bears tend to hibernate.

'You can just tell me about the parade tomorrow. I'm hiding in my apartment."

Lisa had urged Will to be "bright eyed and bushy tailed" for the parade on Sunday so Will called it a night himself. At his apartment, he left a key for Lisa and Jo on the front porch.

Even without a late night out, Will naturally slept until about ten. He'd never been a morning person. He heard Lisa and Jo stir in the living room and they looked cute with their short mussed hair, sacked out on their air mattresses as the morning sun came in. Betty made herself at home in their things and Frida cautiously snuck glances at them as she fearfully scurried past, her short black legs in blur motion like little wheels and her gold, saucer eyes huge with fright.

Everyone took their time with showers and didn't bother with brunch. The girls' top priority was getting to midtown early enough to secure good spots for watching the parade.

"You really think it will be that hard to find space? " Will asked.

"Yes" They said in unison, without hesitation.

"Will, are you still on Athens time?" Lisa, half laughing, asked toward the backseat. Jo drove Lisa's car, speedily, down Piedmont Road toward Midtown.

"What do you mean?"

Lisa turned around in the passenger seat.

"Remember how you and Stephanie used to think you could get anywhere in five minutes and then park anywhere you wanted. Which is why you were both always late to class and had stacks of parking tickets."

"Oh yeah" Will said.

"Oh yeah" Lisa kidded him, like she had in college. She smiled back at him. "You'll be glad we got there early."

In the car, they told Will they'd been doing a lot of GHB in Athens. He'd heard of G, in the alphabet of recreational drugs – G, X, K – but he'd never tried it.

The three of them, girls with lawn chairs and a cooler in tow, walked down tree-lined streets among anti-bellum homes, among a growing number of same sex couples all heading the same direction. A disco beat that grew louder as they walked. The music was coming from event size speakers outside of Outwrite Books on the corner of Tenth Street and Piedmont Avenue, Atlanta's gay epicenter. There were shirtless, chiseled chests in abundance as well as short haired girls and drag queens. Will had never seen so many public displays of affection, gay or straight, at one time and in one place.

"BJ!"

Lisa had called Will BJ since college when she learned that his dad called him BJ after Will attempted to say blue jay when he was a toddler.

"BJ, are you listening to me!"

"Sorry" Will said "I just can't believe all this!"

"Seeeee."

Lisa grabbed his hand.

"So you won't wander off. I know how you are."

Lisa and Stephanie settled into a spot at the corner of Piedmont Avenue and Twelfth Street on the side of the street opposite the park.

Ultra Nate's *You're Free* poured out of the booming speakers in front of Outwrite. The crowd was rowdy and excited and Will couldn't help but want to be a part of it. Though it was hot, and though he wanted to, Will didn't take his shirt off.

Jo ran around like a lab puppy in water. She wanted everyone with a super soaker to point it directly at her and when she saw someone she knew she ran up to them and jumped on them, wrapping her arms and legs around them. Will would have been miserable if someone had done that to him but at the same time he was envious of the way she expressed her excitement so freely. He was brimming over with excitement but no one would know it, reserved and watching. Lisa split her time between letting go with Lisa and hanging back and watching with Will. Even though were in close distance, with that many people crammed together, it can seem like worlds flash by with every second

Lisa excitedly grabbed Will and pointed up at the sky.

"Look BJ!"

A plane circled overhead with a banner floating behind it that read "God Abhors You." Will felt his elation begin to sink until he saw a plane right behind it with a banner that read "Happy Pride 1999!" It took Will's breath away. He was electrified and the hair on the back of his neck stood up as it had only a few times before, after seeing a great and inspiring performance.

Will recognized the same loud, revving engines of the choppers approaching that he'd heard Friday night with Daniel, followed by cheers and screams. Jo jumped up and down and kissed Lisa. The dykes on bikes, popping wheelies and riding in circles, kicked off the parade.

While everyone watched, excited for the next group to approach, Will turned around to look up at the apartment building behind them and all the people on the decks, covered in beads and holding drinks having a good time. On the top, fourth floor balcony of the apartment building directly behind them, he saw Greg leaning over the balcony, drink in hand, casually watching the activity below. Will wasn't sure if Greg had spotted him or not. Will made a mental note to tell Kim about Greg's denim, hemmed shorts when a man came up beside Greg and put his arm around him. The man was taller than Greg, appeared a few years older than Greg, and he had an olive complexion, dark hair and masculine good looks like you'd see in a *Honcho* magazine or gay porn. Greg laid his head on the man's shoulder affectionately. Will turned back around to face the street. A moment later, Will turned around and looked again. Greg and his friend were kissing. Will quickly turned back toward the street.

Will whispered to himself "why did I have to see that? There are so many people here. Why?"

The sight of Greg and his friend ate away at Will for the rest of the weekend. After Lisa and Jo had said goodbye and left for Athens, Will went to a few different bars and drank alone. Men hit on him and he blew them off. Instead of relishing the fresh attention as he had been, Will drank it in bitterly, only seeing what he wasn't getting.

Will had seen Greg with different men at different times. All of those men had been things that Greg effortlessly maneuvered or tossed aside on a whim. This man, Greg had chosen to spend his weekend with. Show affection toward. Will's elation over the parade and the planes with their banners had drawn Will toward Jo's uninhibited way of soaking it all up. He watched and calculated and wondered and wanted. He tried to put it all together in his head to see if he could maybe be that way. The sight of Greg, with the man who was taller, built, and in command – Will allowed it to terrorize him. To push small, clumsy, and trapped in a baseball cap in and overshadow thinner, fitter, and glowing as he had been feeling for weeks. It chipped away at Will, and added to a Will that would have laid on the beach, staring up at Kim's grandmother's condo, and silently damned her and the world because he didn't have a condo like that rather than feel like he owned it and the world because he had health, vitality, and a newfound confidence. It can all be a bright, wide open heaven until the quickest and slightest bite with poisonous venom begins to seep in from an unexpected, less than a minute long scene of two people in a crowd of three hundred thousand worthwhile individuals gets replayed and slow motioned until all the good is gone from your world. Will lived in his head a lot, and now his world was comprised of a scene that wouldn't go away. When you're in love, and it's not returned, it can seem like a person's last name, or the city they are from, or their favorite entertainer, is on the TV and radio every time you turn them on. Every rainbow colored banner with the words "CELEBRATE" that Will had loved so dearly just hours before and every gay person wearing beads or holding hands or relishing in their freedom – it was as if all those things suddenly stopped healing and soothing and comforting Will and immediately began biting and tearing and ripping at him. Momentum and direction had instantly been replaced with still and lost.

The next day, Monday, it was still on Will's mind. After he showered and got dressed for work, he grabbed the phone and called Greg. Will tried to recreate the carefree tone he'd used the last time he called Greg up, but the lightheartedness he'd felt that day couldn't be faked. Will stumbled for words.

"I guess – well – I saw you yesterday but I don't think you saw me."

Greg put his hand over the receiver. Will could hear him laughing softly while talking to someone. Will recognized *that* laugh and he was immediately taken back to the Looming on New Year's weekend. Will remembered the night Greg came over to his apartment when Kim and Zach called. "You could have fucked me all night and into tomorrow" he'd said. All the pieces fell together at once and Will realized who was there with Greg and that Greg was in a mood to torment.

"Oh, I must not have seen you" Greg said, condescension in his voice.
"Will" Greg's voice trailed off. "Isn't it about time for you to go work?"

"YOU FUCKING COKE WHORE!"

Will turned the phone off, threw it across the room, and left for work.

Chapter Sixteen

"You're going to The Manhole?" Kevin said.

"Yep."

"But you've stayed away this long. Why go back?"

"He doesn't own the fucking place" Will said.

In the hallway, the lights were up and the orgy like traffic jams were no more.

A disheveled, mussed haired Greg stumbled down the two steps that dump the poolroom out into the hallway. Clenching his shirt in his hand and looking angry and 80's, like Pat Benatar in her *Love is a Battlefied* video, Greg pushed his way through a clusterfuck of horny men who were just beginning to get it on at the bottom of the steps. Greg looked straight at Will, or rather his crotch, and began walking toward him. As Greg got close, Will could see it on Greg's face as he realized who it was he was approaching. Greg stopped in his tracks and held his hand up toward Will as if they were on the *Jerry Springer Show*.

"*He* walked toward *me*, realized who I was, and gave *me* the fucking hand?" Will whispered to himself.

Shaking his head, Greg walked the other way. Some guys nearby saw how Greg acted and looked Will up and down as if he'd done something to Greg. Will wondered if they knew about the apology letters and phone calls, all unreturned by Greg. He thought the guys had looked at him like he was a stalker.

After getting some air on the back porch Will went back inside and ordered himself another drink. Greg's reaction to him only made him more determined as he made his way through the push and shove Saturday night crowd and back toward the end of the dance floor. He leaned on the bench attached to the wall facing the dance floor, but quickly got bored. He walked around the wall and Greg was on the other side of it making out with some guy. Greg saw Will just as Will saw him and pushed the guy off of him. Will couldn't get a word out before Greg had taken off toward the hallway. The guy looked at Greg walking away and then looked at Will, confused. Will offered no explanation and walked the opposite direction, leaving the guy standing there by himself. Five minutes later, same exact scenario, different guy in the hallway. This time Greg pulled his shirt on and started toward the front of the bar. Will stomped after him and outside the front door.

"I'm sorry! I should have never said that to you!"

Greg kept walking.

"You said we were friends. Why can't you forgive?!"

Greg stopped but he was silent. The only sounds around them were the muffled thump of the disco beat from inside the club and the sound of traffic on Cheshire Bridge Road. Will was aware of two guys sitting in a car parked in front of the Manhole. They were tuned in and ready for a show. Greg turned to look at Will, his light blue eyes pierced through him and moved to his chest, his stomach, his crotch.

"Will" he said, looking defeated "we didn't make it to a year."

Will's heart sank.

"Why can't you forgive me? You've said things to me before. Maybe not as terrible and maybe you didn't scream them but—"

"Will."

"Just please forgive me. I'm sorry I ever said it."

Will looked at him, pleading. A minute that seemed like a year went by. He felt sure Greg would give in.

"Will, stop looking at me like that."

Greg turned and started to walk away.

"You said you loved me! You said we were friends and you said you loved me! Why can't you forgive me?"

The guys in the car were quiet, watching avidly. Will realized they were the same ones who'd looked him over in the hallway.

Greg stopped again and turned around. He looked over Will's body again and then looked into his eyes. Greg's own eyes still flashed with anger.

"Forget about me" he said, and turned to walk away.

Will watched him walk away and start down the sidewalk. He heard the guys in the car say "tell him, tell him!" Will walked down Cheshire Bridge Road and over the bridge to the Sundown Café parking lot where Greg was about to get in his car.

"Greg I just got so jealous when I saw you with that guy at Pride. I know I wasn't supposed to but I did. I'm sorry."

"That guy isn't around anymore!" Greg shot back. It was rare that Greg shot back. Usually, his hand was in the air, making a fist, fighting what he wanted to say to Will.

Greg looked down and struggled for composure. His voice softer, he said "he was just playing house."

Greg's eyes cut into Will and Will took a step back. "It's just a fantasy Will. That's all it ever is."

It was rare for Greg to raise his voice, and it was rare for Will to, even momentarily, put himself in someone else's shoes. He saw that Greg was in pain.

Quietly, Will said "I'm sorry - I'm sorry."

Will backed up, turned around, and walked toward his own car.

Will was barely out of the parking lot before his cell phone rang.

"Get your ass over to Backstreet right now."

It was Kim. He heard Devin in the background.

"Is that my boyfriend? We're rolling our asses off, get over here now!"

Will asked Kim if she thought she could find him a pill.

"Yes, now get over here."

Will parked on a side street and stood in a long line that spilled into the parking lot of Backstreet at two A.M. He tried to imagine what one might think, if they weren't accustomed to late night Atlanta, if they happened to drive past Backstreet in the wee hours of the morning. Big jeaned raver kids, tanned straight couples, shirtless or muscle shirt wearing gay men, and drag queens were all coming and going and standing in line to get in. Hookers and drug dealers could be found on any street corner within a five block radius.

The entrance to Backstreet was on Juniper Street and if someone left through the back door on the Peachtree Street side of the club was a stretcher after a drug overdose. It didn't happen often and when it did, the music didn't stop.

Once Will was inside, he dialed Kim's number. She and Devin were on the porch on top of the entrance waiting for him among the coked up, methed out, ecstasy rolling beautiful people with the Atlanta skyline as their backdrop. Kim slipped Will a pill which he ate half of and slipped the remaining half into the tiny hip pocket of his jeans.

Kim and Devin were riding high on the ecstasy lovey doveys and told Will repeatedly how glad they were to see him. They'd had more than one pill each.

"I like that shirt" Kim said. Devin nodded in approval.

"Have you lost more weight?"

She grabbed Will's arm.

"Make a muscle".

Will loved to show off his work and Kim knew it.

"Damn Will!" Kim said.

"Well, since I'm showing off" Will said and pulled up his shirt to show off his abs.

"Damn Will!" She said again. Kim felt his stomach.

"I hadn't realized you'd gone this far. When did this happen?"

"I don't know. I'm just into it now and it's not all that hard. It's coming pretty easy to me."

It meant a lot to him that she'd noticed and approved.

Kim's expression turned serious. "I hope you're doing this for you and not someone else."

"It's hard to tell anymore. And don't be mad—"

"You went to The Manhole didn't you?"

"Yeah."

"I knew something was wrong" Kim said. "Is it alright if Devin hears this?"

"Of course."

Devin said "It better be. I want to know who's been doing you wrong."

Will began telling Kim and Devin what had just happened at the Manhole.

"Wait. You called Rose on the way over here?"

"Yeah?"

"Will" Kim laughed and looked at Devin who was getting droopy eyed. "That was two in the morning. Rose is such a good friend. Go ahead, sorry I interrupted."

"No, no" Will said. "You're right."

"Will, you have to get over him. Really you do."

He could see that Kim was getting droopy eyed too.

"Are you going to be able to drive home?"

"Yes." Kim could barely keep her eyes open. "I don't know what happened. We were ready to roll all night when we called you."

"I know. It can go this way or that" Will said.

It dawned on Will that he had taken whatever they were on and he was fearful that he might fall into a horrible mental self beating like he had that last time on New Year's weekend. When he couldn't stop staring at the ass of a muscle guy standing next to him and wanted to throw him down and fuck him right there, Will guessed this might be more like that first time he took X. The already pretty skyline seemed to shine even brighter than it had when he first sat down.

"What are you going to do if we leave?" Kim asked, her eyes still droopy.

"I think I'll go to The Looming".

"Be careful. I wish they'd make you wear armbands that say negative or positive when you're in there so you don't get in trouble."

"I don't want my boyfriend getting sick" Devin said before laying his head on Will's shoulder.

At The Looming, Stephen unlocked the door and let Will in before he even knocked.

"Looking good."

Stephen's smile was prurient.

"Haven't seen you in a while."

As soon as Will walked through the hanging beads that separate the front where Chris sat at a podium, Will could hear moans and slapping in the jungle themed section. It took a moment for his eyes to adjust and see a muscle guy bent over and getting fucked by a leather guy. Will was instantly halfway hard. This was going to be a good pill and he guessed that as long as he didn't try it again a second night in a row, he might be fine. Will made his way toward the lounge area and recognized *The Chemical Brothers* song coming from the hidden speakers.

Music
Response
Music must get some kind of response

Will stood at the edge of the area where the widescreen TV was and watched some guys get it on on one of the sofas. Then he turned his attention to the porn playing on the big screen. In the porn, three muscled guys were in a pick up truck outside fucking. You could see cars going by on a rural road in the background, presumably unaware of the porn being filmed so close by and in broad daylight. The idea of the danger of it gave Will a full hard on. Not caring that it showed, he walked through the thick rubber curtains to the back. He stopped in his tracks and his jaw dropped when he saw Stephen's new addition to the construction zone area. Right in front of Will, inside the Looming, was an old white pick up truck with bails of hay in the back. He couldn't believe his eyes. A truck right inside the club and there was a guy standing up in the truck bed behind the cab with another guy on his knees giving him head. Will watched them go at it and the one receiving head nodded at him. He stepped closer to the side of the truck and the reached down and tapped Will's baseball cap. Instinctively, Will jerked back but smiled at the guy as he did. The guy smiled back as Will walked away.

Will walked through the motorcycle area and peeked into the sling room where several guys stood around a naked guy in one of the slings. He watched for a few minutes as they took turns fucking the guy in the sling. Not only was Will was getting used to how good the pill felt, and the pick up truck that had stopped him in his tracks, but he was also getting used to how many opportunities were now open to him. Someone from every group he'd walked past so far had nodded or motioned for him to join. Since he didn't want any of them like he wanted Greg, they were all easy to resist. Will realized the indifference he felt toward them and to him, it felt as good as the pill. Will enjoyed the tease as much as anything and he kept Daniel's rule of four riskiest behaviors in mind.

Will went back to have another look at the pick up truck. The two muscled guys who'd been there earlier were gone. A cute, well built guy was standing beside the truck and he smiled at Will as he walked up. The guy put a finger in Will's belt buckle and led him inside the cab of the truck. Will sat in the passenger's seat and the guy sat in the driver's seat, unzipping Will's jeans and going down on him. As soon as Will felt the guy's mouth around his dick, the good part of New Year's weekend all came rushing back. Greg had been right – there's no feeling in the world like sex on ecstasy. Not even close.

When Will finally got home it was almost five A.M. He slept soundly until after noon and he awoke to the sounds of Betty and Frieda scratching at the door to get out of his room. He heard Brandon's TV in his bedroom which meant that he and his hot retail boyfriend were probably in bed watching a movie. The hot retail boyfriend had grown more flirtatious as Will became more lean. The last person Will would fool around with would be his roommate's boyfriend. Will had his own, albeit unconventional, moral code that he'd tailor made for himself. Free sex with strangers was fine. Getting it on with a good person's boyfriend was not.

Will got out of bed and let Betty and Frida out into the living room. He closed his door behind him before crawling back into bed. He loved how he felt even thinner the day after taking X. He thought about everything that had happened the night before – the encounter with Greg, Kim and Devin at Backstreet, and finally The Looming. And that pick up truck. Was that real? It seemed like a never ending night. He got up to look in the bathroom mirror and it was like seeing his new body for the first time. He understood why Greg had been looking at himself so much that night he'd come over wired.

"Fuck yeah" Will said to himself, twisting and turning, admiring his newly uncovered abs. He laid back down and without even thinking about it started stroking himself. He looked down at his abs and his dick. Maybe those guys weren't just feeding him lines when they made comments. He liked what he saw. He grabbed one of the little packets of lube that Stephen had given him at The Looming and twisted it open. As soon as he felt the lubricant on his dick it was like the guy putting his mouth around it the night before. It might as well have been the first time he'd ever whacked off because nothing before compared. He remembered Greg at his apartment that last time, how he'd said "You could have fucked me all night long and into the next day." If this is what it would have felt like, he thought he could have fucked him into the next day too.

"Why did I have to scream at him?" Will thought, the idea that he'd never get to fuck him all night like he'd said mingling with the ecstasy and the ecstasy he was feeling. He shot thinking about Greg's ass.

Chapter Seventeen

"We got our notices" Craig said, standing at the end of Will's cube.

"We did?" Will said, still settling in and turning his computer on.

"You'll see it all in your e-mail. They're giving us two weeks pay for every year that we worked here, plus a lump sum bonus at the end that's accrued since they first announced the sale".

"When is the sale complete?"

"Three months. Frank told us our group will be here until the end of the year."

From his window seat, Will could see past Craig's cube and down to Laura's window seat. She'd been working feverishly on her upcoming September wedding for months. If her wedding didn't come off without a hitch it wasn't because she didn't work as hard as an army of wedding planners. If she noticed or cared that their company had been sold it didn't show. When Will saw her at their apartment building she was either going for a jog or getting in from one. She was glowing, thin, and ready for her big day. He thought about how she let him cry on her shoulder in January. It felt like a million years ago. He watched as Laura multi-tasked her job and prepared for her wedding with endless energy. He hoped her big day was more brilliant than she'd ever imagined it could be.

Will's phone display lit up and it was Susan. Crisply and fashionably dressed, perfectly poised and soft spoken Susan. Outside of work, and to his friends, Will referred to her as Susan Beautiful Susan. She was also a generous resource of product knowledge. Susan trained Will on their products when he first started his job. After she was promoted to sales, Susan still answered her phone like it was a hot line when Will didn't know an answer, whispering the correct response so no one would hear.

"You didn't forget Laura's wedding Saturday and make plans with some guy you met at The Manhole did you?" Susan said, laughing.

"No" Will said "She's been racing around here. Some of our more bitter co-workers can't wait til it's over."

Susan laughed. "They'll just have to get over it won't they."

"Yes they Will" Will said. "What time are you picking me up Saturday?"

"Since the wedding's at one we should leave your apartment around eleven. I don't know where this place in North Georgia is exactly so we should give ourselves plenty of time. Can you get up that early?"

"Susan!"

"Just one night of not going out. You can do it Will!"

Will did not go out that Friday night before Stephanie's wedding. Since Greg had stopped talking to him altogether, every Friday and Saturday night that he didn't go out felt like a missed opportunity. Would he run into Greg and catch him in an alcohol or chemical induced weak moment where he decides to forgive and wants to have sex? Will wondered what sort of things Greg would be up to later in the night as he walked past the Rich's jewelry counter where Greg had worked over the holidays. Will was on his way up to the Men's Department. Will had never owned a suit. This would be his first one. Even though he'd promised his mother he'd be more financially prudent and not ask for any help, she allowed him to put his new suit on her credit card. His mom was finally selling his childhood home and buying another house. She didn't want Will's "I'll pay you back next week" going on while she was in the midst of it.

It was almost closing time when Will picked up the suit and when the man behind the counter asked for a phone number so that he could verify the credit card, Will warned him that she wouldn't be happy about it. By nine, Will's mother, a bus driver who worked long hours and was a rock to many, had already had her drinks and would be fast asleep, not getting nearly enough rest. The look on the department store clerk's face as he handed the phone back to Will made it difficult for Will to resist laughing. The impeccable and polite Rich's associate (and the ones that sell suits are always extra impeccable and polite), standing in the department store in Lenox Square Mall in Buckhead, had met Faye Turner, who was undoubtedly in her bed, in the decaying ranch house that Will had grown up in, on a county road in Rome, Georgia, in her tee shirt and panties, tired from her life, from Will's hand out, her mother's incessant worrying, her eldest son and his wife and their kids and their juicy juice, and her on again off again girlfriend who no one referred to as her girlfriend because it was Rome, Georgia and her boss who she loathed and last but not least, Will's father, who Will's mom trudged through a mountain of unresolved pain and abuse daily so she could drive the bus and take care of everyone else - most likely said to the stricken appearing man "I don't care what you do with the goddam card but don't ever call my house again this late, do you understand me?" The men's suit sales associate quickly and nervously finished the transaction and Will was out the door and in his car with only ten minutes to spare before the mall closed.

The next morning Will woke up feeling rested and refreshed – rare for a Saturday morning when he'd usually be getting in around five and still rolling hard. As he lay in bed slowly waking up, Will remembered he was out of deodorant and shave cream. He quickly put on his jeans from the night before and a fresh tee shirt before shooting out of the apartment like a cat with the rips and rushing to Disco Kroger, less than a mile away. Several Kroger stores in Atlanta had nicknames that stuck. Disco Kroger on Piedmont Road in Buckhead was next door to a space that had once been home to the Limelight Club, a 1970's disco where a lion could be seen walking beneath a glass floor. A glittering disco ball may have looked more at home at Gay Kroger at Ansley Square, where muscles and flirting are part of shopping for groceries. Kosher Kroger in Toco Hills on Lavista Road is where beautiful, fresh faced Jewish boys saunter along in the golden, early evening Saturday light in their black suits and black hats, sometimes gathering around and propping against street signs that say Merry Lane, Christmas Lane, and Jody Lane, three successive streets that are rumored to be Christmas gifts from a real estate developer to his daughter, and are now at the center of Atlanta's Jewish community. One only has to drive into the parking lot of Murder Kroger on Ponce De Leon Avenue in Poncey Highlands to understand it's nickname.

After Will checked out, a cute guy who'd been in the next line grabbed Will's small waist, turning to smile at Will as he walked out the door. Will said, to himself, "you just got hit on at Kroger, in a predominantly straight part of town, in the morning, and before a shower. You are there."

"Look at you!" Susan beamed walking in the front door. "You clean up nice Will!"

"Thanks Susan. You look gorgeous but you're always dressed to the nines –"

"Stop it Will. I see you broke out the hair."

"It itches already."

"So this is where you and Laura have been living all this time" she said "I always wonder what these look like on the inside when I ride by. They're really cute."

Susan insisted on driving and Will put his jacket in the backseat of her BMW with his baseball cap on top of it.

"You'll be out of that hair and in your baseball cap before we're even back on the highway after the wedding won't you."

"You know me."

"Your suit really is nice by the way. Did you run out and pick it up last night?"

They laughed.

"You *do* know me. I got measured last week and picked it up last night just before closing."

"Will! That's cutting it close even for you!"

"The clerk called mom to verify that it's okay for me to use her card. It was close to nine and I knew she'd be asleep. Who knows what she said to him but from the look on his face --"

"I've got to meet your mom one day" Susan said, laughing "and aren't you supposed to be laying off her bank account right now until she gets her houses straight?"

"I did sort of promise her" Will said

"Then you need to do it, Will." Susan looked over at him.

"You're right."

"Hey, I brought you something" she said "Look in the backseat and hand me that Vogue magazine."

"You brought me a Vogue magazine?"

"Look inside."

Susan had carefully cut out a Britney spread from Elle magazine.

"I know you've probably seen it already because you stay on top of celebrities."

"I saw it in Waldenbooks downstairs during my lunch break one night" Will said "I haven't read it though. Thank you."

"I have a subscription to Elle" Susan said. "I didn't mind cutting Britney out of my magazine for you. You know how I feel about her. Now Madonna, I can see why you gay guys love her. But Britney Spears?

"I can't speak for the others, but I see something" Will said "I was exercising one night after work and I saw her on VH1 – some making of the video show or something. At one point in the video she looked into the camera and I saw something. I think she's got something."

"I don't see it" she said "that drawl of hers."

"The tan" Will said "I hope young girls who want to be like her aren't racing to tanning beds."

They both laughed.

"Our generation can thank Madonna for making it cool not to have a tan. What are these kids doing?" Will said "maybe, one day in the future, after Britney's been a star for a while, we'll see her grow and refine herself. Rise above her legacy. Isn't that what it's all about?"

"I think you give her too much credit Will."

"I can't believe you're letting Britney dominate this much of the conversation" Will said.

"We've got a long drive and I know your attention span. I have to keep you entertained!"

"I hate to ask you this when we haven't been on the highway very long" Will said.

"Already! I know you've joked that you have the bladder of an eight year old before."

"Well—"

"What is it?"

"My stomach feels kind of weird" Will said. "I think it'll be better after we stop."

"Don't worry" Susan said "I don't feel too good today either."

Will knew what it meant when a woman said she didn't feel good.

As he walked back to Susan's four door BMW he heard the ca-clink of the doors unlocking.

"Feeling better?"

"I think so" Will said. "Why'd you have the doors locked?"

"Haven't you heard stories about places like Forsyth county, Will?"

"Oh, yeah" Will said "I don't think it was that terrible in Rome though."

"Well you guys have three colleges up there" she said "so it may be different. I just felt better with the doors locked."

"But they don't like gays any better than black people" Will said.

"But all you have to do is keep your mouth shut!"

"And stay perfectly still and take off the hair" Will said.

They both laughed.

"They'd still know I'm gay" Will said.

Susan mostly kept her personal life under lock and key. Will felt secure the things he told her would stay "in the vault" as she said. She didn't like talking about herself and Will loved talking about himself. They were the perfect travel companions.

"So tell me about Search" she said. "Are you all staying on the tenth floor?"

"So far, yes, Search will stay on ten."

"The customers *are* annoying" Will said "they're mostly people who sign up for the service long enough to do some people finder searches and you know where that information comes from."

"They're still pushing that old stuff." Susan laughed.

"It was rare that I'd get more than ten calls when I was on eleven" Will said. "Now I answer at least forty e-mails a day from internet customers who don't understand the service. The canned responses they have us send back are ridiculous."

"I knew you'd hate it" she said. "How are you getting along with Linda."

"You were right about her. I saw her through rose colored glasses."

"So Frank wasn't so bad after all?"

"You don't know what you've got til it's gone" Will said.

"Is he still bitter that you left?"

"He's softened up."

"Surely he understands that you're just trying to survive" she said.

"So why don't you like Linda?"

"She micro manages."

"You'll never last with those types of customers *and* someone who micro manages, Will. What are you going to do?"

"Well" Will said "I have a plan".

"Will! Have I raised you right after all? Don't tell me you're going to get a real job."

"Oh God no" Will said "remember how Greg told me that –"

"Greg? Are we still talking to him?"

"No, he hates me. He stopped talking to me."

"What? I didn't know about this?"

"Can we start looking for another place to stop?"

"Yes, but I'm remembering this Greg thing and after you've told me your work plan I want to hear what happened."

The next gas station was even more rural and just as before, Susan waited in the car with the doors locked.

"How are you feeling?" she asked when Will plopped into the passenger seat, hands on his stomach.

"About two pounds lighter. My stomach still doesn't feel good."

"Didn't your friend Kim say on your trip to the beach last summer that it's all about your butt."

He laughed even though he still felt sick.

As soon as they were back on the road, Susan said "so back to your plan."

"Last summer Greg got a job as a Computer Operator in a data center. He works three to eleven. It's laid back. He even gets to read a book during the slow parts. It sounds like heaven."

"So that's what you want to do?"

"Yes. I don't want to think about a real career. I like *not* waking up to an alarm, taking my time in the mornings for errands and appointments, and then having plenty of time to work out after work. And it looks pretty casual in our data center so I could probably still wear my baseball cap to work."

Susan laughed.

"So this is your criteria for what makes a good job."

"Quality of life" Will said "it means something different for everyone."

"Yes it does. You've thought about this, I can tell" Susan said. "have you looked around for a job like this?"

"Well - - "

"Will! I knew you were up to something already!"

"There's a guy in operations that I used to chat with downstairs on the patio when I still smoked—"

"I'm so proud of you for quitting!"

"Thank you. The guy, Herb, told me that the manager in operations just fired four people because she caught them sleeping at work. They were third shift weekend people."

"So you think that even though there's a hiring freeze she'll have to replace them?"

"He said the manager wouldn't be able to replace all of them but they'll at least have to replace one."

"How long do you think the data center will be operating?"

"That's the best part! Herb said that they will be operating for at least eighteen more months with the final payout bonus still accruing *and* the immediate raise still in place."

"That makes sense" Susan said "usually when a company is sold, sales and marketing are the first to go and the nuts and bolts like operations are the last."

"Have you met any of these people?" Susan asked. "People have said before it's a snake pit in there" Will said.

"I've heard it's a different world in there" Susan said "you might want to find out more."

"Thirty five percent! That's a lot of money and at the end of a year and a half!"

Susan laughed.

"So you're saying you can handle a few snakes for that much of a raise."

"You bet I can."

"So are you going to talk to the manager about getting a job there?"

"I already talked to someone but not the manager. I went to Josh."

"Will!" Susan laughed and looked over at him. "You went straight to the top didn't you!"

"Well, I remembered one day a while back, as I was going to the elevator and he was coming back from lunch with some people, I overheard him tell one of them he liked my sense of humor."

"So you talked to him?"

"I went to his office and asked for the job."

"What did he say?"

"He set up a time to talk to me next week."

"Will, I'm proud of you. That was a brave move going to the director of technology. But what about David and Ruth in HR? You *just* started at Search and now you're asking to come back upstairs? Will they let you do that?"

"I hope so. Thirty five percent *and* a bonus at the end! No micro managing and no internet customers!"

"Would you be working weekends? You know you love to go out."

"It's a crazy schedule. Friday, Saturday and Sunday from seven at night until seven in the morning."

"You're already up at that time on the weekend anyway aren't you?" Susan joked "you might as well be getting paid for it."

After one more stop they drove into the Young Harris campus with it's rolling green hills, fall foliage, and a white church. The wedding had started thirty minutes earlier. Susan and Will quietly slipped into the standing room only church and watched from the back as a beautiful and radiant Laura and beau exchanged their vows. As soon as the ceremony was finished, Susan and Will slipped back out and found a place to sit while waiting for the newly married couple to bust through the church doors. Minutes later, they drove off in a 1920's era car. The day, the wedding, the car, the scene – everything came together perfectly. Will could feel the magic in the air that he'd hoped Laura would have on her big day.

The reception was also on campus and just as much of a perfect fall scene. There was even a tire swing hanging from a Willow tree next to a sparkling creek. Beautifully set, round tables with white table clothes dotted the manicured, lush green lawn.

Will and Susan sat at a table with a group from work, including Ruth from HR. Soon, Will would be asking her to undo all the work she'd done to get him started at Search. Will moved a few appetizers around with his fork, pretending to eat. He didn't want to ask for any more stops than necessary on their way back to Atlanta. Susan and Will feigned as much light hearted gaiety as they could muster before quietly disappearing into the crowd, and into the parking lot, and into her car, and down a curvy country road.

"I hope I can get us out of here" Susan said.

Will held the directions up in the late afternoon sunlight, and starting from the bottom, read them backwards to Susan.

At the first stop sign, Will said "don't look."

Susan covered her eyes while he quickly switched the hair for a baseball cap, stuffing the hair into his jacket pocket before neatly folding his jacket and putting it back in the backseat.

"That was quick."

"I got the kind that snaps. I won't be a prisoner in that thing."

Will was slouched in the front seat, holding his stomach when a four lane highway came into sight, delighting Susan."

"You are a city girl, aren't you" Will said.

"I sure am. I like for everything to be within just a few minutes."

"I think I understand" Will said. "When I go to Rome for a visit, it's so quiet I can barely fall asleep."

"See" she said "even if you don't want to be around anyone, isn't it nice knowing you have the option with plenty of people around."

"Yes it is" Will said.

"Now tell me about Greg."

"That was quite a segue."

"I want to get the whole story before we get back so I figured we better get started."

Will told Susan about Pride, seeing Greg with the guy, calling him a cokewhore, and stomping after him at the Manhole.

"Will, do you really think that was the way to get back into his good graces?"

"I sent him letters apologizing but he didn't respond."

"Maybe it's better that way. I wish you could find someone less –"

"Dangerous?"

"I was going to say destructive but dangerous is good too. I know how it is though. It's the dangerous ones that get us hooked isn't it."

"I'll be alright for a while" Will said "but then I'll see him out."

"What is it about him?"

"He's hurt. Angry. Inaccessible. You know I'm not into dating one of *those* types of gay guys – the ones who are only concerned with what they drive, how big their houses are, who they're being catty about. Greg's not like all the others."

"Why don't you hang out somewhere he doesn't frequent?"

"After working out during the week I love it when he sees me in a tight shirt and loses himself for a second. The more I work out and the more attention I get – I keep hoping he'll crumble one night."

"You know that's not going to work though."

"I know. I guess I know. I don't know. All I know for certain is that I want a job in operations making more money and not having to deal with Linda or Inform."

It was dark and the first golden tips of the Atlanta skyline came to view in the distance.

"I always get excited when I see the skyline as I'm driving back into town" Susan said.

"Me too."

Susan said "I'm going to take the West Paces exit and show you my favorite house on the way back to your apartment".

West Paces Ferry Road, where the Governor's mansion as well as other prominent Atlanta homes could be found, must be a street that inspires people to pick a house that's their favorite. A guilty pleasure like watching Robin Leach and dreaming. Susan's favorite house was a subdued tudor that looked like it might be more at home on the French country side rather than surrounded by displays of wealth.

"What's your favorite one Will?"

"The pink terra cotta one next to the Governor's Mansion."

"I wouldn't have guessed that. And you can barely see the roof over that fence that surrounds it."

"I know. It'd be like having your own world carved out right in the midst of everything. I won't tell you the kinds of things that I imagine goes on behind those walls."

The scenery changed abruptly when they got to the busy Roswell Road and Piedmont Road intersection where there was an outdated orange apartment building with a green roof crammed awkwardly in between. Susan pulled into the parking lot and Will thanked her for driving and making so many stops.

"I'm happy I got to spend the day with you" Susan said "I hope you feel better."

Betty and Frida greeted him at the door. The apartment was dark except for the light over the stove which was always on. Brandon must have been at home in Alabama or with his hot boyfriend.

Will put food out for the girls and went back to his room where he pulled the chain on the worn bronze lamp with hanging fringe next to his bed. It made just enough light so as not to shock him out of the relaxing ride home in Susan's car that felt like floating on a cloud.

He hung up his jacket, tossed the hair on a closet shelf, and plopped on his bed – still in his suit pants and tee shirt. Frieda and Betty jumped on his bed and sniffed his whereabouts on his clothes. They purred and cuddled up beside him.

Will replayed the day for a while in his head, like he does, before getting up and braving the bright light of the bathroom. When he pulled off his tee shirt, he knew for the first time in his thirty years what it meant to lose a couple of pounds of water weight.

His stomach ache went away – probably because there couldn't possibly be any more food in it. He wondered if I could squeeze into a tee shirt that he hadn't had the nerve to wear yet and went over to his closet.

"Oh yes".

An hour later, he was at a sex club – rolling on ecstasy and getting it on.

Chapter Eighteen

Mr. Woods, the director of I.T., was pale, his hair was mostly white, and his eyes were inquisitive and intelligent. Probing. Like many I.T. people, he wore pull over shirts though he was less perpetually casual Friday than many other I.T. people. Though his hair was white, he was youthful acting and appearing.

Will dressed in crisp, flat front khakis, a dark dress shirt, and the hair.

"I'm dependable and I work hard" Will told him, pushing a hard sale on himself the way he'd learned to in Rome in his younger years. Instilled in him by his family - if you work hard and keep your eyes on the prize everything will come together. Josh sat back comfortably in his chair, rolling a pen between his fingers, watching the show.

"I'll do a good job" Will said.

Without moving or moving his eyes off Will, Josh said "Yes, I was able to acquiesce that from Frank."

Will made a mental note to look up "acquiesce." He figured Frank was probably being an asshole while still helping him out. Statistics would back that theory up.

"Have you ever worked an overnight shift before?"

"No, but I know I can adjust".

"It is quite an adjustment" Josh said "But some people get used to and even like those hours."

"Years ago when I worked a shift like this one" he said "I grew to like it."

Mr. Woods chatted about how he adjusted to third shift hours, his own ease and comfortableness put Will at ease.

"Will, I understand you went to work for Search a few weeks ago."

"I did" Will said.

Mr. Woods hesitated, looking at Will and rolling his pen. Will began to wonder if dramatic pauses, intended to keep someone on the edge of their seat, were taught in managerial school. Mr. Wood's pen rolling pause was similar to Frank's. Will didn't know what to expect and he began to hold his breath.

"I would like for you to go to the director of Search, Lisa, and tell her that we talked about the position in Operations. Explain to her that you just started at Search, and that you'd like to come back to work at Inform on eleven. Let me know what she says."

Will went straight to Search on the tenth floor and to the director's secretary, who he knew and liked. She was a sharply put together lady who'd moved down from Boston for the job. Though Will was a study in bad manners and impulsiveness, this lady was always warm and kind to him. The director, Lisa, came around the corner behind her secretary's desk hurriedly with her sport coat and brief case in tow.

Lisa looked at Will and seemed to faintly recognize him. The secretary nodded toward him and said "Will would like to speak with you if you get a chance."

"You can talk to me on the elevator ride down" Lisa said as she handed some papers to the secretary and pointed a sticky note out to her.

Will told Lisa what he wanted and what Mr. Woods had said as they rode the elevator to the ground level. Lisa looked at Will a couple of times on the elevator. He still wasn't sure she knew who he was.

Lisa stopped at the security desk to sign out and turned to look at Will again.

"Will Turner" she said. "you're the one that Linda hired recently?"

"Yes."

"Who have you talked to in the Data Center?"

"Only Mr. Woods" he said.

Lisa continued looking at him.

"And he sent you to me?"

"Yes."

Lisa sighed. Will couldn't tell if she was frustrated at Linda for hiring him, Mr.Woods for sending him, or just the audacity of his request.

Lisa paused before saying "please make sure you give Linda a notice as soon as possible."

"Thank you, thank you" Will said.

Lisa's heels made hurried and determined taps and echoes on the shiny, white, marble floors as they mingled with other purposeful taps of heels worn by attorneys and business people, all on their way someplace. It was the sounds of those purposeful footsteps at work, and the sounds of traffic and horns on Piedmont Road, that made Will feel alive every day in his new world. Everything else, to him, was crickets.

On the elevator ride up to ten, Will rehearsed a look of sad remorse, hoping to keep his elation in check for the five minutes it would take to tell Linda he was leaving Search.

"You sure look nice today Will. What brings you here on your off day?"

Linda didn't look Will in the eye as she normally did. He hoped she wasn't going to act like a bitter divorcee like Frank did a few weeks prior when he left Inform to work at Search. Will worked to contain his excitement long enough to tell her his news.

"I appreciate it that you hired me and I know you went to a lot of trouble to get me in quickly—"

Linda's expression was morose as she nodded in expectation of more.

"I'm going back to work at Inform."

Linda's eyes got big and her mouth fell open. She looked at him like he was joking.

"You're leaving a future with a company that is growing and has promise to go back to work for a company that you know is closing down?"

"Yes." It was a staccato yes. Will rarely reached in and pulled out a stoic poker face. It only happened when he felt cornered.

Linda looked at him for a moment, gained her composure, and went back to her paperwork.

Without looking up, she said "next Friday is the end of the pay period, so why don't you make that your last day."

"And Will, what will your title be so I can let everyone know."

"Computer Operator."

Will knew what she was saying to him, and he didn't care. He was free to leave Linda and her battered housewife routine on ten and go tell Frank the good news. Frank stopped Will before he could get to Mr. Wood's office.

"Will, I didn't mean to steal your thunder but I told Craig you were coming back to Inform in the data center."

Frank's smile was genuine. He was glad to see Will back and Will was glad to be back.

The next day, as Will waded through a sea of irate e-mails about errant one dollar people searches, he saw a group e-mail from Linda: "Will Turner will be leaving us in order to pursue a career as a Data Loader at Inform."

Chapter Nineteen

Will's new boss, Sue, was a tall, large, neatly dressed light skinned African-American woman who looked as if she could strangle Will every time she saw him. It hadn't dawned on him that going above her head to get the job might instigate a game of cat and mouse if he were hired.

To begin, Will would work two weeks on the night shift, eleven PM to seven AM, and train with Larry, a tall bright skinned African american man who looked like he had bets on how many minutes Will might last in the data center. The third week would be spent training on second shift from three PM to eleven PM. After that Will would go to the toughest schedule – Friday, Saturday, and Sunday from seven PM through seven AM.

Will's first Monday night, staying up until seven A.M. without stimuli of any sort except Larry's naturally voluminous voice spouting off dry material was a battle for Will. Larry reminded Will repeatedly to take notes while Will fought the urge to nod off.

Will found that falling asleep after a night of working is much more difficult than falling asleep after a night of partying. Perhaps it's the tension that is built up as opposed to the tension that was released. Will couldn't relax enough to fall into deep R.E.M. sleep and every little noise sounded like it was in the day lit room with him. Not one that can function without sleep, he was even more of a D student as Larry tried again on Tuesday night to communicate the dry information to him.

"Apparently you must have remembered everything from last night since you didn't bother to bring any notes with you" Larry said as Will's next night on third shift began.

Larry's voice boomed off the walls of the small office they trained in as he sat back in his chair, smug, smiling at Will. Larry handed Will a clipboard with a notepad attached.

Halfway through the night, at about three A.M. when everything seems it's darkest, most isolated, and most miserable, Larry moved in closer to Will's seat. He lightly ran his fingers up and down the clipboard which was resting on Will's lap as he talked.

After two nights without sleep and two days with minimal restless sleep, Will felt ill. He called his mother on Wednesday night and told her about the clipboard.

"Move. The. Clipboard." She told him.

"You can't live without sleep. You got that from me."

"I know" Will said miserably, feeling exhausted.

"Don't forget - if he does it again tonight - move. the. clipboard."

The lack of restful sleep prevented Will from exercising or walking at Chastain Park, heaping misery on top of misery.

In the afternoons, Will drove downtown to the office, sat at Craig's desk, and typed his notes from the night before into a word document. He hoped that typing them would help make the information stick. The next afternoon, before work, he drove downtown again and typed the previous night's notes into his document. From then on, he brought a fresh printout of updated notes for that night's shift.

On his lunch breaks at three A.M., Will left the concealed world of the glass enclosed data center and walked down the aisles where he'd spent his days with Ginger, Craig, and Laura. He missed them. Walking past their cubes in the quietest dead of night punctuated how vastly different it felt from the light, activity and laughter of days.

Will's second week of training was better than the first. He was allowed to do more work on his own using his notes. There was an end in sight to his time training with Larry. Though the log files were overwhelming at first, Larry taught him the few key words he should look for - "fatal error" or "competed successfully". Depending on the outcome of the "job", he either noted the time it completed or paged an on call person who would get online and straighten things out. Will took notes on every single thing that was shown to him, no matter how inept it seemed.

On his third week, Will worked on second shift with the second shift supervisor, Mark. When Will still worked with Craig and Ginger, he was alone one night, or so he thought, when he heard a deep, gravelly voice directly behind him. He turned in his chair to see Mark, over six feet tall, probably two hundred pounds, and very dark skinned. It must be what people feel like when they look out of their sliding glass doors and see a bear on their patio. Will's heart jumped and as Mark introduced himself, Will instantly knew that while Mark was harmless and kind. Will liked his sense of humor.

Will's week working with Mark on second shift, followed by going home afterward and getting a good night's sleep, made Will feel brand new. It also made Will realize he had to find a way back to working daytime hours. And soon.

On the Friday night of his third week, Will celebrated the end of his training with Kim and her roommate Diana at Mary's in East Atlanta. Mary's was the only gay bar in Atlanta that catered to alternative gays who, though well into their thirties, were still determined to undo the damage inflicted to their geek personalities in high school. No matter how many times in their adulthood they could manage to be the first kids on the block with a big wheel, it seemed it would never be enough. Kim and Diana were impressed with Will's still changing physique and he decided to go to the Manhole that Sunday night on take your shirt off night. He'd always wanted to go back in the back on take your shirt off night, but still hadn't done it. Sunday would be his test run.

That Sunday, at the Manhole, it was as decadent a scene as Will had ever seen there. Bugged eyes, water bottles and sweaty, naked chests abound, it looked like many drugs had been consumed already. Will found himself a spot near the wall with the bench to watch the madness and someone immediately grabbed a handful of Will's crotch. Will looked up to see Greg looking back over his shoulder at him. When Greg realized it was Will, his face contorted in anger as he walked away.

"Whoa" Kevin said "Is that Greg. He looks like he's been rode hard and hung out to dry all weekend."

Will laughed it off and kept his place, watching the hot men with their water bottles relive their lost adolescences all around him. Kevin knew Will wished he'd been the one riding Greg hard all weekend.

Will noticed Greg approach a couple just outside the poolroom. He walked up to them, as he had Will, and grabbed their crotches. The guys each brushed Greg's hand away. Greg walked right past Will and Kevin again, not even appearing to know who they were. Will heard him breathing labored as we walked by. He recognized the way Greg's breath sounded and he looked at Kevin.

"I think you're right" Will said "all weekend."

Kevin nodded, half in agreement, half in I'm sorry we ran into him.

But for a moment, Will allowed himself not to care. Cut, shirtless men had been coming over to him and pinching his nipples or rubbing his abs since he'd walked in while Greg, acting base and desperate, waded through one rejection after another.

"See" Kevin said "you didn't need me to hold your hand tonight."

After Kevin left with a fellow bear, Will went to the hallway and began chatting with someone he recognized from U.G.A. As they talked, Will saw Greg go into the poolroom and approach a guy that had already rejected him. When Greg came out of the poolroom and saw Will engaged in conversation with the U.G.A. guy, he hung back in the shadows and watched. When they were finished talking, Will went behind the wall at the end of the dance floor where there was sort of a small orgy taking place. Someone immediately unzipped Will and went down on him while someone else rubbed his chest. Greg, who'd moved just in front of him, reached behind and grabbed Will's dick.

"Are you from out of town?" Greg said softly.

"—Yeah."

Will thought Greg was joking, but he wasn't sure. Greg turned to look at him.

"Will."

"Like you didn't know" Will said.

Greg finally got someone to talk to him and left Will standing in the midst of the orgy, shirtless and with his jeans now around his knees. Will rushed to pull his jeans up but couldn't find his tee shirt. Someone had taken it.

It was Will's first time taking his shirt off on take your shirt off night. He didn't realize he wouldn't be putting it back on as he walked across the bridge over Peachtree Creek, shirtless, at three AM, toward his car at Sundown Café. He was glad for the late hour if he had to be driving home shirtless, embarrassed when he first started his car, but relishing by the time he parked in the parking lot in front of his apartment. He had nothing to hide as he sauntered up the steps to his apartment.

Chapter Twenty

A three day work week sounded like a breeze to Will's friends, but these three days were twelve hours long – and they were nights. It was always a struggle for Will to stay awake, and during those three days he did nothing but work and sleep. The sleep, a lot of times, wasn't very restful.

The first day of his four days off, Monday, was usually spent in a deep sleep. He'd wake up in the afternoon, around three or four, and lay in bed for at least half an hour. It never stopped being strange to wake up on a Monday afternoon, after a deep sleep, and realize it was Monday afternoon and you were off work until Friday evening. Will took his time getting up, getting showered and getting dressed. He often times met Kevin for dinner, anxious for details about his weekend which Will now coveted.

Most always, after dinner and after Kevin went home to go to bed early for his nine to five that Will now coveted, Will would go to Burkhart's. It became a routine and Will loved to stand by the railing that wrapped around the second floor and watch the karaoke singers down below. There was one couple in particular that he loved to watch. Will thought they were probably in their mid twenties. The guy was tall with dark hair. Smooth skin. He wore what Will considered to be a staple straight man's ensemble for that time. He saw it a lot at Backstreet – dark dress pants with just enough stretch fabric to show off their ass and thighs, square toe'd black dress shoes, and a dark dress shirt with just enough stretch fabric to show off their chest and nipples. The girl looked and sounded like Shirley Manson. She wore skirts in 1960's lengths, fur jackets that were about as long as her skirts, knee high boots, and she rarely, if ever, put down her cigarette before she began singing, and it often times became part of her performance. Both of them commanded the microphone with authority and the spotlight with as much charisma. Will was mesmerized by the couple like he had been as a five year old watching Cher vamp and tramp on top of a piano on the Sonny and Cher Show. Once, while someone else was performing, the couple stopped chatting and looked up at Will leaning against the railing. Anytime that anyone who Will had been looking at returned a look then or later, he darted off like Carrie Bradshaw after she'd farted in bed with Big, most times bumping into something as he turned around and shot off in a direction without looking where he was going first.

Almost without fail, a kid would try to sing Cher's ubiquitous *Believe* and, bless his heart, his determined but insecure performances would instantly stagnate the electricity in the air from the luscious performances he followed. It made Will fear microphones and stages even more, and he kept his own cat with an illness belting of *Believe* safely in the privacy of his car.

A strawberry blond kid wearing dirty jeans and a wife beater would take the stage, strutting and singing, tapping and gripping the microphone like he owned it. Will loved watching the kid sing and when he sang *American Pie* he'd start slow and soft and when he got to the part that said "dig those rhythm and blues" his voice boomed off the first and second floor walls as he sang, erasing the time to go buy a drink performance of *Believe*. Will sometimes tried to mimic the strawberry blond kid in his car, driving up a mostly empty Piedmont Road back to his apartment. The speakers drowned him out while he tapped the steering wheel like a microphone.

Though it was always in the back of Will's mind that he might be missing something on the weekends while he was at work, he also enjoyed the comfortable ennui of his weeknights out while most were at home resting for their day jobs. There were colorful characters out and about on weeknights and Will didn't feel that Friday night must get laid urgency all around. Will rarely saw Greg out and he began to feel like weeknights had become his own sort of playground.

Sometimes Will drove to Rome for a visit and he liked popping in on weekdays before his brother and mom had gotten used to his new schedule and didn't expect to see him. He'd paid his mother back for the wedding suit weeks before and he hadn't asked for anything else.

His mother, notoriously resistant to change, still hadn't packed anything to move into the house she'd bought. On one of those visits to Rome, Will sat in the living room of his mom's new house, in the one chair that she'd brought over, looking around the empty living room and putting things in place in his mind. Will's brother, Jim, drove up and walked in. He wore khaki shorts, tennis shoes, a pull over shirt and baseball cap, and usually walked into their mom's house and looked in the refrigerator, plopped down in the living room, grabbed the remote control and put his legs on a footstool and began what would later be called restless leg syndrome. The house was mostly empty and Jim stood at the bar in front of the small kitchen.

"She doesn't want to move over here" he started.

He'd brought a large, black trash bag with him and opened a kitchen drawer, locking the bag in place as he closed it.

"She gets like that" Will said "you know how she is."

"Yeah" Jim said, leaning against the bar with both hands and a defeated look on his face "but how are we gonna get her over here?

"Let's go get her furniture."

Jim laughed.

"Why not?" Will said.

Jim pulled his hat off and rubbed his forehead. He opened the refrigerator and pulled out a two liter bottle of Sprite.

"Of course she'd have that over here" he said "gotta have something to mix her drinks with."

Will normally interrupted, spoke out of turn and blurted out his first thought. He did, however, remain quiet when a family member talked about Faye's drinks. Most times he remained stoic.

"I don't have time to get it all tonight" Jim said. One of his three sons, at any given time it seemed, had a ball game they all had to get to.

"Let's go get her bed then" Will said "then she'll sleep over here."

Jim looked at Will and laughed.

"You know she's gonna get mad."

"For a little while" Will said. "Later on, she'll be glad we did it."

"Are you gonna stay in town and be here when she gets off work?" Jim asked.

"Yep" Will said."

Within an hour, the bed was there and set up.

After Jim left, Will sat quietly in his mom's new living room, looking through the dining room and out the sliding glass doors at her pool. He was hopeful about this new chapter of their lives. He had a new body. His mom had a new house. He hoped the new walls would hold happier memories than the ones they'd occupied when he was a kid. Breaking him from his reverie, his cell phone rang. It was Kim.

"Will, this is big but I need a quick answer".

"Yeah?"

"I can get round trip tickets to London for two hundred fifty dollars each but I have to order them in the next half hour."

"London?"

"For the end of March."

"London?"

"You, me, and Zach."

"How long?"

"I was thinking ten or eleven days."

"Hmmm. With my work schedule I'd have eight of those days clear after asking for three off."

"So you're going?!" You're kidding? Really, you'll go?"

"Yes!"

"I can't wait to tell Zach we get to start a London journal!" Kim said.

Will figured he could do this without asking for any help from his mom. He planned to wait a week or so before telling her. Over the phone. From Atlanta.

Later that evening, after Will's mom had shown up, still wearing her bus driver's uniform and looking tired, Jim came back over with her sofa and some other things. Ten minutes later, Jim's wife Trudy drove up in their van. All three boys were with her. Faye hugged Trudy and beamed at "her boys."

"Justin helped me load the stuff in the truck" Jim said "Will, you get to help me bring it in."

Faye said "Will, you can spend the night here tonight instead of going back to Atlanta." She stirred the ice in her drink and laughed a "you didn't think you were going to just up and move me into this house without telling me and there wouldn't be consequences" laugh.

"I like the garbage can" she said.

As they were taking Faye's things out of the truck, Will said "you brought her TV?"

"Yeah, why" Jim said.

"That was smart" Will said.

"I figured if she had her bed, her sofa, and her LifeTime movies" Jim said "she'd be glad we did it."

Will spent the night on the sofa at his mother's new house. The next morning, his mom was in the kitchen, saying things like "I'll have to do this to this stove" and "I'll have to go get this for". She was happy they'd pushed her into moving. Will stood at the sliding glass door, the sun pouring in from the east, and stared out at the pool. He was lost in thought when his mom said from the kitchen "don't worry Will. No one's going to take it from you."

*

Not long before Thanksgiving, Will took a Friday and Saturday night off. He was anxious to see what he'd been missing – especially at The Looming. From the looks of the guys coming and going at one A.M. and the full parking lot, he'd been missing a lot.

Inside The Looming, the smell of the nag champa incense, the sex, the porn all around – it was as enticing as Will expected. Along with the pick up truck, they'd added a van in the back of the club where it was darkest.

Will went to the refreshment area and took a pill that Kevin had given him.

"A friend of mine found these" Kevin said "they're gonna rock your world". They both chuckled at the phrase Kevin wouldn't seriously use.

The pill hit Will fast and hard and he felt like raping everyone in sight - repeatedly.

As Will walked back through the maze toward the area with the big screen TV, he ran into Greg walking the other direction through the tight hallway. Greg stood still and took in Will's long, lean torso in his now staple tight tee shirt. Will locked his eyes and held them.

"Will, just consider me a ghost" Greg practically whispered and then walked away.

Will walked through some black rubber curtains and joined a group of cute, collegiate looking kids who were in a circle. They reeked of bi-curiosity in their sweaters. Will wrapped himself around a dark haired, fresh faced, twenty something guy and ground his round ass through his khaki's. The kid pulled Will's dick out and started stroking it while Will reached in his pocket for lube. When the guy pulled his pants and boxers down for Will, one of his friends put his arm between them.

"Hey, don't you need to wrap that up?" he said in Will's ear.

Will was momentarily stunned, unable to believe that he was *that person* – who would put someone in danger. He knew he was negative but they didn't and why would they? His unbelted, unbuttoned, and unzipped jeans fell to his ankles. Will got tangled in them and fell down, causing the guys in the circle to step back.

"It's Saturday night!" he heard someone say from the group just next to theirs and laugh.

When Will stood up and finally got his jeans fastened, he saw Greg in the shadows, still and watching.

With his tee shirt hanging out of his back pocket, Will stumbled through the black rubber curtains and across to the area with the big screen TV. There was an orgy on all three sofas and in between. The porn on the big screen was hardcore and he could barely take his eyes off it when a cute, shirtless couple pulled him into their group. Through his haze he kept Daniel's rule of four in mind, only climbing to number two. He made no effort to resist the muscular thighs and asses in front of him as he put his dick in two different guys before breaking away and going to the front. When Stephen asked him if he could get him anything, he'd forgotten he'd walked up front to ask for a condom. He made a goofy smile and said something inaudible before walking back through the beaded curtains and back into the jungle themed area.

Will went into a far corner bathroom in the jungle area that was largely overlooked. Inside, with the door locked, he cleaned himself and realized why Greg had been admiring himself so avidly in his bathroom mirror that night he was at his apartment in the summer. Just like he'd loved his car like he'd never been in it, or had never seen a Krispy Kreme store lit up at night, he stood in the bathroom, staring at his newly transitioned body in the mirror with the utmost in self indulgence. Maybe that was a hallmark of drugs – they can mess with time. Like when you see someone every day, or yourself every day, you don't realize the changes. But if you go a while without seeing them, the changes are more pronounced. Will had not taken time to really stop and look at the work he'd been doing. It was hard for him to believe it was himself that he was looking at in the mirror. His veins bulged with life and at the same time, they bulged with speed. He stood still, looking in the mirror with the jungle noises just outside the door. The room was lit only by a black light, but it was a large restroom with a full length mirror. It seemed separate from the rest of the club. At once, in the mirror, Will saw someone he didn't recognize, someone he'd desperately wanted to be, someone he was proud he'd turned into, and someone he didn't know – and he saw *himself*. He saw muscles bulging off his small frame that had been made fun of in school for being too small, veins popping on arms and hands that didn't look like his own, and an intense look in his eyes that even he almost had to look away from. He stood straight, legs wider, arms as if they were ready for action.

His eyes softened. Quietly, almost inaudibly, Will whispered "Will – is that you in there?"

Will walked into the little room with the multiple TVs. He'd been afraid New Year's weekend when he'd seen Roger draped over three guys, all sharing in afterglow. Now, he scanned the room with confidence.

Will went back through the jungle room and out the other side to the main area with the big screen TV. Through the unseen speakers, Bernard Sumner's haunted voice resonated in him like it had since his teens. But this time, more than a decade later, Bernard Sumner's voice was backed by a relentless, driving, Chemical Brother's beat.

Sometimes I feel that I'm misunderstood
The rivers running deep right through my thought
Your naked body's lying on the ground
You always get me up when I'm down
And it always seems we're running out of time
We're out of control
Out of Control
Out of control

Will walked through the black rubber curtains and past the pick up truck. He saw Greg - not in a theme area or in a sling, not in a standing box with moons cut out or in the bed of the pick up truck - but right in the middle of the floor, face down, getting fucked. Will was as stunned as he was that night he'd seen the pick up truck the first time, when it seemed like the porn and reality were blending. Will stopped in his tracks and did not attempt to hide as he watched Greg and the guy go at it. Will barely got a glimpse of the guy's face while he pounded away at Greg's ass. They were like two wild animals and a crowd had formed around them. Only a couple of minutes passed before Greg began looking for his clothes. It looked like the growing crowd around them began to get to him. Will backed into the shadows and walked away, almost wishing he hadn't been seen.

As New Year's Eve 1999 approached, the manager of Operations, Sue, made it clear that everyone was to be on site the entire weekend. Many feared that because of code written long ago which didn't take into account the new millennium, major disruptions or even outages might occur at midnight on New Year's Eve. Will understood that and it is was talked about on the news regularly. What he didn't understand was why Sue insisted that Richard (his counterpart who worked Friday, Saturday, and Sunday from seven AM through seven PM) and he would not get paid double time and a half like everyone else that would be in the data center New Year's weekend.

"Because it's your regularly scheduled shift" Sue told them before abruptly ending the conversation.

Will wasted no time telling Ruth and Rachel in HR about Sue's Nazi attitude and the holiday pay. The next Friday when Will came in for his shift, Sue pasted on a perm-a-grin while telling Richard and Will they would be paid extra, just like everyone else, on New Year's weekend. Though she was smiling on the outside, Will could tell that Sue was ready to implode on the inside. Will had worked for her for almost three months and thought he'd seen every trick up her sleeve already. This one, he felt, had to be addressed and he was glad he told Ruth and Rachel. Will knew it would always be a cat and mouse game with Sue. He'd gone over her head to be brought into the data center, rose to the occasion to stay there, and now caused one of her ruses to be foiled. He suspected Sue would be out to get him and often felt like the Road Runner cartoon, often times barely escaping her clutches before punching a time clock so they could do it all over again the next day.

That Friday night, the beginning of his work week, was also New Year's Eve. At Fellini's on Ponce De Leon Avenue, he pouted to Kevin about having to go in on New Year's Eve. That palpable Friday night, New Year's Eve excitement in the air that wasn't meant for Will was killing him.

"But look at all the extra money you'll be getting." Kevin tried to console Will. "And besides, neither one of us has any pills, the Looming won't be any fun because the world won't be here after midnight. I'm staying home, hiding under the covers with Meredith (his cat), and watching the news until it's all over. You'll be safer at work anyway and you won't have to worry about what you're missing on Friday and Saturday nights anymore because the Y2K is making the world end. Don't you even watch the news? Go get me some more coke."

It was cold, gray, and windy out as Kevin and Will sat in Fellini's talking and eating among the fresh faced Emory students and hipster staff.

Will resigned himself that for this year, and this time, the excitement in the air wasn't his to grab onto. He went into work at seven PM with a good attitude, ready to do his job through the uneventful, over dramatized, transition into the new millenium.

After eleven but before midnight Rachel showed up unexpectedly and poured champagne toasts for everyone. This being the first company Will had worked for in Atlanta, he didn't realize how extraordinary that was or how rare it was for Human Resources to do something like that.

The company reserved rooms next door at The Marriott Marquis Hotel for some who were staying overnight but not on their regular shift. That explained where Larry, who Will had not been looking forward to working with, had been all night.

Larry, who Will referred to as Ike Turner among his friends outside of work, stumbled into the data center at midnight to slur a Happy New Millenium wish everyone's way. It was out of character for Larry, who didn't strike Will as a person who would even smoke a cigarette or drink a beer. Larry was barely coherent and blamed it on cold medication. Will was happy to see the beast heavily intoxicated and down for the count. He figured the cold medicine excuse came straight from Sue's seemingly infinite arsenal of transparencies, and no one cared because who wanted Larry breathing down their necks anyway.

Just after midnight Will's cell phone started ringing. Since the world hadn't shut down and no one was running around the data center in a hurried panic, he took the calls and exchanged Happy New Year's. Later on, Kevin called to tell him he was still hiding under the cover with Meredith watching T.V.

"It's still not midnight everywhere yet so it's still not safe" Kevin said.

Will laughed at the thought of Kevin, a big hairy bear, his youthful face, at home under the covers with his cat, watching T.V.

"There's something wrong with you" Will said, laughing. "A good gay would be out fucking in the new millennium right now".

Kim called after Kevin, sounding more serious and sober than Will expected. He told his co-worker that he was taking a break and went to the TV Lounge with the red, yellow, and blue Jetson's chairs on the twelfth floor. He turned on a channel that was showing a rerun of the X Files and settled into the middle chair like he always did in that room. He turned the sound down so he could talk to Kim.

"Are you alright?" Will asked, concern in his voice. He hadn't even heard her light a cigarette which she never fails to do for a phone call.

"No."

"What is it?"

"Zach's in his room and won't talk to me" she whispered "I think I'm going crazy."

"Oh God" Will said "Have you two been to Backstreet?"

"No, we've been in Athens all night. We did acid".

"Oh. You know I'm terrified of that stuff. I don't know how it makes you feel and I don't want to know. Oh wait. You know Patricia did it once about ten years ago and she just showed up at my house randomly. I don't think she knew who she was."

"I don't know—" Kim whispered, sounding genuinely frightened. Will understood being in your own head and being frightened of what you saw.

Will tried a trick Rebecca had taught him once – just start chatting about whatever crosses your mind until the person calms down.

"Well" he said "If this is anything like I felt at the Looming that night then you'll be fine. I know you're better about getting your mind off of something than I am."

"What do I do?" she said.

"Well, what are you doing now?"

"I'm in Zach's living room."

"Turn the T.V. on" Will said. "Maybe that'll help."

He heard the phone shuffling as she moved around.

Kim whispered "Oh God. It's so bright. Hold on."

Will heard her lay the phone down and it was a couple of minutes before she came back.

"Okay" she said. "I went out to my car to get my sunglasses."

"I was starting to get worried" Will said "What's on T.V.?"

"Infomercial."

"Turn the channel. That could make a sober person spiral down."

"Zach has the Brady Bunch movie."

"Perfect" Will said. "Harmless. That lady from Cheers. RuPaul. Should be safe in there for a while."

"Are you going to be okay?" he said "I should get back to the computer room."

"I think so" Kim said, sounding unsure.

"Call me back if it gets too bad" Will said.

Kim called back about an hour later. Zach had finally come back from his own bad acid ledge and cracked up at the site of her in his living room wearing sunglasses and watching the Brady Bunch Movie.

"We're feeling so much better" Kim said. "I can't thank you enough Will".

Will laughed. "It was nothing. Now I'm glad I'm at work instead of out."

The rest of the night, while there were no jobs to run and Will's only task was to be an awake, warm body in a chair, he and his co-worker watched *The Matrix* on a T.V. that Sue had brought into the data center just for the night. Throughout the night Will's mind went back to the things he'd been doing at the Looming, and how he'd feel if he were ever told he had H.I.V. - how the body he'd been working so hard on might begin to break down. He swore to himself he'd get tested that very week and if he found out he was negative, then he'd have to go a different way.

He did get tested that week and he was still negative.

Chapter Twenty-One

On rare occasions when Will saw Greg out on a weeknight, he noticed Greg talking to someone named Eddie. Eddie was tall, in his mid forties, and had thick brown hair. He looked to Will like the definitive coach or dad type. Eddie had hit on Will before but Will hadn't thought about it. Now that Will saw Eddie talking to Greg, he decided to exploit that first encounter when Eddie had approached him. The next time Will saw Eddie out, he picked him up.

Will went out with Eddie a couple of times and he introduced Will to coke and taught him how to buy it from the bartenders at the Metro. Will couldn't get his mouth around Eddie's dick and by some fluke of gay genetics, Will wasn't into big dicks. Nor did he like someone pushing him down to his knees aggressively and demanding he put his mouth around it. Will was, however, struck at how Eddie, a nurse, examined his dick thoroughly in the bright fluorescent bathroom light of his apartment before giving Will head. Will was impressed that Eddie was unapologetic for his germaphobe tendencies. Like Andrew, Will and Eddie quickly moved along that age old, well worn trail between gay pick up and friendship.

It seemed that Will was getting what he wanted, in several ways. He wanted to go back to Inform – he got it. He wanted a body like Andrew's – he got it. He wanted to make a friend that might help him penetrate Greg's circle and hopefully ingratiate himself with someone in it who might soften Greg towards him – and so far he had that too. The more Greg got to the things he wanted, the more he convinced himself that would be one of those things. The more Will got what he wanted, the more of a jaunty kind of strut appeared in his now sturdy, man-boy gait.

Kim kept after Will to apply for a passport, knowing it could take six weeks to process. Will was always down to the wire when it came to money and time. His right arm was full of bruises where Kim had pinched him whenever she'd asked him in person if he'd remembered to go apply. He was certain his eardrums were bruised from her reminders over the phone.

In early February, Will finally went to the post office in Buckhead, had his photo taken, and applied for a passport. It arrived in the mail just days before their trip.

In early March, Will visited friends with Kevin who lived in a small one bedroom apartment in an older, brick apartment building nestled among large, craftsman style bungalows shaded by huge canopies of old trees whose roots grew through the hexagonally shaped stones in the sidewalks. During their visit, Will mentally arranged his own furniture in their apartment which was only two blocks from Piedmont Park. Will imagined no longer jogging at Chastain Park to build a better body in favor of jogging at Piedmont Park with that better body.

The next day, Monday, Will called to inquire about the apartments. One would be available just seven days after he, Kim, Zach and Lucas (a friend of Kim's) were to return from Europe. On Tuesday, Will was shown an empty apartment like the one that would be vacant, paid a deposit and signed a lease. He told Brandon that he was moving out at the end their lease which coincided with the move-in date. Brandon had settled into Atlanta, made a name for himself at work, and found a not only cute, but genuinely nice boyfriend all in just a little over a year's time. Will respected what Brandon had done and Brandon was too polite to say to Will "do you think of anything besides protein powder and Greg?"

*

Friday nights, when his work week started, were the only nights that Will and Herb, the one who'd first told him about the job in operations, had overlapping schedules. Herb was finishing up his work week and his three PM to eleven PM shift while Will poured over e-mails from the previous week. Herb caught Will up on the politics that Will was glad to have missed. Herb also told Will about Sue's almost daily drama. Will was glad to know that he wasn't the only one who's work life Sue sought to complicate. Herb and Mark, the second shift manager, saw through Sue as well. Herb told Will that he'd been thinking of moving to first shift to fill the job of Sue's best friend and right hand man, who Sue had recently fired presumably because of a personal squabble, but it seemed no one knew for sure. Will told Mark and Sue that if Herb went to first shift he'd very much like to have Herb's open spot on second shift. Soon, plans were made for Herb to go to first shift and for Will to go to second shift as soon as Will returned from Europe.

It did seem that Will was getting everything he wanted, and now it looked like he would have the normal sleep schedule he'd been missing as well.

Like the overlap with Herb's Monday through Friday schedule, there was a small overlap with Larry's schedule as well. His work week began on Sunday nights at eleven, so Will worked with him for eight hours once a week. Sunday nights were slow with only a few jobs running. Will sat in a desk that was in the back and out of Larry's sight. It felt to both like a mutually beneficial arrangement.

Larry napped every Sunday night between two A.M. and four A.M. On one of those Sunday nights, or Monday mornings rather, during Larry's regularly scheduled naptime, Will heard an odd, clicking noise coming from the office Larry sat in. When Will walked by later, he saw Vince inside, his cheap sock tucked inside his cheap shoe, oversized nail clippers in hand, clipping his long yellow toe nails. It was a sight that Will wished he could erase from his memory immediately.

Will liked to take short, five to ten minute breaks, in the twelfth floor TV Lounge which was behind the aquarium at the far end of the larger lounge with the pool table, bar stools and exercise room that Will still used on weeknights. Will loved catching part of the X File reruns in the dead of night, periodically staring down at steam blowing up through grates on the sides of Peachtree Center Avenue and swirling as it collided with the cold air above the street. It was one of the things Will liked about his shift and the periodic visits to the TV Lounge broke up the monotony of twelve hours in one room. On this night, Larry appeared in the doorway, his voice booming, and startled Will.

"So Will, do you think you can just come in here and take a break whenever you feel like it?" Larry's voice was mocking.

Will ignored Larry and Larry stood still. Larry stared at Will until Will finally stood up and left. Will, furious, breathed deeply on the elevator ride back to eleven. Within five minutes, Larry was standing in front of Will's desk.

"Will" Larry said, drawing his name out condescendingly "I need to see you in my office."

Larry had a way of, when he wanted to, speaking someone's name in such a way that screamed "who do you think you are? I'm going to cut you down to size". He hadn't said Will's name like that since training and the sound of it instantly stoked Will's already incensed anger.

Will didn't correct him by telling him it wasn't *his* office.

In the office, sitting across from Will, Larry said "Will, we get one thirty minute lunch and two fifteen minute breaks."

Will didn't abuse this and he took several small five to ten minute breaks through the long twelve hour shift.

"Since you don't seem to understand this, it's my job to tell you about yourself."

"No Larry, it's not."

Will kept Larry's gaze locked. A minute passed before Larry spoke again.

"What did you just say?"

"Will said "no it's not."

"Well, I believe it is."

Will said "it is your job, as a supervisor, to tell me about my job. And how to do it. And answer any questions I might have. But you will *never* tell me about my *self*."

Will kept Larry's eyes locked and did not look away. To Will, it felt like there was no black or white skin, no gay or straight, no boss or employee. Only two eyes locked between right and wrong.

Larry quietly said "that's all. You can go back to your desk."

That was the last time Larry hassled Will. He settled back into his nap time routine, leaving Will free to read whatever book he'd brought to work.

Will began reading Bill Phillip's *Body for Life,* and he was convinced that if he followed the step by step instructions and illustrations, he could make a remarkable transformation of his own. He'd not been able to get out of anyone exactly *how* they'd built their incredible bodies because when they tried to explain they assumed Will knew more than he did. He had no idea what a row or a military press was. Bill Phillips, in his book, broke it all down.

"I can do this", Will said to himself, under his breath and sitting alone at the desk in the back. But like the book says, if you're not getting the proper amount of rest at night, the exercise is almost pointless. Will planned to begin *Body for Life* as soon as he returned from Europe when he was to begin his new Monday through Friday, three to eleven shift.

Every time he thought of the trip, the new apartment and his new work hours, he almost forgot how excited he was to go to Europe – he was so excited about what awaited when he returned. Will was about to go overseas for the first time, live alone for the first time, and embark on a physical transformation that he knew in his gut he would be successful at. Everything was going his way and because of that, he also convinced himself he could get Greg too.

As the end of March drew near, during those few hours that Will and Herb worked together on Friday nights, Herb began making comments to Will that rubbed him the wrong way.

'I'm not so sure I want to go to first shift" Herb said, almost teasingly "second shift is so much quieter."

"Why don't you come over here, get under the table, and suck my dick."

The first comment bothered Will so much, he barely wondered why the second, so out of left field it was barely comprehensible, comment came about.

Sue sometimes dialed into the computer room from home on Saturdays or Sundays to check in and say hello. She did this because with staggered schedules, weeks could go by when she had no face time with some employees. She asked Will if he was excited about his trip and the new shift he would start when he returned.

Will said "Oh - Herb says he doesn't want to go to first shift now." Will thought of the teasing way Herb had said "he just didn't know if he wanted to go to first shift of not now" as he delivered the news to Helena. Will had a feeling he knew how well that would go over with Sue and he was right. That Friday evening, Herb didn't say one word to Will.

No sooner had Sue fallen into Will's prediction of her reaction with Herb than she turned her tactics back on Will. Though his vacation time for the upcoming trip had been scheduled and approved months in advance, Sue feigned that she'd thought he was due back on Monday and said he'd need to deduct those hours if he wanted the day off. Will told Ruth about it and again, HR intervened. They explained to Sue that if he had not been going on vacation but rather working his regular Friday, Saturday, and Sunday week, they wouldn't have expected him to finish a shift on Monday at seven am and then be back at work at three pm the same day to start his new hours. Monday was free and clear – not necessary to use personal time. Sue gritted her teeth again as she told Will the good news.

Chapter Twenty-Two

The only thing Rebecca asked Will to bring her back from Europe was recordings of the sounds he heard – street noise, crowded restaurants and trains. The flight was scheduled to leave early on a Wednesday morning. Will cabbed to the nearby MARTA station in the middle of the night and stood waiting with a huge backpack that Devin had loaned him as well as his regular suitcase and travel bag. He was the only one in the MARTA station and when a security guard came along Will asked when the next train would be by.

"They don't start til four" he said.

Like the trip to Los Angeles the year before, Will began a trip wasting money because of a lack of planning. He grabbed a cab and paid twenty bucks for a ride to the airport. He found that Kim, Zach and Lucas had made the same assumption and were starting the same way.

"We've been trying to call you" Zach said while Kim quickly herded everyone toward an escalator.

"I thought she was gonna get me" Will whispered to Zach.

Zach laughed and said "she's already worried we're gonna miss the flight even though we're twelve hours early."

"What are you two talking about back there?" Kim interrupted.

"Hi Lucas."

"Hi Will."

Lucas was quiet and unassuming while the other three, even at the early hour, began verbally bouncing off of each another.

Kim pinched Will's still bruised arm. "I was pissed when we got here and then couldn't get you on the phone. I told Zach if you didn't show up we'd get on the plane without you. You better not have been somewhere having sex with somebody."

Walking briskly now with the others, Will said "I didn't bring my cell phone because I thought it'd be useless where we're going and I didn't realize MARTA doesn't start running until four."

It was around ten or so when the four of them landed at Newark. Zach, who still stuck militantly with his vegan diet and workout routine, was already struggling with his bags. Will was surprised and it occurred to him that Zach had inspired him, with his biceps and abs, to begin his own workout routine. Will wanted to catch up to Zach and because they were friends, the feeling of readily handling the huge backpack that Devin had loaned him along with his regular suitcase and travel bag while Zach struggled and periodically put his bags down to repack and shift weight – it made Will's own success taste less sweet. He didn't get it and Lucas noticed.

"They got pretty drunk last night" Lucas quietly, and with a note of concern, confided to Will.

It was late in the afternoon when they flew out of Newark on a large Boeing with a row of seats on either side of the airplane and one down the middle. Between movies, overhead screens displayed a map with a small white airplane, miles already travelled, and miles still to go. It quickly grew dark outside and it wasn't long before Will felt relaxed and fell into rhythm with the reassuring hum of the engines and the steady confidence of the stewardesses. Those things, combined with the overhead reading lights, glowing lights that lit the aisles, periodic dings over speakers and whispers of passengers, was as much, if not more, as comforting to Will as a warm fire in a fireplace. Night time flights were Will's favorite.

The uneventful six hour flight to London was Will's longest flight. When they all got to Heathrow and he tried to buy a ticket for the tube with the credit card his mom sent with him, the card was rejected because Will's name wasn't printed on it. Everyone was tired and Kim gave Will a look. Lucas stepped in and bought Will's ticket, telling him they could balance it later on the card.

"Will, how do you always get in these messes?"

"Will, how do you always luck your way out of these messes?" Kim laughed, exhausted.

Readily, Will balanced Devin's backpack, his own suitcase in one hand, and travel bag in the other. He stood straight and carried the load with apparent ease while Zach heaved and dragged his unorganized luggage around, spilling on escalators and stairways as they went. Zach, with his big guns and six pack, had inspired Will the just the year before. Will didn't understand what was going on with Zach now. Will had wanted to catch up to Zach and walk beside him – not trip over him.

At King's Cross, at the flat Kim had reserved, their rooms were simple and clean. On their budgets, they'd all expected hostel like conditions.

"Because it's almost the end of off season" Kim explained, "everything, including plane tickets, will cost more in just a couple of weeks."

Even after the long day of travel, Kim and Zach were determined to drink like frat boys.

"Good. Night." Will said, closing his door behind him.

Kim wanted to stop by the office and discuss their flat early the next morning. The first thing Will noticed was how soft spoken the locals were. He loved it. For once, everyone around him spoke at a volume he could relate to and he didn't feel like he was mumbling.

Kim came back with the news that they'd all been moved to another flat on the same street. This one had two bedrooms – one with three beds and one with one bed. Will would be getting his own room and all at the same cost – as if by magic. And Will believed it.

Kim and Zach spent copious amounts at the Diesel and Paul Frank stores in Picadilly Circus while Lucas and Will perused items neither of them wanted even if they could buy them.

"Don't forget you're gonna have to carry all that stuff home" Lucas quietly advised Kim. Kim and Zach looked at each other with "like that's going to stop me" expressions.

"We know" Zach said, laughing.

Lucas and Will stepped outside and watched the local fashions in motion. Most everyone wore black clothing on slender bodies that glided hastily and confidently among architecture that was in itself a feast for eyes that had seen too many streets lined with stucco strip malls and asphalt parking pads. Like prisoners who after years forget there are worlds made of anything but cinder block, Lucas and Will, with their eyes, devoured even the most seemingly insignificant moments, exchanges, and daily routines that took place all around them. Moments in time, soon forgotten by those doing nothing unusual, etched into Lucas's and Will's minds forever simply because those moments were new and fresh and everywhere for them to lap up. They were sitting in the middle of a magazine ad, swirling all around them, while Kim and Zach fetched components of it to live their lives in.

At dinner, Will checked to make sure the credit card would be accepted. He bought Lucas's meal, paying him back for the train ticket the night before. Lucas, quiet and gracious, said he'd go along with Will like that for the duration.

The subject of Will's high maintenance was quickly forgotten as a waiter approached. Still determined to carry on his vegan diet, Zach and the waiter searched the menu for something he could eat.

On the way back to their flat, Will saw two guys wearing skimpy clothes disappear into a bar just two blocks away. Back at the flat, he looked in his guide to gay Europe and found that their flat was just two blocks from London's version of the Manhole. He knew it would push Kim to madness. And he planned to go.

He thought about Kim and Zach at Piccadilly Circus, buying clothes, and "coveting what you see every day". He'd done it too, he realized. He'd turned himself into one of those Heretic guys, dressed in skimpy clothes, looking like an easy trick.

While Zach and Kim rooted through their designer loot (everyone predicted Zach would grow tired of his and either give it away or throw it away in a year's time) and Lucas kept them company, Will napped. He feigned sleep deprivation while the others got ready for dinner. After everyone left, Will took his time with a tub bath. He sat in the bath tub, in the middle of the room, marveling that it was in the middle of the room – and that hot water came from one spout and cold water came out of another.

Relaxed and clean, Will walked to the bar and ordered a drink. He smiled when he saw poppers prominently displayed behind the bartender rather than hidden in a drawer where they would be pulled out if someone asked for video head cleaner. A sign that read *Beware of Pick Pockets* was prominently displayed behind the bar as well.

King's Cross didn't make Will want to hide his money and stay near people like he did when walking through Atlanta's homeless panhandlers at night, but he did sense that the patrons I this particular bar didn't have much money. He noticed that these British boys' shoes, and their other clothes, were very worn. At the bar, they carefully counted out every coin as if each drink were the last one they could afford. Will felt like an ass for having sixty euros in his pocket.

The London version of The Manhole made Will feel at ease away from home. He relaxed, enjoyed a drink, and watched. Gay boys snorted their poppers unapologetically on the dance floor and seemed to almost brawl with each other – which Will found to be a turn on. He wanted a reprieve from the self imposed prison of his baseball cap, a blaring notification that he was American. He wouldn't take it off.

Will half expected to get his ass kissed like he now did at bars at home, but not so. It seemed he was as invisible as he'd felt in Atlanta just two years before until a handsome man approached him on the dance floor. After a minute or so, the guy said to Will "It' so loud in here. I can't hear you. Let's get down a little lower, closer to the floor so I can hear you."

Will fell for it and the guy chatted with him like that for a few minutes, low and awkward. Will left shortly afterward and back at the flat, as he undressed, his sixty euros was of course gone.

Kim wasn't angry that Will had gone to the gay bar and said she'd known what he was up to. She said she *would* be angry if he didn't go to a party they'd seen advertised on the way to dinner.

"There is no ecstasy like the ecstasy you can get here" Kim and Zach both said.

Aggravating Kim even further, Will declined the party. The promise of potent ecstasy would have tempted him at home, but he didn't want to try a new drug while so far away from home. At times he was reckless. At other times, he held on tight. It didn't make sense to Kim and Zach who felt like Will had no interest in connecting and sharing the experience of the trip. Kim's anger grew though she kept it just beneath the surface.

The next night, while Kim, Zach and Lucas were at a party in London enjoying ecstasy that people back home rave about, Will went back to the club a block away. He got picked up by a cockney accented Brit who hassled the cab driver on the way back to his small apartment several blocks away. Will tried to pay close attention to street markers while the guy yelled at the cab driver about the fare.

The guy, cute and lean with a sense of humor that tempered his anger, talked about Americans and how they always had the Brits' backs.

"Fuck me ass mate" the guy said, abruptly changing the subject.

His apartment was simple and neat and his black combat boots stayed in a corner as he sat on top of Will's unwrapped dick.

The guy talked excitedly about showing Will around the bathhouse the next day. Will didn't tell him it would be his first trip to any bathhouse and that he had no plans to go with him. If Kim had been aggravated at Will's going to the gay bar instead of taking X with her, Zach, and Lucas - Will imagined what might happen if he spent their last day in London at a bathhouse with someone he'd picked up the night before.

Later, in the early morning hours, Will left the guy sleeping peacefully on his twin size mattress, on the floor in the corner of his room, while he dressed quietly, wrote him a short thank you, and slipped out.

The sun was coming up as Will walked in the direction he hoped would take him back to their flat. He looked for the street markers he'd taken note of earlier but saw none. He saw lawn ornaments and children's toys outside of quaint homes where he imagined that later in the morning pale, soft spoken women would be smoking, watching British T.V. and complaining about parliament in that quiet, sing-song lull he'd grown so fond of. He saw a cat in someone's yard and slowed to say hello and give it a pat but it wouldn't go near him. When he saw a marker he recognized, he began to walk faster down the street so far away from home in Georgia that was still asleep on what was becoming a bright, sunny Sunday morning just like the one when they'd taken the watermelon to Daniel. He knew he'd climbed all the way to two again on the rule of four sexual risks and this time without even taking ecstasy. He'd stuck his dick in a guy who never asked for a condom and who also frequented the local bathhouse. Will began to jog, the taps from his boots growing louder on the street pavement. He saw the next marker that he recognized, and his jog turned easily into a run that barely winded his healthiest ever body. When he saw what he recognized as their street, he sprinted as fast as he could before he stopped just outside the door, panting healthily and quietly, and let himself in with the stealth of a seasoned thief.

The four of them spent Sunday doing tourist things - Buckhingham Palace, Big Ben, London Bridge.

Monday was dreary and overcast. A perfect London day, Will thought. Zach urged him to throw out the poppers he'd bought at the club just before boarding the train to Paris. Zach feared they'd all be thrown off the train if Will were caught with them. He tossed the little brown bottle into a garbage can and the four of them, with their headphones, settled into their own worlds on the way to Paris.

The English country side zoomed past in streaks as Will meticulously recorded figures in his little notebook. He'd been frugal except for the sixty euros that were stolen from him at the gay bar and he was caught up with paying Lucas back with dinners. He had a feeling that merchants in Paris would be even more of a pain in the ass about the credit card.

At the train station in Paris, a very nice fellow approached Will, Zach, Kim and Lucas and generously offered to sell them tickets for the metro. All four looked at each other with "wow, can you believe our luck" expressions. They could barely understand the fellow but they thought he said that tickets for the train were sold out. They each paid him one hundred euros for a ticket and thanked him profusely. The bored attendant at the metro didn't even look the four of them in the eye as he explained that the tickets they were attempting to use were expired. The generous man who they'd bought the tickets from was nowhere in sight. The four of them looked at each other with "did we really just fall for that" expressions that, almost as if choreographed, seemed to register all at once "that was one hundred euros."

Tired, and now deflated, they all found a vendor and paid twenty euros a piece for new tickets.

Their cheap hotel in Paris was near the Bastille and to them, even the Bastille was eye pleasing architecture. The walls and floors of the hotel were paper thin and as if by magic, again, the layout of the rooms was the same – three to one room and one for Will - all for the same price. Still, when Kim and Zach decided to drink and scream all night, banging on Will's door periodically and demanding that he join them, they were met with acerbic irritation. When Kim used a transparent excuse of needing a towel at three A.M., Will opened his door and threw a towel in her face – only instead of her face, the angrily tossed towel flew directly into Kim's always running video camera. A moment in time, captured forever.

The next day they visited Pere LaChaise Cemetary, Will felt like the inhabitants of the cemetery may have been the only Parisians who didn't look down on him. Bill took photos of the graves of Oscar Wilde and Jim Morrison. Will soaked up the quiet and the space, and tried to pet the stray cats that slinked around and hid behind tombstones. Perhaps the calmness of the cemetery confirmed what he already knew – it was time for some alone time.

Will bailed on everyone again as they were ready to go over to The Louvre. He was tired and he felt filthy. All his clothes had been worn at least once and travel had made them feel like they've been worn much longer.

Will took all of his clothes to a Laundromat near their hotel and figured out how to do his laundry with the French dials and detergents. The peace and solitude he found in the empty French Laundromat, not unlike Laundromats at home where the sound of a washing machine or dryer can lull someone into a sense of security that even smells good, the only difference being the sing songy, seemingly stress free French voices coming through the television speaker. Will flipped through French entertainment rags that were scattered about, looking for French words he recognized and laughing at the photos that, to him, said no matter what the language, sensationalism is universal in it's instant gratification.

No one came in the Laundromat while Will took his time folding his clothes and placing them neatly back into the backpack. The quietness of the cemetery followed by the solitude and mundane activity recharged Will in ways he didn't realize he needed to be recharged.

Back in his room, he took a delicious afternoon nap, satisfied his clothes were fresh and clean, while his recorder, next to the TV, recorded a French soap opera for Rebecca.

When Will met the others downstairs later, he expected Kim to be angry. Instead, she smiled.

"You look refreshed" she said. "And guess what."

Zach and Lucas looked at him, both anxious for Kim to finish.

"You lucked out again. The Louvre is closed on Tuesdays." Her voice sounded sing songy like the voices on the TV in the Laundromat. "I have to admit I wish we'd checked somehow. Now I wish I had a backpack full of clean clothes." She shook her head and laughed. "You're such a brat."

Will, Lucas with his always present camera, Kim and Zach walked easily along Parisian streets while the sun set with no real plan of where to have dinner. Since none of them were fluent in even reading French, they decided to forego the vegetarian and vegan search and just look for an inviting place.

They happened upon a tiny restaurant delivered pizza. It was operated by two gorgeous men who looked to be in their late twenties or early thirties. One of the presumable owners confidently cooked while the other came and went on his bicycle, an order to deliver as he left and a new one as he left again, the bell on the door to the restaurant ringing and clanking against the door as he came and went. Will got caught up in their fluent pas de das while the four of them sat at a small, candle lit table in the dim little restaurant, looking out of the window and into the night. Will gathered from the body language of the two owners that they must be lovers and he silently prayed that one day he would have what they did – a missing puzzle piece that would be his other half. He hoped that if he ever found him, they would work in harmony so beautifully as these two.

The next day, Wednesday, Will, Zach, Kim and Lucas all boarded a train headed for Amsterdam. Will went through receipts and recorded purchases in his notebook. The frugality was unfamiliar to him. Even after being swindled out of one hundred euros upon first arriving in Paris, he felt good about the amount he'd spent, and better about the amount he had not spent. When finished and looked up, Kim, Zach, and Lucas were wearing headphones, watching France, with all of it's beautiful treasures, zoom past.

When they stepped off the train in Amsterdam, It was that time of day when artificial lights pop against the dusk sky as the sun is setting. With renewed excitement, easily strolled past the hustle and bustle of street vendors. They hadn't been out of Central Station long when someone approached them and asked if they wanted to buy ecstasy.

"Will, are you sure you don't want to change your mind?" Zach asked, laughing.

They walked along the canal and up the hill toward their cheap hotel. It was dark when they began climbing, luggage in two, the tall, steep stairway.

As if by magic, again, the rooms were three to one and one for Will. His was on a separate floor.

Kim grew concerned they may have found themselves in a bad section of Amsterdam since the hotel was further up the hill than she had realized. None of them had seen such a steep and narrow staircase as the one leading up to their rooms.

"Will, I know you'll have to have a shower so come knock on our door when you're finished" Kim said as they stopped at the door to their room.

The room was small with thin paneling. A thin tin ashtray and a bowl of fruit sat on top of a small Formica table next to the window. Will relished the warm shower and alone time, then dressed quickly. He knew the others were excited to smoke pot in a public coffeehouse and after, as they all strolled along in the Red Light district, their trashy jokes lingered in the air, made heavy at the sight of girls standing in windows that were really lit with red lights. They were for sale and when they looked in your eyes, you knew it was real.

The next night, after dinner and marijuana, Will said he wanted to go explore some gay bars. He went to the Eagle first and then to a bar across the street where he saw a man wearing a gas mask cruising in a darkened room down below. Since it was Thursday and still early, both bars were mostly empty.

On Friday night Will went back to The Eagle and picked up a cute blond guy who lived just a couple of blocks away. On the exterior, the apartment seemed crammed and Will expected it to be tiny. Inside, it was a different world – large fresh and modern. When Will had enough of observing the guy's apartment, he pulled the guy off him and told him he was ready to leave.

Will went to a bar called the Cockring where he saw a bartender use a helium machine to fill a balloon before handing it to a shirtless patron who breathed from it as he danced. They were called whippets back at home and like poppers, they gave an instant rush. Will thought the others would love it, but a sign at the front said *Men Only.*

Will didn't consider walking back to the hotel alone and late at night. He stopped along the way at a phone booth, where he used a prepaid card his dad sent with him. He talked to Rebecca for almost an hour while people strolled and rode their bikes along the canal. No one seemed to have their guard up, even at the late hour. It was almost two A.M. when Will began sauntering back toward the hotel. He liked this city. There was something about it that reminded him of Athens, Georgia – it felt very innocent, like people were up late simply because they were nocturnal and wanted to socialize.

Further up the hill and closer to their hotel, the couples strolling and holding hands and the people on bicycles seemed far behind him. It got darker and Will heard footsteps on the other side of the street but they weren't just from one person. It sounded like several people - all those sets of footsteps, yet Will didn't see anyone around. The footsteps grew faster and more hurried, and perhaps because they were heard but not seen, Will felt something sinister in the air. He looked again at the other side of the street and saw about ten guys, all watching him and walking parallel to him. He turned his head forward again and pretended not to notice, but the group of guys ran across the street. One of them jumped in front of Will and pushed him. Will tried to walk around but another guy grabbed him from behind and picked him up so his feet were off the ground. He held Will like that while another guy went through Will's jeans pockets.

"Quickly, quickly" Will heard one of them say in a tone was so polite, it struck Will, even amidst what was happening. He felt like a gay being robbed by a brit. None of them ever raised their voices.

Will kicked and twisted until he was free and ran across the street to the front of the hotel. Someone grabbed him again but Will was able to press his finger to the buzzer beside the locked front door. When the attendant looked out from the second floor Will said "Call the police!" The crew of guys started laughing, saying "Call the police!" as they all took off running further up the hill. The one who'd been going through Will pockets turned around and threw Will's bottle of poppers (he'd just bought at the Cockring) at him. A darkly ironic punctuation mark, the bottle of poppers hit Will right in the head, making a thump threw his baseball cap. The attendant let Will in and appeared not to hear as Will relayed his story of what had happened.

The next morning, down in the room with the others, Will told Kim what had happened. Kim's eyes turned huge and she yelled for Lucas and Zach.

"Tell them what you just told me" she said.

"That's exactly the same guys who got us yesterday afternoon!" Lucas said. "We went walking around to take some pictures while you were still napping and those exact same guys came after me and Zach.

"I hid behind a car" Kim interjected, laughing "Big help I was. I hid there watching the whole thing."

"They didn't want my camera" Bill said "they just wanted money."

"Did they get your money?" Will asked.

"It wasn't much. I'm just glad they didn't take my camera."

Zach said "Did they get money from you Will?"

"It was the end of the night" Will said. "I'd spent my cash on drinks and poppers. They didn't like that very much."

"What do you mean 'they didn't like that very much?'" Kim asked. Will made a face.

"They threw my poppers at me as they walked away."

"The bottle hit me right upside the head."

"They hit you in the head with your poppers!" Kim clapped her hands and laughed. "Will Turner, you finally got what you deserved!"

Everyone laughed, including Will.

Kim, forever irritated that she couldn't go in the back to the dance floor at The Manhole on dress code nights, was just as let down when Will told her about the *Men Only* sign at the *Cockring*. Zach was feeling the pull of the gay bars himself, and since Lucas wanted to visit the red light district again, alone, Kim didn't see why she couldn't do whippets on the dance floor at the *Cockring*.

Dressed in a pair of Zach's jeans (as if one hundred and fifty dollar jeans would make anyone look masculine) and one of Will's baseball caps pulled low, a pair of Lucas's work boots and a flannel shirt, Kim walked with Will and Zach down the Canal and to the *Cockring*.

The surly attendant at the entrance saw through the ruse immediately and denied Kim entry. Pouting and arguing did not win him over and he threatened to deny Zach and Will entry as well. Zach and Will walked with Kim back to the hotel and promised to be back early.

Will and Zach shared whippets they'd bought from the bartender until the balloon got away from Will and blew across the dance floor. Panicked, Will chased it down and tried unsuccessfully to resume an incognito position next to Zach.

"That was real masculine Will" Zach said, deadpan. Will instantly felt like a clown, as he often had during his college years when he and Zach were roommates.

At the Eagle, two men sitting on a pool table upstairs tried forcefully to pull Will into a bathroom in the corner as he passed them. He yelled for Zach who was too far way to hear over the music. When the guys realized Will wasn't feigning resistance in this impromptu rape scene, they finally let him pass. Will locked the bathroom door behind him and breathed deeply. He straightened up his ripped jeans and tee shirt. Looking in the mirror, he guessed the hole in the seat of his jeans made the guys think he really would give it up just like that in a bar.

"I'm ready to go back home where you can dress like a slut and not really mean it" Will said to himself before unlocking the bathroom door and opening it just enough to peer out. Satisfied the guys were gone, he walked back to the bar and found Zach.

Back at the hotel, Will and Zach found Kim slumped in the floor with a water bottle cradled to her chest. Will had poured poppers into the water bottle before they left. The sight of Kim, still wearing the man get up, slumped in the floor and high on poppers had Will and Zach laughing so loud it woke Kim up.

"I don't know what you get out of these" she said 'I can't even tell they're doing anything".

"Oh, they're doing something" Zach said. "You just don't know it."

That Sunday evening was their last night in Amsterdam and in Europe. The mood and atmosphere in the cramped pubs felt like Atlanta bars on Sunday nights – one last go round with no expectations before the monotony of the work week begins. That impromptu Sunday evening pub crawl was the most fun Will had with Zach, Kim, and Lucas on their trip – full of light hearted laughter and one liners flying.

That night he lay in the twin size hotel bed with the new memories of their trip swirling around in his head – the pick pocket in London, the rip off artist in Paris, and the muggers in Amsterdam, the beautiful couple in Paris running their little restaurant together, the fights with Kim, *Mind the Gap* and fuck me ass mate, the cats slinking around the cemetery in Paris and the Van Gogh Museum in Amsterdam, the jog back to their flat in London on the Sunday before. He loved their trip but he also loved his home. It wasn't much, but he'd always loved his home base – neat and clean with Betty and Frieda waiting for him. He wanted to go to Raging Burrito with Kevin and hear what deviant things he'd been up to. He couldn't wait to get moved into his new apartment in Midtown and begin *Body for Life* with his new second shift hours and sleep during the night. He wanted to finish building a body that Greg couldn't resist. Why, he did not know. He didn't know anything beyond wanting his own bed and to hear his cats purr.

The next day when they all boarded the plane someone asked Lucas if he'd switch seats with them. Lucas agreed, though he'd be seated separate from Will, Zach and Kim who sat together in a middle row.

About halfway into the flight, over the Atlantic Ocean, the plane bounced with turbulence. Quickly, the turbulence got bumpier and the plane dropped suddenly. Will, having never experienced any turbulence in a flight, thought it felt like an amusement park ride. The three of them held on and heard screams as the lights in the cabin went off and on. The movies on the TVs were replaced with snow. The plane stabilized and a collective sigh was heard throughout. Will, rigid with fear, turned to look at Kim whose eyes were big. Her hands were dug into Zach's upper arm and Zach, still staring forward, didn't move.

Will picked up his fork and started for the first bite of the dinner the stewardess had served before the turbulence began again. Before he could get the fork to his mouth, the turbulence started again – the bumps and tilts and sudden drops. The lights went out again and there was another drop – longer than the last one. Will put his fork down, held on, and silently prayed – or rather demanded. He'd never sent a prayer up that sounded like a demand before.

I'm not finished yet!

The voice in Will's head screamed, and begged, and screamed – repeatedly.

The turbulence continued and finally stopped. A few minutes later, and when Kim's face was no longer buried in Zach's arm, the captain's voice came over the speaker.

"We apologize that we didn't let you know beforehand there may be some bumps along the way because of the weather".

The three of them looked at each other.

Kim said "I thought we were going to die."

Zach said "Did you see that stewardess over there? She fell into someone's lap and couldn't get up. She said she wouldn't fly again."

"Will, your eyes are huge" Kim said, finally letting out a small laugh.

Will could barely speak. He shook his head instead.

Lucas turned around in his seat, found the three of them, and gave a peace sign.

Though the rest of the flight was uneventful, Will was damp with sweat when they landed in New Jersey. He swore he'd never get on another plane.

The flight to Atlanta from New Jersey was smooth. Exhausted, Will unintentionally eyed (from a few rows behind) a fit, muscular young guy in an outer aisle seat. Will tried not to stare, but watched as the guy ate a protein bar and drank a bottled water. Will missed his routine. He looked down at his own arms, and he thought the veins looked less than they had. It had been twelve days since a workout. He couldn't wait to get home and get back to it.

Will thought about what Kim had said. He thought they were going to die too. It somehow made him wish even harder for a second half to run home to and tell them about the horrible thing that had happened - a soul mate. Someone who cared.

Chapter Twenty-Three

Myrtle Street Apartments, built in 1959, is comprised of three red brick buildings nestled among large, well cared for homes in Midtown. The three buildings are in a U shape like Will's apartment in Buckhead. The building Will moved into comprised the middle of the U with the other two buildings on either side of his. Instead of backing up to traffic-choked Roswell Road, Myrtle Street Apartments sat on a quiet street where the branches of large trees canopied the sidewalk that ran around the buildings. Instead of the sounds of traffic and car horns, Will could hear bird's chirping and an occasional car or jogger pass so he kept his living room windows open often where Betty and Frieda lay perched on top of his sofa, bird watching. He'd sometimes hear a loud thump and knew that Frieda had momentarily though she could jump threw the screen and out to a bird that she'd been watching intently, having not moved herself for several minutes.

Will's one bedroom apartment was less than seven hundred square feet accessible by a front door facing Eighth Street and a mostly glass door in the kitchen facing the parking lot. The living room and adjoining bedroom faced Eighth Street and the bathroom and kitchen faced the parking lot. Piedmont Park was two blocks away and Marquis One Tower, where he worked, was less than two miles away in the opposite direction. To Will, the set up was unbeatable.

On the first day at his new apartment, Will stood in the corner of the living room beside the front door and surveyed the unpacking he still had to do. Exhausted, he slid down a corner between two walls and sat on the floor. Betty and Fried walked over to him, purring. Frieda got in his lap, as she often did when he only intended to sit for a minute. He began petting her and was instantly lulled into reverie.

"What will happen within these walls?" the thought, the not knowing, and the positive momentum he'd been gaining, made him feel like he couldn't wait to find out.

Kim told Devin about Will's plans to begin a more serious weight lifting routine. Devin offered to sell Will his weight bench and weights which he said had sat untouched in his parent's basement for years.

Will spent his afternoons lifting weights with Devin's weight set and carefully following the illustrations in *Body for Life* which lay open on his bed as he worked out. Now that he was confident in his physicality, Will didn't just exercise - he worked out.

He printed the meal plans and exercise routines at work along with the daily worksheets.

"Will's in there documenting away at something" Derek said that Friday evening as it was just his co-worker Barbara. It was just be the three of them for the rest of the evening. Derek and Barbara had been in the Jetson's Hallways with it's shiny black tiled floor, talking and watching Will through the round glass panes that had the effect of making the small hallway seem like a fishbowl instead of a data center.

"What's all this you've been copying, Will?" Derek asked in a jovial tone.

Will was too embarrassed to show them.

"Just some stuff" he said, not realizing that any kind of secret documenting, at the workplace, might raise eyebrows.

"Did you hear that Barbara?"

Derek liked to joke. Especially on the Friday night home stretch. Barbara was Will's replacement for the weekend shift and at seven P.M., her workweek had just begun. While she went through hundreds of e-mails that had accumulated Monday through Friday, like Will had done, Derek and Will wound it down and took on the relaxed vibe that the rest of the world had been enjoying since about lunch time.

When Barbara wasn't around, on weeknights, Derek would tell Will regularly how much money he'd made during the eighties and into the nineties.

"Hand over fist, Will. Hand over fist" he'd say. "I made all this money ya see, but I spent it."

"You know I like the ladies Will" Derek would say, shaking his head. "Dang I wish I'd saved some of that money".

Will nodded politely while Derek tried to impart his experience. Derek could see that Will, who had the illusion of immortality normally reserved for teenagers, was anxious to get back to the book he was reading. Derek didn't ever take it personally and laughed a warm, defeated laugh.

"I know Will, you can't wait to get out on that street."

Derek shook his head and laughed some more, rolling backwards in his brightly colored office chair (they were all either bright yellow, blue, red or chartreuse) toward his own work station.

"We almost got it made Will" he said, pointing to the simple school room clock that was on a wall in the middle of the data center just outside of Sue's office "we almost got it made."

Will Xeroxed a copy of the *Body-For-Life* diet and kept it on his refrigerator. He mostly stuck to what Bill Phillips suggested for diet as well as exercise, substituting lean meats for vegetarian alternatives. Since he'd lost seven more pounds in Europe, he didn't want to lose any more weight – just add muscle. He drank whey protein religiously between fifteen and forty five minutes after a workout. That was *the window* according to Bill Phillips and the Men's Fitness magazines Will read at Waldenbook's downstairs.

The first thing Will noticed was a vein that ran along his forearm and up his biceps. He could see and feel other results after the first week. His arms felt stiff and rigid as he shaved his face before work. The looked better than ever. He could *feel* the muscles he'd been working for the first time it seemed. Every little movement felt good and reminded him that he was *building his body for life.*

Will slept deeply and restfully, waking every morning feeling more refreshed and energetic than ever. It seemed that every morning, when he looked in the mirror, his body was visibly more muscled.

Since he didn't have the proper equipment for leg exercises, Will paid for a membership at Fitness Factory on Amsterdam Avenue in Midtown. The no frills gym (no sauna, no pool) was close by and since Will worked second shift, working out between nine and three to stay within the parameters of the matinee membership was not only easy, it was his preference.

The gym was mostly empty at one in the afternoon and Will was free to learn about the equipment with no pressure to move on. His confidence grew so that if a machine was in use, he sometimes asked guys much bigger than him if they were almost finished with it. He knew his legs would not get big, but did they ever feel powerful with each step he took. He could *feel* them when he moved, and he loved that new feeling.

As he rode a stationary bicycle one afternoon, Will noticed a man on the leg press at the other end of the gym. Will watched as he lay on his back, looking at himself in the mirror, pressing hundreds of pounds away from him then bringing his knees back up to his chest – each movement showing a little bit more of his powerful thighs where they turned pale above the tan line. Will could have fucked him right there. Will couldn't take his eyes off the guy's thighs as he brought his knees to his chest, revealing the beginnings of his white ass past the tan line. The guy looked Will in the eye, in the mirror. Embarrassed, Will looked away.

The tips of Atlanta's Midtown skyline was visible from the glass kitchen door of Will's apartment. He loved looking out and seeing the tips of skyscrapers illuminating the night sky as he drank one more protein drink before bed each night.

One night after work, Will, in an old pair of faded jeans and a plain white tee shirt (he loved it when he realized that it was the body underneath that made the clothes look better) went by himself for a drink at Burkhart's. He missed Monday nights there as well as the karaoke singers. Will stood just outside the pool room, sipping his drink and watching the Monday night crowd. He leaned against the wall that was between the pool room and the railing that overlooked the downstairs part of the bar where the karaoke singers and drag queens performed. He felt someone's eyes on him and turned to see someone he didn't recognize standing next to him and looking up at him.

"You probably wouldn't even give a guy like me the time of day would you?" the guy asked.

He was short, bald, overweight, and apparently bitter.

Will said "it's almost twelve."

The guy glared at Will and stepped closer.

"You think I'm a toad - don't you."

Will couldn't help but laugh a little.

"I don't even know you —"

The guy didn't let Will finish his sentence before skulking away, stopping just long enough to look back over his shoulder and glare at Will one more time.

Will was both baffled and flattered by the surprise attack by the complete stranger. When he'd begun working out, he did it to get Greg's attention. Now, someone had imploded right in front of him. Not only reassuring Will he was going in the right direction, the man's bitter comments satisfied, at least for the moment, Will's need to be objectified. Compliments, no matter how sincere, do not actualize someone's fleeting time on a pedestal as powerfully and assuredly as jealousy.

Will almost felt bad for the man, but then reasoned that nothing was stopping him from picking up a book and buying himself a weight set.

"If someone isn't making the most of their own body, why should it be my problem?" Will wondered. "And if someone's not making the most of their own body, why would they expect me to share mine with them. I didn't expect to get to touch one until I had one." Will was sure this man wouldn't understand that concept and chided himself for wasting so much thought on the guy.

As Will started toward the upstairs bar again, he saw the leg press guy from the gym talking to someone. Leg press guy looked at Will and smiled, not breaking from his conversation. Will made eyes with him while he chatted. Will guessed from the body language it was a friendship like the one he shared with Kevin or Kaleb.

When their conversation was over and the friend left, Will walked over to him. As if on cue, Dolly walked over, her balloon breasts perpetually begging for a needle stick, and said "you two look good together" before rubbing Will's chest and sauntering away in her mile high heels and floor length black dress.

Leg Press Guy's name was Aaron. He revealed nothing about his personality except that he seemed surprised at Will's audacity when he asked him to go home without offering to buy him a drink.

At Will's apartment, both hands around Aaron's round bubble butt and Aaron gripping Will's hard dick, Aaron whispered in Will's ear. "There's my man."

Aaron was reserved with his personality, but he didn't hold back with bedroom talk. Aaron talked dirty and Will liked it. He pulled Will's dick out just in time to keep Will from shooting in his ass. He did the same thing the next morning. Will felt inexperienced, and he didn't mind.

The next time Will saw Aaron out, Aaron pretended he didn't know him.

"Who's that guy you're looking at?" Kevin asked. He and Will were upstairs at Blake's on another Sunday night, having a drink.

"Nobody, I guess."

Kevin said "oh, I'm sorry. You gotta get used to it though. They do it all the time."

Chapter Twenty-Four

It was May before Will Went back to the Looming. He went on a Friday night and sat down in the area with the big screen T.V. He watched porn and waited for his ecstasy to hit. To his left were two guys, probably mid-20's, chatting in a hushed tone while a lean and muscled blond got fucked on the sofa beside them. The blond was the only one naked of the seven or eight who were either stroking themselves or in line to fuck him.

Unaware he was even doing it, Will began stroking himself through his jeans while watching the blond get passed from one guy to the next. The blond smiled at Will, and Will walked over and stood beside the guy who was fucking him. The blond grabbed Will's erection through his jeans and unzipped them.

Will didn't mean to come in his ass, or come as fast as he did. He felt like an inexperienced kid, again, and he was a little embarrassed as he pulled up his jeans. He bent over and whispered in the blond's ear. He said he was sorry for being so quick.

"I liked it that the lean boy in the baseball cap came inside of me so quick. It was hot" the blond said, watching with approval as Will zipped his jeans and fastened his belt.

In the bathroom, eye level with a tarantula that lived in a glass box on a shelf above the toilet, Will didn't take his eyes off of it. He always pee'd right after he stuck his dick in someone's mouth or ass because Rebecca had heard on a radio show (Dr. Drew? Dr. Ruth Westheimer?) that it clears out anything that may have made its way up the urethra. The tarantula didn't move during Will's bathroom visit and if it had of, he would have hurriedly zipped up and rushed out.

Will noticed the blond sitting alone as he walked past. The blond smiled at Will again, and Will sat next to him.

The blond's name was Ben and his light blue eyes and white teeth shown through his dark, golden tan. He asked Will if he'd like a bump.

"Of what?" Will said.

Ben smiled and said "Tina."

"Oh no" Will said.

"You're not on anything?"

"Just X".

"Is that all you do?"

"Yep."

"Really--?"

The blond looked at Will.

"Yep".

Ben smiled at him.

"You're serious?"

"I don't get it" Will said. "Is that really so hard to believe?"

Ben smiled at him again and grabbed him through his jeans.

"Come to the bathroom with me."

Ben pulled on his jeans and led Will to the bathroom he'd just been in, but Will pulled him toward the further one in the corner of the jungle room that was rarely in use. It was bigger and there was not a tarantula in it.

Ben pulled a little vial out of his jeans pocket and said "just a little."

It made that first hit of ecstasy feel like an appetizer.

Ben, in his little convertible, followed Will the short distance to his apartment. Ben pulled off Will's cap and clothes, rubbed his bald head, and smiled at him. They sixty-nined and fucked for hours and Will used the dirty phrases he'd learned from Aaron. They finally took a break as the sun was coming up.

While Ben was in Will's bathroom, Will put his jeans and baseball cap back on. He envied how comfortable Ben was hanging out naked. Will was coming out of his shell, but he wasn't sure about hanging out naked. Ben took out a vial when he got back into Will's bedroom and offered him more meth. When Will said no, Ben insisted.

"You really don't like getting fucked?" he asked Will, as they lay side by side on Will's bed.

"I really don't" Will said, not wanting to reveal that Dr. Newman's surgeries had left him afraid of venturing into that territory.

"Why don't you have a boyfriend?" Ben asked next, lightly running his hand up and down Will's stomach.

"I don't want one".

Ben looked at Will and raised an eyebrow.

"Well I do want one but that's just it – I want just this one. I haven't been able to get him and I don't want anyone else."

"I don't want one either" Ben said "but for different reasons".

They lay still and silent for a few moments longer.

Will said "tell me how you work out."

Ben took a drink from his bottled water.

"My bosses, who I live with, just started a new training program. It's very intense and they've taught me much of the routine."

"What's it called?"

"I'm not sure" Ben said "they have a personal trainer who came up with it and they shared it with me."

Ben ran his fingers up the line that was forming down the middle of Will's chest.

"Have you tried creatine?" Ben asked, nodding toward Will's weight bench.

"No, Will said. I just started *Body for Life* a few weeks ago and I drink whey but not creatine. What is it?"

"It's used primarily by athletes."

"Circuit boys use creatine a lot" Ben said "It fluffs up your muscles."

Ben lightly moved a finger down the vein that ran from Will's bicep down his forearm.

"You've got such great veins. I think you'd like the results you'd get from creatine. It would pump them up even more."

"Do you drink it with your protein?"

"No, you drink it before your workout. You'll get an extra push so you can lift more and you know that pumped feeling you get after a workout? When your muscles still look bigger? That will stay with you. You'll go around looking like you've just worked out, all day long. You have to cycle though. I use creatine for four weeks and then stay off of it for four weeks. If you don't cycle off you'll start holding on to water weight. I know you wouldn't like that any more than I do."

He gave Will a smile and patted his abs.

"You live with your bosses?" Will asked.

"I'm their administrative assistant and yes, I live with them too."

"So you're their houseboy?"

"No, I'm their administrative assistant."

Will said "one time, when I was eighteen, I was very close to moving in with someone who'd rented a house for us in Fort Lauderdale. I would have been his houseboy in return for him paying for my college education."

"What happened?"

"I chickened out" Will said.

"It might have been fun" Ben said. "Imagine - and just imagine because this is just fantasy - that I'm naked under the breakfast table in the mornings while my bosses, fully dressed, sit reading the morning paper while I crawl between them, sucking their dicks."

Will was hard again. They fucked again until afternoon, only stopping because the bed slats came loose and the mattress slid off.

Chapter Twenty-Five

On a Sunday night in early summer, Kim called Will on her drive back from Rome where she'd been visiting her dad. Kim drove a mid nineties navy blue Nissan Pathfinder with thick tires. Kim, with her precision cut bangs, laundry basket in the back of the SUV and brindle Labrador Retriever in the backseat. Kim moved through her days with such determination, one could easily imagine her bouncing over obstacles in her SUV with those thick tires, barely noticing what might have got in her way while smoking a cigarette and absorbed in conversation on her cell phone.

"Kiki (her grandmother) wanted to go to lunch and then I had dinner with dad and his girlfriend. My laundry basket is still in the back of my car where it's been all day."

Will laughed because that laundry basket full of dirty clothes, specifically, jeans that had probably been worn and febreezed each a few times, was always in the back of her SUV.

Will offered the laundry room in his building if she wanted to stop by.

"I was planning to bribe you with a drink at *Blake's* if you'd let me do laundry" Kim said.

Will put on one of his growing number of muscle shirts before Kim showed up.

Walking into Blake's on a packed and festive Sunday night, people Will recognized and others he didn't recognize grabbed his biceps or patted his chest as he and Kim walked by. When they finally got upstairs and found a spot to talk, Kim grabbed his arm.

"Will, make a muscle" She said.

"Will!"

He beamed.

"Well, you do have bragging rights now. You are there. When did this happen? I know you've gotten fit but Will!"

He didn't attempt humility, still beaming.

"Did you see how everyone looked at you when we walked in?" she said, her eyes still big.

"It felt good" he said.

"Have you seen Greg?"

"No. And you know I'm hoping he'll fold when he sees me."

Kim looked at Will with pure empathy that only someone who was putting themselves in the other person's place could feel.

"Will" she said.

He looked at her, questioning.

"I just wish."

He kept looking. Still questioning.

"You're not going to stop are you?"

Kim looked serious.

"No."

"Will. I hate to see you come this far and --. Look how they wanted your attention out there. Isn't that enough?"

"I can't help myself - I just can't" Will said.

"You didn't send him another letter did you?"

"Wellllll."

"Oh God" Kim said, laughing. "Did you bring a copy of it?"

"It was short" Will said "I know what I said."

"Hold on" Kim said "I have to have a cigarette for this one."

"Okay" she said, blowing smoke. "Go ahead."

"It said 'Greg, I live in by myself in midtown now. I'll keep a stash of drugs here just for you. I still want to fuck you three ways from Sunday'."

Kim looked astonished. Finally, she shook her head.

"Only you Will" she said "Do you have drugs for him?"

"No" Will said. I better get some huh!"

They both laughed.

"I really don't think he'll go for it but I guess I should have something around just in case."

Kim shook her head and laughed. Then she got quiet.

"You shouldn't be doing this. I know you want Greg but please be careful."

Kim said "Haven't you been tested like five times this year already?"

"Yeah" Will said "usually after an especially crazy weekend."

"You've been lucky so far."

"I know" Will said.

"And how many letters have you sent him?"

"I don't know. A bunch."

"Will, let me ask you something" Kim said, serious, her gaze intent, holding her cigarette tight and annunciating every word with staccato period.

"How long. After you wake up. Do you start thinking about Greg?"

She turned her head to exhale smoke but didn't look away.

"I can't believe you just asked me that" Will said.

"I'm sorry, I didn't mean—"

"No, no" he said. He looked like he was far away for a second.

"Just this week, I thought of that too. And wished I could do something about it. It's hard to explain.

Kim looked at him. "Go ahead."

"He's in my head within minutes of waking up – every day. I try to steer my mind in a different direction. But imagine a huge, huge piece of metal. Like a water tower I guess. And my mind is a gigantic magnet. I try and try to think of something, *anything* but him. But my mind goes right back like to him, and how to get him to talk to me again. Like the gigantic magnet flying into the water tower and making a loud clank."

"I think we both have some OCD here" Kim said "I know how hard it can be. I like the way you put that by the way."

"Will, do you ever wonder how he feels when he reads these letters from you?"

Will felt like her intense eyes were looking through him. He stumbled for words.

"No, I guess I don't. I just think that eventually something I write in one of them will get to him and he'll soften."

The next week, Devin, who usually didn't chat on the phone, surprised Will by calling him at home one night after work. Devin wanted to tell Will that he and Kim weren't going to be friends anymore. Kim had already told Will she thought this might happen. Will didn't ask Devin any questions.

"Will, I've always enjoyed hanging out with you. You keep everyone laughing. I hope we can still be friends."

That Saturday night, Will and Devin walked along the cement hexagons, with roots in between pushing them up, that were the sidewalk next to Myrtle Street. A person could easily slip in and out of the shadows of the huge old trees and not ever be seen between Will's apartment and Tenth street, if they wanted to. But not in the orange tank top Will wore.

At Blakes, Devin took a long look at Will.

"You look good Will." Devin half laughed. "And that's a gay as hell shirt."

"I'm enjoying the weight set" Will said proudly. They tipped their glasses.

Though Kim had wanted Will to try and find out as much information as possible about why Devin had decided to stop talking to her (though she knew it was about his girlfriend Gina), Will sensed it wasn't the time. It seemed like Devin just wanted to hang out.

By the end of their second drink, Devin said "well, it's almost midnight. Time for me to turn into a pumpkin so you can go out and look for Greg and have lots of gay sex."

"Well, yeah" Will said, smiling.

"Will—" Devin stopped. "be careful. I don't want to end up going to your funeral."

Will met Daniel at the Eagle and Daniel immediately raised an eyebrow at the muscle shirt. He'd been crabby since the weight started coming off and Will had written that off to a little jealousy, maybe. He guessed Daniel might just be competitive. Daniel wouldn't acknowledge the hard work Will had been doing on his body, and attributed the changes to ecstasy. It irritated Will.

"I'm a weekend warrior, at my worst" Will said.

Daniel didn't laugh.

Someone came up to Will and slipped him a card – an invitation to a sex club he'd never been to. "For Masculine Men Only" it read. Daniel took the card from Will, read it, and handed it back to him.

"Well well well."

"Do you think Greg will be at The Manhole tonight?" Daniel asked.

"Probably" Will said "do you want to go over there?"

"Yes. I think it's about time I see what this person looks like."

At The Manhole, Daniel took a walk round to see if he could spot Greg in the Saturday night crowd by Will's description alone. Two shirtless guys, a couple Will had played with at I.T., came over to hug Will as Daniel walked away. Daniel looked back at Will, disapprovingly.

Will stepped outside for some air, hoping to calm down before he said something to Daniel. It was crowded on the deck and Will walked right past Greg and his dealer, Avery. Greg coldly ignored Will and started toward the door that led inside. Avery conspicuously observed Greg's abrupt departure and walked over to Will.

"So you're Will" Avery said, smiling.

Avery was cute with dark hair, intelligent eyes, and a quick wit.

"Yes" he said nervously "I'm Will."

"Didn't Eddie introduce us one night?"

"I think he did" Will said unconvincingly. They both knew he did.

Avery rubbed one of Will's pectorals.

"You're looking good".

"Hey, Greg, get over here" Avery said when Greg peeked back outside. Begrudgingly, Greg walked over to them, looking around but not at Will.

"Greg, do you know Will?" Avery asked, his dark brown eyes gleaming with mischief.

Greg stiffened even more and nodded in Will's direction.

Flatly, Greg said "Will."

Avery looked at them both with feigned confusion, chewing his drink stir. He personified a John Hughes movie character.

"I better get back inside" Will said, ready to end Greg's torture as well as his own.

Daniel saw Will walk inside and walked over to him.

"I think I saw him by the dancefloor. What's your Greg wearing?" Daniel asked.

"I just saw him" Will said "he's outside."

"I guess that's why you look so tense" Daniel said.

Will saw Greg walk inside and unaware, past them on his way to the dance floor. Will grabbed Daniel and said "follow me". They made their way past the growing push and shove Saturday night crowd and to the end of the dance floor. Greg was already behind the wall making out with someone. Will quickly and subtly told Daniel who to look for before walking away.

Back up front, Daniel said "I think you're crazy."

Daniel's usual puppy expression was replaced with fatherly authority. He locked eyes with Will until he turned away. Will kept quiet, not wanting to say something he'd regret.

"Will, I think you're crazy."

After a few moments of awkward silence, Daniel said "I saw people in Los Angeles who'd done so much meth they thought they had bugs crawling on them and they kept reaching around their bodies to slap them off."

Will looked at Daniel with a look that must have been like a teenager who wanted to argue the irrelevant, grasping at straws, last ditch effort reasons he felt he shouldn't be grounded.

"But I don't do meth."

Daniel drew Will in and hugged him. When Will started to break free, Daniel held on a little longer.

"Be careful Will."

Daniel left and Will stood in the corner of the front bar where he'd met Daniel two years, thirty pounds, and a mess of hair ago, thinking he was in love with with a man who would rather make out publicly with a stranger than acknowledge him. Will went looking for Avery and asked him if he had any pills.

Avery said "wait right here" and left Will on the side of the dance floor.

Will stood still in the push and shove crowd, watching everyone dance their jobs, bosses, and cares away. In his head, he tried on Daniel and Devin, knowing they both loved him, and knowing it wouldn't work with either of them. Daniel loved pot, and Devin loved Gina, and Will loved Daniel and Devin both too much to put them at risk for an STD. Will thought "even if it could work with someone who loved me, and wanted me to come in out of this, I'm a risk now. I'm damaged. I have an STD. I'm unlovable. I'm trash."

Avery appeared and put his arms around Will, covertly shoving a pill into his back pocket. Will made his way to a bathroom, waited in line for a private stall, and washed the entire pill down with the rest of his vodka cranberry.

Chapter Twenty-Six

He would be speeding down Horseleg Creek Road in Rome, the pop up headlights on his white Celica spotlighting the prominent homes with lush, green landscapes and rolling hills. He'd get to a curve in the road. Every time. And every time he came to that curve, he'd press the gas and go even faster. As the little white car went flying off the curve and into the darkness, Will would wake up. Every time.

The sight of the rainbow colored Pride banners exhilarated Will, just as they had the year before. Lisa would be there again with Jo, but this time they planned to sleep at Piedmont Park in sleeping bags.

The week before Pride, as Will drove along Myrtle Street on a weekday morning, he saw an old, wooden sewing machine table that someone had thrown on the curb. Will stopped his car, got out to have a look, and found that the table had no sewing machine inside. From the noise and workers, it appeared the 1920's era home was being renovated. Will put the table in his trunk and drove away.

That night at work he thought of colors, or lack of color, in his small kitchen with black and white floor and white walls. The only color was the orange glow of an orange lamp he kept on the counter. You could see it from the parking lot through the mostly glass door – his white kitchen glowing orange like the windows where the hookers stood in Amsterdam.

On his lunch break, Will drove to Home Depot and bought the richest, thickest orange paint he could find. It wasn't fluorescent orange like a pylon but beautiful like – an orange.

The next morning, excited about the discarded table, the first thing Will did was paint a coat of orange paint on the empty sewing machine table. After his workout and shower, and just before work, he added another coat. The next day, he added two more coats of paint. By the end of the week the newly painted sewing machine table was dry. He put his microwave, which was still on top of stacked boxes, on top of it. He did things like that when he lived in Rome and Athens. Will loved taking nothing, and turning it into something.

That Friday night, Will met Kevin at The Eagle. "For just one drink" they always said.

"Rebecca will be here tomorrow so I planned on behaving myself tonight. I don't want to be dragging during her visit" Will said.

"Didn't you say she would be here in the afternoon?" Kevin said.

Will answered with a devilish smile.

"Go find us pills" Kevin said "while I go get another drink. Want one?"

With ease, Will found them both a pill. Kevin left soon after with a bear fuck buddy that showed up.

The Looming wasn't as full and raucous as Will had hoped, but his pill hit him hard. He was just about to give up on the Looming and go over to I.T. when someone grabbed him from behind.

"You're looking good, Will'.

Greg, from behind, wrapped an arm around Will's chest.

Greg led Will to one of the stand alone boxes with the stars and moons cut out. He stood in front of Will, reaching behind to unzip Will's jeans. Greg lubed up Will's dick and slid it in.

"Did you miss that?" Greg asked, over his shoulder.

Will shoved his dick in deeper and said "did you miss *that*?"

Someone tried to come into the box and Greg put his hand up, stopping them. Will lost his hard on.

"Losing it already?" he asked.

"It's just the pill" Will said.

"I have some friends with me who are in town for Pride" Greg said. "Why don't I take them back to my apartment and then come back over to your place for a bit."

Greg followed Will out to his car. Will wrote down his apartment number for Greg.

"Give me about an hour" Greg said.

At his apartment, Will showered and tried to relax, but he was nervous. When Greg got there, smelling like a fresh shower himself, they quickly got into bed. The moment, at the Looming, was gone.

Will and Greg lay side by side on Will's bed. Greg sat up first.

"Give me your phone number" he said, looking Will in the eyes. "I *will* call you."

"Will said "I said I'd have something here for you. But I'm always taking the pills. Or giving them away".

"Will, you think this is all so glamorous. But it's not."

Greg's eyes looked tired. He looked over at Will's weight bench and then back at Will, smiling. He wrapped his hand around Will's bicep.

"Will, you can do whatever you want to do. Don't you see that?"

Greg started to say something else but then stopped. He rubbed his head, frustrated. He turned to Will, his eyes glowering.

"*You. Are so. Stubborn.*

He looked like he could have hit Will.

"Will."

Greg balled his hands into fists and raised one to Will's face. Will didn't flinch and Greg flipped the bill of Will's baseball cap.

Greg laughed a little.

"You know vanity" he said "I know you do, and I know it too."

"Give me your number" Greg said "I will call you".

Will wrote down his number while Greg petted Betty, who sat between them. He gave Greg the piece of paper.

"You have to pay attention Will."

Greg looked Will in the eyes. He was serious.

"Will, you *have got to learn* to pay attention."

Greg stood up and hugged Will for a long time.

"Do you think you can act sensibly this time?"

"Yes" Will said, ashamed of himself and remembering the Pride weekend before.

The next day, or, later the same day really, after a delicious, long, afternoon nap, Will woke up feeling unbelievably refreshed and chipper. Ecstasy can do that sometimes.

It was late afternoon when Rebecca, thinner than he'd seen her since their youth, walked up the front stairs to his apartment, lugging her huge suitcase and endless keys and gadgets dangling from her key ring. Redolent of perfume, her pale skin glowed. Rebecca, sapient, had kept herself out of the sun in high school and beyond. A decade later, her wrinkle free skin glowed with youthfulness. Year after year, she still looked fresh and at thirty, she'd shed the alternative girl image of her college years (dyed black hair, Doc Marten boots and leggings) and seemingly overnight, a physically fit woman had emerged who had advanced in her career and now sported tailored dress pants with heels, shoulder length copper red hair that wisped like only hair that has been doted on with expensive colorings and cuts can wisp although she did it all herself.

Rebecca had, in college, managed to spend tireless hours in a graphic design studio while still, on weekends, drinking and having a good time with her boyfriend and her gay friends, including Will. She could still drink men and women twice her size under the table, often times a pool table, on weekends. She smoked Marlboro Reds because, as she said, a lighter cigarette would necessitate more powerful draws which might result in smile lines.

Rebecca didn't visit without showering Will with gifts. This time, she'd brought Stoli vodka, candles, books and magazines.

"Little Betty" she'd practically sing, hugging Betty close and whispering in her ear "my littlest angellllll." In college, when Will and Rebecca were roommates, Betty had been her cat. When he moved to Atlanta, he left Betty with Rebecca. Betty and Frieda mourned each other so thoroughly (and Betty so vocally) that Will made the one and half hour drive to fetch Betty one night after work. Happily reunited, he didn't try to separate them again.

The only thing Rebecca loved more than mid century modern and fiestaware were gay men. And the feeling was mutual.

"Oh honey, look at that red hair" and "oh honey look at her skin. It's like porcelain." It had been the same in college, Rebecca holding court with her gays and drag queens like she did that Saturday night at Burkharts. The next morning, clothes spilled from Rebeccas suitcase into the living room floor with smells of cologne and soaps filling the air. Betty and Frieda lounged among Rebeccas things while she slept on the sofa.

After showering, Rebecca liked to sit Indian style on the sofa with a glass of water, a cup of coffee, drama TV playing in the background, a small mirror in one hand and lipstick in the other. Bright eyed and now looking fresh but not made up, it would be difficult for one to imagine that just hours before, at he end of the night, last drink and cigarette in hand, she'd said, about someone, "goddam 'em all" in a voice that sounded like a hardened butch prison warden or a two hundred pound chain smoking drag queen.

Rebecca loved treating Will to brunch and when he passed through in the third tight shirt he'd tried on and wasn't sure about complaining of a head ache from the night before, she mock yelled in her drunken sailor voice "Grease! We need brunch. It'll soak up the alcohol!"

At brunch, as they caught up, when Will mentioned throwing Herb under the bus so he could get the shift he wanted or throwing Sue under the bus to HR like he sometimes did, Rebecca would, unsympathetic to anyone else, say "Oh Darlin', I'm sorry you had to go through all of that." If it had been money laundering or fraud, her response would have been the same.

Sunday at one, Will and Rebecca walked to Tenth Street and watched the Parade from the corner of Tenth and Myrtle. Kevin ventured out to join them but soon went back to his apartment, frightened by all the gay pride. Rebecca was inundated with beads, fans, lube, condoms, and other gay pride and she loved it all.

Will scanned the crowd for that turn of the head and sparkle of the earring against the jaw line that he would instantly recognize. It did not appear.

After the parade, Will and Rebecca went back to his apartment for a change of clothes. The heat and humidity would always win, but they battled it fiercely. They freshened up and joined Kevin before walking back over to the park.

Will was struck at how a place where he found solitude on weekday jogs, was now an ocean of people that now seemed vast.

They ran into James, a thin, cute aloof guy who Kevin had known in Rome. After he and Kevin said hello, James pinched Will's nipple and said "you look good." Will had been interested in James, years before, and it was unexpected validation.

"You know him?" Kevin asked afterward.

"He knows him" Rebecca said with an impish grin and laughed. "Why can't you have a thing for him now! He's so cute!"

At the lower part of the field, next to Park Tavern's parking lot, was a grove with shade trees which was heavily occupied by women in wifebeater shirts, spiked hair, and wielding super soakers. These were lesbians.

Jo ran up to Will and wrapped herself around him like he'd seen her do to her friends the year before. Lisa was right behind her, and she lifted Will's obnoxiously tight tee shirt so she could see his abs.

"He loved it. When Lisa complimented Rebecca's svelte figure, Rebecca pointed it back at Will.

Lisa said "I know. Gay guys like to hear it more" and winked at Will.

At the end of the field which is encircled by a track, a stage was set up for The B-52's. Fred Schneider, in his denim Daisy Duke's, camped it up for the Gay Pride festival as he, Kate, Cindy and Keith performed their inimitable songs. Not long into their performance, a muscle boy sitting on his taller muscled boyfriend's shoulders leaned down to Will and said "you can see great from up here." Will shied away, but the guy kept on. He got down low spoke in Will's ear.

"He wants you to" the guy said, smiling.

The taller boyfriend smiled at Will.

The shorter muscle boy slid down and they both introduced themselves. The shorter guy lifted Will up as the taller one bent down so he could climb on his shoulders.

255

Will loved the idea of sitting atop the tall one's shoulders so close to the stage. If Greg were somewhere in the crowd of three hundred thousand, maybe this year it would be him that recognized Will instantly.

When the tall muscle guy stood straight, Will felt dizzy like he might have vertigo. The shorter one knew from Will's expression and said something to his boyfriend, who stood very still and told Will to hold on and breath. Will crouched down, afraid. The tall muscle guy bent over and Will slid off him as Lisa walked over.

"BJ, it's easy. Look."

Lisa jumped on the guy's shoulders and he stood up straight, allowing her to see over the forest of people.

Lisa turned and said "you can do it. You're not going to fall."

Will thought of Jo, running free and loving everyone and how he'd envied her the year before, knowing that would never be him. Will held on tight, to whatever it was that he was holding on to, and he wouldn't get back up on the guy's shoulders. He was afraid to climb up high.

Chapter Twenty-Seven

Devin called Will on Friday nights and sometimes on Saturday nights, and usually between eleven and twelve. He knew Will would be getting dressed to go out. He'd tell Will to be careful.

On a Saturday night at Burkhart's, a bartender who Will recognized but didn't know stepped around from where he'd been working behind the bar. He stood in front of Will, stopping him in his tracks. He grabbed Will's shoulders.

"Slow down" the bartender said, looking Will in the eyes and holding onto him.

Will shook his head. He didn't get it.

The bartender continued to look in Will's eyes. He held onto Will's shoulders.

"Slow. Down." He said again before letting Will pass by.

Over lunch, Eddie asked Will - practically begged Will - to get over Greg.

"He's not all that you think he is" Eddie said. "you should be above this, Will. You're acting desperate."

"What am I doing?"

"You're always out. He knows you're out because he is."

On a Saturday night in late July, Greg watched from the shadows in the back of the Manhole as two muscled guys looked Will over.

"He's hot" one of them said.

"He's too small" the other one said.

The first one kept looking at Will.

"No, he's hot" the guy said. "Look at all the muscle he's packed on that little frame."

The other guy looked Will over again.

"He's too little" the other guy said, irritation growing in his voice.

The guy kept looking at Will until his friend pulled him away to the dance floor.

Greg came over to Will and ran his hand down Will's chest.

"Got any X?"

"No. Yes. Let me go get it."

"No, that's okay" Greg said "if you don't have it with you."

"I'll drive home and get it" Will said.

Greg put his hand up and walked away. Will stomped off and watched the two muscle guys dancing. One eyed Will's crotch while the other ignored him.

Will found Greg behind the wall making out with someone. Will pulled Greg off the guy who stood still, confused, watching as they walked away.

"Let me go get it. I've got it I swear" Will said.

"No" Greg said "I don't need it"

Like Kevin had said on another night, Greg looked he'd been rode hard and hung out to dry. He must have had a fun Friday night, Will thought.

"Give me a ride home" Greg slurred.

The muscle guy that had been watching Will watched on with a confused expression as Will and Greg walked, hand in hand, out the front door.

As Will and Greg got closer to Will's car, Greg stopped in his tracks and shook his head.

"You, you" he said, wagging his finger at Will.

"What?"

"No. I'm not going with you."

"Greg –"

Greg cut Will off and blabbered incoherently.

"Greg, do you really think I'd harm you?" Will said.

On the short drive down Cheshire Bridge Road, Greg erratically twisted in his seat and pulled on the door handle as if he might jump out. Stopped at the next red light, Will said curtly "Greg, there is a cop behind us. I will *not* get a DUI because you're acting crazy. Get normal and stay that way until I get you home."

Greg straightened up and remained calm the rest of the way. In the parking log, he reached over and grabbed Will's hand as he was turning off the ignition.

"Not tonight Will" he said. "it won't be tonight."

"Can't I stay?" Will asked, holding his hand.

"No. This isn't the night."

Will took Greg's hand, pressed his lips to it, and said good night. Will missed the days when he and Greg had first met and "no, you're not coming home with me" meant "I'll put my ass in the air for you." That night, Will wasn't sure Greg could do much beyond pass out. He drove back to his own apartment on Myrtle Street, looked in the little box on top of his stereo, and found a pill.

At six A.M., just after the Looming closed, Will walked outside to his car only to find his keys were locked inside. A man in a bright red, Mercedes convertible who was speeding by slammed the brakes and screeching tires, stopped the car when he saw Will outside of his car.

The guy, who was kind of queeny, pulled his car into the parking lot. He drove slowly across the gravel and stopped beside Will's car. The guy slowly slid his sunglasses down his face and took a long look at Will in his ripped jeans and tee shirt that looked like another layer of skin.

"Goddam" he said "where are you headed?"

At the guy's apartment, they lay in his bed and filled up balloons with whippets and breathed them in. The guy excused himself every few minutes to answer the doorbell.

"It's Sunday morning" Will said in between visits. "Who keeps showing up at your door?"

The doorbell rang again.

"I sell Avon dear", the guy said over his shoulders as he walked away, leaving Will alone in his bedroom with the whippets again. Will noticed what looked like a huge piece of white chalk, illuminated in the morning sun on the bed beside him.

"Oh, that must be coke" Will said to himself, breaking off a chunk and shoving it in his jeans pocket. When the guy realized Will wasn't going to have sex with him no matter how many whippets he gave him or how much coke he offered him, he offered to drive Will home.

"We have to stop at Krispy Kreme first" the guy said.

Will still felt the ecstasy he'd taken the night before as the guy sped along the empty Sunday morning streets in the red Mercedes convertible. The guy, wearing sunglasses, his hand hanging out the side of the car with cash in it, and Will, in his obscenely tight tee shirt, ripped jeans, and eyes bugged in the passenger seat, pulled into the drive thru window at Krispy Kreme.

"Mind holding this?" the guy said, waiting for his change. Will thought the smell of the freshly made donuts was nauseating and he kept that thought hidden behind a poker face.

"Want one?" the guy asked.

"No thanks."

"You don't like Krispy Kremes?"

"I love Kristy Kremes. But they're not on my diet" Will said.

The guy looked Will over again.

"I bet they're not."

The guy dropped Will outside of his apartment and sped down Eighth Street, through the quiet neighborhood, and back into the quiet, empty streets of downtown Atlanta with his dozen donuts.

An on call maintenance person made the Sunday morning drive to Will's apartment and let him inside. Will showered and cabbed back to the Looming where his car still sat in the otherwise empty parking lot. Will unlocked it with his spare key and, without sleep, drove to Rome.

Painting a house in the hot sun after taking X the night before will undoubtedly make a person quick tempered. Will's grandmother, who'd slowed down considerably during the past year, came over to the empty house where Will had grown up. His grandmother did not know she was walking into a hornet's nest as she, hips and stomach hurting, took tiny, pained steps up the driveway that she'd walked up so many times during Will's youth, often times with freshly cooked or purchased food in hand. She slowly walked around to the back yard where Will painted. She looked weak and tired.

"You're so thin" she said.

Will sighed.

"No I'm not" Will said, and kept painting.

"I just wanted to see you for a minute while you were here. You never come up anymore".

"Yes I do" Will said, in the tone of an exasperated teenager.

"Well honey I'm sorry" his grandmother said "I'm sorry I bothered you."

Will kept painting and growing more irritated as she looked at him like she didn't know him.

"Will you come by my house before you leave?"

Will stopped painting and looked at her. Bluntly, he said "when have I ever *not* come to see you before I left to go back?"

She took a pained step back, almost losing her balance. Hurt poured out of her eyes and made Will even madder. She slowly turned around to leave and as if forced by someone else's hand, Will kept painting instead of running after her and putting his arms around her and saying I'm sorry.

Chapter Twenty-Eight

On Labor Day weekend, as summer 2000 came to an end, Will made sure to have pills in his pocket in case he ran into Greg. The crowd at the Manhole was thick and it took time to move from one part to another. On Will's third time around, Greg stopped him.

"Will" Greg said, frustrated. "Stop and say hello to me. You're trying to act coy and I know you saw me."

Will laughed nervously as his pill hit him hard. He could barely speak as the mirrors and brutal self exam began. He wanted to tell his grandmother he was sorry for the way he treated her the last time he saw her. He could barely stay still and he left the Manhole. He decided to drive to Rome, still in his club muscle shirt, rolling on X, and with cash, lube, ID, pills and a new bottle of poppers in his jeans pocket.

After Forty minutes on Interstate 75N, a heavy fog set in and Will slowed to ten miles per hour on the four lane stretch of highway that leads into Rome. He could barely see.

Will dialed Greg's number, though he thought Greg would still be out.

"Greg, uhm—I—I was glad to see you tonight. Let's hang out soon." Will barely recognized his own voice.

It was three A.M. when Will pulled into the driveway at his grandmother's house where his mother had been staying nightly. When his mother let him in the door she didn't have to say a word. Her Indian brown eyes glowered at him as she asked him to sleep in the bedroom across from his grandmother's and listen for her to call out.

"I'm going home and taking a break" Will's mom said. "Don't you leave here before Jim or I get back to look after her."

Just as ecstasy had amplified all the senses the first night Will had taken it, making everything more beautiful, it also amplified the opposite. It was the first time Will had smelled sickness, and just as the X had made the lights glow brighter, it made the sick smell sicker, and the darkness even heavier. He couldn't sleep. He was still wired, hearing the beats from the Manhole in his head as he lay in his great grandfather's old bedroom, cash and poppers falling out of his jeans pocket onto his great grandfather's old bed. He tossed and turned and mentally tortured himself for the message he left on Greg's machine.

His grandmother called out for Will's mom, and Will went to see about her.

"Will, what are you doing here?"

She barely sounded like herself. She asked for a pan and began to heave. Will thought he might be sick himself.

Will hadn't slept when his mother got back the next afternoon. Brisk, she asked how his grandmother had been during the night.

Will sat with her in the afternoon and she spoke to him like she was waiting for him to say something important. Instead, he grew more and more impatient, the drugs still flowing through him.

"Will, please" she said, sounding tired. "Please be nice to me. I don't feel good, honey."

Instead of the "I'm sorrys" and "how could I talk to you that ways" he'd thought of during the week, Will found himself saying, unexpectedly "I went to California last year."

"California?" she said "Why didn't anyone tell me?"

"Because you'd worry" Will said.

That Thursday night after work, as the MTV Video Music Awards silently flashed across Will's TV, he dialed Greg's number. Will's bizarre, late night phone message from the previous weekend had gone unreturned. Greg's hello sounded more like a goodbye. He'd expected the call.

"It's Will, did I catch you at a bad time?"

"I'm eating" Greg said "but I can talk for a second."

"I just wanted to apologize for the call over the weekend. It was the X and—" Greg cut him off.

"Will—"

"Will. It doesn't matter" Greg said.

Greg's tone was curt and final. Will didn't know what to say next. He heard Greg put his fork down on his plate.

"Will, why couldn't you have just talked to me when you saw me at the Manhole? Asked me if I wanted to get together?" Greg said.

Will had no answer.

"You send letters. You left that message."

"I don't know. It was the X."

"Will, this is a merry go round and I'm getting off of it."

Tears came fast and Will held the phone upside down so Greg wouldn't hear.

"It's like beating a dead horse" Greg said.

Standing in the doorway between his bedroom and the living room, Will slid down the door frame and sat against it on the floor. Betty and Frieda came to his side.

"Will, say goodbye to me."
Will didn't speak.
"Will. Say goodbye."

Will got out a weak "goodbye" and heard Greg say goodbye as he hung up. Will pressed the off button and curled up in a fetal position, sobbing.

Chapter Twenty-Nine

On a sunny September day with crisp autumn in the air, Kevin called Will around lunchtime.

"I know you don't like straying from your routine" Kevin said "But can I come over?"

Kevin sat awkwardly on the end of the sixty-nine chair. (There is no way to sit on the end of the sixty nine chair except awkwardly). Will couldn't think of a time when he and Kevin had talked, in person, at that time of day on a weekday – it made the visit feel serious.

"I just came from the health department" Kevin said.

Will noticed Kevin's eyes looked red. He wished it wasn't happening.

The sun sparkled through the leaves outside Will's living room window and Will heard the word "positive" in the sentences he didn't want to hear, hoped he'd forget, and tried to be present for. It was the first time he'd seen Kevin cry.

Like someone who's been on a long flight and has no interest in sitting down or sitting still afterward, a body still in motion, Kevin worried how the news might affect a love interest.

"I guess I can forget about anything ever happening with Allen now" he said.

As Will hugged Kevin, he realized he'd never hugged him before, though they saw each other several times in a week. It was numb and robotic. Will didn't feel him.

Will went back to his workout, and he stared at the veins in his arms that he'd been so excited to see grow when he'd started the *Body for Life* plan. With every thrust of the barbells and dumbbells, he considered the blood running through those veins.

That beautiful September day, like Laura's wedding day the year before, was another before and after day for someone Will loved. Days where the actions and choices that lead up to them culminate in permanence.

"Don't ever tell my parents" Kevin had said. "they would worry themselves to death".

In early October, on a Wednesday night, the phone in the computer room had been quiet most of the night. It was almost eleven when it rang.

"Will" Derek said, half standing up in his work station and holding the receiver out so Will could see.

It was Will's brother Jim.

"You better get up here".

Derek said "Who was that?"

Will told Derek who it was and what he'd said.

"You better go then" Derek said "you may not have another chance. Get out of here. I'll tell them what's going on."

Will drove to Rome that night in a 1988 white and red Dodge Dakota pick up truck with over two hundred thousand miles that his brother had loaned him while he repaired Will's car. He'd loved driving the truck and until then he'd been unaware how many stares from gay men he'd get simply because of his biceps in the blue collar vehicle. He'd always thought a new BMW would get him those kinds of looks but instead, he found, he was getting those kinds of looks from the drivers of new BMWs. Will rolled the windows down and listened to sparkly, late 90's pop music on the truck's factory radio that was barely audible over the air. The drive, on a weeknight, with no alcohol, no drugs, and no disco beat, was such welcome clear headedness that Will, at times, forgot the reason for driving to Rome. The ninety minute drive felt like it'd flown by in the blink of an eye when Will pulled the truck into the driveway of his grandmother's neat little house where the lights were all on, making it look as if someone were having a party in a house that normally, on a Wednesday night after midnight, would be bolted tight with the lights out.

Will's mother, normally unflappable, looked shaken like he'd never seen her look.

"Will" his mom said "before you go back – she doesn't look like herself."

Will stopped in his tracks and at once the clear air filled drive was replaced with blunt reality.

"She's lost so much weight. Her hair is completely white" his mom said, tears filling her dark brown eyes.

They walked through his grandmother's house and to the guest bedroom his grandmother now stayed in. She was in a hospice bed.

His mother was right. The perfectly coiffed and dyed yellow hair, the make up, the meek smile and the kind, worried green eyes were gone, replaced by frail sickness, closed yet restless eyes and white, white hair.

"Go talk to her" his mother said.

Will stepped toward her bed and said softly "Maggie."

After a few moments, eyes still closed, she spoke back.

"Will?"

'Is that you?"

He still heard his grandmother in the voice that had once been sing songey. She busily twisted something imaginary between her fingers. Will looked over at his mom and her friend.

"She's getting her hair rollers ready" his mother whispered "to do her hair."

Maggie said "Will - go get my pocketbook".

"It's okay" he said "I don't need any money."

"No, no" she said "You might. You never know."

Will looked at his mother again.

"It's okay. Keep talking to her."

'Maggie" Will said.

"Yes honey?"

"I love you."

"I love you too honey."

Back in the living room, Will's mother said "go over to my house and sleep there. We'll be here. Don't ignore the phone if it rings because it might be me. And when I call, be ready to drive back over immediately. Don't mess around and take your time."

His mom called around ten that morning, on Thursday. Ten minutes later, as he drove up to his grandmother's house, cars were parked in the driveway and on the street in front.

Will's mother introduced him to the hospice nurse and asked him to sit down beside the hospice bed. The nurse, an early twenties, pretty, Asian-American woman with a reassuring presence, listened to Maggie's heart. Will's mother and her cousin stood to the side and watched.

Will had read somewhere that the hearing is the last thing to go. Softly, he said "Maggie while holding her tiny hand that had worked so hard for him. Her hand looked frangible against his vibrant veins.

"Maggie" he repeated, a little more quietly each time, as the morning sun shined in and his tears silently fell on top of her hand.

When the hospice nurse said "she's gone" his mom buried her head in her cousin's shoulder and sobbed.

"My best friend just left me" Will's mom said, her voice shaking like he'd never heard it.

Ten minutes later, Will's mom had pulled herself together for the growing number of visitors now filling the house.

Chapter Thirty

On the Wednesday night before Thanksgiving, Kaleb called Will. They hadn't seen each other in months.

"You know the Manhole will be fun" Kaleb said "it's a holiday tomorrow.

Around Kaleb, Will could soak up attention unapologetically because no one understood wanting attention more than Kaleb.

"Don't wear much for a shirt" Will said. "I want attention tonight."

At the Manhole, when Kaleb saw Will, his jaw dropped.

"When did all this happen?"

Will shrugged and said "you know. It just did".

"Uh huh" Kaleb play pouted "you're gonna get attention away from me."

"Kaleb!" Will playfully mocked "Never!"

A guy Will had gone home with on a weeknight once stood on the side of the dance floor with his friend. They watched Kaleb and Will dance. Will looked the guy in the eyes while mimicking Andrew's dancing.

"Will!" Kaleb said 'I like this side of you!'.

"I have to admit it's a lot more fun than hiding on the sidelines" Will said, drinking his vodka cranberry.

"I told ya so" Kaleb said, laughing and coquetting.

"What's this?" Kaleb said, pointing at Will's drink.

"A lot less calories than *that*" Will said, pointing at Kaleb's beer.

"Will – I *do* like this side of you."

Kaleb smiled at him devilishly.

The guy Will had gone home with offered him another marathon blow job.

"Not tonight" Will said "We're just dicking around."

Chained, unable to get over Greg, Will found brief moments of liberation when saying no to others.

On the drive to Rome, Will hoped there would be more nights like this one with Kaleb. Maybe life would be better if he reverted back to a more innocent time before Greg and ecstasy. Will wondered if it were even possible.

It wasn't even Christmas before Will was at Backstreet looking for a pill. Within half an hour of paying the entrance fee and getting stamped, Will was back in his car with a tab of X. He drove toward the increasingly empty Looming. The X hit Will hard, and his dick wouldn't get hard while someone's mouth was around it. He walked from one area to the next, but hardly anyone was around. Stephen as never around anymore and the music wasn't the same. Will saw James, who he'd ran into at Pride with Kevin and Rebecca. James watched from the shadows as Will walked confused from one area to the next in the almost empty club.

The next morning, still unable to get hard, Will found himself at a sex party in someone's apartment.

"Too much meth?" the host asked Will.

"I don't do meth" Will said. "Just X".

"Honey, I hate to tell you this" the party host sighed and looked at his lover who nodded for him to keep going. "You got here five hours ago and you haven't been able to get hard the whole time. Someone may have sold you X, but trust me, it's not X. You took meth."

At work the next week, Will had flashbacks of the weekend before. How strange it was to feel so good while unable to keep an erection. The flashes came over him in waves and he wanted to feel that way again. He wanted more meth and he made arrangements to buy some before New Year's Eve.

On New Year's Eve the Looming was an empty shadow of the lustful lustre it once was. Hardly anyone was around. Will couldn't get hard and he couldn't sit still. He walked up on two people in the furthermost, darkest corner in the back. The one kneeling down and giving a blow job jumped up when he saw Will. It was Greg and he stumbled past Will on his way toward the front. The guy he'd been sucking followed.

Will walked around for a minute more and left when he realized Greg had gone and taken the guy with him. Will didn't see anyone else in the club.

Will went to his apartment, but he couldn't fall asleep. He wanted to whack off, but he couldn't get hard. Will picked up the phone and called Greg. He hung up without leaving a message. Over the next few hours and into the early afternoon, Will dialed Greg's number over thirty times. He didn't leave any messages.

Will left the Looming and drove along empty, snow covered streets through downtown and into Midtown and down Cheshire Bridge Road. When he got to Greg's building, he stopped in the parking lot just outside his apartment and turned off the ignition. Will sat quietly in the old Dodge truck, listening to the snow fall, each flake making everything seem a little bit more unreal. He saw Greg's car and thought of him inside his apartment, warm and in bed with the guy he'd picked up.

Rather than call a friend and suggest lunch or a visit, Will focused whole heartedly and single mindedly on this one man in one apartment where he was no longer invited inside. A feeling of infinite black emptiness enveloped Will like only Meth can while outside the truck the snow kept falling all around, instantly transforming the brick apartment building and dirty parking lot into a picturesque white scene like only a new snowfall can. Every warm, cozy, fireplace feeling that snow can bring when it happens in the south where it doesn't happen often turned on Will like an unfortunately chosen card with a dark and evil flipside.

Will cranked the truck and drove back toward Midtown, down Spring Street onto Fourth Street. Inside the bathhouse was a small area where someone, behind glass, asked for I.D. and explained the cost. Once payment was made, he buzzed the door, allowing the person entrance as the next person in line stepped up to the window. Once inside, the attendant handed that person a folded white towel, a folded white sheet and pillowcase, along with a folded brown bag and the key to a room.

"You're in room twenty" the attendant said "Checkout's at nine o'clock".

Will couldn't imagine staying there for eight whole hours.

The entrance to the bathhouse was well lit like an office. Just past the attendant's area were rows of lockers with benches in front of them. A person could rent a locker to store their clothes in while they walked around only in a towel for less than the cost of renting a room. Both locker and room rentals came in eight hour increments.

On the wall opposite the lockers was an area with cafeteria booths and vending machines. Condoms, lube and plastic cock rings were sold just outside the attendant's station. There were two well lit bathrooms accessible from the vending area.

A Hallway with two steps led up to an area that was significantly darker. Three leather sofas comprised a U in the lounge area where regular cable shows played on a large screen TV.

Metal light fixtures like you might seen on a ship were outside of every room. Men standing around chatting and wearing only towels watched as someone new came through, fully dressed and looking for the room number that corresponded to the key number the attendant had given him.

The rooms were about five feet wide by ten feet long with one wooden bunk built in to the wall with a thin mattress on top of it. A small TV hung in the upper corner perpendicular from the head of the bunk bed.

Will covered the vinyl covered mattress with the clean sheet and slid the pillowcase over the pillow. He stripped, folded his clothes, and placed them on top of his boots in the corner of the room. He wrapped the towel around his washboard abs and still wearing his baseball cap, opened the door to his room. He turned the dimmer down halfway and laid back on the freshly made bed. He watched porn and watched the people walking in the hallway.

Will got up and closed the door, put his key into the little bag with meth in it, like Eddie had shown him with cocaine, and dug some out. Will snorted some of the meth, put the bag and the keys in his jeans pocket, and opened the door again.

"They're thinking about sex, not hair" Kevin had said "and besides, I always see someone around there wearing a towel and baseball cap."

Will got up and walked around, enjoying the attention normally bestowed on fresh meat. Most of the guys around were so wound up on their drug of choice they could barely decide whether they wanted to chat incessantly or have sex. Will couldn't blame them and it was a conundrum he now understood.

Through a steamed glass door and down a set of stairs painted black, Will saw a steam room and pool. The voice of a man he'd seen in front came over a loud speaker periodically, reminding everyone there was no touching in the pool.

Eight hours seemed to fly by and Will checked in for another eight hours. He couldn't get enough of the hungry masculinity all around the private world of the bathhouse, carved in the middle of the city where just outside it's doors people in daylight were having lunch after church.

At ten P.M. on New Year's Day, Will finally left Flex after two eight hour stays. Walking out of the darkened men's only world of indiscriminate sex and drugs and into the parking lot adjacent to eight lanes of traffic speeding by on I-75 with all the noise and horn blowing that went with it was like stepping out of one world and into another.

The blinking lights on Will's answering machine were calls from his mother and his friends. At after ten P.M. on New Year's Day night, they were understandably worried. To Will, it felt like not much time had passed and he acted irritated at the concern.

Monday's workout felt impossibly difficult. Will had no energy to lift weights and he felt like he could sleep for days. He made a pitiful attempt at working out and barely got to work by three.

That evening, while Derek watched the computer room, Will took a late break. He noticed his heart palpitating in a way he'd never felt. It fluttered and flew like it wanted to take off. Will called Zach in a panic and told him about it.

"That stuff messes with your heart" Zach said. "Ecstasy is one thing but I don't know if I'd keep doing Tina. Crystal Meth is kind of a big deal and I've seen people ruin their lives with it."

Will called Kevin next.

"Yeah, you might want to think about not working out the first couple of days after a weekend at the bathhouse" he said "Zach's right but he's probably just being over cautious. Just find an amount that works for you and try to sleep at least a day before going back to work."

Though his heart felt like it was beating out of his chest, Will still liked Kevin's answer better.

During the week, Will felt a deep depression that he'd never known before.

By Friday, Will felt closer to normal and his workout did too. In direct conflict with his new drug of choice, he loved sleep and couldn't survive without it.

The songs he'd heard at Flex were not chosen with care like the ones Stephen played at the Looming, but they had stayed in Will's head all week. Whenever he heard nu jazz, it reminded him of the warmth and easy freedom he'd felt inside the bathhouse around the other towel clad, hungry men. Will decided to let his body recover rather than go back so soon.

Will waited until the third weekend in January 2001 to go back to the bathhouse. He stayed most of the weekend and so did Kevin. Kevin advised Will to have stiff drinks when it was time to come down, and he did just that. Will fell asleep faster and slept longer.

At work that week, the songs stayed in Will's head again. They immediately brought back the smell and the sounds of the darkened bathhouse, and the chemically induced pleasures it held. Will felt drawn to go back, and it came in waves. Now, when Will saw an ass or a set of arms he liked, instead of inspiring him to build his own, the sight of them reminded him that he had to get back to the bathhouse so he could *have* them. The bodies and the sex and the drugs were so intermingled now, he knew he was in over his head. Another first for Will – he didn't care. It felt too good to care.

Will told Kevin about his concerns one night at Raging Burrito and suggested they both just not go there ever again and run the other way.

Will stopped himself and said "But we'd never get to taste how hot that cock or that ass is after that first bump and who doesn't want that?"

Kevin said "I'm glad you've come to your senses. And hey, can you find me some for this weekend?"

Chapter Thirty-One

On Super Bowl Sunday 2001, Will left a buddy's house later than usual. It was almost eleven o'clock and Will was sober. His friend always reminded him about the ramifications of a DUI.

There were no other cars for long stretches as he drove down Clairmont Road. Will noticed a pair of headlights in the distance and up a hill. There was something odd about the position of the headlights and it almost seemed like they were coming right at him. Those headlights were coming right at him and he quickly turned the steering wheel to the left to try and get in the opposite lane. The car hit him head on and his airbag deployed, knocking the wind out of him.

Reflexively, Will reached in the back seat and grabbed his baseball cap. He got out of his car, stumbled to the side of the road, and sat down. Will felt sick and he must have been in shock. He could see another wrecked car on the other side of the road, halfway in someone's yard. Will walked and looked for a house with their lights on. A young, collegiate looking kid, walked out of one of the front doors and asked him if he was alright. The kid was surprised that Will had been in one of the cars and could still walk around. He suggested Will go back and wait for the ambulance.

"We heard the crash. It sounded terrible" the kid said. "They'll wonder where the driver of the car is."

The police and ambulance were at the scene as Will, in a stupor, walked back up. A policeman asked Will if he knew who was driving the white Celica. Will said "that's my car", to the surprise of the policeman. Will's car sat catty-corner in the middle of the road, parts strewn around, and the front smashed except one little strip on the left. The left pop up headlight was still up. That last minute maneuver to the left may have saved Will's life. The policeman, looking over Will in his skin tight shirt and low slung jeans, questioned Will as if he might be the cause of the accident.

Another cop came over and Will heard them talk. They surmised from the black tire marks and positioning of the cars that it had been the other driver's fault.

"Hey" one of cops said "we just found empty beer bottles in this car. We found some more of the same kind in the ditch beside it. It looks like they tried to hide the bottles. That guy was passed out behind the wheel".

Livid instead of frightened, Will railed on the other driver.

"I don't want to ride with the drunk driver who hit me" Will said to the EMT who strapped him down. He took Will's shirt off and examined him for injuries. He noticed a curve in the bottom of Will's left pectoral and asked if it was already like that. When Will said yes, the EMT smiled and said "mine's like that too." The EMT studied Will's face for a while, and as he did, Will calmed down.

Downtown at Grady Hospital, the south's largest and best trauma center, Will lay on a stretcher in a busy corridor while different people came by to check on him. It was almost five A.M. before Will's mother and brother peeked their heads in the temporary room he'd been wheeled to. When Will saw their faces, he cried.

"Hey baby" his mom said, caring and self assured as she surveyed him from head to toe.

His mom said "I can see an impression of the seatbelt across your chest and stomach."

"Everybody keeps telling me that" Will said "and then shaking their heads and reminding me that seatbelts save lives. Do I look like I need to be reminded? I had the thing on."

"Did they give you morphine?" his mom asked, settling into a chair and releasing a sigh while looking at his brother.

"No, why?"

"You're awfully bitchy."

"I know" Will said. "I wasn't feeling bitchy before the wreck. I've been in a shit mood since."

Jim laughed, and asked "who was the other driver?"

"An immigrant. Passed out behind the wheel."

"And you think you're going to sue them?"

Jim laughed again.

"Why not?"

Jim made that dismissive noise that starts with blowing air through your lips. It's a noise that says fat chance.

"They probably don't even have insurance."

"Well I'm suing them anyway. Assholes."

"What kind of car was it?" Jim asked, settling down into one of the flimsy metal chairs in the small room with a dingy tile floor and stained ceiling partitions.

"I don't know. Something cheap. And ugly. It was that horrible light aqua color. Probably a Hyundai or a Ford or something."

A nurse who'd come into to check Will's vitals raised an eyebrow and looked over at his brother.

"He's always like this" Jim said.

"Where were you going so late at night?" the nurse asked.

Will said "take your shirt off night at The Manhole" as if she should know that Sunday is take your shirt off night and midnight isn't really late.

When the nurse left the room Will said "I'm sick of everyone asking *me* why *I* was out so late. I'm sober. I have car insurance. I have health insurance. What's their damn problem?"

Jim looked at their mother, unflappable as Bea Arthur and with the same white hair, dark brown, skeptical eyes and dry wit.

'He's sober" his mom said "I can tell."

She let out another sigh.

"But I wish I weren't. Anywhere to get a drink in this place?"

Ron rested his tired head on his wrist and looked at their mother with the same brown eyes she looked at him with.

"I don't think they have a bar at Grady Hospital mother."

"I'm sorry!" Will said.

Jim laughed. "It's not your fault. Don't worry about it."

Since Will's childhood days when the three of them – he, his mom, and Jim - were together, the one-liners and quips were easy and non-stop.

Throughout the afternoon, at random times, it dawned on Will that he could have been killed in the car wreck. Overcome, he'd look at his mother and cry. She walked over to him and hugged him, letting him cry more.

Jim would say "they might have car insurance. I don't really know".

It made Will laugh every time through the tears.

It was late afternoon when Will was finally released to go home. He insisted he was fine and asked to be dropped off at his apartment. His mother and Jim left for Rome and got there two hours later. Four hours later, Will showed up. He wanted to be with his family.

In late March, Will finished the physical therapy prescribed after his car wreck. After two months away, he went back to the bathhouse for a long weekend of meth, sex and incessant chatter in between. He stayed until Sunday afternoon, his last meal a protein shake on Friday night at work.

Rebecca and Kim didn't say it, but the tones in their telephone voices screamed how saddened they were that Will, who'd regarded the wreck as a wake up call, didn't act accordingly.

On Sunday nights, Kevin and Will went to Burkhart's and plied themselves with vodka drinks so that they'd both get some sleep before beginning their work weeks. Monday workouts were becoming a thing of the past, since Will barely woke up in time to shower and go to work.

The mingling of the alcohol chasing the meth out of Will's system made everything seem funny. The guys who approached them at Burkhart's weren't just flirting – they practically demanded and they acted like Will and Kevin should give it up. Will reasoned that all of the sex of the weekend must be recruiting on the way out of their systems.

Kevin and Will discussed the vibes they were putting off. Neither of them planned to have sex with anyone after a weekend at the bathhouse, and it seemed to have the effect of an aphrodisiac on others. They weren't bothered by the attention as they winded down, or came in for a landing as they called it.

"Who'll buy us drugs and pay for our covers if we don't' make it to work" they joked.

Chapter Thirty-Two

In April of 2001, Atlanta bloomed magnificently and Will couldn't wait to get out among the lean joggers at Piedmont Park and feel like he was a part of all of it. The dogwoods and cherry trees, doted on azaleas and roses. Instead, he found himself dragging during the week after long weekends at the bathhouse. He continued making the owners of Quick Test rich by paying sixty dollars per rapid H.I.V. test. Kevin warned Will about crossing over, as he now called it, though he said it was fun being a member of the club.

"You can do whatever you want and you don't have to worry about it anymore. It's already done."

On a Sunday night at Burkhart's, when Will told Eddie he wanted a stiff drink to take the edge off, Eddie laughed.

"This isn't you Will" he said "you're not over Greg are you."

"The tables have turned now" Will said. "I can get anybody I want and Greg looks worse for wear every time I see him out."

Eddie studied Will. Will couldn't tell if he was shocked at what he'd said, or just sad that he'd said it. Will thought he saw pity in Eddie's eyes. He knew he saw a lack of recognition flash past.

The weeks at work following a weekend at the bathhouse were tough to get through. Time crawled as the meth wore off and Will, who ordinarily loved to crack jokes and brighten days, was simply rotten at times. It was as if he was a different person altogether.

Will's mom told him once "always be nice to security guards and bus drivers and don't forget your mom did those jobs." He'd listened to her, and did as she said. He regularly chatted with cleaning people in his office just because he liked to and less because he'd been taught to. One night, during one of those weeks, a downstairs guard asked Will to sign in twice. The guard had made an error on the sign in sheet. Will signed the sheet, slammed the pen down, and cursed at the guard.

Daniel called but his calls were fewer and their once lively conversations were heavy. One night Daniel called Will at work when Will had felt particularly ill that week. When Daniel chided Will for the drugs and bathhouse, Will shot back.

"You're just a mean, bitter old man and you're jealous of the attention I'm getting." Will said.

Will had never heard Daniel's voice so shaky as it had when he said goodbye. Will could feel his pain pouring through the phone. Later in the week, as more of the meth wore off, Will called Daniel to apologize. Daniel did not answer, and he never did again. Whenever Will thought of him, and what he'd said, his heart sank.

After a rowdy weekend at the bathhouse, Will came home one Sunday night too wired and tired to meet anyone out for a drink. Alone, he made stiff drinks until he fell asleep.

The next morning, on Monday, he was so thoroughly dehydrated he could barely get out of bed. At the advice of a friend who knew about these things, Will went out to buy something containing plenty of electrolytes. It only provided temporary relief.

Will called in sick and made a doctor's appointment.

'You look like shit. What have you been doing?"

Will didn't have an answer for him.

"Your skin is yellow but we'll have to wait for your blood work to get back before we know for sure that it's hepatitis."

Will looked at a mirror in the examining room. The doctor was right. His skin was yellow next to his bloodshot, yellow eyes. He looked like shit.

"Well you called this one right" Kim said that evening over the phone.

"I know how you can be" she said. "I didn't think you'd really have it."

Kim and Rebecca asked Will, gently, to please slow down. He said he would, but not with his workouts.

"You can't workout" Kevin said "You'll make yourself sicker. Just take a week off. At least a week."

Stubbornly, Will pressed on, determined that he wasn't going to lose any muscle tone or gain any fat. His post workout protein drinks made him sick and by mid-week he had no choice but to stop. When his doctor called him to confirm the Hepatitis A diagnosis, Will told him about the protein drinks and how they now made him sick.

"You're not supposed to be working out anyway and drinking whey protein right now is like spending all day in a bar. Your liver needs to heal and you're just damaging it further. You've got to take a month off from work and absolutely no drinking (alcohol or whey) or working out."

Will hung up the phone and sighed.

He laid back on the sofa. Betty and Frieda sat behind him on the window sill, the open windows letting the spring air fill the apartment. Between the bathhouse on weekend, sleeping late and then going in to work, Will had forgotten what fresh air smelled like. He breathed it in and wondered how long it had been.

After one week of not working, working out, or going out to bars or bathhouses or sex clubs, Will's apartment was organized and clean. It became obvious that life – his friends and family, his cats, his apartment, bills, and accounts – had long been neglected.

Will did something he hadn't done since his last surgery – he rented movies and watched them. He spent time at his apartment with his cats. Betty and Frieda lapped up the attention and company.

As Will's yellow skin tone faded, his hard earned physique and vitality went with it.   And sometime, while Will and Kevin were at the bathhouse or asleep, Devin graduated from Georgia Tech and landed himself a good job. He invited Will over for drinks at his new place. Will explained to Devin that his drinks would have to be non-alcoholic and why.

Devin said "come over anyway. I haven't seen you in forever."

Not realizing the implications, Will mentioned his illness around Devin's friends, all considerably younger and straight. They all excused themselves to go check out the yard. Devin stayed inside with Will.

"Will, you look skinny" Devin said. He looked sad, nervously rolling the napkin around the bottom of his beer bottle.

"Do you think it's finally time to slow down?"

"I've been in Atlanta almost four years now" Will said. "I moved here full of hope, and I wanted to fall in love. Build a life. Build a body. I had a lot of friends who all believed in me. Respected me. Things fell into place for me, over and over again. And now, like dominos, they've fallen out of place. It almost feels like I should be graduating, after four years, from something. Instead, I feel like I've been demoted. Knocked down. I didn't learn a thing. "

When Will went back to Burkhart's and the Manhole, the drinks were noticeably weaker. No one kissed his ass. No one noticed him much

Will hadn't yet realized that he could no longer get away with wearing practically anything when he went out. A healthy and vital body carries the clothes it wears and when it is no longer vital and healthy, the opposite is true. The tight shirts that once showcased his bulging muscles and tight abs now showcased a body that had been sick and was now skinny with falling pectorals.

After a few weeks, Will returned to a daily workout regimen supplemented with soy protein. He was not able to return to the level of physical fitness and muscle tone he enjoyed before Hepatitis A. Maybe it was the meth. Maybe it was the Hepatitis. Maybe it was the onslaught of whey protein he'd drank the first week he had Hepatitis. Whatever had happened, his body simply didn't respond to exercise as it had before.

By the end of the summer, Will felt as if he'd been living in a nightmare. He still woke every day expecting to feel refreshed and rejuvenated like he had the year before, but instead, he woke up every day feeling nothing more than bland. He'd rebuilt to a respectable degree of fitness still envied by the average Joe on the street – but the cover worthy torso, abs, biceps and veins were gone and apparently never coming back. Still, perhaps in denial, he tried.

Over that summer, Will didn't go swimming in the pool at his mom's new house. The pool wasn't fresh and clear as it had been the year before. The surface had cracked, and the now murky water had a green tint that wouldn't be cleaned away.

In early September, Will was reminded of September 2000. The crisp, sunny morning that Kevin came over and told him about his H.I.V. test.

On 9/11, another beautiful, crisp, autumn morning, Will's mom called to tell him what had happened. When Will turned on his television, he couldn't believe his eyes. When she told him the plane was bound for California, he began to see.

"So it was full of gas" Will said.

"I suppose so" his mom said. "Why?"

"We're at war" he said. "Someone planned this."

Will listened to George Bush speak on the radio as he went through the motions of a hopeless feeling workout. Will longed for his former body and his former self that didn't know drugs. He longed for the hopefulness and seemingly infinite optimism he'd known when he'd first moved to Atlanta. He even longed for the Clintons.

When Will got to work that day, Ruth from HR told him he could leave if he wanted.

"Since this is an office tower we just can't be sure" she said. "Go be with your family."

Will's mom, his brother, and his brother's family were all in Rome. His dad and stepmother were in Florida. Will talked to everyone on the phone, including Rebecca who'd lit candles in her windows.

Will went to a bar near Burkhart's. Inside the gay bar the gays were doing what they do best in a time of crisis - sallying forth and singing show tunes along with the old movie stars on the big screen.

Will soon found that it would take more than show tunes to forget the outside world. After only one drink, he was on his way to the bathhouse while Kevin, Kim, Zach and Rebecca– everyone was at home with a loved one, watching the news.

Sometime after checking in, Will noticed Greg in the darkened hallway just outside of his room. Greg kept hanging around and Will assumed he must not have recognized him. Will pretended Greg wasn't there, but finally it made him uncomfortable. Will, locking the door to his room behind him, started down the dim hallway. Greg stared right at him and made some kind of grunt that said he was irritated.

Will wondered how it was that someone he'd felt such a spark with years before, was now languishing in the same murky waters of discontent and mediocrity. After so many years and so many little baggies of drugs go by, it gets so intermingled you can't tell who brought who into it. And it doesn't matter anymore.

Will didn't turn around and attempt to talk to Greg, but instead felt pity for him. And for himself. He heard him make that hissing noise at some guy in the hallway – meaning he wanted to suck their dick. It all felt so sick and Will had no desire for Greg. Will had no desire to get both of their rode hard and hung out to dry, regularly up all night and all day, hardly any muscle tone left bodies together in any way.

When they first met, Will wanted to follow Greg - and now he had followed him – all the way down it seemed. Will had lost himself and he didn't know anything for sure, except that he couldn't see where he was going and wasn't sure if he'd ever get out.

"You better stay away from me - before you get yourself in trouble."

Since Will first used meth at the end of 2000, it seemed no one believed in him anymore. The looks he got from Kevin and Kim were incredulous mixed with pity. It felt as frustrating and dirty a trick as his washboard abs disappearing before his eyes. He'd stopped acting as if he'd ever had a muscled body because of those same incredulous looks mixed with pity.

Now, not only had he dropped back down to mediocrity in fitness, his words weren't taken seriously either. It seemed like it'd all happened while he wasn't looking. One minute he was someone who got noticed and people, especially friends, cared what he had to say. And the next, he was a pest and a drug addict with a distorted reality. He struggled to pinpoint the exact moment he'd slipped into such a pathetic state. And that's the thing of it – really the thing of it. You can get stuck. Stuck trying to pinpoint *when, how* did this happen? Where was I looking, what was I thinking, what was I doing when I lost it all and didn't even realize it? How did I go from having everything I'd ever wanted - to having it all turn on me like some waking nightmare? At what point? At what point?!

You start making promises to God, and breaking promises to God, and trying to get back *there*, whatever and wherever *there* is. That place, that thing, that whatever it is where apparently there's no turning back because whatever you did that was such a fuck up was such a fuck up you've been slam dunked into a hell all your own. You start to realize that no matter how hard you wish and hard you want and how hard you cry and how much you tell your mother and your friends and your family and your doctors and – you can even hear it in your own inner voice when you're stomping around swearing to rebuild. You don't know if you can. You don't' know if you've gone too far. At what point? When did this happen? Why can't I change it? Why can't I go back? I've always been able to will my way, to want my way, to get my way, to not take no for an answer my way, to convince my way, to stomp my way, to just want it so much I could make it happen my way – but I can't go back in time. I can't. And I keep swearing to God that if I could I'd do it different. I'd never ever fuck it up so bad. But maybe he knows, maybe somebody somewhere knows that's all bullshit because you would. Wouldn't you? I would, wouldn't I? I'd just keep fucking up the same way over and over again? I'd never get it right. I'd be right back here all the time.

John David Hall lives in Atlanta, Georgia. This is his first novel.

32080724R00162

Made in the USA
Charleston, SC
07 August 2014